Jackie Kabler was born in Coventry but spent much of her childhood in Ireland. She worked as a newspaper reporter and then a television news correspondent for twenty years, spending nearly a decade on GMTV followed by stints with ITN and BBC News. During that time, she covered major stories around the world including the Kosovo crisis, the impeachment of President Clinton, the Asian tsunami, famine in Ethiopia, the Soham murders and the disappearance of Madeleine McCann. Jackie now divides her time between crime writing and her job as a presenter on shopping channel QVC. She has a degree in zoology, runs long distances for fun and lives in Gloucestershire with her husband.

www.jackiekabler.com
@jackiekabler
@officialjackiekabler

Also by Jackie Kabler

Am I Guilty?
The Perfect Couple
The Happy Family

The Murder List

JACKIE KABLER

OneMoreChapter
an imprint of HarperCollins*Publishers* Ltd
1 London Bridge Street
London SE1 9GF

www.harpercollins.co.uk

HarperCollins*Publishers*
1st Floor, Watermarque Building, Ringsend Road
Dublin 4, Ireland

This paperback edition 2022

2

First published in Great Britain in ebook format by
HarperCollins*Publishers* 2022

A catalogue record for this book
is available from the British Library

ISBN: 978-0-00-843400-7

Set in Birka by Palimpsest Book Production Limited,
Falkirk, Stirlingshire

Printed and Bound in the UK using 100%
Renewable Electricity at CPI Group (UK) Ltd

Prologue

*I*t's becoming harder to breathe now.

At first it was just tendrils of smoke, creeping under the door and floating lazily across the room, and for a few moments I sat there, mesmerised, watching them. But now the air is thicker, more acrid, and suddenly there are flames too, chasing each other along the carpet and licking the legs of the chair beside my bed. I can feel the heat on my skin and in my lungs, and I draw my knees up to my chest, head whipping from left to right, eyes scanning the door, the window, the door, the window. The house is on fire. This room is on fire.

From somewhere nearby I hear a muffled shout, and then another, and I uncurl my legs, slide off the bed, take an uncertain step, and then stop. The door is engulfed in flames now, the wood cracking, and suddenly there's a flash, a blinding light, and I stagger backwards as a wall of heat slams into me. There's a sharp pain in my right wrist, and I grab at it, and then gasp. The bracelet I went to bed in just an hour ago is too hot to touch, searing my skin, and I turn in terror and rush towards the window, but there are flames there too now, snaking up the curtains, and my vision is blurring, my chest burning.

I can hear someone wailing, crying, far away in the distance, and then there's the sound of glass splintering, and a crackle close to my left ear, and I realise that my hair is on fire.

I open my mouth, and I begin to scream.

Chapter 1

Christmas Eve

The run-up to Christmas is always a strange time. Not nearly enough dead bodies. Plenty of house break-ins, though: people out partying, leaving gifts visible under Christmas trees, posting on social media about heading off to visit relatives – burglars have a fine old time of it in December. But generally, summer is the best season for murder, it seems. It depends where you are, of course; I've scanned dozens of articles today, looking at the stats, just to pass the time. It varies in different parts of the world, but it seems that, overall, killing is more popular in warmer weather. Riots too. Higher temperatures, higher violent crime rates. In fact, one study from South Africa showed that for every one-degree rise in temperature, there's a 1.5% increase in the number of murders. Interesting, isn't it?

Interesting, but not very festive. I sigh and sign out of my computer.

Shall I just go home?

I glance around the room, wondering if there's anyone

who might fancy a chat, but there are only a couple of other people here this morning, and both are currently on the phone. One of them obviously turned on the Christmas lights when they got in though; in the corner by the window the elegant seven-foot blue spruce I helped Eleanor decorate three weeks ago is twinkling and sparkling, hundreds of tiny white lights entwined in its branches. I only popped into the office earlier to pick up some presents I left here yesterday; I didn't want to lug them all with me in my bag when a few of us went for Christmas drinks after work last night. But with no real plans for today until this evening, I decided to have a quick browse online before I left, hoping there might be something I can get my teeth into when I come back to work next week.

The result? Nothing. Nada. Zilch. It's been like this for a few weeks now, and it's getting a little tedious. I'm a freelance crime writer, and a good one, even if I do say it myself. I work hard, and over the past ten years I've built a reputation for getting to the heart of a story: in-depth interviews with relatives of victims, with detectives – and, on occasion, with the killers and rapists and fraudsters themselves, carried out in prison visiting rooms – have become my specialty. But it's been ages now since I've had a good inside story, one the tabloids and magazines are keen to get their hands on, and I'm getting a little twitchy. I'm OK for money; it's not that. But I like to keep busy, and there's been far too much sitting around recently. I sigh again and tap the screen of my phone to wake it up. No messages, and it's nearly two.

I might as well call it a day. Head home and get glammed up for this evening.

4

'All right, Mary? Gifts from your secret admirers?'

I jump, and turn to see Edward Cooper standing behind my chair, just a little too close as always. He's carrying a mug, obviously on his way back from the kitchen downstairs, and he's wearing a Christmas jumper. It's red, and a tad too small for his tall, bony frame, with a drunken-looking reindeer on the front under the slogan 'on the piste'. There's a faint odour about him today, stale and sweaty, and I swivel round in my chair and edge it away from him slightly as I reply:

'Hi, Edward. Gifts, yes. Not sure about the admirers though.'

I smile, trying to sound friendly. I'm never quite sure how I feel about Edward. He's relatively new to The Hub, the shared workspace where I've rented a desk for the past two years. We're all 'creatives' here – Edward is another writer who joined in October, but he's in marketing, writing public relations copy for sports brands. There are a few other freelance PRs too, including another newish arrival called Satish, who I haven't really got to know yet but who seems OK. Then there's a little group of web designers, nerdy but actually pretty good fun on a night out. And then there's Eleanor, of course. Eleanor is *fabulous*: a tiny Welsh ball of energy who runs a thriving make-up artist agency from her desk by the end window. Her girls – and they are mostly girls – pop in and out now and again to pick up samples or just for a gossip, all glossy lips and swishy hair and practical black sweat suits. I love Eleanor – she makes me laugh, and laughs are often hard to come by in my job.

Others come and go too, and that makes it interesting. I could work from home, I suppose – sometimes it does seem like a bit of an extravagance to pay nearly three hundred pounds a month for a chair and desk here, when I have a perfectly adequate home office in my box room – but most of the time I think The Hub is worth it. I work better in a formal workplace environment, and I like being around other people in this big, bright space. We have two floors of a five-storey building in the heart of Cheltenham; as well as the main office and small, modern kitchen there's a meeting room, a couple of 'break-out zones' with squashy sofas, and even access to a roof terrace where I sometimes take my laptop on balmy summer days. Unfortunately, there's now also Edward Cooper. Oh, he's fine really, I suppose. He just has this habit of looming over people, and I edge a little further away, reach for my handbag and start putting the presents into it. There's a bottle of prosecco – my gift from The Hub's annual Secret Santa – a few boxes of chocolates sent from editors I've written pieces for during the year, and a book-shaped object, probably a desk diary, in a cardboard wrapper. I haven't opened that yet, so I'm not sure who it's from, but I can do that later, I think, as I shove it in my bag, suddenly keen to escape.

'Exciting plans for Christmas?' asks Edward.

I think it's partly his voice that's a bit off-putting; it has a whiny, nasal quality. I don't like his eyes either – they're small, too close together, and so dark they're almost black. Even as I think that though, I instantly feel mean.

He can't help what he looks like, or what he sounds like, can he?

I force myself to smile again.

'Just spending it with friends,' I say. 'We're going out for

6

dinner tonight and then having a quiet couple of days at my place. It'll be fine.'

He nods slowly, his eyes flitting from my face to the handbag resting on my knee and back again. My hair is tucked behind my left ear and I flick it out, letting it fall across my cheek, feeling self-conscious. I know that's my problem though, nothing to do with him, but I really want to leave now, so I zip my bag closed and stand up, reaching for my coat which is draped over the back of my chair.

'No family get-together then?' he whines.

'No family get-together. And I need to get off now, Edward. Have a good one.'

I could explain; could explain that I don't really have a family, that I'm an only child, that my mum died when I was three years old and my dad when I was eighteen, but why should I? It's none of his business. And anyway, he could find out all that for himself, if he cared to pop my name into an internet search engine. It's all there. I'm surprised he hasn't done it already, actually. I don't need to explain it to him. I've already shared more than I should have about my Christmas plans. My past has been well documented. My present, I like to keep private.

'OK. Well, happy Christmas, Mary. See you on the other side.'

He doesn't move though, and I wince inwardly as I have to brush past him, our shoulders touching.

'Happy Christmas, Edward.'

I walk swiftly away, and I don't look back.

Chapter 2

Sunday 31st January

'I'm sorting out a bag for the charity shop – anything you want to chuck in?'

I turn to look at Pete, who's just come in from a run, and he takes a swig from his bottle of water and shakes his head.

'Don't think so. You getting rid of unwanted Christmas gifts? Hope mine isn't in there, Mary Ellis. I'm off for a shower.'

He grins at me and heads for the door, and I watch him go, his thighs taut and muscular in his short shorts. He always runs in shorts, tight and black, even on a cold, frosty morning like this one, and I can't say I object. I don't *fancy* Pete, not really, but you can enjoy looking at someone without fancying them as such, can't you? We're housemates, that's all. Friends for years. And anyway, he has a girlfriend, Megan.

'Megan Walker, although I'm not much of a walker. Prefer to run everywhere, a bit like Pete,' she giggled, on our first meeting.

Despite this somewhat irritating way of introducing herself, she seems nice enough, and she's very beautiful. Blonde, blue-eyed, creamy alabaster skin. I envy her skin – I envy *anyone* with smooth, perfect skin – but she's all right, although I don't know her very well yet; they've only been dating a few months, and she lives alone so when they spend the night together it's usually at her place over in Prestbury.

'Don't want to disturb you. Things might get a bit ... *noisy*,' Pete said with a wink, the first time he told me he'd be staying over.

'Ugh. *Way* too much information, Chong,' I groaned, and threw a tea towel at him, and he laughed, his greeny-brown eyes crinkling at the corners. His face is as nice as his legs – his late dad was Korean and his mum is Irish, and it's an excellent combination. He's six foot two, has thick, dark hair, a sharp jawline, and a smattering of freckles across his nose. He's a good guy, Pete Chong, and I am definitely *not* putting my Christmas gift from *him* into my charity bag – it was the loveliest, softest wool jumper, black with gold and silver stars down the sleeves. I am, however, putting in a cinnamon-scented candle I got from Dinah, our next-door neighbour – Dinah is lovely, but I really hate candles – a second, smaller candle that was included in a very nice hamper of chocolates and hand creams (given to me, to my surprise, by Megan), and a jarful of star-shaped cookie cutters that Virginia who runs the corner shop pushed into my hands when I popped in for a newspaper just before Christmas.

'I got them in in case anyone needed last-minute presents,' she told me. She had a flashing snowman brooch pinned to her navy tabard. 'But I can't shift 'em. Merry Christmas.'

I'd smiled and accepted the squat glass jar, but I'm not much of a baker.

Let someone else enjoy them, I think now, as I put them into the bag. *What else? Ah yes, the desk diary.*

I'm sitting on the little sofa in front of the TV in our big open-plan kitchen/diner/downstairs living space, having gone round the house earlier collecting all the things I want to ditch and piling them on the coffee table. I reach for the diary, the one someone sent to the office for me as a Christmas gift. Along with not being a candle or baking person, I am also not a diary person – well, I am, but I use the diary on my phone these days, not a real paper one – and I haven't even really looked at it properly yet, I realise, feeling guilty. I should have thanked whoever sent it by now, but I don't remember seeing a card or note when I slipped it out of its cardboard wrapping and dumped it on my desk upstairs on Christmas Eve.

'Where did you come from, then?' I ask it, out loud. It's actually a nice-looking diary, a page a day, boxed and bound in black leather. I remove the plastic lid of the box and slip the diary out, opening the front cover, wondering if there might be any clue to the sender's identity inside. Instead, I'm surprised to see a bright-yellow sticky note on the first page.

It says, in block capitals:

READ ME

What?
Weird, I think.
Frowning, I flick through the first few pages containing

the usual calendars and lists of notable dates and religious festivals for the coming year, until I reach the 1st of January. And then I freeze.

What the hell is this?

There's an entry on the page, just three words, in black ink and block capitals just like the sticky note.

MURDER LISA, OXFORD

I stare at the words, and then at the date. The 1st of January. New Year's Day. A little shiver runs up my back, and I slowly lift my gaze to the television screen in front of me. The BBC lunchtime news is on, and I've only been half listening, but I know which story they've just been running. It's the story of Lisa Turner. A story which shocked and saddened a hungover nation when it first broke a few weeks back. Lisa Turner, a twenty-eight-year-old woman who was found dead in Oxford early on the morning of New Year's Day, murdered as she made her way home from a New Year's Eve party. Lisa Turner, whose killer still hasn't been found.

My chest tightens. I look down at the diary, at the words, again, and then turn a few more pages. My hand is shaking, my mind racing.

Who sent this?

It came in the post – landed on my desk the day before Christmas Eve, the 23rd of December, if I remember correctly. Around then, anyway. That was more than a week *before* Lisa Turner was murdered.

So how …?

11

I freeze again. I've reached February now, Monday the 1st. *Tomorrow.* And there's another entry.

MURDER JANE, BIRMINGHAM

What the hell? Is this some kind of sick joke?
I read the words twice, three times, nausea rising. Then I start turning pages again, frantically now. Blank, blank, blank ... then, on Monday the 1st of March, the same black ink, the same neat lettering. Just a different name, a different city.

MURDER DAVID, CARDIFF

I swallow hard. I'm starting to feel light-headed.
What's going on here? What is this?
Flick, flick, flick, more blank pages, my fingers slippery with sweat now. And then I stop, little ribbons of fear curling in my stomach.
Does that say ...?
It does. The black words are stark against the white page. It's another entry, on Thursday the 1st of April.

MURDER MARY, CHELTENHAM

Chapter 3

Sunday 31st January

'It mentions Lisa Turner's murder, in Oxford, but it was written *before* that murder happened,' I say, as I wave the diary at the jaded-looking woman at the front counter of the police station, trying to convince her that I need to speak to an officer, urgently. 'And it contains threats against other people too, one of them dated tomorrow. Please, I need to talk to somebody. It's *really* important.'

There'd been no further entries after the one with my name in it. I'd flicked feverishly through the rest of the diary but it was blank, so I'd gone back to the beginning and found the four marked pages again, staring at the words until my vision blurred. I'd gone upstairs to find Pete then, trying to explain what I'd just found, thrusting the diary towards him then grabbing it back just in time, realising that the police would need to check it for fingerprints and DNA, and that I'd already touched it more than enough. I took some photos though – of the cover, and of the notes inside it, just for future reference, my crime-writer brain beginning to whirr – and then I dropped the diary into a freezer bag and sealed the top, ruing the fact that the wrapping it had come in was long gone, discarded in the recycling box which was emptied weeks ago, its contents now lost forever in the mountains of waste generated by Christmas celebrations. Then, telling Pete – who still looked confused and slightly shocked – that I'd be back in a couple of hours, I jumped into my car and headed for the police station.

By the time I'm finally escorted from reception into a small windowless room to speak to a man who introduces himself as Sergeant Gareth Little, I'm feeling rather frantic, tripping over my words as he asks me some basic questions about myself and the purpose of my visit and notes my answers down on the pad in front of him. I've never met him before; I know a few of the Gloucestershire police officers a little from stories I've worked on, but not him, and I'm starting to wonder if it might have been better to have waited to speak to one of my previous contacts. This guy has a rather sceptical expression on his face.

'I've bagged it for you,' I say, when he's finished making his preliminary notes and finally agrees to take a look at what I'm clutching in my hands. 'I'm the only one who's touched it since it arrived. But look – these are the four entries in it.'

I hold out my phone, swiping through the photos, and his brow crinkles in a frown.

'And you received this when?' he asks. His surname belies his appearance – he's far from little – a tall, broad, muscular-looking man with a shaven head and pale-blue eyes.

'Just before Christmas. I opened it and threw away the

packaging unfortunately. But I only looked inside it for the first time this morning, and look, this is the entry that's concerning me the most right now. It's a threat against a woman in Birmingham, tomorrow. I mean, it's just a first name, and there must be, I don't know, hundreds if not thousands of women called Jane in a city of that size, so I don't know what on earth you're going to do with this, but ...'

He's definitely looking at me suspiciously now.

'Right. And do you happen to know anyone with any of these names, in any of these cities? A friend, a relative, maybe?'

He asks the question abruptly, and I shake my head.

'No. I don't think so. Nobody springs to mind.'

He nods and stares at the photos for another minute, then looks at me curiously, as people often do, and I shift uncomfortably in my chair.

'Can you wait here, please?' he says. 'I won't be long.'

He stares at me for a few moments longer, then stands up and leaves the room, taking the bagged diary with him. He's gone for twenty minutes, and I wait, my stomach churning, fingers tapping on the battered wooden tabletop, mind still racing, so distracted that I jump violently when the door opens suddenly and he reappears.

'Sorry, just needed to make a few calls,' he says. 'And I've arranged for the diary to be sent off to forensics. It's probably some sort of strange hoax, but I agree it is concerning that the first entry mentions a Lisa in Oxford, if it *was* written ahead of time. And yes, worrying that there's a mention of a possible crime happening tomorrow ... and a possible threat to you, if you're the Mary referred to'—he runs a meaty hand over his smooth scalp—'but we can take over now, so thank you for bringing it in. Can I just check – where were you on New Year's Eve?'

'Me?' I frown. *Why is he asking me that? Surely he doesn't think …?*

Then I shrug.

Of course he has to ask. I could easily have written those things in the diary myself, couldn't I? He's only doing his job.

'I was here in Cheltenham all night,' I say. 'My housemate was away – he went to Dublin to see his mum, that's where she lives – so I went out with a few of the guys from The Hub. The shared office space I mentioned?'

I point at his notebook, and he nods.

'Names? And where did you go?'

'At first it was just me and my friend Ellie – Eleanor Lloyd. She runs Sparkle Specialists; it's a make-up artist agency. We were together from about eight until, gosh, probably about 2am. We had dinner at Brasserie Blanc and then went on to Gin & Juice for the rest of the night; they had a band playing. Two of the others met us there, Guy Hamilton and Stu Porter – they both work in website design. They arrived about eleven. Guy and I walked home together around two – he lives down on Bath Road, so not far from here. That should all be easy enough for you to verify.'

'OK. Thanks for that.'

He hesitates for a moment, scanning the notes on his pad, then looks up.

'You said you're a crime writer? This *could* just be a prank. Or it could be someone looking for your attention, or trying to cause trouble of some sort. These may not be real threats at all. The entries are so vague ... but rest assured we will give it our full attention and keep in close contact with you, OK? And please, can I ask you to keep the arrival of this diary to yourself for now, while we make some enquiries? Have you told anyone else about it?'

'Just my housemate, Pete. Peter Chong. But I can tell him not to breathe a word to anyone. I'd trust him with my life, quite literally. He won't say anything.'

He nods and makes another note.

'OK. Oh, and one more thing – are you happy to let us take a sample of your DNA and fingerprints now, before you leave, for elimination purposes? As you've touched the diary. Your friend Pete didn't touch it at all?'

'No. Just me. And yes, that's fine, of course. And thank you,' I say.

But as I head home half an hour later, I feel even more anxious than before, and at the same time oddly deflated. I'm not sure what I was expecting, but Sergeant Little's reaction felt so ... low key. And yet, he was right about how vague the threats were. Jane in Birmingham? David in Cardiff? For goodness' sake.

Isn't David one of the UK's most popular first names for men? How do the police even begin to investigate a threat like that? It's impossible, I think.

It's just after six when I get in, to find Pete waiting anxiously. He tells me to go upstairs and sit down while he opens some wine, and I head up to the big first-floor lounge, where he's thoughtfully turned the central heating up, put some music on and lit the lamps. Tonight, though, the soft pools of light and quiet jazz which I normally find so calming after a long day aren't doing it for me, my brain still feverishly trying to process the events of the past few hours.

Could that diary be some sort of joke?

But ... *Lisa, Oxford.* The words written *before* Lisa Turner's body was found. The diary already sitting on my desk, waiting to be opened.

If I'd looked at it sooner, could I have stopped it? Could I have saved her? And ... 'Murder Mary, Cheltenham'? *Is that me? Or another Mary? The diary was sent to me. But why? Why would anyone want to kill me? And the date – the 1st of April. April Fool's Day. Is that significant?*

'Are you OK? What did the police say? This is *insane*.'

Pete's back, holding out a glass, and I take a large mouthful of chilled white wine and swallow.

'Thanks, I needed that. And yes, I'm OK. It just took ages. I had to wait for nearly two hours while they found someone for me to talk to, and then I'm not even sure how seriously he took it. I think he thought I might have written those notes in the diary myself. I mean, I know it's a strange one. I don't really know what to make of it myself now I've calmed down a bit, but you can't take the chance, can you? Especially with that freaky entry about Lisa in Oxford. That can't just be a coincidence, can it? Now I'm just worried about Jane in Birmingham, whoever she is. If it's not a prank, it's *tomorrow*, Pete. Murder Jane, Birmingham, 1st of February.'

He's shaking his head, eyebrows raised.

'And murder Mary, Cheltenham, on the 1st of April. Bloody

hell, Mary. I'd be on a plane to Australia by mid-March if it was me.'

'Well, it might not be me. Could be anyone called Mary. And anyway, hopefully they'll have caught him by then,' I say.

He rolls his eyes.

'How are you so relaxed about this? Stay there. I don't fancy wine – I'm going to grab a beer.'

He stands up and walks out of the room, heading downstairs to the kitchen, and I pick up my glass again, then with my other hand reach for the soft grey blanket that's draped over the back of the sofa and pull it over my knees. I'm not relaxed, not really. I feel shivery and a little sick, and I take a couple of long, deep breaths, trying to steady myself.

'They might get lucky with forensics,' I say to Pete, as he walks back into the room. He sits down on the other end of the sofa, beer bottle in hand.

'If they find DNA on that diary, and get a match on the police database ...'

'*If*,' he says darkly. 'I'm worried about you, Mary, even if you're not.'

I force a smile.

'Shush, it'll be fine,' I say. 'Oh, and they've asked us to keep it to ourselves for now. Please don't mention it to *anyone*, OK?'

'I haven't, and of course I won't,' he says.

'Not even Megan?'

'Not even Megan.'

He smiles, and I smile back.

'Go on, stick the telly on. Let's find something funny to watch. I could do with some light relief.'

He obliges, and I stretch out my legs and rest my feet on his lap. He promptly uses them as somewhere to lodge his beer bottle, and we both laugh and settle down to watch an old episode of *Father Ted* in companionable silence. I'm glad he's here tonight and not staying at Megan's, I think, and steal a glance at his handsome profile, his white teeth flashing as he roars with laughter at Father Dougal's latest mishap. As I said before, I don't *fancy* Pete, but I do love him, I suppose. He's an accountant, and we met at a house party in London about eight years ago. I'd recently returned from America; I'd spent the previous few years living in New York with my grandmother, while I studied journalism at Columbia University, and Pete and I bonded immediately over our shared passion for the Big Apple.

'I spent my gap year travelling across Europe and America, but New York – well, so far it's my favourite city in the *world*,' he said, with such glittery-eyed, boyish enthusiasm that I laughed out loud.

'Mine too,' I said, and we clinked glasses and spent the rest of the evening deep in conversation.

I'm not really sure why our relationship never developed into a romantic one; friends have commented on it for years, telling us we're perfect for each other, and we've even said it ourselves, once or twice – we are remarkably compatible in pretty much every way. But I suppose that chemistry, that *spark*, just isn't there; we'll happily snuggle up together on the sofa, like this evening, but with no desire whatsoever to rip each other's clothes off, and there's never been any jealousy when one of us is dating. We're the very best of friends, but it's always been a purely platonic relationship, and we're both really happy with that. So when I decided to move out of London three years ago and use some of my inheritance money to get myself on the property ladder, Pete came too, and moved in as my lodger.

I was twenty-nine, and starting to tire of the noise and frantic pace of London, and Pete was two years older and had been thinking of moving somewhere more rural for years. We were both single, and when Pete heard of a great job going at a Gloucestershire accountancy firm, it seemed like a good time to up sticks. I'd lived in the Cotswolds before, in my teens, and I knew how beautiful it was. I fell in love with my lovely modern townhouse in the smart Montpellier area of Cheltenham as soon as I saw it. A three-storey building on The Grove, a sweeping tree-lined street, its big open-plan living area downstairs opens onto a pretty little paved courtyard at the rear, which in turns backs onto the landscaped gardens of Grove Court, an upmarket apartment complex. Upstairs, the elegant first-floor lounge (the estate agent's details called it a 'drawing room') has floor-to-ceiling windows and a beautiful polished maple wood floor; and on the top floor, the master bedroom – mine, naturally – is huge, with en suite dressing room and bathroom and doors opening onto a roof terrace which gets the morning and afternoon sun.

The house is mortgage-free – my late father left me a substantial sum, as did my grandmother – but Pete still pays me the going rate to rent one of the three other airy bedrooms, and while I still have plenty of cash in the bank I've always been a worrier when it comes to money, so it's nice to have that monthly sum coming in, especially as being a freelance crime writer isn't always the most reliable source of regular income. Pete bought himself a place in Cheltenham too, last year: a smart one-bed apartment in a Regency building just off Royal Crescent. But he rents it out, to a colleague at work, and the arrangement suits us both. Maybe the arrival of Megan on the scene will change things one day soon; maybe *I'll* even meet someone special one of these days, who knows. But for now, we're happy with how things are.

I don't date much; there've been boyfriends, on and off, but it takes a while for me to let men get close. I have scars, you see. My left ear and cheek, my right wrist. I was burned in a fire many years ago, the fire that killed my father. I've healed well, but people still stare. Edward Cooper in the office, that police officer today ... You get used to it, but I still hate them – the curious looks, the pity I sometimes see in people's eyes, the unasked questions. Pete never stared though. He didn't even seem to notice; it was me who brought it up, weeks after we met, and he looked surprised, as if seeing those bits of me for the very first time.

'What, you expect me to believe you've never noticed half of my left ear is missing, and what's left looks like a shrivelled sprout?' I laughed, and he laughed back, peering at the side of my head.

'Honestly, I really didn't!' he said. 'I mean, your hearing's obviously not affected?'

I shook my head. I'd been lucky there.

'And OK, I did sort of notice that bit of rough skin on the

side of your face, and the mark on your wrist, but ... well, you're beautiful, Mary. All that fabulous hair and gorgeous dark eyes. What do a few little scars matter? Does my childhood appendectomy scar ruin my incredible six-pack? I think not.'

He pulled his white T-shirt up and flashed his tanned stomach, and I rolled my eyes.

'Any excuse, Chong! Put it away!'

But the exchange had made me happy, my confidence soaring. As the years have passed, I've become less self-conscious, more accepting of my appearance, realising that apart from my cheek, my flaws are easy enough to hide, but I still don't like being looked at by strangers. I don't even like *talking* to strangers sometimes, which is a definite disadvantage in my job.

And, I think now, reaching for my glass again, *I might have to add receiving gifts from strangers to that list too, after this. Who sent that bloody diary? Are people really going to die? Am I going to die?*

I take a large mouthful of wine and put the glass down again.

Stop it, Mary. Don't freak out over this.

Pete's right. *If* the threats in the diary do start to become reality, and *if* I think the Mary in the diary really is me, then I can just ... leave, can't I? I have friends abroad, I have money, it's not going to be a problem.

And what a story.

I've been complaining about everything being too quiet for weeks. And now this has literally landed right in my lap. It's a crime writer's dream, isn't it? I wriggle a little in my seat, adjusting my feet on Pete's lap, and he glances at me and smiles, then turns his attention back to the TV screen.

Yes, I think. *It's a crime writer's dream. Exactly the sort of thing I've been wishing would come my way.*

And I try to ignore the little, faraway voice in my head that's whispering something so softly I can barely hear it. I know what it's saying though.

Be careful what you wish for.

Chapter 4

Sunday 31st January

Cheltenham Central Police Station

'I've put calls in to Thames Valley, West Midlands, and South Wales Police,' says Sergeant Gareth Little.

He's on the phone to the duty inspector, Rob Jones, filling him in about Mary Ellis and her disturbing Christmas gift. Or *alleged* gift, anyway.

'No reports of any other mysterious diaries or any death threats being received by anyone in Birmingham or Cardiff to date. And as far as they know in the Lisa Turner investigation in Oxford, she hadn't mentioned any messages or threats before her murder either. Seems like just this one diary, sent to this Mary Ellis.'

'Hmmm,' says Rob. 'Well, you were right to get it sent straight off to forensics. Bit of a strange one. If it's genuine though – holy crap. Don't really want to think about that. What did you make of this Mary Ellis? The name's familiar for some reason?'

'She's a local crime writer,' says Gareth. He'd got some basic details from Mary herself earlier, but he'd done a little more research after she'd left, curious about her.

'Not a newspaper reporter though – more of a specialist,' he explains. 'She does in-depth interviews for some of the big newspapers and magazines. Victims, families, even perpetrators of high-profile crimes. She moved to Cheltenham from London a few years ago. Works out of a shared office in town and lives in a fancy pad in Montpellier with a friend. The house is worth about a million. And she's single, no kids.'

'Ah, yes, I know who she is now. She was the one who did that interview with Stoney Linehan in Wakefield last year, wasn't she? Pretty impressive, actually. She managed to get him to talk about things he'd never told anyone before. It was grim reading.'

'Yes, that was her. I read it. Pretty chilling stuff.'

Gareth is silent for a moment, remembering the case of Stoney, who played lead guitar for the chart-topping indie band Pineapple Metal, until he was convicted of multiple child sexual offences spanning at least a decade.

'Sickening,' agrees Rob.

'She's also the daughter of Gregor Ellis,' says Gareth. 'Remember him? The famous American crime novelist? He was huge in the 90s. He wrote a string of bestsellers. A couple of them were even made into movies.'

'Oh wow, is she? That's interesting,' says Rob. 'Wasn't he a bit of a recluse? He's dead, isn't he?'

'Yep. I read up on it earlier. He brought her up on his own, as far as I can make out. His wife, Mary's mother, died of cancer, I think. Gregor pretty much hid away from the world after that, although they moved about a lot. He was always looking for inspiration for his books in new cities and countries, according to Wikipedia. They were living here in the UK when he died, not far away actually – some country mansion in the Cotswolds. There was a fire one night, and Mary escaped with burns, but he was killed. She was only eighteen.'

He pauses, remembering the self-conscious way Mary Ellis had kept pulling the sleeve of her jumper down over the scar on her wrist as she'd sat across the table from him. There'd been something on the side of her face too, but he'd been more interested in looking at her chocolate-brown eyes. Her accent had also intrigued him: a soft mix of American and English.

Mid-Atlantic, was that what they called it?

'And now *she's* a crime writer too, of a different kind. Interesting,' says Rob. 'Which brings us back to the diary. Do you think it's genuine?'

Gareth shrugs.

'I've asked her about her whereabouts on the night of the Oxford murder, which we can check out, just in case. But yes, actually. I got the feeling she was quite unnerved by the whole thing.'

Rob nods.

'I wonder if her occupation is the reason it was sent to her, specifically, then?' he says. 'Some sicko who wants their story written? A death threat to a well-known crime writer is certainly one way to grab attention.'

'Maybe,' says Gareth. 'But if the Mary in the diary *is* her, she's not the only one being threatened. There are two more before her. Who are they? And what else do we do now? Wait for forensics, obviously. But anything else, in the meantime?'

There's a moment's silence.

'I kind of hate to say this,' says Rob slowly. 'But, as tomorrow is the 1st of February, I think what *we* do is ... well, we wait. We wait and see what, if anything, happens in Birmingham. And then in Cardiff. And then, if we have to, we can really start to worry.'

* * *

Cardiff Central Police Station

'Well, let's see if anything kicks off in Birmingham first, before we panic, right? We're not up until March after all, according to this, and it's probably all bollocks anyway. I'm off for a coffee – want one?'

Inspector Rhys Williams heaves his not inconsiderable bulk out of his chair and looks questioningly at his colleague.

'Yeah, cheers, boss. Black, please. And I'm sure you're right. Still, I don't envy the lads up there in the Midlands. Not much notice, is it? And sod all to go on, if it's for real.'

Sergeant Hari Hughes and the duty inspector had been discussing the diary handed in to Gloucestershire Police for the past ten minutes and, while it was definitely disconcerting that it had mentioned a Lisa in Oxford, they'd decided it wasn't worth putting too much into in the way of resources. Not yet, anyway.

'David, in Cardiff? That's bad enough, but if you throw

all the blokes called Dafydd, Dai, Dewi and so on into the mix too, well ...'

The inspector had thrown his hands in the air in despair, and Hari had nodded his agreement. The Welsh spelling of David, and its diminutives, might double the number of men called David in the city, although neither of them had any idea what that number might be.

'It's been one of the most popular names in the UK since the 1930s,' Hari had told Rhys, after a quick Google search. 'And here in Wales, well, he's the patron saint, isn't he? Even worse. Hopeless, eh?'

Now though, he watches the boss lumbering off towards the coffee machine with an uneasy feeling.

'If something does happen in Birmingham, it's us next,' he mutters to himself. 'And what the hell do we do then?'

He shrugs. That's a worry for a higher pay grade than his. *Let's just see what happens, eh?*

* * *

St Aldates Police Station, Oxford

'We need that forensics report, and fast.'

DCI Linda Lake, senior investigating officer in the Lisa Turner case, is pacing up and down the incident room. In the month since the murder, every single lead she's had – and there haven't been many – has led to dead ends, and she's been starting to feel a little desperate. The call this afternoon from Gloucestershire has been like manna from heaven.

'If there's a fingerprint, *anything* ... and I want to speak to this Mary Ellis, too,' she says, reaching the far wall of the room and turning abruptly to march back across the stained blue carpet again, weaving her way between the desks.

'If this diary's legit, this could be the break we've been waiting for. Does Mary have any connection with Lisa? And we need to go back to Lisa's family and friends again, ask them about any associates in Cardiff and Birmingham ...'

She stops pacing suddenly, aware that she's sounding a little hysterical and that the other officers in the room are watching her warily.

'Could still be a hoax, ma'am,' says the nearest detective sergeant cautiously. 'Although, I agree it's a massive bloody coincidence if that diary really was in the post before Lisa was murdered ...'

Her voice tails off.

'Exactly,' says Linda. 'And it's all we've got right now, isn't it? All eyes on Birmingham tonight and tomorrow. And we'd all better start praying for something good to come out of that forensics report. This could be it, guys. Keep everything crossed, OK?'

* * *

Birmingham Central Police Station

'Jane? Jane in Birmingham? That's all we've got? And it's tomorrow? Gimme a break.'

Detective Chief Inspector Priya Thomson of West Midlands

Police pushes a strand of loose, dark hair back off her forehead and frowns at her colleague. Detective Inspector Jason Butcher shrugs.

'I know,' he says. 'That's all this diary has, apparently. Three dates and three first names. Well, four if you include the one that's already happened, which is why it's sparked a bit of concern. And that's all it says for Birmingham. Jane, tomorrow.'

'Well what the hell am I supposed to do with that? And why send it to this Mary woman in the first place?' Priya knows she sounds as exasperated as she feels, and she takes a deep breath.

I really could have done without this today, she thinks.

She didn't sleep well last night, and she can feel a headache brewing. She glances at her watch. It's already nearly six o'clock. 'Tomorrow' starts in about six hours' time.

'Not sure. Gloucestershire are looking closely at her, but their gut feeling is that she's not lying about it, and they've asked forensics to fast-track the diary,' says Jason. He's a short, wiry man with a neat red beard, which he has a habit of stroking when he's thinking hard about something. He's doing it now.

'But even so, on a Sunday night ... it could be Tuesday before we get anything back. And that's going to be too late, if it's a genuine threat. But, well, we can hardly ask local news to put out a report telling everyone called Jane to lock herself in her bedroom for the next thirty hours, can we? Can you imagine the mass panic?'

Priya rolls her eyes.

'No, we can't do that. I don't even have a clue how many,

well, how many Janes there might be. Is it any old person called Jane, or a specific person? I mean, she could be a baby or a granny or anything in-between, couldn't she? And what if it's a specific Jane, but she decides to go on holiday or away for business or something tomorrow?'

She pauses, her mind racing.

'And what if it's someone whose *middle* name is Jane, or someone who was christened Jane but later changed her name? I mean, the possibilities are endless. We could search the electoral roll but that would just give us the ones registered to vote ...'

She pauses for breath, aware that she's on somewhat of a rant, and rubs her temples for a moment. They're starting to throb.

'And *Birmingham*? Does that mean just the city, or the whole metropolitan area? It's just impossible, Jas,' she says.

He nods.

'I know. I know. It's a friggin' joke.' He shakes his head, then looks over his shoulder and calls:

'Frankie? Any luck with those numbers?'

Two desks away, Detective Constable Frankie Tanner turns in her seat. Her white-blonde pixie cut is tousled, tufts sticking up at strange angles, as if she's been running her hands repeatedly through her hair.

'It's a surprisingly tricky search, actually,' she says, and gives a small sigh. 'I've got a ballpark figure, but it's very rough. I mean, we could try asking for data from the most recent census, but in theory the records are all anonymised and kept secure for a hundred years, so, you know ...'

She rolls her eyes.

'The Office of National Statistics might help us out, but they might not, and we certainly won't get anything tonight. I've done some number crunching though, from what I can find online. I've used female population estimates, and ONS historic baby name rankings ...'

She reaches for a piece of paper on her desk and taps it with a slender forefinger.

'And, well, as I said, this is an incredibly rough estimate, and Jane is *such* a common name. Although it's not as common as it once was, actually. It was very popular from the 1950s through to the 70s, and then began to decline a bit. But my very vague guess is that in Birmingham there are probably at least ...'

She hesitates, frowning, then continues.

'... two to two and a half thousand women called Jane. Most likely to be in their fifties and beyond. Fifty-something to eighty-something. But a friend of mine actually called her new baby Jane just six months ago. Jane Amelia. So ...'

She lifts both hands in a gesture Priya interprets as *who knows, really?*.

'Right. Well, thanks Frankie.'

She thinks for a minute. The victim in Oxford, Lisa Turner, was twenty-eight. *If* – and she still thinks it's a big if – there really is some sort of deranged serial killer targeting people in different cities, there'd usually be some sort of pattern. Young women walking home alone late at night, for example. And yet, one of the supposed prospective victims is David, Cardiff, which doesn't fit at all. A mix of male and female victims? All the same ...

'OK, Jason, this is what we're going to do. It's not much, but I think it's all we *can* do, given the vague nature of this threat and the massive number of people and the huge area it covers. I'm still hoping it's some sort of sick prank, but I'm going to ask for some extra manpower until midnight tomorrow. More patrols tonight, especially after chucking-out time. They all need to look out for women walking home on their own, be extra vigilant. Give them lifts if necessary. And any 999 calls from women in distress – domestic violence, even anyone hearing a noise outside, whatever – have to be given highest priority. What do you think?'

Jason nods slowly.

'Agreed, ma'am. It's something, at least. And as you say, it's probably a hoax. The Lisa, Oxford thing was most likely a coincidence. What killer warns his victims in advance, eh?'

They stare at each other for a moment, and Priya is pretty sure he's thinking exactly what she's thinking.

Please, let it be a hoax. Because if it's not, we're in big trouble here.

Chapter 5

Monday 1st February

It's happened already. *Overnight.* It's 10am. and I'm sitting at my desk at The Hub, constantly refreshing the online news pages, anxiety gnawing at my stomach, and suddenly there it is.

> *West Midlands Police have launched a murder investigation after a woman's body was found in Edgbaston. The victim, believed to be in her fifties, was found in her back garden early this morning by a neighbour; she was pronounced dead at the scene. More to follow.*

Scant details as yet, and no name. But she's going to be a Jane: I can feel it in my gut.

MURDER JANE, BIRMINGHAM.

The 1st of February.
This is it, isn't it? It's happening, just as the diary threatened. Or is this just a horrible coincidence?

I take a deep breath, trying to calm myself.

What do I do now? Don't panic, that's the key. Wait until this poor woman's been identified, for a start …

'All right, Mary? Want a biccie?'

I jump as Eleanor zooms up behind me, one hand skilfully manoeuvring her wheelchair, the other proffering an open packet of fig rolls. I look quizzically at the biscuits and smile.

'Fig rolls? I didn't even know they still *made* fig rolls. I'm OK, thanks. You really do have the most retro taste in snacks, Ellie.'

Eleanor tosses her long red hair back with a flip of her head and grins. She is, as always, exquisitely made up, her eyeliner in perfect cat-like flicks, her full lips a deep burgundy.

'Got to keep my energy up. Two weeks until Valentine's Day, and the phone hasn't stopped,' she says. 'Speaking of which …'

Down at the far end of the office, her desk phone has started to ring, and she drops the packet of biscuits onto her lap and whizzes off again, calling 'Later!' over her shoulder. Moments later she's grabbing the phone and proclaiming:

'Good morning, Sparkle Specialists, how can I help?' in her lovely, sing-song Welsh accent. Her agency is thriving, it seems. Eleanor – or Ellie, as most of us call her – and her team travel far and wide: red-carpet events, fashion shows, magazine shoots, the lot. But their bread and butter is just normal women who like to have their hair and make-up professionally done for a night out. It's not something which would ever occur to me – I'm happy with a heavy-duty concealer, a slick of mascara and lip gloss and a dab of blusher – but apparently it's a growing trend, and things always get a little crazy for Ellie at certain times of the year:

Christmas, graduation time, wedding season. And Valentine's Day, of course.

I turn back to my computer screen, clicking onto the West Midlands Police website and navigating to their *Latest News* section. There's nothing more there than I already know, and there probably won't be for a while. It's beyond frustrating, and I wonder if it's worth putting a call in to Sergeant Little, the local police officer I spoke to yesterday, because surely he's been keeping an eye on Birmingham overnight too? Then I change my mind. It would be a waste of time; he's not likely to know the victim's name yet either, and even if he does, he won't share it with me. I'll just have to wait, and try to keep busy. I'm so tired though. I slept badly last night; at around nine, as we'd just started watching an old episode of *Miranda*, Pete took a brief phone call from Megan, and after saying goodbye he looked at me with an expression which was a combination of sheepish and hopeful.

'She says she's really missing me. She really wants me to go over and stay the night. I mean, I'd like to, but I don't want to leave you if you're feeling shaky ...'

'Oh don't be silly, go! I'm fine. Enjoy your night of debauchery,' I said.

'Are you sure? Really?' he asked.

'Yes! Get out of here, go on.'

But, alone in the house, my anxiety had flooded back, and I'd spent a restless night, sleeping fitfully and waking at the slightest noise. I had nightmares too; I've had them for years, on and off, but this was darker, more frightening, than any I've had in a long time, and twice I sat bolt upright in bed, gasping for breath, my pyjamas soaked with sweat. Now, I stand up, stretch my tense, stiff neck and shoulders and walk down to the kitchen to make a strong coffee. When I get back to my desk, mug in hand, I reopen the document I started working on first thing this morning, and stare at the photograph I've copied onto the top of the page. Lisa Turner, the young woman who died in Oxford on New Year's Day.

She stares back at me, and I swallow hard, suddenly feeling as if I want to cry. Twenty-eight years old, a glossy dark-brown bob, soft fringe swept across her forehead, and quite remarkable eyes, yellow-brown like a tiger's. She'd recently become a barrister, working for a leading chambers in Oxford city centre and specialising in insolvency and company law.

Such a waste, I think.

Every death is tragic, of course. But when it's someone so young, with so much to give ... I pick up my coffee and take a sip, then jump again as a voice behind me says:

'A bit macabre, your job, isn't it? Looking at photos of dead people again?'

Could people just stop *creeping up behind me?* I think, with a wave of irritation, and turn to see Edward Cooper peering over my shoulder at the photo of Lisa. I close the document and roll my chair away from him.

'I'm a crime writer, Edward. It's what I do,' I snap, not even trying to hide my annoyance, and he backs away, raising both hands in the air.

'Sorry, sorry, just passing,' he says. 'That was that lawyer who was killed in Oxford at New Year, wasn't it? Very sad.'

I say nothing, turning back to my screen, and he stands

there for another couple of seconds, then walks away. When I look up again, I see that he's stopped to talk to Satish on his way back to his desk. I can't hear what they're saying, but suddenly Satish turns and glances at me, abruptly turning away again when he realises I'm watching him. Edward looks at me too and smiles, looking a little embarrassed, I think, then heads back to his own desk further down the room. I stare after him for a moment, then realise I really can't be bothered, and reopen my file on Lisa Turner.

I'd been aware of the case, of course, ever since the murder investigation launched a month ago, but it hadn't struck me as one I might want to delve more deeply into. Until now, of course. Now, I desperately want to find out everything I can, every tiny little detail. If she really was the first in what is to be a string of related killings – still a *big* if, I keep telling myself – and *if* I really am a potential victim too, then Lisa's the key, isn't she? Or at least, she might be. Some killings are just ... well, just random. But what killer chooses a random name in advance, and then seeks out a victim to match? Nobody would do that, surely? Which means that these names – Jane, David, Mary – aren't random. They're the names of specific people, people the killer has already selected. Probably.

'I don't know. I have no idea, not yet,' I whisper to the photo of Lisa Turner. 'But you, I want to know everything about you.'

I spent an hour this morning gathering as much information as I could, and now I scan my notes again. Lisa Turner had been single at the time of her death, and had one older brother, an Oxford GP called Alastair. Both of their parents are dead; I couldn't find much on their father, Alan, who passed away fifteen years ago. But their mother was interesting. She died two years ago – a heart attack – but she was Alice Turner, better known as The Honourable Mrs Justice Turner, one of very few women to be appointed as a supreme court judge. I found a fascinating article when I looked further into that: Lisa, interviewed in *The Times* not long after her mother's death, talking about how 'out of step' the UK is in its judicial diversity, both in terms of race and gender.

'This is the highest court in the land – the final court of appeal for civil cases in the UK and criminal cases from England, Wales, and Northern Ireland, and yet where are all the female judges?' she's quoted as saying. 'Less than a third of British judges are women. My mother felt passionately about that, and so do I. It has to change.'

Outspoken, then. Did that draw the attention of whoever killed her, maybe?

The police, it seems, have had little to go on in terms of suspects. Lisa had been making her way home, alone, from a New Year's Eve party, and had seemingly taken a short cut along the Oxford canal towpath; her body had been found with serious head injuries near Wolvercote Lock, three miles north of the city centre and just minutes from her home on Godstow Road. There was an appeal for witnesses in the days following the murder, one news article mentioning that there were no CCTV cameras on that stretch of the canal.

Did the killer know that, and choose that location deliberately? And it's so difficult to identify people in winter anyway, especially on a cold January night. Everyone's bundled up in coats and hat and scarves. Even where there is CCTV coverage, faces can be tricky to see ...

A smart, forensically aware killer then, avoiding cameras and, presumably, leaving nothing for the forensics team to go on. If he had, surely the investigation would be further on by now? It seems to have completely stalled, as far as I can gather anyway.

I want to look further into all of this, but I can't concentrate until I know what's happened in Birmingham. And, more importantly, *who* it's happened to. I click back through the news pages again. No further updates.

Come on, I urge silently. *Come on. Tell us her name. Please.*

And if it is Jane, as I strongly suspect it will turn out to be, what then? *What the hell do I do then?*

Chapter 6

Monday 1st February

Edgbaston, Birmingham

'Jane Holland. Her name is *Jane* Holland, guv. *Christ.*'

DI Jason Butcher runs a hand across his cropped red hair, his eyes wide. Priya stares at him for a moment, suddenly feeling sick, then in her peripheral vision sees someone approaching and turns to see who it is. It's Mia Whitehouse, the crime scene manager, who's just walked around the corner of the house and is peeling off her facemask.

They're standing in the wide paved driveway of 6 Oaks Road in Edgbaston. It is, Priya knows, one of the most prestigious streets in Birmingham, average house price £1.4 million, and number 6 is probably worth a lot more than that: detached, seven bedrooms, with half an acre of south-facing gardens to the rear. She'd been round there earlier, crossing an extensive terrace with steps leading down to a central lawn surrounded by beautifully tended borders. There are two magnificent oak trees, one at either end of the expansive space and, on this bright February morning, the sky a duck-egg blue for the first time in weeks, under one of those trees there's a dead body. The body of a woman, her identity now confirmed. Jane Holland. *Jane in Birmingham.* Not a hoax after all, then. Priya swallows hard, the feeling of nausea increasing.

But what could I have done? There've been extra patrols on the streets all night, officers on high alert, but this … I couldn't have prevented this, could I? In the poor woman's own garden? Or could I? Did I do enough? Could I have handled it differently? Should I have—

'Hi.'

Mia's face wears a sombre expression, and Priya takes a deep breath.

'Hello, Mia. How's it going? What can you tell me?'

Mia, now taking off her latex gloves, glances over her shoulder to where a private ambulance has just pulled into the drive, ready to take the body to the mortuary.

'Just about finished,' she says. 'And honestly, I hate to say this but there's very little here to go on. Cause of death was a single blow to the back of the head, by the look of it. No sign of any sort of weapon, no sign of a break in. The attacker enticed her out into the garden somehow, maybe? Not sure why she'd be out there on a winter night otherwise. She was in her pyjamas and dressing gown. Could have been someone she knew and let in? These houses all have private CCTV, so we're getting hold of that, and house-to-house may come up with something, hopefully.'

'OK. Who found her?' asks Priya.

'The victim lives alone apparently – it was the next-door neighbour who found her, and she says she didn't see or hear a thing last night. She let her dog out into the garden around 7.30 this morning and wandered down to pick up his ... his *doings*. She glanced over the wall between her garden and the victim's and saw what she described as a "strange shape" under the tree. She took a closer look and realised it looked human. She came round and banged on the front door for a few minutes, then tried phoning the victim; when she got no joy she dialled 999. She's in a bit of a state, as you can imagine, but she's in no doubt that it's her neighbour, Jane Holland. They're friends – they've lived next door to each other for the past six years.'

Priya nods, taking it all in, thinking. The decision's been made not to tell anyone else about the diary right now, but she needs to know if it fits.

Jane, on the 1st of February.

'Time of death?' she asks. 'How long was she out there?'

Mia frowns.

'We'll know more after the postmortem, but best guess is she died seven to eight hours before she was found. So the time of death, to answer your question, would have been around midnight. Just after, most likely. Between then and 1am. Right, back in a mo.'

She walks off towards the ambulance, and Priya and Jason exchange glances. *Before* midnight would still have been the 31st of January. But *after* ...

'He didn't mess about, did he? Only *just* the bloody 1st of February,' says Jason.

She nods.

If only they'd had more time. More time to consider the best course of action, to issue warnings maybe. They'd had a matter of hours, and it had been impossible, ludicrous really, but … OK, stop, Priya. Stop this.

She forces herself to focus. She can't, *mustn't*, go down this road right now; the feeling that she's failed this woman, the woman who's now lying dead in her back garden, is threatening to overwhelm her, and today she needs to concentrate on the investigation. Concentrate on finding whoever did this, and stopping him doing it again.

'Better hope we get something from that CCTV footage then,' she says briskly. 'And we need the forensics from that diary *now*. Can you get on to Gloucestershire, see what's happening? Plus, I want to know everything there is to know about Jane Holland. Why her, Jason? Why *this* Jane? It looks like we may well have a serial killer on our hands now, God help us. This can't just be a coincidence, can it? But I don't believe he's just picking random victims. There's got to be some link, some connection. We need to look closely at the Oxford murder, and speak to this writer, journalist, whatever she is, who was sent the diary. Mary Ellis? These people *must* have something in common, right?'

'You'd have thought so, wouldn't you?' he says. 'Right, I'm on it. And South Wales need to get on it too. They're next in line, aren't they?'

* * *

Cardiff Central Police Station

'It's happened. Jane in Birmingham. Look, here. Her ID hasn't been made public yet; they're still trying to trace her family, but they thought they'd better let us know ASAP. Jane Holland, fifty-five years old. Found dead in her back garden early this morning. Holy shit.'

Sergeant Hari Hughes waves the sheet of paper in his hand at the inspector, who stares at him for a moment then gives a low whistle.

'Woweee,' he says. 'Gonna be a bit of a job for us, then.'

Hari nods. Someone somewhere in Cardiff Central has done a bit of research and a few calculations since the threat in the diary was made known to them last night, and the news, as he and Inspector Williams had guessed, wasn't good. At least two thousand *Davids* in the city alone, plus hundreds more *Dafydds*, *Dais*, *Dewis* ... They were talking maybe three to four thousand men being potential victims, and that could well be an underestimate.

'I can't get my head round this one,' he says. 'If it *is* a serial killer – and I know you have to have three deaths, normally, to qualify, but he's threatening to do four, isn't he? Anyway – it's got to be unusual to target both men and women, eh? They usually stick to one or the other. And in random cities all over the place too? What do you make of that?'

Rhys Williams shrugs.

'No idea,' he says. 'Fortunately, it's no longer our problem. Wonder who'll get this one? Rather them than me.'

'I wouldn't mind working on it myself,' says Hari, a little

wistfully. He hopes one day soon to join the ranks of the detectives in the Criminal Investigation Department, and wonders which of the DCIs will be assigned to the case. Helen Andrews, maybe? She's young, but good. Or maybe Bryn Lewis. Whoever it is, he vows he will watch, and learn. This one is going to be *very* interesting.

Chapter 7

Monday 1st February

I'm still at The Hub, trying to research some potential stories but struggling to concentrate, when the news alert finally flashes up on my phone.

> *The woman who was found dead in Edgbaston, Birmingham, earlier today has been named by police as 55-year-old Jane Holland. Officers were called to her home this morning after her body was discovered in her back garden by a neighbour. Police have launched a murder investigation …*

There are more words, the usual appeal for witnesses and for anyone who might know the woman's movements over the previous day or so, but they blur in front of my eyes. I put the phone down, my hand trembling.

Jane. Jane Holland.

It's not a surprise, not really – my gut has been telling me all day that her name would be Jane. I knew it, I *knew* it, but even so, the confirmation is making me feel wobbly. It's happened. And now what? David in Cardiff, and then ... me? Or another Mary in Cheltenham? I jump violently as my phone starts ringing. It's an unknown number, and for a moment I consider ignoring it, then tell myself not to be so ridiculous and accept the call.

'Hello?'

My voice sounds thin and reedy and I swallow, my throat dry, and repeat the word.

'Hello? Who is this, please?'

'Mary Ellis? This is Sergeant Little. We met yesterday?'

Relief floods my body.

'Sergeant, hello. Yes, this is Mary.'

'Great. I was just wondering ... have you seen the news? From Birmingham?'

I swallow again. I need some water, but there's none on my desk.

'I have. Just now, yes. A woman called Jane. It's ... well, it's pretty scary ...'

I pause, looking around the office, but the nearest desks are all empty. Even so, I keep my voice low.

'So, what now?' I say.

'Well, it's early days, but as this no longer seems like a coincidence and as there are several parts of the country involved, things have moved pretty quickly in the past hour or so. We'll all have to stay across developments in each other's cases, which we can do via our IT system of course. But there'll also be regular briefings involving key members of each investigation team, via video conferencing. I'm going to be upfront with you, Mary: there will still have to be some investigation of you personally. But the first team meeting is tomorrow, and we'd like you to attend, if possible? Here in Cheltenham, at 10am?'

'I understand. And of course. No problem.'

'They all want to ask you a few questions, plus see if they can establish any patterns, any links between the potential victims, that sort of thing. Oh, and Mary, there's a strict media blackout on this for now. Not on the actual murders, obviously, but on the diary and the possible links between the cases. Can I assume you still haven't shared any details with anyone, other than Peter Chong?'

'Nobody,' I say. 'That's why I'm talking so quietly. I'm in the office. There's nobody within earshot though.'

'Great. OK, well tomorrow you'll meet the detective assigned to the case here in Gloucestershire – I don't even know who it's going to be yet, actually. And they'll be appointing an FLO too – that's a family liaison officer. Oh, sorry, I didn't need to explain that to you, did I?'

He laughs lightly, and for some reason the sound makes me feel a little better.

'I'm familiar with the term, yes. Thank you,' I say.

'That's OK,' he replies. 'They'll be your point of contact, keep you updated on the progress of the investigation, you know the drill. Anyway, I'll let you go. We'll see you at ten tomorrow, OK? Just come to where you came before. Somebody will be there to meet you.'

As I end the call, Eleanor hurtles past my desk again. A moment later she's reversing her chair, coming to a halt next to me.

'Gosh, are you OK, Mary? You're so pale. You look like you've seen a ghost.'

'I'm fine, Ellie.' I force myself to smile at her. 'Just a bit tired – I didn't sleep very well last night.'

'I feel your pain,' she says. 'Same here. I never sleep well in the run up to bloody Valentine's Day. Rushed off my feet. Not that I was ever on them, of course.'

She winks and speeds off again, skilfully manoeuvring her wheelchair around a briefcase someone's left sitting on the floor and then around Satish, who's walking towards her with his head down, engrossed in reading something on his phone. Clearly startled, he lets out a little yelp and a 'Whoops, sorry Ellie!', and I smile again, with genuine amusement this time. She's pretty incredible, I often think; she was born with a congenital spinal cord injury, and has never been able to walk, and it hasn't held her back one tiny bit. She has a lovely rooftop apartment in Vittoria Walk, not far from my place, her successful business, an *amazing* social life ... I watch her zip neatly back into position behind her desk just as her phone starts to ring for the umpteenth time today, then turn as Satish, who's just reached my desk, pauses and grimaces at me.

'You look knackered, Mary. You OK?' he says, and then, not waiting for me to reply, adds: 'She's a right little speed demon, isn't she?'

'She is. And I'm fine, thanks,' I say. 'Busy. You?'

I don't really mind Satish, as I've said before. He seems quite nice; he never stares at me and my burns, like so many people do. He doesn't even seem to notice them. He's pleasant to everyone, but he and Edward seem to have become particularly pally recently, which probably means, I've reluctantly decided, that Edward is basically OK too, if it wasn't for his disconcerting habit of invading my personal space.

'Yeah, busy, busy,' Satish says, and waves his phone at me. 'Just catching up on the news while I go for a coffee. I'll let you get on. But you do look really tired, so take it easy, right?'

He looks at me with a concerned expression, as if assessing the level of my "tiredness", then wanders off, head down again, scrolling on his phone. I sit there for another few moments, wondering what to do, then look at the time. It's after four.

Sod it, I'm going home.

When I get there, via Tesco to pick up some pasta and a couple of bottles of wine – I'm *definitely* going to need a drink tonight – Pete's already home, chopping tomatoes in the kitchen. I feel a little put out suddenly – he hasn't rung me today, and I thought he might, considering – but I suppose he's been busy at work, and now he's not alone here either. He's chatting to Megan, who's sitting on one of the high stools at the breakfast bar, looking lithe and toned in tight leggings and sipping water from a glass.

'Oh, hi Mary,' she says. 'I'm not staying. I'm off to class in a bit – just popped in for a quick catch-up with this hunk.'

She winks at me, and we both smile as Pete rolls his eyes dramatically. I sit down next to her, and we chat for a few minutes about not very much: the weather, and how busy her work is at this time of year, mostly. As well as being a fanatical runner, she's a yoga teacher, so when she says she's 'off to class' she means she's teaching at one of the big gyms in town. She tries, not for the first time, to persuade me to come and join one of her lessons ('It would do you so much good, Mary. You look a bit pale and stressed, if you don't mind me saying, and it really helps ...') and I sigh inwardly, wondering how many more people are going to comment on my appearance today, and politely decline, as I always do. I don't mind a long walk or a swim, but bending myself into all sorts of weird positions in a hot sweaty room with no windows and huge mirrors everywhere? Really not for me, no matter how pale, stressed or tired I may be. When she excuses herself to nip to the loo, I make sure the kitchen door is closed then turn to Pete.

'You haven't told her, have you? About the diary?' I hiss.

He looks up from the pot he's stirring on the hob – I'm not sure what he's cooking, but it smells delicious – with an indignant look on his face.

'Of course I haven't. I told you I wouldn't. Why? And I'm so sorry I haven't been in touch today, I was in non-stop meetings and then Megan was waiting for me in reception when I finished work, I didn't have a second to myself ...'

'It doesn't matter. Shush, listen. Because I've just spoken to the police again, and they've told me there's a media blackout on this now, and absolutely nobody else can know about it, OK? It's because ... well, it's happened. The second murder. Jane, in Birmingham. In the early hours of this morning.'

His eyes widen.

'Christ, Mary! Are you serious? This is—'

He stops speaking abruptly as the door opens and Megan reappears. She hesitates, looking at us, clearly wondering why we've stopped talking the moment she enters the room.

'Everything ... OK?' she asks, a look of suspicion on her pretty face.

'Fine, fine,' says Pete. 'Just a disagreement about ... household stuff. Whose turn it is to put the bins out this week.'

'Yep,' I agree hastily. 'And it's definitely *yours*.'

I wag a finger at Pete and he shrugs.

'Fine. I'll think of it as an extra workout, lugging all your empty wine bottles out to the road.'

'Oi, cheeky!'

Megan's still looking uncertainly at us, but now her expression clears and she smiles.

'You two. You're like an old married couple. I'm off anyway.'

She crosses the room and kisses Pete firmly on the lips.

'See you later in the week?'

'Try and stop me,' he says, and they grin at each other, then Megan skips from the room, calling: 'Bye, Mary! Bye, babe!' Moments later the front door slams and she's gone.

Immediately, Pete puts down his stirring spoon, walks to the fridge, pulls out a half-empty bottle of white wine and sloshes some into a glass. He plonks it down in front of me.

'You look like you need this. Right, tell me!'

I sigh.

'Honestly, I don't know that much yet. It's only just happened.'

But I tell him everything I know so far about the death of poor Jane Holland, and my upcoming return visit to the police station tomorrow morning, and when I've finished he shakes his head slowly.

'Mary, you can't risk it now. Not after this. I know the

threat to "Mary in Cheltenham" isn't for a while, and yes, yes, before you say it, I know we don't know for definite that it's *you*. But you need to start making plans, OK? And, as I've said before, this is what I'd do: why not just get on a plane to somewhere nice and hot at the end of March, and not tell anyone where you're going? I'll come with you, in fact. I could do with a holiday.'

I pick up my wine glass and take a sip, then another.

'I don't know, Pete. Not yet. I've thought about it, of course I have. Maybe go abroad, yes. Or maybe the police can sort of take me into custody or something on the 1st of April. Put me in a nice safehouse for twenty-four hours, where nobody can get me?'

He frowns at this.

'Maybe,' he says slowly. 'I'll come there with you too, if you like. I don't want anything to happen to you. I think I'm more nervous about this than you are.'

I reach out and touch his hand.

'You're sweet. Look, it'll be OK. I'm sure the police will protect me if it comes to it. Well, once they start *trusting* me; at the moment they're clearly still a bit suspicious I might have something to do with it all. Hopefully when they check out my alibi for New Year's Eve that will reassure them. And they might catch him quickly, who knows? There's ages yet. A month until poor David in Cardiff, whoever he is. And two months until the Cheltenham threat. So let's not panic. I *am* nervous, of course I am. I felt completely freaked out when I heard the news about Jane. But at least *I* know what might be coming. She didn't. So I've got a massive advantage.

Stop worrying, OK? And remember, don't breathe a word, to anyone.'

He shakes his head, mouth set in a grim line.

'I *won't*, I told you. But you're my best mate, Mary Ellis. I love you. Of course I'm going to bloody worry. You've been through tough times before though, haven't you, and come out the other side? So I'll keep the faith. Don't let me down, right?'

'I won't let you down. Love you too,' I whisper, suddenly feeling a little tearful, and he takes a big stride towards me and pulls me in for a hug.

'Anything you want me to do, just shout,' he murmurs into my hair.

'Can you pour me another glass of wine?' I mumble back, and he laughs and lets me go, heading for the fridge again with a cheeky wiggle of his bottom which makes me laugh too. After dinner though – Pete serves up a yummy, spicy chicken arrabiata – I start feeling jumpy again, and retire to my room on the top floor to try to call Lucinda. She's one of my oldest friends, one of the very few people I've kept in touch with from back in my teenage years, but I don't see her very often because she's a zoologist, and now lives in Africa. Over the past few years she's worked on a lion conservation project in Zimbabwe and at a gorilla sanctuary in Uganda, and now she's just signed up for a year at a wilderness centre in Botswana, helping a team who are monitoring changes in the wildlife population in the Okavango Delta. It sounds incredible, and I know she loves her job, but it does mean I can't speak to her as often as I'd like to; her mobile phone signal can be patchy, to say the least. Tonight, I manage to get hold of her for about ninety seconds, so the conversation doesn't involve much other than 'how's it going out there?' and 'I miss you!', but just hearing her cheery voice makes me feel better. *Maybe I'll fly out and join her for a couple of weeks in April*, I think, as the signal fades and we lose the connection. She's always telling me they need extra volunteers, and what potential killer is going to find me there? I'm not even sure where the Okavango Delta is myself.

'Things will be absolutely fine,' I say, aloud and resolutely, as I head back down to the lounge again to watch an hour of TV with Pete before bed.

Just think about what an incredible story this is, landing right in my lap. The story of a lifetime. And Pete's right. I've been through tough times before, haven't I, and survived? This is nothing.

My left hand moves automatically to my right wrist, the skin rough and ridged under my fingers. Then I take a deep breath, push the lounge door open, and go and join my housemate.

Chapter 8

Tuesday 2nd February

Cheltenham Central Police Station

'Right, let's all introduce ourselves, and then we can begin. I know we don't have much time, so hopefully we can keep this nice and snappy,' says DCI Steph Warden.

It's 10.15 on Tuesday morning, and I'm sitting in a small, rather stuffy meeting room, nursing a surprisingly good coffee in a cardboard cup.

'We used to have bloody awful coffee, until I got a new coffee machine at home and brought my old one in here,' the DCI told me as she handed me my latte. She's the SIO, the senior investigating officer, assigned to the Gloucestershire police side of the operation last night. She's shorter than me and lean, and I can see muscular biceps under the thin white cotton of her shirt sleeves. As she walked me briskly from the reception area to the room we're now sitting in, she told me that she's worked two previous serial killer cases in different parts of the UK, both of which ended in successful prosecutions and both of which I'm familiar with. I'm impressed – she looks young, maybe early forties, with a neat dark bob and just the start of fine lines around her eyes. She transferred to Gloucestershire just two months ago, to be closer to her elderly mother who's in a care home in Cirencester, she confided. I felt horribly anxious on the way here this morning, but already I'm feeling calmer.

This is in safe hands, I think.

'Can you move a bit nearer, Mary? I need to get us both in shot. Hang on ...'

DCI Warden, sitting to my left, angles the large monitor that's sitting on the desk in front of her slightly more towards me and I pull my chair a few inches closer to hers.

'That's perfect, thanks.'

On the screen, below the image now showing me and her, are just three other faces, two women and one man, the SIOs from the other forces involved. But DCI Warden has told me that others are also present in each room, out of shot, including deputy SIOs, senior forensic staff and other detectives who'll be working on the cases.

'This is big,' she said. Now she clears her throat.

'Right, well I'll kick things off then, shall I?'

She has a hint of a Geordie accent.

'I'm DCI Stephanie Warden, SIO here in Gloucestershire. Please call me Steph though. Only my mother and my old French teacher ever call me Stephanie.'

There are smiles from the three other boxes on the screen.

'I'm accompanied today by Mary Ellis, who as you know is the crime writer who received the diary with the entries about the four murders.'

She gestures at me, and the others all nod. I nod back, feeling a little self-conscious, and hoping that my scars aren't too visible in the harsh light of the meeting room.

'Mary, as you'd expect from someone in her profession, is very aware of the need for a media blackout and for the utmost discretion about everything we'll be discussing today, just in case anyone has any concerns. She's happy to answer any questions you may have, and then we can let her go and talk operational matters. Oh and just to let you know, my deputy will be DI Mike Stanley – he's unable to attend today but he will watch this back later. DC Jess Gordon is also in the room. She's the FLO.'

I glance to Steph's left where, along with a handful of other people, the family liaison officer is sitting, sipping a mint tea. We chatted briefly before the meeting began, and my first impression was that she was quiet and serious and – dare I say it – a little dull. She looks to be in her late twenties, a petite woman with high cheekbones and strawberry-blonde hair pulled back into a tight, low bun. She glances over at Steph as her name is mentioned, her face expressionless.

As I thought … a barrel of laughs, I think, then turn my attention back to the screen in front of me.

'West Midlands?' says Steph.

'Hi,' says the woman in the middle box. 'DCI Priya Thomson. Thanks for arranging this so quickly. The Jane Holland case is not proving to be an easy one at this early stage.'

She has long black hair tied in a ponytail, a touch of eyeliner emphasising big, dark eyes. There are shadows beneath them, and for some reason this calms me further. It's not just me who's losing sleep over all this, clearly.

'Thanks,' says Steph. 'South Wales?'

The man to the right of Priya raises a hand.

'Mornin',' he says. Even though he's only said one word, his strong Welsh accent is instantly recognisable.

'DCI Bryn Lewis. Pleased to meet you all. Hell of a case, this one, isn't it?'

His voice is deep and loud, and from what I can see of him he looks huge, like a stereotype of a Welsh rugby player, broad shoulders filling the frame.

'Certainly is,' says Steph. 'Good morning to you too. And finally, Thames Valley?'

'DCI Linda Lake. At my wit's end with the Lisa Turner investigation here in Oxford, and hoping you lot can help me out, if indeed these cases really are linked. Because I have nothing here at the moment, and it's doing my head in.'

'I feel your pain,' says Priya Thomson in Birmingham, and Linda Lake nods and grimaces. She has ash-blonde hair, almost grey, cut short, and even though the picture quality isn't great, her eyes stand out – a striking green, almost cat-like in appearance.

'Right, well now we're all acquainted, let's begin,' says Steph. 'As I think you're all aware, this is now Operation Shearwater.'

Shearwater. I don't have a notepad in front of me – I didn't like to ask if I could make notes; I'm here as a witness, not as a journalist, after all – but I file the codename away in my head.

'Obviously, with the Lisa Turner murder in Oxford and now

the Jane Holland murder in Birmingham, we're being forced to take the contents of the diary sent to Mary seriously,' Steph continues. 'I think we're all agreed these deaths now appear to be no coincidence.'

There are nods and murmurs of assent from the faces on the screen.

'And just to update you on that diary, I received the forensic report first thing this morning. No good news, I'm afraid. Completely clean. Not a hint of a fingerprint or a speck of DNA, other than Mary's.'

'Shit,' says Linda Lake. And then: 'Sorry. Carry on.'

Shit indeed, I think. *That's a blow.*

'It is pretty unfortunate, agreed,' says Steph. 'We've looked into where it might have come from, but it seems these diaries are widely available on the High Street. Most branches of WHSmith stocked them in the run-up to Christmas, as well as a number of other stores. And I'm talking across the UK – Scotland, Wales, and Northern Ireland as well as England. Thousands were sold last year. So he – I say *he*, but of course it could be a she, although my gut tells me otherwise – he could have bought it absolutely anywhere, which is of no help to us. So my first question to Mary – and forgive me if you've been asked some of these questions before, Mary, but we just need to be completely clear about all of this – my first question is, do you have *any* idea who might have sent it to you? I know you said it was sent anonymously, and you sadly threw the envelope, the packaging or whatever away, but do you have *any* clue?'

I shake my head.

'None. I'm so sorry. It arrived in the post on the twenty-third of December, but I was busy and didn't bother opening it until Christmas Eve, which was when I threw away the wrapping. I just assumed it was a gift from an editor I'd written a piece for last year; they tend to send stuff like that at Christmas. And even then, I didn't take it out of the box it was in until Sunday, so nearly a month later. I don't use a paper diary, so I was about to give it to the charity shop, and I felt a bit guilty about not thanking whoever sent it, so I opened it up to see if there might be a card or something inside. That's when I noticed the diary entries.'

'Hmmm. And I suppose your work address would be quite easy to find out?' says Steph, frowning.

I nod.

'Pretty easy. I've rented a desk there for the past two years. Tons of people have the address – editors, other journalists, finance departments, the usual. It's my contact address on my online profile too, so it's not hard to find. I keep my personal phone number and home address very private, but not my office details.'

There's silence for a moment. Then Linda Lake says:

'He took a chance, though, didn't he? Assuming you'd flick through the pages when you got the diary, and see the entries he made? And I can't work out why he wants you for some reason to know in advance that these murders are going to happen, and that you're on the list. Or that *someone* called Mary in Cheltenham is, anyway. Lisa and Jane weren't warned in advance, as far as we know anyway. It's odd.'

'I have no idea,' I say. 'As you say, I could easily not have read it at all. I suppose he doesn't know even now that I *have* read it, does he? As the existence of the diary hasn't been made public?'

'True,' says Linda. 'If you'd given it to the charity shop without opening it, we wouldn't know about it at all. It was pure luck. Definitely a bit of a gamble on his part.'

There's another short silence. Then Steph says:

'This is all guesswork right now. But what are we all thinking about the *reason* behind sending Mary the diary? That this killer, whoever he is – let's stick with *he* for now for simplicity – has sent these warnings to Mary because of her job, maybe? He wants her to write his story, or to try to track him down, to try to stop him maybe? Is it part of the thrill for him, to give someone like Mary these clues? He must know she'd go to the police, surely? So is it us he's playing with, too? Giving us tiny hints about what he's planning, knowing they're so vague there's almost nothing we can do to protect the potential victims?'

'Except Mary,' says Bryn Lewis. 'You can protect her, because she's had a direct warning, or at least we assume she's the Mary he's threatening. So maybe that's part of his plan too. You can be protected, Mary, so you survive and write his story. Makes sense to me, if anything about this makes sense. Are you *planning* to write about this, Mary?'

I shrug.

'I mean, I'd like to, yes. It's a hell of a story,' I say honestly. 'But not yet, obviously. When it's all over, whenever that might be. And I won't write anything without letting you all know first.'

'That would be appreciated,' says Steph.

'Good. But of course, he might not give a toss whether his story's written or not. We just don't know *what* the motivation behind sending the diary was, do we? And that's the problem, we're all just guessing,' says Priya. 'And meanwhile, Linda and I have two dead women on our hands, and virtually nothing to go on. What we need to do here is concentrate on those victims, because he's not picking people at random. It wouldn't make any sense. He chose them for a reason, so even though we haven't found it yet, there must be a connection between them, and with you too, Mary. Can we talk about that for a minute?'

'Of course,' says Steph. 'Mary, can you think of *anything* you might have in common with Lisa Turner or Jane Holland, based on the little you probably know of them at this point?'

I shake my head.

'Nothing, I'm so sorry,' I say. 'I don't know either of them; I'd never heard of either of them. And obviously I don't know much about Jane yet at all, but I've been reading as much as I can find online about Lisa and there's just nothing that strikes me. I can't think of any link between us. Schools, career, interests ... there's nothing. I've never even been to Oxford.'

'What about David in Cardiff?' asks Bryn. 'Know anyone of that name? Unusual name, obviously.'

He raises his eyebrows, and everyone smiles.

'I don't, I'm sorry,' I say. 'I mean, obviously I know quite a few Davids. But none are from Cardiff, or have lived there, as far as I know. It's not much to go on.'

'Tell me about it,' says Bryn drily.

'Any more questions before we let Mary go?' asks Steph.

A few seconds of silence are followed by shakes of the three heads on the screen.

'OK. Thank you, Mary, for coming in. We'll be keeping in very close contact with you, of course – in fact, I think Jess wants to arrange a meeting as soon as possible, right, Jess?'

I look over at the FLO, who nods unsmilingly.

'I do. And I also need to ask you another few questions before you go. Another alibi check, for the Birmingham murder, I'm afraid,' she says.

'Sure,' I say. 'No problem.'

'Thank you, Mary, for understanding. And please, please let us know as soon as possible if you think of anything, no matter how seemingly small or insignificant, that might link you and our Oxford and Birmingham victims, OK? Or if anything at all out of the ordinary happens in the coming days. We're working blind here, but for some reason it does seem that the killer has reached out to you with those warnings. So we need your help. *Anything*, OK?'

'OK,' I say. 'I'll do my best.'

'Thank you. Right, we'll say goodbye then. Jess will have that quick chat and then see you out.'

There's a chorus of 'bye, Mary' and 'thank you' from the faces on the monitor, and I give them an awkward wave.

'And as DCI Warden said – *anything*, Mary,' says Linda Lake. 'Like Priya, I'm certain that there has to be a link between our victims. If we can find that, we can find the why. *Why* they were killed. And if we find the why, we might just find the *who*.'

Chapter 9

Tuesday 2nd February

Cheltenham Central Police Station

'OK, everyone back? Let's move on. Can you update us on the Jane Holland investigation, DCI Thomson?'

Steph turns away from the monitor for a moment to nod at Jess Gordon, who's just re-entered the room. She gestures for Jess to take the now-empty seat next to her, then looks back at the screen, checking that everyone is in position again after the short pause in the meeting.

'Of course,' says Priya. 'But first, now she's gone, how sure are we that Mary Ellis is for real?'

'Yes, I'd like to quickly discuss that,' says Linda. 'Look, my gut feeling is that she's probably not going round killing people. In fact, everything she's told us feels genuine. But we still need to ask the questions. What if she's an accomplice? What if she has some *connection* with the killer, maybe? She could still have written those names in the diary herself. She's already said she wants to write about all this, and it's a hell of a story, isn't it? Call me cynical, but I don't trust journalists. I still think it's odd that a serial killer, if that's really what we're dealing with here, would warn any of his victims in advance like this. Anyone else?'

Steph nods slowly.

'I know. I agree there must be a reason she's been selected as the victim he's decided to give information to. We'll keep a very close eye on her, and we are currently checking out where she was on *both* nights in question now, just to cover ourselves. I'm assuming her New Year's Eve alibi has already been checked, although I'm not sure why I haven't heard anything yet. I'll report back as soon as I can.'

'Great,' says Priya. 'OK. Jane Holland. Well, unlike in Oxford where you didn't have any luck with CCTV, Linda, we do actually have some footage of the suspect. But honestly, it's not great.'

She sighs.

'There was a CCTV camera at the front of the victim's house only. There's a secure side gate, with code entry, which is the only official access to the rear of the property, so maybe she felt safe enough with just that, because she had no cameras at the side or rear. If you wanted to burgle the place, you could easily hop over the wall from one of the neighbour's back gardens, although I suppose you'd be taking a chance as quite a few of the properties on the road do have cameras front and back ... Anyway, I digress. It's irrelevant, because it seems the attacker simply strolled up the driveway and rang the doorbell.'

'What?' says Linda Lake. 'But you said the footage isn't great? Why not?'

Priya sighs again.

'There are two cameras, one angled to cover the entire driveway and one pointing downwards, covering the front door. At ten minutes past midnight, we see somebody jog up the drive. I say somebody, because it's impossible to tell if it's a man or a woman. Black clothing; a bulky padded jacket, black gloves, and a baseball cap pulled down low over their eyes. They keep their head down, and they're moving quickly. They ring the doorbell several times, and then it seems they flatten themselves against the wall or something, because they're out of sight of the cameras until Jane opens the door about ninety seconds later. There's a brief conversation on the doorstep, which we can't hear – the cameras are vision only – and then, well, Jane lets them in.'

She shrugs.

'So was it someone she knew, or at least recognised?' she continues. 'Or did a stranger persuade her to let them in for some reason? We simply have no way of knowing, because that's where our footage at the house ends. We have nothing from inside or from the rear garden – nothing from the neighbour's cameras either. Next door does have a security camera at the rear of the property but it's only capturing footage of its own garden, understandably. Anyway, Jane and the killer clearly went outside for some reason and then he obviously hit her. Cause of death has been confirmed as a single vicious blow to the back of the head. She would have died pretty quickly.'

There's silence for a few seconds. Then Jess says:

'Why take her outside? Why not just bop her over the head

indoors? She lived alone, didn't she? No witnesses. Why risk doing it in the back garden, where one of the neighbours could have seen what was happening?'

'No idea,' says Priya. 'Just one of many questions we have about this. It makes no sense. There's some CCTV footage from other houses along the street too, by the way. We see him enter Oaks Road on foot a minute or so earlier, running. As in, jogging. Like somebody out for a late-night run, which might sound odd to some but it's actually relatively common in Birmingham.'

'In Cheltenham too,' says Steph. 'I've seen people out running at all sorts of odd times. Four in the morning, for example. I'd say they must be bonkers, but I've actually done it myself now and again before an early shift, or if I can't sleep. It's quite a nice time to run. Quiet.'

'So have I, actually,' says Jess. 'Especially in summer.'

'Right. Well, fair enough, although it certainly wouldn't be my time of choice for exercise,' says Priya. 'Anyway, at about 12.20, so only ten minutes or so after he rings Jane's doorbell, he's off again, running down the road. No sign of any weapon, although as I said, the jacket looks quite bulky so maybe he was concealing it under that. Still no footage that shows any clear pictures of his face. The peak of his cap conceals it, and he keeps his head down, and runs fast. He's fit, that's about all we know. It's hard to even guess at his height. Probably between five-five and six foot though.'

'So, a person of indeterminate sex, indeterminate height, and fairly fit. Great. Not much to go on, is it?' says Bryn. 'Anything at all at the scene? Footprints, maybe?'

'We do have a couple of footprints, yes,' says Priya. 'Not many, and not very clear though. It was a dry night, and we haven't had any rain here for days, which is unusual for Birmingham in January. It was cold and frosty though, so there were imprints in the grass – two sets of footprints, Jane's and her killer's, walking down the garden, and one set leaving again. They show he left via the side gate, which doesn't require a code from the garden side, by the way. He didn't go back through the house. But he was clever: as he left he more or less retraced his steps down the garden and it looks like he deliberately scuffed his footprints. You know, sort of shuffled his feet in the grass, so they're not clear? We got a couple of half-decent ones, enough to be able to identify the brand. They're Adidas, and unfortunately a really common style. I've got a pair myself. So, again, not much help.'

'It's something though. We didn't get so much as a single print here. What size?' says Linda.

'We're not certain, due to the way he made sure to mess them up,' says Priya. 'Not tiny, though. Probably between a size six and a nine, maybe ten maximum.'

'Oh crap,' says Linda. 'That doesn't help much then. As far as I can remember, the average male shoe size in the UK is nine and female is six. Dammit. Where does he go, Priya, once he leaves Oaks Road?'

'We pick him up on a couple of cameras on nearby streets,' says Priya. 'But we lose him about ten minutes later. He runs into a CCTV blackspot, and that's it. He's clearly smart, and organised. The cap, the head down, the speedy entrance and exit, leaving nothing at the scene except messed up footprints. He may have left a vehicle somewhere out of view of any local cameras, who knows. It's beyond frustrating.'

'It is,' says Linda. 'But it does give us *something* to go on here in Oxford. As you know, there were no cameras around the spot where Lisa Turner was murdered. But I'm going to go back to the footage from adjacent streets now and see if we can see anyone out for a run in dark clothing. You never know, right?'

'True,' says Priya. 'Good luck. Keep us posted.'

There's another few seconds of silence.

'Well, we're no closer to the *who*, then, for now,' Steph says. 'So what about the *why*? What do we know about Jane Holland?'

Priya shuffles some paperwork.

'Right. Jane Holland was fifty-five, single – never married, no kids – and lived alone at the address where the murder was carried out, 6 Oaks Road, Edgbaston. For those not familiar with the area, Edgbaston is a pretty affluent suburb of Birmingham. Nice and green. Home to the Botanical Gardens and the Cricket Ground of course. And birthplace of former prime minister Neville Chamberlain, for those who like a fun fact. Anyway, Oaks Road is a *very* nice one; Jane's house is worth close to two million.'

'Phewwwww.'

There's a low whistle from Bryn.

'How did she make a living?' he asks.

'Gambling,' says Priya. 'As in, she owned a couple of casinos – the Topaz Group. One here in Birmingham, and one in

Coventry. High-end places with cocktail bars and good chefs. Little goldmines, by all accounts.'

'Nice. So who inherits?' asks Steph. 'Any possible motive there?'

'One of the first things we checked,' says Priya. 'But there's no one big beneficiary. She was an only child and both parents are deceased. The casinos will keep going for now – there's a board of directors, and her will, made some time ago, requests that they continue to run the business as profitably as possible for ten years, after which it's to be sold. They'll all get a decent payout for doing that, but they're all wealthy anyway and the sums wouldn't be life-changing for them. She's left some money to a handful of close friends, and to three cousins, and she's put some cash into university funds for their children. But the bulk of her estate, once the casinos are sold, is to be divided between a number of charities. They get a bit now too, but they'll get more down the line. She supported about a dozen, mainly ones that work with underprivileged or abused kids, plus a couple of foodbanks and two of the smaller cancer charities. They'll all do very nicely out of it, but not for a while yet. There's nobody who benefits big-time immediately, that's the thing. So would someone kill her now, for a payout in ten years' time? Maybe, but we're just not sure. We're still working our way through interviews with all of her friends, those three cousins, and the people she dealt with at the charities, but so far they all have solid alibis for the night of the murder. And none of them *feel* right, if you know what I mean? I could be wrong, but I just don't get the feeling that money was the motive here. Nothing appears to have been stolen from the home either. Nothing disturbed at all indoors.'

There are nods from the other officers, who've been scribbling notes as Priya's been talking. Then Linda says:

'Nothing was taken from Lisa's person either. Her phone, her purse, everything was still in her bag when her body was found. And this Jane sounds like a very good woman, as was Lisa, which makes this all even shittier. And still no obvious links whatsoever between them. I mean, they were both single with no children, and both comfortably off, although Lisa wasn't in Jane's league. She had a good job, but she hadn't even bought her own home yet – she was still renting – so her prospects were good but she didn't have much to leave anyone. But other than their single status and their good careers – nothing. We have, without explaining why, asked Lisa's friends and family if they knew if she had any friends or acquaintances in Birmingham, and in Cardiff or Cheltenham too. But they don't think so, so I don't think these two knew each other or anything. It's so bloody frustrating.'

'So why the hell have they been targeted?' says Bryn. 'It just doesn't seem to make any sense. There *must* be a connection between them all, guys. We just haven't found it yet. And if we're going to stop him killing David here in Cardiff, whoever *he* is, we need to find it in the next few weeks, don't we? Priya, how about a press release asking for anyone based in Cardiff, Oxford or Cheltenham who might have known Jane to come forward? That might help, if we word it carefully? It might throw up a connection without necessarily alerting anyone to the fact that we think we've got a serial killer on the loose?'

'Yes, OK,' says Priya. 'Worth a try.'

'It is,' agrees Steph. 'But honestly, I think the answer lies with Mary Ellis. Assuming for now she's an innocent in all of this, she's also single and reasonably well off, so I suppose there's that small similarity between her, Lisa and Jane. But there's obviously a lot more to it than that. The killer sent her that diary for a reason. Yes, because of her job and because he wants the notoriety, maybe. But he's also saying she's on his hit list, unless it's a different Mary he's talking about. So she *must* have a proper connection with our two victims, and with this "David in Cardiff", whether she knows it or not. There's no way this is random. It's far too organised. On that note, do we have any thoughts about where this killer might be based? Considering the locations of his crimes and planned future crimes?'

Bryn raises a hand.

'I've been thinking about that. Best guess is probably not a northerner, as all the locations are south of the Midlands. But other than that, who knows?'

'Agreed. And I've been wondering about something else,' says Priya. 'He's warned us about four possible killings, but where's the guarantee that that will be the end of it? What if another diary appears once he's got through this first lot? He's managed to kill two women already and get away with it – with the best will in the world, we have sweet Fanny Adams to go on here, don't we? He must be feeling pretty cocky right now, and that scares me. There's no way of knowing how far he might go, and how long this might go on. And threatening to kill on the 1st of April? I bet that's deliberate. April Fool's Day. He thinks we're all idiots.'

There are nods from all the boxes on the screen, and a deep groan from Bryn.

'And it's our turn next,' he says. 'Deep joy. I'm with you Steph – I think the key lies with Mary Ellis. Watch her, OK?'

Steph turns to look at Jess.

'We will, won't we Jess? Keep in very close contact with her. You OK? You're very quiet.'

Jess nods.

'Just thinking. And I'm on it,' she says.

Chapter 10

Wednesday 3rd February

'*Police in Birmingham investigating the murder of fifty-five-year-old Jane Holland in the early hours of Monday morning are appealing for witnesses who may have spotted a late-night runner in the Edgbaston area ...*'

I'm sitting in the kitchen, coffee cup in hand, when I hear the story on the Radio 4 nine o'clock news. I've taken the day off work; my focus is entirely on this story right now anyway, and Jess Gordon, the family liaison officer, is due to come round at eleven, along with the deputy SIO, who I haven't yet met. They want to check the house for security, she told me as I left the police station yesterday, and have a 'general chat'. I'm hoping that means she'll tell me that my alibis for the nights of the two murders have now been checked and I'm finally in the clear; I'd sighed inwardly yesterday as I'd told her that I was alone here, at home, on Sunday night.

'Pete, my housemate, was with me until sometime between nine and ten I think, but then he went off to spend the night with his girlfriend Megan over in Prestbury. So I was home alone after that I'm afraid, which I know isn't of much help to you,' I said, and she'd raised an eyebrow, then thanked me and told me I was free to go.

I get it, I do. I'm the one who was in possession of dates and victims' names, written *before* the crimes occurred. Of *course* they have to consider me as a potential suspect. They'd be stupid not to. Even so, it's not nice. But then, none of this is nice, is it?

Now, I reach over and turn up the volume on the digital radio sitting on the countertop.

'... *police are keen to trace the runner, dressed in dark clothing, who was seen in the Oaks Road area between midnight and 1 am. They're also interested in hearing from anyone currently based in Oxford, Cardiff, or Cheltenham who might have known the victim. The body of Jane Holland, a well-known local casino owner, was found in her garden ...*'

Interesting. They've decided to risk naming the three places mentioned in the diary, I think.

I listen to the rest of the bulletin, but there's no other new information, and I switch the radio off and sit sipping my coffee and thinking.

So the killer was in running gear then? Captured on CCTV, maybe? It doesn't sound as if they have much on him at this point then, does it? I wonder if they're any closer to knowing why Jane Holland was chosen as a victim?

I've done my own research of course; it didn't take long to find Jane online. She was wealthy, the owner of the Topaz casinos in Birmingham and Coventry, but it's her philanthropy which has really struck me. There are numerous newspaper articles about her generous donations to local charities, accompanied by photos of her, a petite, slender brunette with a broad smile. Seeing her face, reading about all the good things she did with her life, makes this even more horrible, and scarier.

Why choose her? Why did she have to die?

I discussed it with Pete last night, as we had a quick cup of tea together when he got in from work before he headed off to spend yet another night at Megan's.

'They're calling it Operation Shearwater,' I said.

'Shearwater? That's some sort of seabird, isn't it? And I think it's a lake at Longleat Estate too, if I remember correctly. Why have they called it that? Do they think this killer has some connections down in Wiltshire?'

'Quite the opposite,' I replied. 'They pick operation names randomly, and they always have nothing whatsoever to do with the actual case, just in case someone who shouldn't overhears a police conversation. Anyway, I probably shouldn't have told you that, but hey, you already know about the diary, so ... hush hush, you know the score.'

He winked at me and smiled.

'Don't worry. My lips are sealed. How are you feeling now, after this Birmingham thing? Are you OK?'

I nodded.

'Just about. It's awful though, isn't it? Pretty spooky. And Jane seemed like such a good woman too.'

'Yep. I had a look at the BBC website at lunchtime. And you know what? I've been to the Topaz in Birmingham – do you remember? I wonder if she was there that night? I didn't recognise her from her photo online, but I was pretty drunk, to be fair. I might have actually met her, which would make it even spookier.'

I stared at him.

'You've ... you've been to her casino? When?'

'A few weeks ago. In January, when I went away for Rob's birthday?'

'Oh. I do remember that, yes. I just forgot you went to a casino ...'

'Oh. Well, does it matter?' he said.

'No. No, it doesn't matter,' I replied.

But I frowned, thinking. It had been the week after New Year's Eve, and Pete had headed off to spend the night in Birmingham with some old friends from London including Rob, who was celebrating his thirty-fifth birthday. I vaguely remembered Pete telling me about their dinner and drinks, followed by a trip to a casino and on to a club, but I hadn't paid much attention. It had just sounded like a pretty standard boys' night away. Now though, the coincidence made me a little uneasy. And yet, thousands of people must visit the Topaz casinos every week; they are, by all accounts, popular venues for birthday parties, stag parties, celebrations of all kinds. A slightly odd coincidence nonetheless, although maybe not, as Pete hadn't actually met Jane Holland that night – or, if he had, he'd been too drunk for it to register.

I'm still thinking about it this morning though, wondering if it can mean anything, and I'm browsing through articles about Jane again when the doorbell rings. I close my laptop and go to open it. DC Gordon is standing on the doorstep, hair pulled back into an even tighter little bun today. She's wearing a pin-striped navy skirt with a pale-blue blouse, and she's accompanied by a man in a grey suit. He has short black hair and a round, cherubic face, and he looks about sixteen.

'Mary, good morning,' she says, and smiles. A small, tight smile, but a smile nonetheless.

A little friendlier than yesterday, then. Making an effort. That's progress.

'This is Detective Inspector Mike Stanley,' she continues. 'We thought we'd have a quick look around and check out your security first, if that's OK?'

Detective Inspector? He must be at least thirty then, I think, and I immediately feel old.

'Good morning, Mary. Nice to meet you,' he says, in a surprisingly deep voice.

'Likewise. Come in.'

I put the kettle on while they tour the house, and when they walk into the kitchen ten minutes later DI Stanley is scribbling in a little notebook. He rips out the page he's writing on and hands it to me. There are two names on it, with phone numbers.

'A couple of locksmiths we recommend,' he says. 'You need better window locks, and a good mortice lock for the front door. The ones you have now are adequate, but they could be a lot better. And I notice you have a spyhole in the door but no security cameras.'

I shake my head.

'I've never really felt the need. It's such a nice area, and it's quite a busy street and this is a mid-terrace so no side access, so you only really have to worry about the back, you know? But my rear courtyard leads on to the apartment block gardens, which are behind a security gate, so I wasn't too worried. But – OK, yes. I'll think about changing the locks, if you think it's necessary.'

They both nod.

'It's just a suggestion for your peace of mind really,' says Jess. 'We have no reason to think that there'll be any threat to your safety ahead of the 1st of April, but, well ...'

I nod, feeling an unexpected little shiver of fear.

'In case he decides to change his timetable, and not tell anyone?' I say.

She shrugs.

'Just in case. And of course, as we keep saying, you may not be the Mary in Cheltenham he's after at all. But better safe than sorry and all that.'

She pauses, looking around the room.

'Can we sit down for a minute for a quick chat?'

'Of course. Tea or coffee?'

They both ask for tea – Jess black and weak, Mike white with two sugars. When I've made the drinks we all sit down at the breakfast bar, them together on one side, me facing them. They both sit in silence for a few moments, looking at me and, suddenly feeling self-conscious, I pull my hair out of the band that's holding it back in a ponytail and let it fall around my face, then tug the sleeve of my black jumper further down over my right wrist.

'So, Mary, anything you want to ask us?' says Mike.

'There is actually. Have my alibis been checked yet? I promise you, every single thing I've told you is true. That diary came to me in the post. I know you have to tick all the boxes, so I totally get why I'm being checked out, but I'd love for us to be able to move forwards without this suspicion hanging over me.'

Jess nods.

'Yes, your New Year's Eve alibi checks out. We had a few issues getting hold of your friends but so far we've managed to speak to two of the three people you said you were with and they've confirmed you were together as a group here in Cheltenham until after 2am. That's around the time Lisa was murdered. And over forty miles away. Checks on your whereabouts on Sunday night are happening as we speak. We're a bit short-staffed at the moment, which isn't helping. For what it's worth, I think you're telling us the truth, Mary. But we'll make that official later today and then, as you say, we can move forwards more easily.'

She smiles, her second of the visit.

She's trying, isn't she? Maybe she's OK, really, underneath that stern exterior, I think.

I smile back.

'Good. That's a relief. Thanks, Jess.'

'OK, well, assuming now that all is well in that department, Jess will, as you know, be your main point of contact,' Mike says. 'And we're very much hoping you'll be able to help us out, Mary. I'm sure you're keeping up with the news online, and honestly we can't tell you much more than what's been released to the press right now, which as you'll be aware isn't a lot. A figure dressed in dark clothing – running gear – was seen knocking on the door of the Holland home just after midnight and then running away again shortly afterwards. There are no decent CCTV images and, as yet, no witnesses. Thames Valley are now looking at footage from the night of Lisa's murder again to see if they can spot a similar figure, but, well ...'

He shrugs, and rubs a hand across his pink plump-cheeked face.

'Everyone's flummoxed,' says Jess.

'There's been a subtle request for information from anyone living in Cardiff, Oxford, or Cheltenham, as you probably heard,' Mike says. 'But we're not hopeful. The only even vague similarity between the two victims so far is that both were single and both were comfortably off. But money doesn't really seem to be the motive, and we simply have no idea what is, and that's the problem. One of the many, many problems.'

There's silence for a few moments. I pick up my mug, take a sip of tea, and put it down again.

'Any clues on their social media, anything like that?' I ask.

'Nothing that we can find,' Jess replies. 'Jane didn't really use it, other than a private Facebook account she just used to keep in touch with friends and family. Lisa had an Instagram account which she posted the occasional photo on but nothing very personal, and she didn't interact with anyone on there much. So that hasn't been of any help either. Nothing has.'

'I don't use it either,' I say, and I see Jess raise an eyebrow, as if surprised, but she doesn't say anything. I'm glad; it probably *is* unusual, for someone my age, but I've never been a fan of putting myself out there on Twitter or Instagram or whatever. My scars, my background – it's not for me.

'OK. So, what now?' I say.

'Well, I know we have a couple of months before the threat against "Mary",' she says – she draws inverted commas in the air as she says my name – 'but have you thought much about what you want to do on the 1st of April? We can put you in a safehouse, somewhere nobody can get to you. Would you like me to start arranging that? I'd be there with you; you wouldn't be on your own, if that worries you.'

It's my turn to sigh.

'I just don't know,' I say. 'As you can imagine, I've been thinking about this non-stop. If the threat *is* against me – and let's just assume it is, because I think we have to, for now – then he must know that by warning me so far in advance, he's not going to be able to kill me, is he? He's made it impossible for himself. He must know that I'm going to hide away somewhere he can't find me.'

Jess and Mike both nod.

'So,' I continue, 'I'm half tempted just to stay here in the house and see what happens. It might be your best – maybe your only – chance of catching him. Use me as bait, almost. Let him come for me, if he dares.'

I pause, feeling a little surprised that I've actually said it out loud. This idea, to stay put instead of running away, has actually been something that's been slowly forming in my brain for the past twenty-four hours or so, although this is the first time I've actually said it to anyone.

But, well, it might work, mightn't it? He'll know police will be watching, but he's got away with two murders already. Might he be cocky enough, determined enough, to try? And could I risk that? With police close by, I might not actually die. They might actually catch him. And the story ... What. A. Story.

Mike is raising an eyebrow.

'Well ... I don't know, Mary. But I'll pass on your willingness to do something like that to the team. Your safety is our top priority, obviously. And ideally, this person will have been stopped long before the 1st of April. We'll get a safehouse lined up too though, OK?'

I nod.

'Sure. As you say, we have lots of time. I've also considered leaving the country, by the way. An old friend of mine, Lucinda, is working in Botswana at the moment. I thought I might head out there, possibly. I've messaged her and she says it would be fine. She's working on a wildlife project literally in the middle of nowhere ... I can't imagine he could follow me there.'

Jess grimaces.

'OK, well, travelling could be risky but we can discuss that nearer the time,' she says doubtfully.

'Indeed,' says Mike. 'The important thing is that we have options. Good. We'll stay in close touch though, right? If we find out anything we think you need to know, we'll tell you.'

'And if you think of anything, or anything happens, or ... well, you know the score,' Jess says. 'You have my number, don't you? Call me anytime, day or night.'

I nod, wondering if I should mention the coincidence of Pete's visit to Jane Holland's casino only a few weeks ago. She did just say 'if you think of *anything*', after all. Then I immediately decide against it. Pete didn't, to his knowledge, even lay eyes on Jane while he was there. It was just that, a coincidence, I'm sure of it.

They leave shortly after that, Jess actually patting my arm as she walks out of the front door, leaving me feeling a little guilty about my original assessment of her.

She's just a quiet, serious woman doing a tough job, isn't she? She's OK. We're all on the same side, after all. We all want to find out who's behind this. We all want to stop him before he can hurt anyone else. So, onwards. What now?

I reach for the piece of paper DI Stanley gave me. It will do no harm to change the locks, and it might even help me to sleep a little more soundly, especially if Pete's going to be spending more nights with Megan. The nightmares were back last night, my sleeping mind taking me to dark places I haven't visited for years, my body rigid with terror when I woke, heart thudding, tears running down my cheeks. New locks won't banish the bad dreams, I know that. But they might help me feel a bit less vulnerable, and it's one thing I can do right now, to make me feel a little better. To make me feel like I'm doing *something*. I pick up my phone and call the locksmith.

Chapter 11

Wednesday 3rd February

Cheltenham Central Police Station

'Right, everyone's here, I think. West Midlands, do you want to start? Any joy from your appeal for witnesses or any connections in any of our other towns and cities? Anyone spot your mysterious midnight runner?'

It's 5pm and DCI Steph Warden has just arranged a quick Operation Shearwater conference call, the officers involved all agreeing that a daily catch up, or as close to daily as they can manage, is probably a good idea right now. She's sitting at one end of a long table which takes up most of the meeting room, phone in front of her, loudspeaker on so she and the others in the room, four members of her team, can hear the conversation. There's silence for a few seconds, then the sound of rustling paper, and finally DCI Priya Thomson says:

'Sorry ... with you now. First of all, nothing useful yet from our appeal to people who might have known Jane – a few have come forward from all three places but they haven't told us anything helpful so far. And as for our midnight runner, well, I'm frankly amazed at how many people seem to be as mad as you and Jess, Steph. We've had more than twenty calls since we put the appeal out this morning, all saying they'd either seen someone running on Sunday night or had actually been out themselves and wanted to eliminate themselves from the enquiry. We're working our way through them but so far nothing jumps out; we'll keep you posted though. And nothing else to report at all, I'm afraid. We're looking closely into Jane Holland's life and background, just to see if there's anything there, anyone who might have held a grudge, but nothing so far. No links to Lisa Turner either, or to Mary Ellis, that we can find. It's getting bloody depressing, I can tell you that.'

'I bet,' says Steph, with feeling. She's worked on enough big murder cases to have had her fair share of dead ends too, and she knows what it feels like. It's soul-destroying.

'Thames Valley? Linda, any news from you?'

DCI Linda Lake coughs, then says:

'We've been going through all the CCTV footage from the night of Lisa's murder again with a fine-tooth comb. We haven't spotted any runners at all though, unfortunately. I suppose it *was* very late New Year's Eve into New Year's Day – maybe even the most dedicated runner takes a day off. Or maybe he did this one differently. Anyway, whatever the reason, no joy here.'

Steph nods, then remembers Linda can't actually see her.

'Bummer,' she says. 'OK, well just to update you on what we're up to here, Mary Ellis does, as we all hoped and indeed generally thought, seem to be for real, as I'm sure you'll all know by now. We'd already ruled out her being in Oxford at New Year, and as for the 31st of January into Monday the 1st of February, it does appear that she was at home here in Cheltenham all night as she claims. We have mobile phone analysis on her number now and it pinged all night right here in town. So, unless she went off to Birmingham to kill Jane Holland without her phone – and we really don't think she did, do we Jess?'—she turns to look at her colleague, who shakes her head—'then we believe she's in the clear. Unless anything else turns up to contradict that, obviously.'

'Fine. I'm happy to consider her as nothing more than another potential victim, but one who for some as yet unknown reason the killer chose to forewarn,' says Linda Lake, and there are murmurs of agreement from Priya and Bryn.

Steph nods.

'Yes, I think she's being straight with us. I do believe the first she knew of any of this was when she received that diary in the post. What do you think, Jess, having spent a bit more time with her today?'

Jess, who's sitting opposite her, nods.

'I agree. She's pretty unsettled by it all, I'd say. I can't see her having any involvement. We're still discussing what to do on the 1st of April, by the way, and she's actually suggested potentially staying put at home and acting as bait for the killer, if he dares to come for her, knowing she's bound to have police protection. But I've told her we can talk about that nearer the time.'

There are expressions of surprise from the voices on the speakerphone.

'Interesting,' says Linda.

'It is. And something to think about,' says Steph. 'And we've had no leaks to the press about the possible connection between our two murders, or about the existence of the diary. So, I'm hoping that means we can trust her, and her housemate, who's the only other person who knows these details.'

'Great,' says Priya's voice from the speaker. 'Is Bryn with us? What are you doing in Cardiff?'

'I'm here,' booms DCI Lewis. 'And we're a bit unsettled now too, if I'm honest. We may be less than four weeks away from our own murder and we currently have no way of protecting the potential victim, other than the prospect of telling thousands of men and boys to lock themselves in a cellar or whatever for twenty-four hours on the 1st of March. And I can't see the powers that be sanctioning that, can you? We need to find this killer, guys.'

There are a few seconds of silence. Then Steph says:

'We do. Let's speak again tomorrow. Good luck all.'

'Cheers, Steph,' says Bryn. 'I think we're going to need it. Luck, or a bloody miracle.'

Chapter 12

Thursday 4th February

Thursday morning, and the office at The Hub is quiet, just a handful of other people busy at their workstations. I make myself a coffee and settle at my desk, my first task an email to Jess, copying in DCI Steph Warden. I tell them that the locks at home are being upgraded tomorrow, but the main reason for my email is to let them know that I've decided to officially start working on an article for when this is all over. Steph replies almost immediately, asking me if I can call Jess to discuss the details, and when I ring her direct line, taking my mobile down to the empty staff kitchen to ensure I won't be overheard, she answers promptly. After a little polite chit-chat, I get to the point.

'I know I mentioned that I probably would be writing something at some point,' I say. 'But I decided last night that I might as well get on with it and start getting some interviews in the bag and some thoughts down on paper. That way, if I'm murdered in April, at least I'll leave the bones of an article behind for someone else to finish.'

I laugh lightly, but on the other end of the line I hear Jess give a little tut.

'Mary, we're going to keep you safe,' she says, sternly. 'Stop that.'

'Sorry,' I say. 'Look, I just wanted to keep you in the loop, as I promised. I'm going to try to interview friends or relatives of the first two murder victims, starting with Lisa Turner this week, hopefully. Then I'll go to Birmingham and do Jane Holland. Obviously we all hope there won't be a third lot of grieving relatives in Cardiff in a few weeks' time, but if there are, well ...'

I don't finish the sentence. It suddenly feels horribly grisly to be discussing interviewing the devastated relatives of a man who isn't even dead yet. Instead I say:

'I assume Lisa and Jane's friends and families have now all been asked if they received anything like my diary before their murders, but I presume nobody's been told any specifics? Or that the two murders are thought to be linked?'

'Correct,' Jess says. 'The existence of the diary, your involvement, and the possible connections between these killings have not been made public in any way. And we can't stop you doing these interviews, Mary – they may even be helpful; they may throw up some link between Lisa and Jane that we haven't discovered yet, who knows? But I am asking you to be very discreet. This is literally a matter of life and death, as you well know. How are you planning to play it?'

'I'm going to keep it really simple,' I say. 'I'm a reasonably well-known crime writer; I was just going to say I'm writing a series of articles on recent murders that have stumped the police. I doubt anyone would question that. I'll just be a writer, doing a straightforward crime story. Is that OK?'

There's a pause, Jess clearly thinking. Then she says:

'Yes, that's fine. Thanks, Mary, for being so up front about this. And you will pass on anything of interest, won't you? By the way, we've started calling him the Diary Killer, in-house. Just for your information. Might make a good headline, when this is all over.'

'It would, yes. Thanks, Jess. Speak soon.'

The Diary Killer, I think, and shudder. *Who the hell are you, and why are you doing this?*

I need to focus on the job in hand though, so I take a coffee back to my desk and get stuck into some more research into the Lisa Turner case, trying to decide the best person to approach for an interview. Her brother, Alastair, seems a good bet; as a GP in Oxford, his number is easy to find, and I'm about to dial it when a cheery voice behind me makes me jump.

'Mary! I've been hoping you'd be in today. I had a bit of a strange phone call – Stu did too. From the police. What have you been up to then?'

I turn to see Guy Hamilton standing behind me with a goofy grin on his face. He's one of the nicest of the four or five web designers who use The Hub, in his mid-twenties with a neat goatee beard and a quirky sense of humour. I'd suspected he'd approach me today, and I'm ready, having decided to stick as closely to the truth as possible without actually telling him anything at all.

'Hey, you,' I say, and smile back. 'A call about New Year's Eve, I assume?'

'Yep.' He nods, eyeing me quizzically.

I smile again and tap the side of my nose.

'Guy, I'd love to tell you, but I really can't. Not just yet. But I promise you, I haven't done anything wrong! It's to do with a story I'm working on, and I'm working quite closely with the police on this one because we both have some involvement in it; that's about all I can say at the moment. They needed to know where I was on New Year's Eve because it's significant for the story, so I told them, and they needed to confirm it, that's all. I'll tell you more when I can, in a couple of months' time probably. Can we just leave it there for now?'

He shrugs.

'Sure. I know what you're like with all your secret squirrel stuff. I'm intrigued though.'

'Sorry. I know it's annoying. Thanks, Guy. Will you explain to Stu too, when you see him? And Ellie, if you see her before I do?'

'What about Ellie?' says Ellie, suddenly appearing beside us and stopping her chair abruptly just an inch from Guy's left foot. He looks shocked for a moment, then deeply impressed.

'You should enter some sort of chair agility competition or something,' he says. 'I have no idea how you control that thing so ... so precisely.'

'Agility competition? I'm not a *dog*, Guy. But, in response to your comment about my immense skill, I used to play wheelchair basketball,' she says, flicking her long hair back off her face. 'Speed and accuracy, that's what it's all about. I don't have time to play these days, but I've still got it.'

She winks at me and grins, and Guy's eyes widen.

'You have. You should get back into it. Olympic-level skills, I'd say.'

Ellie shrugs.

'Maybe one day. Anyway, why were you two talking about me? And Mary, I had a phone call from the police about you. I didn't want to disturb you on your day off by calling to ask you about it, but what's going on?'

'Ahh, nothing much, don't worry,' I say, and give her the same spiel I've just given Guy. She looks as intrigued as he did.

'Wow, OK,' she says. 'I look forward to hearing all about it at some point then. Right, better get on.'

She waves a hand and zooms away again, heading for her desk.

'I'd better get on too. See you later,' Guy says, and ambles off. I take a breath – that was easier than I thought it might be – and reach for Alastair Turner's number again. I've had a quick look at his surgery website; he's based in North Oxford, just off the Woodstock Road. I've never been to the city but from my research I know that this is a nice area, and that Woodstock Road – one of the main routes into the city centre – is wide and tree-lined, with some of the most expensive properties in Oxford. I dial the number for Milton Street Surgery and when a friendly-sounding receptionist answers, ask to speak to Dr Turner. My luck is in; he's just about to take a short lunch break, and when I explain that I'm a journalist, calling about his sister's murder, he agrees to speak to me, although he sounds a little wary.

'I haven't really spoken to the press much so far,' he says. His accent is refined, upper-class Oxford, his voice deep.

'But I've heard of you, I think – I may have even read some of your work. And to be honest, I'm starting to lose hope. It's been five weeks since my sister died and the police seem to have absolutely no leads whatsoever. But what do you think *you* can do? Why have you chosen Lisa's case to write about?'

'For that very reason,' I say. 'Because it seems to be such a difficult case. There are a couple of others I'm hoping to feature too, where the police just can't seem to get anywhere. Publicity often helps, and Lisa's case has really resonated with me. I'd love to see justice done, for her and for you and your family of course.'

And none of that's really a lie, is it? I think. *Lisa's case does resonate with me, massively.*

There's silence on the line for a few moments, then he speaks again, sounding decisive now.

'Right, well, it can't hurt, can it? Are you free tomorrow by any chance? I try to take Friday afternoons off and I don't have much in the way of plans. Could you come to Oxford, around 2.30? I'll give you my home address. I have a two-year-old son so I can't guarantee complete quiet while we chat but I'd rather do it there than here at the surgery.'

'Wonderful. Yes, 2.30 is perfect. Thank you, Dr Turner,' I say.

'Oh, call me Alastair, please,' he says, and gives me his address. I scribble it down and we say goodbye, just as a text from Ellie pops up on my phone.

Fancy nipping over to the Brasserie for a quick lunch or are you too busy? X

I look down to the far end of the room where she's sitting at her desk, and she raises a hand and first gives me a thumbs-up and then a thumbs-down sign, a questioning look on her face. I hesitate for a moment. I love Ellie, and normally I'd jump at the chance of a gossipy lunch, but with everything that's going on, and the fact that I can't talk about it …

Oh, sod it. Lunch won't do any harm, will it?

I give her a thumbs-up, and she grins, and holds up both hands, wiggling her fingers at me.

'Half an hour?' she mouths, and I grin back and nod.

And lunch does me good. Over club sandwiches, sparkling water, and a shared portion of French fries, Ellie makes me howl with laughter with stories about her most recent, and disastrous, online dating experiences.

"The last one was thirty-five and still lived with his mother, Mary. He talked about her *constantly*, from the minute he arrived. And then he left me sitting on my own in the bar at nine o'clock because, apparently, they always watch the ten o'clock BBC News together and he had to get home. I mean, *seriously?*"

Other than asking if I'm sure I'm OK, she doesn't ask for any more details about the so-called 'secret story' I'm working on, and although I dearly wish I could confide in her, I know I can't, and so I'm extremely grateful for her lack of nosiness. We've been there for nearly an hour when Satish wanders in, spotting us across the room and making an immediate beeline for our table.

'Oh, hi, you two,' he says. 'I just fancied a quick sandwich out of the office – would you mind if I sat with you for a few minutes?'

I hesitate – I'm enjoying it just being me and Ellie – but she's already nodding and smiling and pointing at the empty chair next to me, so I can't really object, especially as I can see the way his face has lit up.

He was probably expecting us to say we were just leaving, I think. And it's fine, quite fun really. Ellie carries on sharing her hilarious dating stories, and he reddens at some of them, making me wonder if he's also been guilty of similar faux pas, but he laughs along with us, and we end up staying in the restaurant for far longer than we should. By the time we get back to The Hub I'm feeling more relaxed than I've felt in days. I hug Ellie and smile at Satish and we head back to our respective desks, where I make some notes ahead of my chat with Alastair Turner tomorrow and then, as it's still only mid-afternoon, decide to look into flights to Botswana, just in case. Right now, I'm still not sure *what* I'm going to do as the 1st of April draws nearer, although I'm definitely leaning towards staying in the UK now; I'm not sure why I'm even considering this, and I haven't dared to tell Pete yet, but the prospect of meeting this killer, of him turning up despite warning me in advance of his intentions is just *so* tempting. Little quivers, a mix of dread and excitement, run through me every time I think about it. But I would dearly love to see Lucinda too, and I'm sure Botswana would be an incredible adventure. Maybe I can go afterwards, instead, when this is all over.

If you're actually still alive after the 1st of April, of course, a voice in my head whispers, but I ignore it.

I'm scrolling through flight times when I hear a familiar, nasal voice.

'Going on holiday? Hmmm, Botswana, eh? Sounds ... different.'

I turn to see Edward Cooper peering over my shoulder, his tiny, almost black eyes staring at my computer screen. I close the page and swivel round to face him. He's wearing a blue shirt so rumpled it looks as if he slept in it.

'Just browsing,' I say lightly. 'I might go away at the end of March. I haven't decided yet.'

He nods and smiles, then looks down at my desk, eyes sweeping over my notebook and the notes I've made about tomorrow's Oxford trip.

'And off to Oxford too,' he says. 'You get around, don't you? It's a nice city, Oxford. Satish and I spent New Year there, actually. We went for a run along the canal on New Year's Day, to blow away the cobwebs, you know? We had to stop earlier than we wanted to though because there'd been that murder in the early hours, and they closed the towpath. You know, the woman lawyer, the one you were looking at a photo of the other day? Anyway, I'll let you get on. Laters.'

My heart thuds. I open my mouth to reply, but he's strolling slowly away, not looking back. I watch him go, my mind racing.

Hang on – what did he just say? He and Satish were in Oxford on New Year's Eve?

I knew they were friendly, but I didn't realise they were close enough to go away together. And I didn't know they were runners either. Both are lean, I suppose, and Satish looks pretty fit, but Edward? He's never struck me as the running type, although I suppose runners come in all shapes and sizes. But it's that last bit that's making my heart rate speed up. That last thing he said.

'There'd been that murder in the early hours, and they closed the towpath ...'

Edward and Satish were in Oxford the night Lisa Turner was killed. I suppose there's been no real reason for Satish to tell me about that – we haven't had any conversations about what we did over the holiday period, not today or previously – but why on earth didn't *Edward* mention it when he saw me looking at Lisa's photo on Monday, and commented on how macabre my job was?

And the running thing, I think. Police in Birmingham are looking for a runner, who they suspect of murdering Jane Holland. A coincidence, or something else?

There's a knot forming in my stomach now, my breathing quickening as I try to process what's just happened. Is it just another coincidence, like the one of Pete recently visiting Jane Holland's casino? I sink my head into my hands, trying to calm myself.

Am I overthinking all this?

Pete was in Birmingham *weeks* ago, ages before anything happened to Jane Holland. And Oxford's exactly the sort of place people visit all the time for mini-breaks. Hundreds of people probably went there for New Year's Eve, and loads of people like to run on New Year's Day. It's a first day of the new year starting-as-you-mean-to-go-on thing. So should I tell the police about Edward and Satish and their trip? Or would that just be a waste of everyone's time, and the perfect way to really piss off people you have to work with every day?

I'll think about it, I decide. *I'll think about it, on the way to Oxford tomorrow. A day or so won't make any difference, will it?*

I take a deep breath and sit up straight in my chair, then swallow hard. At his desk halfway down the room, Edward is now chatting animatedly to Satish, who's standing over him and leaning in close, nodding. As I watch them, they both turn simultaneously and look at me, then quickly look away again and my breath catches in my throat.

Is something going on here? Am I being ridiculous?

But Satish is walking back to his own desk now, and Edward's head is down as he flicks through some papers on his desk, then reaches for his keyboard and begins tapping it. My eyes flit from him to Satish and back again, and then I look around the room, and everything looks normal, just another ordinary afternoon at The Hub. People working, chatting on the phone, typing, sipping coffee.

It's just my imagination, working overtime, isn't it? Stop it, Mary. Get a grip.

I take another deep breath, pack up my bag, and head for home.

Chapter 13

Friday 5th February

Cheltenham Central Police Station

'Everyone happy to start?'

DCI Steph Warden angles her big monitor so that everyone in the room can see it clearly. On the screen, DCIs Priya Thomson and Linda Lake both nod, and DCI Bryn Lewis raises a thumb.

'Happy as always,' he says, although he sounds rather morose.

'Right, good. OK, so as it's Friday morning and I'm hoping at least some of us are going to try and take some time off over the weekend, shall we try and make this as brief as possible? I believe it's just you, Priya, who said you had something to share today? Has there been a development in the Holland case?'

Priya nods, tucking a loose strand of dark hair behind her right ear.

'Maybe,' she says. 'We've been doing a little more research into Jane's background, her family and so on. And there's something ... well, it was actually one of our Detective Constables, Frankie Tanner, who spotted a possible connection between Jane, Lisa, and Mary. Let me bring her in.'

She shuffles off to one side, so she's only partially in shot, and another woman slides her chair into the vacated spot. She's young, with a striking white-blonde pixie haircut, and she smiles and clears her throat.

'Right, well ...'

She sounds nervous, and she pauses for a second or two, then swallows and starts again, her voice a little stronger now.

'It may be nothing at all, just a coincidence. But when I pointed it out to DCI Thomson, she thought it was worth a closer look, as it's the only even vaguely possible connection we've found to date.'

She pauses again, looking down at some notes in front of her.

'It started when I took a closer look at Jane Holland's father. He died some years ago, but when he was alive he was ... well, I suppose *notorious* is a good word. His name was John Holland, but he was always known as Big Johnny. It was him who opened the original casino, the one here in the city. Jane opened the second one in Coventry when she took over the family business about twelve years ago. But Big Johnny was rumoured to have had a lot of other business interests over the years, and shall we just say that not all of them were exactly legit, if the rumours are to be believed anyway.'

'Oooh,' says Linda Lake in Oxford. 'This sounds interesting. What sort of stuff are we talking about?'

'Well, this is where it gets tricky,' says Frankie. 'He was

never actually done for *anything*. It was all just rumour and supposition. But I've spoken to a number of senior officers who were around at the time and they all say the same thing. Big Johnny was rumoured to be involved in all sorts, using his law-abiding casino as a front. Drugs, a bit of people smuggling, even a few pretty lucrative armed robberies. The only problem was, nobody could ever pin anything on him, even though it sounds like they tried pretty hard from time to time. He was, apparently, very, very good at staying one step ahead of the law. He always had an absolutely water-tight alibi, and there was never any actual evidence to link him to any of the crimes he was suspected of being involved in. The man never got so much as a parking fine. When he died – suddenly, of a heart attack, I believe – he left everything to Jane, his only daughter. His wife, Jane's mother, had died some years before. And at that point, when Jane took over, all the rumours just started to fade away. If he *was* involved in organised crime, she clearly decided not to go down the same road. As far as we can make out, she was all completely above board. And as we know, charity work was incredibly important to her. Making up for the sins of her father, maybe, although of course I'm just speculating now, as nothing was ever proven.'

There's silence for few moments.

'Ohh-kaay,' says Linda slowly, dragging out the word. 'But I don't really see how this gets us anywhere. There's no suggestion that Mary Ellis or Lisa Turner have possible criminal elements in their families, is there? Quite the opposite in Lisa's case; her mother was a prominent judge, remember.'

Frankie nods.

'Yes, and that's the thing. *Prominent*. Look, as I said this is just guesswork. But all three of the victims – and I'm including Mary Ellis here, as a potential *future* victim – had at least one famous, prominent, whatever you want to call it, parent. And all connected – or rumoured to be connected – to *crime* in some way. Jane Holland's father was, as I said, notorious here in Birmingham, even if nobody could ever prove he was a criminal. Lisa Turner's mother was a renowned and outspoken judge. And Mary Ellis's father was Gregor Ellis, one of the most famous crime authors of the 90s. Now, as I said, I don't know yet if all this is just a coincidence. I'm looking into it a bit more, and also trying to work out if any of these parents knew each other or had any dealings with each other in any capacity. Who knows? Maybe Gregor Ellis contacted Alice Turner with some questions about the British legal system while researching a book at some point. I don't think he ever wrote about a casino in any of his novels but maybe he knew Big Johnny in some way too. Maybe Big Johnny and Alice Turner had some dealings with one another – maybe he needed to consult a lawyer at some point. I have no idea, and as I said there's a lot more work to be done here. But, well, it's something, isn't it?'

She shrugs, and glances to her left, and Priya Thompson moves back into the shot, so the two of them fill the frame now, sitting close together.

'I think Frankie just might have something,' she says. 'Gregor Ellis died fourteen years ago. Lisa's mother was already a successful lawyer at that time, and John Holland – Big Johnny – would have been at the height of his notoriety. The

Ellis family moved around quite a lot but they were definitely living in the Cotswolds for a while before Gregor died, so not that far from either Oxford or Birmingham. So maybe these three did meet at some point, who knows? It's worth looking into a bit more, don't you think? And maybe it can help you out a bit down there in Cardiff, Bryn. I mean, not a lot, at this stage, maybe, but it's *something*, right?'

Bryn is nodding slowly.

'Maybe. OK, so we're saying we could now be looking for a potential victim called David who has at least one well-known parent with some sort of crime connection, then? I mean, it's a still a bloody ridiculously common name. But yes, it's something. We'll get our thinking caps on.'

'And remember, it doesn't have to be a living parent. All three so far are actually well-known but *dead* parents,' says Frankie.

Bryn nods.

'True, yes. Thanks.'

Then he sighs.

'Oh bugger it, I don't know, guys. It seems a bit far-fetched, really, doesn't it? Why would someone be going round killing the adult offspring of long dead, well-known people? There's no logic there really, is there? Yes, the crime connection is interesting. But they're all in such different fields. We need to find out more, as quickly as we can. Mary Ellis might know, possibly, if her late father did any research that might have brought him into contact with either of the others, eh? And Linda and Priya, you'll go back to Lisa's and Jane's families and see if they know of any possible connection between the parents? All with the utmost discretion of course.'

'I will,' says Linda. 'I'll do it right now, in fact.'

'On it,' says Priya.

'And I'll talk to Mary,' says Jess. 'This afternoon, if I can.'

'Thanks, Jess,' says Steph. 'Well, it's certainly a very interesting development. Good work, DC Tanner.'

Frankie beams.

'Thanks,' she says.

'And we'll try to find some Davids who fit the bill here,' says Bryn. 'Even though I still think it's unlikely to narrow it down nearly enough. I wonder if it's time to start thinking about releasing some more information to the public? Very carefully, obviously. Because we have exactly twenty-three days now until we're promised a murder here in Cardiff, and that's not something I'm relishing, I can tell you.'

There's another few moments of silence. Then Steph says:

'You might be right, Bryn. But we still have a few weeks. Let's not panic yet, OK? We've got a direction to explore now, at least, haven't we? Let's try and do that first and reconvene early next week. Because we're getting closer, guys. We're getting closer to working out his motivation, I can *feel* it.'

'And once we know what that is, we're one step closer to finding out *who* he is,' says Priya.

'*Exactly*,' says Steph.

Chapter 14

Friday 5th February

It's after one o'clock on Friday and I'm cruising along the A40 on my way to Oxford when my mobile rings, Jess's number flashing on the display. I have, in fact, just been thinking about her; as planned, I've been mulling over my concerns about Pete's casino visit and Edward and Satish's Oxford trip as I drive. Three people I know suddenly seem to have vague connections to the two murders; is that somehow linked to the fact it was *me* who was sent the diary, and am I being stupid not taking the information to the police? I'm just so tired of worrying about it all, but I'm still trying to decide if I'm overreacting when the call comes in.

'Mary, we've had a little development in the case,' Jess says.

'A development? Do tell,' I say.

'OK, well first, this might sound like a very random question, and I know I'm going back a bit here, but would you know if your dad might have visited a casino at any point, as research for one of his books maybe? One of Jane Holland's casinos in particular? Or whether he ever consulted a lawyer, again for research?'

I frown, hitting the brakes as I approach a red light.

'Errmmm ... I mean, maybe,' I say, doubtfully. 'There aren't any casinos in any of his novels though, as far as I can remember. But the lawyer thing – possibly. There was quite a bit of legal stuff in some of his plots so he may well have needed to check some details. Why?'

'Do you have any way of checking? Any of his old notes, documents, early drafts of manuscripts, anything like that?'

The light changes and I move off again, shaking my head at the speaker Jess's voice is booming from.

'Nope,' I say. 'Everything was destroyed in the fire. The one he died in, as I'm sure you're aware? He was pretty old-fashioned – he still used an old electric typewriter to write his books. And so everything, including all his notes, was just on paper. There were no electronic back-ups or anything like that. I'm amazed his publishers allowed it, and they probably wouldn't have for much longer, but it was over fourteen years ago and he was a really big name back then, so, you know ... anyway, everything was lost. I have nothing left at all, except his finished novels and screenplays of course. But why, Jess? Why do you want to know?'

'Well, it's just a theory at the moment,' she says. 'But one of the DCs in Birmingham has spotted a possible – quite tenuous, but *possible* – link between you and the first two victims. It's to do with having a famous parent, or certainly a parent well-known in *some* capacity, and with a connection to crime.'

She explains further, and I listen, fascinated.

'Gosh,' I say, when she's done. There's a little tight feeling developing in my chest, and I swallow hard before saying, 'I mean, yes, a bit tenuous. But there might be something in it. Are South Wales Police taking it seriously? It could narrow things down for them, couldn't it?'

'It could, and yes they are,' Jess says. 'Still a bit of a needle in a haystack, and of course we could have this all wrong. It could just be a coincidence. But think about it, will you? And let us know if you remember anything about your dad that might help. Trips he might have made to Oxford or Birmingham, maybe? I'll email you photos of John Holland and Alice Turner too, see if their faces ring a bell. Anyway, speak soon.'

I drive the rest of the way to Alastair Turner's house in a bit of a daze, somehow managing to follow the instructions barked at me from my sat nav. My mind is racing.

More coincidences? What's going on? And could this really be about our parents? Has whoever's doing this picked us out not because of who we are, but because of who they are?

It's a thought that's simply never occurred to me until now, and as I turn onto Painton Road and slow down, looking for number eleven, something starts pinging in the far recesses of my mind, a new idea suddenly beginning to form. I don't have time to think it through at the moment though, and I spot the house I'm searching for and pull into the small paved driveway, tucking my little Audi in next to a smart black Jaguar SUV.

Alastair Turner's house is a handsome semi-detached

Victorian property, a date stone above the porch telling me it was built in 1896. The front door is painted deep blue, and when I ring the bell I hear a rich, deep peal, followed moments later by rapid footsteps. The man who opens the door is dressed in charcoal suit trousers and a black and white checked shirt, the top button open, no tie. He's tall and dark with a neat beard and he looks, I think immediately, very like his late sister – the same striking yellow-brown eyes.

'Dr Turner? I'm Mary Ellis,' I say, and hold out a hand.

He takes it briefly, his grip firm, then smiles and stands aside to let me in.

'Please, as I said on the phone, call me Alastair,' he says. 'Go through – second door on the left. We have the house to ourselves for an hour or so, fortunately. My wife has taken our son to the park. Would you like a tea or a coffee?'

'Oh, a coffee would be lovely,' I say. 'Black is fine, thank you.'

'Won't be a minute,' he says, and walks briskly off down the hallway, presumably to the kitchen. I push open the door he indicated and find myself in a bright reception room, presumably once separate sitting and dining rooms but at some point knocked through to make one big, open-plan living space. It is tastefully decorated and has comfortable-looking, modern furniture; bi-fold doors open out onto a surprisingly large and very neat rear garden, crocuses and early daffodils bobbing their heads in the breeze in tidy borders.

I stand there for a moment, admiring the view, then turn away from the window to look around the room. There's a long L-shaped white sofa and two large, matching armchairs with a low table in-between them. I choose a chair and sit down, pulling a notebook, pen, and voice recorder from my bag. Gathering my thoughts, I remind myself not to let anything slip about the fact that I'm a potential victim of whoever killed Lisa too.

Stick to the story, I think. *Just try to find out if there's anything else that might link us all. The police might be right about the parent thing, but they might not …*

'One black coffee. And a couple of chocolate digestives on the side. I always think coffee just isn't the same without a little bit of chocolate,' says Alastair, suddenly reappearing.

'Mmm, I agree, thank you,' I say, and smile, and he smiles back, his eyes crinkling at the corners.

He takes the chair opposite me, and we both take a sip of our drinks. Then he carefully puts his mug down on the table and looks at me expectantly.

'So. What can I tell you, Mary? Oh, I had a call from the police a short while ago, by the way. They wanted to ask about my mother, rather randomly. They were wondering if I knew if she might ever have encountered a character up in Birmingham – a casino owner known as Big Johnny. They said they couldn't really explain, but clearly they're investigating some sort of lead. I can't imagine what my mother's work years ago could have to do with my sister's death though. I don't suppose you can shed any light on that?'

I shake my head.

'No idea, sorry,' I say, and instantly feel guilty for lying to him. 'Did she, though? Your mother, I mean. Did she know this guy?'

He shrugs.

'I don't know. I've referred them to her former chambers. Somebody there may know. She never really talked about her work at home, or indeed with us even as grown-ups. Anyway – I'm sure I'll find out what it's all about eventually.'

'Probably,' I say.

Clearly, the police didn't also ask him if his mother knew my father, I think with relief. *They know I'm here with him today, and that might make him suspicious. Hopefully they can discover if there's a link there from one of her former colleagues, maybe …*

'OK, so shall we make a start? Do you mind if I record our chat?'

I point at the voice recorder lying on the table, and he nods.

'That's fine,' he says.

'Great.' I switch the machine on, then pick up my notepad and pan, glancing down at my list of questions.

'Right, well, can we just start with a quick look at Lisa's younger years? Where she went to school, university, her hobbies and so on? A little potted history? I know some of it from her online biography, and from various news articles I've read, but it would be good to hear it from you, as her brother.'

'Sure. OK, well, I was actually ten when she was born, so I remember it well. I'm not sure why my parents waited so long to have a second child – my mother's career maybe – but I do remember how happy they both were, to have this gorgeous new baby daughter. I was pretty thrilled too, to have a little sister, after so many years as an only child …'

He spends the next few minutes telling me all about Lisa's early years, and while it's nice to build up a more detailed picture of her life, I'm soon listening with a growing feeling of despondency. Lisa had been a lively, outgoing child, star of her school plays from about the age of six, and later an active member of her secondary school debating society. She loved horse-riding and camping and had a judo black belt by the age of sixteen. It's all fascinating stuff, but the more I hear, the more I realise that if I'm looking for a connection between us, it's certainly nothing to do with her early life or interests. We couldn't be more different. I'd been a quiet kid, spending most of my spare time escaping into books. By the time Alastair has, in his story, reached his sister's university years, where she was a star of the Drama Society and the Debating Union, I've pretty much made my mind up.

If there's any link between me and Lisa, I can't see it.

When he's finished, I ask a few more questions, making a note of places she liked to visit on holiday, her favourite restaurants – again, nothing there that I can relate to at all – and writing down some basic details about some of the most high-profile legal cases she'd worked on in the year or so before her murder.

'Unlike my mother, my sister loved to chat about her work. It was all pretty dry – insolvency cases and such like – but I found it quite interesting for some reason,' Alastair says. 'Maybe because it was so different from what I do. And we were close, so we met up often, and we talked a lot. That's what I miss the most, you know? Just ... just sitting around with a coffee or a glass of wine, catching up with my little sister. I was so proud of her, and everything she achieved. I miss her, every day.'

He swallows, and turns his head abruptly, staring out of the window into the garden. I can see from the set of his jaw that he's struggling to keep back tears, and my heart twists in sympathy.

'I'm so sorry,' I say quietly. 'To have her ripped away from you like that must have been just horrendous.'

Alastair is silent for another few moments, then he takes a deep breath and turns back to face me.

'I suppose you went through a similar thing, with your father. I'm aware of the grim circumstances of his death,' he says, and I nod.

'Yes,' I say.

'I'm actually a big fan. I've read most of his books,' he says. 'I recognised your name, as I said on the phone, and then I realised who your father was. He was a huge talent.'

He smiles, his rather lovely eyes crinkling at the corners again, and I smile back.

'Well, that's nice of you,' I say. 'And thank you for being so open with me. I don't know yet when this article will be published – as I said, my chat with you is part of a series of interviews with relatives of victims of unsolved crimes. But I'll keep you posted, OK? And who knows, there may even be some detail in here'—I tap the voice recorder—'that might be of some help in the investigation. You never know, eh?'

He nods and smiles again, and I thank him once more and start putting my things back into my bag, asking him about his plans for the weekend and commenting on how lovely his garden is as I stand up to leave. As I drive away, I try to quell the feeling of disappointment now sitting like a weight in my stomach, replaying my conversation with Alastair in my head just in case I've missed something, although I'm pretty sure I haven't.

I was really hoping I might spot a connection, but maybe there just isn't one. Is it a waste of time to keep looking? Should I start looking at the parents now too, instead?

'Oh, bugger.'

I sigh as I see a long line of stationary traffic up ahead, and hit the brakes. I'd forgotten how early the afternoon traffic can build up on a Friday, and the A40 is a busy road at the best of times. I turn the radio on, scrolling for a minute before settling for a 90s music station. Christina Aguilera's 'Genie in a Bottle' is playing, and suddenly I'm ten years old again, singing into my hairbrush. The age of innocence, an age when I had no idea what lay ahead in my teenage years, and how my life would turn out.

I inch forwards, and then hit the brakes again, groaning. As I wait for the car in front to start moving, Jess's words from earlier run through my head, and I realise that the idea that had begun as a shadowy outline as I arrived at Alastair's house has suddenly become more solid in my mind. If the police are right, if this killer *has* selected his victims because of something to do with our parents ...

I feel a rush of adrenalin, and I know it's part terror, part exhilaration. I know I need to think about this some more – really, really think about it. But if it's true, if they've got this right ... well, this could change everything. This killer thinks he's smart. And he *is* smart, clearly – he's killed twice already and got away with it, after all.

But the thing is, I might, quite unexpectedly, be one step ahead of him now. I look in the rear-view mirror, into my own eyes, and I can see the spark of excitement in them.

He may not be as smart as he thinks he is. Because I know something he doesn't.

Chapter 15

Friday 5th February

The traffic eases as I get closer to Cheltenham, and I'm about half an hour from home when I suddenly decide to make a detour. It's to somewhere I haven't been for a very long time, and as I drive though the small, picturesque village of Thornton and pull into the parking area outside the cemetery, I feel a lump forming in my throat and realise I'm fighting back tears, memories more than a decade old racing through my mind, the emotions unexpectedly strong. Sometimes, these days, I think I've almost forgotten all about it – the fear, the pain, the long, dark months that followed that cold March day fourteen years ago, the day my life changed forever. But, deep down, I know that of course I'll *never* forget it, not really.

How can I? Impossible.

I walk slowly through the graveyard, empty of living people right now, the path meandering past weathered, moss-covered headstones with indecipherable inscriptions and new, shiny black granite tombstones; long-dead Victorians and the recently deceased lying side by side. It's peaceful here, a gentle breeze rustling the leaves of old oak trees, the rich, fluty call of a bird – *a blackbird, maybe?* – high above. And then, there it is. I haven't been here for years, and yet it looks exactly as I remember it.

> *GREGOR ELLIS*
> *1957-2007*
> *Sail on, my love, sail on*

I stand there, motionless, staring. He was just fifty when he died. No age, really, and with so much potential still ahead of him – so many books he could have written, so many screenplays. So many people he could have made happy with his words, his talent. The line on his headstone – *sail on, my love, sail on* – was the final line in his last novel, the one published just weeks before he died. It had seemed apt somehow, to also use them at his final resting place, a place which has now become somewhat of a ... well, *tourist attraction* isn't exactly the right phrase. Maybe pilgrimage site is more accurate. His fans certainly come here, hundreds of them a year, or so I'm told, leaving flowers, taking photos of themselves holding their Gregor Ellis paperbacks, his grave in the background. I've seen them online, these pictures, and I've never quite been able to decide if it's weird and ghoulish, or rather sweet – a testament to the continuing, powerful impact of the work he left behind. But the photos, the fans, are one of the reasons I don't visit here often; I haven't, as I said, been here in years – three, maybe even four now. It's the main reason I don't use social media, either. I don't want to be drawn into conversation, to be asked questions, to be gawped at.

The daughter. The one who survived.

My hand drifts to my left cheek, my fingers running over the scarred, lumpy skin, and although the afternoon is mild for February and I'm bundled up in a thick padded jacket, a scarf wound round my neck, I shiver. If I let myself, if I allow the memories to trickle back into my head, I can still hear the crackle of the flames, and feel the heat slamming into me, solid as a wall.

There's a bench just a couple of metres away, at the edge of the path, and I sink down onto it, remembering. Remembering the house, not far from here. My father had rented Furnbury Hall for a year. He was even thinking of renewing the lease for a second year, which was remarkable for him, since he rarely stayed in one place for much more than six months. My mother, the love of his life, died of cancer when I was just three years old; months after her funeral, he sold the house in Connecticut where I'd been born, packed up everything including me, and moved us to Sweden. And that was it, for years; Germany, South Africa, Brazil, Italy ... he never seemed to be able to settle anywhere for long, and for me that meant innumerable first days at new schools, and a rootless, lonely childhood. He said the travelling inspired him, that his creativity became stagnant if he stayed in one place for too long, but now, as an adult myself, I don't believe that anymore. I think he was trying to outrun the pain, to somehow keep one step ahead of his anguish over my mother's death, never able to truly find peace. He was a cold, angry man for nearly all of those final years, but in the final months of his life, something changed, just a little. A thawing maybe, of the icy hand of grief which had clutched at his heart for so long, the beautiful fifteenth-century manor house we were renting working some sort of magic on him. He was still cold and angry, but he was a cold, angry man who was thinking of staying in one place for a while, which was something.

And then came the fire. It started just after midnight, and it took hold horrifyingly fast. It took more than twenty hours for the fire service to completely extinguish the blaze, even though at its height there were more than a hundred firefighters tackling flames so high that the local newspaper reports said they could be seen three miles away. I shiver again, the memories coming back with a vengeance now: the shouts in the dark, shrill with terror; my panic, my heart thumping, my lungs burning, my hair on fire ...

'No! Stop it!'

I gasp and stand up abruptly, aware that I've just shouted the words out loud, and that I'm sweating now, my armpits clammy under my coat, my palms damp.

Don't think about it, don't ...

I take a deep breath, then another, trying to steady myself, to slow my racing heartbeat, and look around, hoping I'm still alone here, hoping nobody is going to approach me to see why I'm shouting at nobody, at nothing, in this place of sanctity, but there's no one here. Relieved, I swallow hard, take another breath, and move the few steps back to the edge of the grave.

The graves.

Because there are two of them here, of course. Gregor Ellis

was not the only one to die in that fire. I crouch to pull a weed from between the cracks on the large York stone slab that covers his burial spot, then turn to look at the headstone on the right.

AMANDA ARCHER
1989 – 2007

It's simple, unfussy Italian white marble, and I reach out a hand and run my fingers across the smooth surface, across the letters of her name.

Amanda Archer.

My friend – one of the few I'd ever had in the nomadic life I'd led back then. She'd been staying with us that night, the night the flames consumed Furnbury Hall; she was just eighteen, like me. We'd bonded in our first year of college over shared experiences – I didn't remember my mother, and she had never known her father. And while I had struggled with my lonely, although massively privileged, childhood, travelling the world with a famous, wealthy single parent, she had known the same loneliness in very different circumstances. Her late mother had been violent, and a drug user, and Amanda had been in and out of foster care for years. Like me, she had found it hard to make friends, had been lonely, had craved a stable, normal life. She had finally left the care system and moved out into her own little bedsit in Bristol just weeks before that fateful night; starting her life, trying to plan her future. And then ... the fire. The end of everything.

I'd insisted that she be buried here. She had no family; it

was the very least I could do. I run my fingers over her name once more, and feel tears pricking my eyelids. I clamber to my feet, fumbling in my coat pocket for a tissue as I walk quickly along the path towards the cemetery gate, not looking back.

I shouldn't have come here. Why did I? It always makes me so … so sad, I think, as I get back into my car, pulling my scarf from around my neck and tossing it onto the passenger seat. And right now, I know I can't afford to feel like this; I can't afford to get distracted. I need to concentrate, need to think, need to focus on the matter in hand, on this man, this person, who's threatening my life, who's already taken two, maybe more.

Because if this really is something to do with my father, the great Gregor Ellis, I could be holding a winning card, I think as I turn the engine on and move slowly back out onto the road.

I just have to figure out how to play it.

Chapter 16

Monday 8th February

Monday morning is cold and frosty, the clouds steel grey. Yet again, my sleep over the weekend was sporadic at best, the now depressingly regular, terrifying, flame-filled dreams – yes, they're always about fire – leaving me exhausted, hating the night. I'm struggling to switch off at all, my mind running repeatedly over everything that's happened in the past few weeks. I *think* I know what I need to do now – if I dare – but I'm driving myself to distraction trying to work out how to do it, my thoughts a jumble. It's all too big, too scary, and if I get it wrong ...

I tried to take a break from my own head with a wander round the shops in town followed by a meet-up with Eleanor for coffee and cake on Saturday afternoon, and then a few drinks and a film at home with Pete and Megan in the evening. They headed over to her place yesterday afternoon, though, leaving me to spend a restless night alone, but Saturday was pleasant enough, with lots of wine and a Thai takeaway. If I'm honest, though, I am increasingly finding Megan a bit ... well, a bit *annoying*, I suppose. Maybe it's just my current anxious state of mind, and more my fault than hers, but I'm getting a sense that she's feeling a little differently about me too; I actually think she's started becoming a little jealous of mine and Pete's friendship, that she's not quite sure if there's more to it than us just being old mates. She hasn't said anything, not exactly; it's just the odd look, the occasional slightly sarcastic comment. And yet, she's always friendly enough when she's here, always makes an effort to include me, and that makes me feel bad for sometimes wishing she *wasn't* around, and guilty for thinking that actually I'd rather be sitting in our cosy lounge with just Pete, my feet on his lap. Because Pete does really seem to be very fond of her, and she makes him happy, and that makes me happy. So, it's all a little confusing really. But this weekend, I kind of wanted to chat to Pete properly, and I couldn't, not with her here.

There's just so much in my head right now. I've been thinking more and more about Edward and Satish at work, not just about New Year's Eve but about how they always seem to be chatting together in low voices these days. Am I imagining that often, when they do that, they glance my way, looking at me for a moment before resuming their quiet conversation? I just can't decide if I'm being paranoid. I mean, they're friends, after all. And I have chats just like that with Eleanor, when we're exchanging bits of silly office gossip and don't want anyone else to hear, don't I? And Satish really does seem genuinely nice; I enjoyed his company very much when he joined me and Ellie for lunch. And so I probably *am* being paranoid, but I still feel as if I need to talk it through with somebody. I nearly did on Saturday, deciding to run it past Pete when Megan went downstairs to the kitchen for a few minutes to make a phone call. Just as I was about to tell him, though, she came back into the room, complaining that her mobile was dead and that she'd have to charge it up before she could phone anyone. I was about to point out that she could plug it in and make the call *while* it was charging, but she'd already moved on to another topic, shivering theatrically.

'I'm so chilly. Why don't you light the fire?' she asked, snuggling up to Pete and pulling the sleeves of her grey hoodie down over her hands. 'It seems such a shame to have a lovely open fireplace like that and not use it.'

Over her head, Pete looked at me and grimaced, an apologetic expression on his face, and I shrugged.

'It's me, Megan. I don't like fires. Or fireworks, or anything like that really. You know, because of ...'

I gestured vaguely at my left ear, and for a moment she looked at me a little strangely, and then her eyes widened.

'Oh ... Oh GOD, Mary, I'm so sorry! I just didn't think, that's so insensitive of me, I'm mortified. Sorry. Urgh, I can be *such* an idiot!'

She sounded so genuinely horrified that I laughed.

'Don't worry. Just don't ever give me a candle as a birthday present. I can't be around *them* either. The local charity shops are always happy to take them luckily.'

I winked at her, and she clapped her hands over her face and groaned again.

'There was one in that pamper hamper I gave you for Christmas, wasn't there?' she mumbled through her fingers.

'I am *so* thoughtless. I'm really, really sorry. I'll remember in future.'

'Honestly, don't worry. It was a lovely hamper,' I say as Pete rolls his eyes. 'It's fine, Megan. Stop it. Go and pour me another glass of wine and I'll let you off.'

I waved my empty wine glass at her and she uncovered her face and leapt off the sofa, still muttering apologies, and I felt guilty again then, wishing I'd just made up some excuse about why our lounge fireplace holds a glass vase filled with fairy lights instead of a pile of brightly burning logs. Although she *does* know about the fire of course, and about what happened to me. Pete told me he explained it all to her in the early days of their relationship, when she asked him about my scars after the first time we met. Maybe she just forgot when she gave me that candle, because to be fair, I've never really talked to her about it, or about the fears and the nightmares it left me with. I don't speak about it to anyone really, partly because I don't really need to; as I've said before, it's all there on the internet for anyone who wants to read about it.

At the time, it was in every newspaper, both here and in the US, for weeks; the famous American writer Gregor Ellis, dead in a massive house fire in the Cotswolds, perishing along with his teenage daughter's best friend. It was a huge story, a tragedy and a miracle all in one. My survival was the bit dubbed the miracle – the daughter who survived, despite being dragged unconscious from the flames with severe burns. I spent a few weeks in the burns unit at Southmead Hospital in Bristol and then, when I was deemed stable enough to travel, was flown to the US, to my grandmother in New York. There, she arranged for me to have treatment at one of the best trauma and burns facilities in the city; not only that, but she took me in, taking care of me, giving me the stability I'd long craved: a lovely home, a routine, an ordered life. She was a clever and practical woman too, helping me to manage my father's estate for the next four years until I graduated, keeping me out of the spotlight, away from the journalists who initially clamoured for an interview and then, eventually, when it was clear I wasn't interested, leaving me alone. Added to all that, she was funny, quirky, and glamorous, and I loved her and the time I spent with her dearly. She made it to my graduation ceremony at Columbia University, a vision in a white designer trouser suit and a wide-brimmed hat, and then died from a massive stroke just three weeks later. It was after that that I decided to come back to the UK. It's home, for some reason. And despite the fact that with my inheritance money I could live pretty much anywhere, and even despite everything that's happened since I opened that *bloody* diary, I know this is where I want to be. I'm content here. I have good friends and work that I enjoy; I love the history and culture and sense of humour; I even like the weather, the changing seasons. Although today, I think, as I glance out of the kitchen window at the glowering sky, is *not* my favourite kind of winter morning. There's no sign of any sun to melt away the white frosting on the pavements and the icy jackets on the leaves of the London plane trees that line the street outside.

It's nearly 11am, and I should head into The Hub really, but I'm just debating whether to have one more coffee before I go when I hear the clang of the letter box. I walk into the hall and pick up a small handful of mail: our electricity bill, what looks like a bank statement for Pete, a flyer about a new pizza delivery place, and a brown envelope addressed to me. Back in the kitchen, I flick the kettle on *–I think I will have that last coffee after all* – and open my letter. There's a single plain white sheet of paper inside the envelope, just a few lines handwritten in block capitals in the centre of the page. Frowning, I read them, and my stomach flips.

What? What the hell …?

I stare at the words, my heartrate speeding up, and suddenly I feel dizzy and grab onto the kitchen counter for support. Blinking to clear the spots before my eyes, I read the note again.

TWO DOWN, TWO TO GO.
DON'T TRY AND RUN, MARY ELLIS.
I'M WATCHING YOUR EVERY MOVE.
YOU CAN'T HIDE FROM ME, NO MATTER
WHERE YOU ARE.
TWO DOWN, TWO TO GO …

Chapter 17

Monday 8th February

Cardiff Central Police Station

'Three weeks today. *Three weeks*. Shit.'

DCI Bryn Lewis sinks his head into his hands, then rubs his eyes and sits up straight again, turning to look at the colleague who's just been updating him on the latest research into possible victims of the promised March the 1st murder. Sergeant Hari Hughes is sharp and keen and is working towards joining CID, and he had begged to be involved in the investigation – *'somehow, anyhow!'* – a plea which Bryn hadn't had the heart to turn down. He remembers what it was like to be on the sidelines when a major case was going on, and Hari has already proved himself. The information he's just handed Bryn may not, in the end, result in a life being saved, but it's certainly a good start.

'I know. Three weeks is pretty scary. But, well, we can only do what we can do with such limited information, can't we?' Hari's saying now. He's a short, stocky man with a neatly trimmed goatee and a gym-honed physique. They both have mugs of coffee on the table in front of them, but while Bryn has already nibbled his way through three ginger nut biscuits, Hari waved the plate away when it was offered to him, focussed instead on his notes.

'I mean, there are probably three to four thousand adult men called David in Cardiff, and that's likely a low estimate,' he says. 'It was a really popular name here between the 1930s and 1990s, then dipped a bit. But it started to grow in popularity again from 2007 onwards, I'm not sure why. Anyway, there's a *lot* of them. But if we're going with this theory for now, that this could be something to do with a parent with a crime connection, well, it's helped narrow them down a bit. We'll have missed loads of people off this list, there's no doubt about that. But if we can warn some of them at least ... I mean, if it *is* one of them who's being targeted, and we can somehow get them out of the city for the twenty-four hours in question, we'd foil this killer, wouldn't we?'

Bryn smiles, trying to look a little more positive than he's feeling, and wipes a biscuit crumb from his lower lip.

'We would. It's a massive long shot though. And I'm still not quite sure how we're going to do even that without causing mass panic. Here, let me see that list again.'

Hari pushes a sheet of paper across the table, and Bryn slowly reads down the list of names. It's an eclectic one: there's David Evans, son of Alwyn Evans, crime reporter for BBC Cymru Wales for the past thirty years; David Morgan, son of Helen Morgan, a notorious brothel madam who made millions running a string of massage parlours in Cardiff and then famously went on the run after being accused of human trafficking; Dai James, whose father Gwyn runs James and James Solicitors with his brother Martyn, their criminal defence firm specialising in money laundering, drugs, and robbery cases. Further down the list are sons of crown court judges, a documentary film maker, a well-known criminal psychologist, an award-winning Welsh fashion designer who committed suicide in prison after being jailed for sexually assaulting young models ... Bryn nods slowly as he reads the rest.

All good suggestions, good possibilities, he thinks. *But only if this 'well-known parent, alive or dead, with a crime connection' theory is true ... and even if it is, how do we even begin to find them all, all of these Davids, in the next three weeks? And then somehow protect them all? It's madness ...*

'It's good, Hari,' he says. 'What about *us*, though? If the David in question is a police officer's son, we're stuffed. There'll be loads of us who've called our kids that name, but we'll need every last man and woman on duty that day; it's not like we can give them all the day off to protect their offspring, which is what they'll want to do if we tell them about this.'

'I know,' says Hari, and sighs. 'We did think of that too, obviously. But, if the theory is correct, it's well-known, *prominent* parents. We looked at all the highest-ranking officers in the force, from Chief Superintendent upwards, and there's only a handful who've actually got adult sons called David, as it happens. A few with younger kids with that name, but we're assuming this killer isn't targeting children, aren't we? The names of those officers are on a separate page. Here, look.'

'We're assuming a lot at the moment,' says Bryn gloomily, taking the second list. 'All we can do, I suppose.'

'It is,' says Hari. 'And it's how far you go, too. For example, what if one of our police officers is called David *himself*, and he had a parent who was also a police officer and well-known back in the day? It could be a serving police officer who's at risk from this killer, not just his offspring ... It makes my head hurt.'

'Christ. Mine too,' says Bryn, again feeling beaten by the futility of what they were trying to achieve. 'OK, well thanks for that anyway. Good work, Hari. In terms of the force, this threat is still being kept largely under wraps as you're aware; it's on a need-to-know basis right now. But I think we will have to warn those more high-profile officers with sons called David at least, to tell them to be on guard on the 1st of March ... Leave it with me. We need to work out how best to do that without causing undue alarm, and even more so when it comes to alerting those civilians you've identified. But your thoroughness is much appreciated.'

Hari grins, looking gratified.

'And who knows?' he says, as he stands up to leave. 'Thames Valley or West Midlands might even track him down before he gets here, eh? There's still three weeks, as you say. A lot can happen in three weeks.'

Bryn holds up his right hand, and firmly crosses his index finger over his middle finger.

'Fingers crossed,' he says. 'Fingers bloody crossed.'

* * *

Cheltenham Central Police Station

Family liaison officer Jess Gordon has just got up from her desk to make a cup of tea when her phone rings. She tuts and wonders whether she might ignore it – *after all*, she thinks, *they'll call back if it's important, won't they?* – then sighs and reaches for the handset without looking at the caller ID.

'Jess Gordon,' she says.

'Jess? Jess, I need help, I'm sorry ...'

The voice on the other end of the line is shaky and tearful, and for a moment Jess doesn't recognise it. Then it clicks.

'Mary? Is that you? What's happened?'

'Yes, it's me, sorry. It's Mary, Mary Ellis. I need to talk to you, urgently ...'

Mary gulps, as if trying to catch her breath, and Jess sinks slowly back down onto her chair.

'OK, Mary, don't panic. Are you safe? Do you need urgent assistance? What's going on?'

'No, it's OK,' says Mary, and Jess hears her gulp in more air. 'I'm safe. It's just ... something's happened. Somebody's sent me something else, this morning, in the post. And I'm frightened, Jess. I'm *really* frightened now.'

Chapter 18

Monday 8th February

Cheltenham Central Police Station

'Right, so who knew you were thinking of leaving the country around the 1st of April? Apart from us? Who did you tell? Here, have another sip of water. Are you feeling OK?'

DCI Steph Warden leans across the table and touches Mary Ellis briefly on the hand. Her skin feels cold and clammy, and Steph scrutinises her face for a few moments.

She doesn't look well, she thinks. Mary's hair is tucked behind her ears, the scarring on her left cheek more livid than usual against the paleness of her face. When she'd spoken to Jess earlier to tell her she'd received something unsettling in the morning post, Jess had asked if she could bring it straight into the station, and Mary had been in reception within twenty minutes, her hands shaking as she'd handed over the brown envelope containing the single piece of paper with its disturbing message. It's sitting on the table between them now, and Steph looks at it again as she waits for Mary to answer her question.

TWO DOWN, TWO TO GO.
DON'T TRY AND RUN, MARY ELLIS.
I'M WATCHING YOUR EVERY MOVE.
YOU CAN'T HIDE FROM ME, NO MATTER
WHERE YOU ARE.
TWO DOWN, TWO TO GO …

'Mary? Who else knows?' Jess, sitting next to Steph, says gently.

Mary picks up the glass of water in front of her, takes a sip, then another, then slowly puts the glass down again. She wipes her mouth with the back of her hand.

'Hardly anyone. I mean, apart from Pete, obviously. I've told him I might go away.'

'OK,' says Jess. 'Anyone else?'

'Well …' Mary hesitates, frowning. 'Look, I wasn't sure if I should mention this, because I wasn't sure there was anything in it, but now …'

She points at the note on the table, and Steph nods.

'Go on,' she says.

Mary looks at her for a second, then her eyes flit to Jess, then back to Steph.

'Right, well now I feel really stupid for not telling you about this before,' she says. 'I should have. I know you said if there was *anything* …'

She sighs.

'So, there's this guy at work, at The Hub. His name is Edward Cooper. He's single as far as I know, mid-forties; he's a freelance PR guy, for sports gear companies mainly. He started working with us a few months back, around October time. And he's ... well, maybe I'm being unfair, he's generally fine, and nobody else seems to have a problem with him. But I find him a little bit ... well, *creepy*. He's always appearing out of nowhere and sort of ... looming over me. Standing far too close, you know what I mean?'

'Sure,' says Steph. 'We've all met them.'

'Definitely,' says Jess. 'But what's worrying you about him specifically?'

Mary puts her elbows on the table and clasps her hands together, resting her chin on them for a moment, then says, 'Well, last week I was at work and I started looking up flights to Botswana. I think I told you, Jess, that one of my oldest friends, Lucinda, is living there at the moment, and it's one of the places I've thought about going if I do decide to get out of the country? Anyway, I had some time to spare in the office, and I know, I *know*, I probably shouldn't have done it there, I should have done it at home or somewhere private, but I just didn't think ...'

She sighs again, and rolls her eyes, as if in despair at her own foolishness.

'Anyway, suddenly there he was. Edward Cooper, creeping up behind me again, and he saw what I was doing, and he asked me about it. "*Oooh, off to Botswana, that's different,*" he said, or something like that.'

She imitates her co-worker in a whiny, nasal-sounding voice which sounds quite comical, and Steph suppresses a smile.

'OK. What happened next?'

'Nothing really, because he was distracted by some notes

on my desk. It was just before I went to Oxford, to chat to Lisa Turner's brother for my article. I had some notes on a pad, and Edward asked me about that too. But then – and this is the thing I really should have told you sooner – *then* he told me that he'd been in Oxford for New Year's Eve. He'd gone for the night with Satish Patel, another guy who works at The Hub. I mean, I know loads of people would have visited Oxford over the Christmas period, but ...'

She takes a deep breath.

'Edward even told me they went for a run along the canal on the morning of New Year's Day. He said they'd had to cut the run short because the towpath was closed because of Lisa's murder. I didn't even know they were into running. And he and Satish always seem to be having little quiet conversations these days, muttering away to each other. And now this ...'

She waves her hand at the note again.

'I'm so sorry, I know I should have mentioned it to you a few days ago. I just thought it was a coincidence, you know? And it may still be, but ...'

Her voice tails off, and she looks from Steph to Jess and back again, her eyes anguished.

'Well, yes, you should have mentioned it sooner really,' Steph says, trying not to sound too exasperated. 'But at least you've told us now, and we can make some enquiries. What else can you tell us about this second man – Satish, was it?'

Mary nods.

'Satish Patel, yes. He started at The Hub not long after Edward, November I think, I don't know exactly. He's a bit younger, mid-thirties. He does PR too. He seems nice enough, and he and

Edward seemed to hit it off pretty quickly, although I didn't realise they were friendly enough to spend New Year together. Not until Edward mentioned it last week. And this running thing ... you know, with the police in Birmingham asking about anyone who might have seen a late-night runner ...'

Her voice tails off again.

'Right, well, thanks for telling us now. Especially in the light of this letter,' Steph says briskly. 'Is there anyone else you mentioned going away to? Anyone at all?'

Mary shakes her head.

'Nobody. That's it. And ...' She hesitates. 'Well, I suppose this puts an end to any speculation now, doesn't it? That it might be another Mary in Cheltenham the killer's after. He's used my full name in that note and sent it to my house. It's definitely me. And that writing – the block capitals. It's exactly the same as the diary entries. This is definitely from the Diary Killer, isn't it?'

'Yes, so it seems. Look, try not to panic. I know that's almost impossible, but try, OK? We're going to do everything we can to protect you, and if he sticks to his timetable – and we have no reason to think he won't; he's been bang on so far – then we still have plenty of time to catch him. And Mary, please, in the coming weeks, if there's anything ... I mean *anything*, OK? No matter how small or insignificant it may seem, we need to know about it.'

'I'll tell you, I promise. I'm so sorry. Thank you. Do you think ... well, will you be speaking to Edward and Satish now?' Mary says. Her voice wobbles a little as she speaks.

'Yes,' replies Steph. 'But don't worry, we'll be discreet. We won't mention that it was you who told us they were in Oxford for New Year. We'll work around that somehow. And we'll get this note off to forensics and see if we can find out where it came from. And I think we should check your computer, your laptop, tablet, whatever you use, for spyware too. In case someone is monitoring your online activity remotely and that's how they figured out you were possibly making plans to go away. But for now, you go home and rest, OK?'

Mary takes a deep breath, sinks her face into her hands for a moment, then looks up again.

'Thank you so much. And yes, I think I will. I was going to go into work but I think I might just go home instead. Thank you, both of you.'

'Of course. Look after yourself and we'll be in touch. Jess, can you see Mary out?'

'Sure.' Jess pushes her chair back and stands up, and Mary follows her out of the room, her face a little less pale now. She waves a hand at Steph and is gone. Steph stares after her, thinking. A minute or so later, when Jess returns, she says:

'At least that note implies there are only two more murders to come after all, doesn't it? The Operation Shearwater team were getting worried there might be another diary on its way at some point, but maybe not.'

Jess shrugs.

'Maybe. Can't trust a serial killer though.'

'True. Right, I'll pay The Hub a little visit straight away then. Have a word with these two characters.'

She taps the pad on the table in front of her, where she scribbled down some notes while Mary was talking.

'She's very anxious, isn't she? Mary. What do you think? You probably know her better than any of us at this point.'

Jess nods. Her strawberry-blonde hair is in a high ponytail today, and it bobs as she moves her head.

'She is. That's the most anxious I've seen her,' she says.

'Yeah. I think she's pretty tough though. She'll be OK. Anyway, the pressure's more on Cardiff right now,' Steph says, as she stands up and picks up her notebook and pen and the mug that's also been sitting in front of her, half full of cold, greasy-looking coffee.

'They've only got three weeks left. Did you hear they're going ahead with warning selected individuals that there may be a threat against them and advising them to leave the city for twenty-four hours? Bryn sent an update through just before Mary arrived. Good luck with that one, that's all I can say.'

Jess nods.

'I saw that, yes. It's going to be interesting to see how it goes, isn't it? And, more importantly, if it actually makes any difference to the outcome. We'll see, I suppose.'

'We will,' says Steph. 'Anyway, I'm going to update Operation Shearwater on this latest interesting development, and then I'm off to The Hub. Let's see what this Cooper and Patel duo have to say for themselves, shall we?'

Chapter 19

Monday 15th February

Cheltenham Central Police Station

'Nothing. Absolutely sod all, in fact, yet again. Sorry, everyone. Other than a nice little newspaper report over the weekend, criticising the lack of any developments in the case.'

It's just after ten on Monday morning, and the police officers who've joined the virtual Operation Shearwater catch-up meeting are sharing their latest news.

And that's not going to take very long, at this rate, thinks Steph who's chairing the meeting, but she decides not to voice that observation. No point in making everyone feel even more despondent than they already are, so early into a new week. Instead she smiles sympathetically at DCI Priya Thomson, who's just told the group that, other than the damning newspaper headlines, she has nothing whatsoever to report from Birmingham.

'I know what that feels like,' says Linda Lake. 'We had

a few journalists on our case here for a while. They'll be onto the next big story soon, don't worry. Memories like goldfish.'

Steph smiles at that too, then looks at Jess, who's been sitting next to her, nibbling on a croissant. She frequently looks rather disinterested in the proceedings, Steph has noticed.

She's so quiet. Rarely voices an opinion or asks a question. Bit of a strange girl, really, she thinks.

'Well, we don't have anything new here either. Do we, Jess?' she says.

Jess, who's now sipping from a cardboard coffee cup, puts it down on the table in front of her and shakes her head.

'No,' she says. 'Nothing new. It's been a week since Mary Ellis received that note from, we assume, the Diary Killer. No further contact since then, and no further reports from her of anything out of the ordinary. I've been in contact with her almost daily. She's bearing up well, considering.'

'Good,' says Steph. The note in question had been rushed through forensics but, just like the diary before it, had yielded nothing of any use; no DNA or fingerprints, the pen and paper used of types found in pretty much every office, supermarket, and home in the country.

'It was a black Bic ballpoint, similar to the one the diary entries were made with – but that's not particularly helpful. It's reported to be the most widely sold pen in the world, if you're interested in trivia like that,' said the forensic scientist who, unusually, had popped in to deliver the results in person. He was a huge man, over six feet tall and weighing, at a guess, around twenty-five stone, Steph thought, and he lived, apparently, just around the corner from Cheltenham police station. He had introduced himself to her, but she'd been eager to hear his findings and hadn't paid much attention to his name; it still escapes her now.

'And the paper is just a page from a bog-standard A4 wire-bound notebook. Again, available everywhere. We think this is from a brand sold in Sainsbury's, so again, not very helpful.'

He had, however, shared one small piece of potentially useful information, which had been gleaned from the (again, widely available, nothing special), envelope the note had been in. The stamp had been postmarked:

Royal Mail
BA, BS, GL, TA
Mail Centre

'That means the stamp was cancelled – in other words the letter was processed – at the Royal Mail centre near Filton,' he said. 'It processes mail from the Bath, Bristol, Gloucestershire and Taunton areas – that's what those letters stand for. It doesn't indicate where the letter came from any more precisely than that I'm afraid. So, again ... not much help to you. Sorry.'

He had sighed lugubriously and lumbered off, but it was at least *something* to discuss at the next Operation Shearwater meeting.

'It's a huge area though,' DCI Bryn Lewis had said. 'I mean, as we've mentioned before, our killer may well be from some-where south of the Midlands, seeing as Birmingham is the furthest north he's ventured, or threatened to venture, so far. But knowing he posted the letter in one of those areas isn't a huge help. There are good motorway and A-road links right across this region, aren't there? Pretty easy to jump in a car and drive for an hour or two from where you live to post a letter and send us off on the wrong track.'

They had all nodded, agreeing. The region, and all the towns and cities on the killer's list, did indeed have good road links: the M4, the M5, the M40, and A40. The cities he'd already killed in, or was threatening to kill in, were all only a couple of hours apart, and the area the letter was posted in just a little further south. The postmark wasn't really of much help at all. Nothing was.

The chat Steph had had with Edward Cooper and Satish Patel from Mary's office had been a waste of time too, the team had concluded. She'd taken DI Mike Stanley with her, and once they'd got past the rather officious security guard at The Hub's reception desk, they had found the two men both at their desks in the spacious, open-plan office. Looking puzzled – and in Satish's case, a little scared, Steph noted – at suddenly being confronted with two police officers wanting to speak to them urgently, the men led them down a corridor and into a conference room, offering them two of the numerous comfortable black leather chairs which surrounded a long grey table. The room was bright and clean, with one glass wall, two painted white and the fourth emblazoned with what, Steph assumed, were supposed to be motivational words and phrases stencilled onto it in foot-high capital letters.

QUALITY WILL ALWAYS TRUMP QUANTITY
DETAILS MATTER
COLLABORATION REQUIRES COMMUNICATION

Steph and Mike had looked at the wall, looked at each other and simultaneously rolled their eyes. The two men sitting opposite them hadn't seemed to notice; they were both shifting uncomfortably in their seats, clearly waiting to find out what the police officers were so keen to discuss with them. Edward was wearing a tight blue jumper which looked too small for him, the sleeves finishing several inches above his bony wrists. Satish was in a jacket and tie, his face flushed.

'Right,' Steph said. 'I hope not to keep you from your desks for too long, but your names have come up in an investigation that's currently ongoing over in Oxford, and I've been asked to pop in and have a quick word. It's just routine, nothing to worry about, but I believe you were both in the city together for a night, on New Year's Eve?'

Satish's eyes widened, and Edward's narrowed. He glared at her, then turned his head to the right for a few seconds, peering out through the glass wall into the corridor beyond it as if searching for someone. Then he looked back at her and said, 'How do you know that?'

Steph cleared her throat and launched into the cover story she'd come up with. The team didn't want Mary Ellis to be publicly associated with the Oxford murder in any way, not just yet.

'The police there have been investigating a murder which took place in the early hours of New Year's Day, a young woman called Lisa Turner – I'm sure you've heard about it over the past six weeks?'

There were brief nods from both men, frowns furrowing both of their brows.

'Well, during the course of this investigation, which is proving to be a tricky one, they decided to look at hotel records to identify men who checked in for just one night on New Year's Eve. They're working on a theory that it was probably someone from outside Oxford who carried out this murder, and made his getaway the next morning.'

Out of the corner of her eye, she could see that Mike's gaze was fixed on the table, his face expressionless, but she could tell he was thinking the same as she was.

What an absolute load of nonsense.

It was, but it had been the best she'd been able to come up with at such short notice, and anyway, what did it matter?

These two wouldn't know police investigation procedure from a dental procedure, she thought, and ploughed on.

'Anyway, your names came up as a result of this trawl of the hotel records. Can you confirm which hotel you stayed at that night, please?'

Edward and Satish exchanged glances.

'I think it was called ... The Bellingham? Is that right, Ed?' said Satish. There was a little quiver in his voice; he was looking more terrified every second, Steph thought with interest.

'Yes, The Bellingham,' Edward said calmly.

Excellent. Thank you for that, Steph thought. The police had, of course, no idea where the two men had stayed that night, no such trawl of hotel records having taken place; with no evidence whatsoever that it was someone who had stayed in a hotel that night who had carried out the murder, it would have been a mammoth and probably entirely fruitless task. Still, it had been good of the two men sitting in front of her to give up the information so freely.

'Great, that tallies with the information we've received,' she lied blithely, and sensed rather than saw Mike stiffen next to her.

'And, bearing in mind that we'll be able to check this on CCTV, can you give me a brief account of your movements that night, and the following morning?'

Edward and Satish exchanged glances again.

'Well, we arrived about 3.30, and checked in. Then we went for a few beers at a couple of pubs near the town hall, The Bear Inn one of them was called – it's quite famous? And then we went for some food at, ermm …'

Satish pulled at his tie, loosening it, a bead of sweat running down his forehead.

'At Zizzi,' Edward said quickly. 'We just wanted something quick, and pizza seemed like a good idea. Lines the stomach, you know.'

He smiled, a genuine enough smile, Steph thought, although she'd already noted how accurate Mary's impression of his voice had been. He spoke in a peevish, nasal manner which she knew she would find most irritating if forced to listen to it for too long.

'And after dinner?' she asked.

'After dinner we went to an Irish bar, O'Neill's. They had a band on; we bought tickets a couple of weeks before. It was a good night. We saw in midnight there and then went back to the hotel. It wasn't a late one – we'd been out since four so we'd had enough by then. Neither of us are massive drinkers. We would have been back in our rooms around ... 12.45?'

Edward looked at Satish, who nodded.

'About that, yes,' he said quietly, and wiped the back of his hand across his forehead.

'The next morning we went for a run around nine, and ended up on the canal towpath. It was blocked off at one point and that was when we heard there'd been a murder. So we just went back to the hotel, showered, and had some breakfast and then came home. Not sure what else I can tell you,' Edward said, and smiled again.

'OK. And, why Oxford? Why did you decide to go there for New Year, in particular?' asked Steph.

Edward shrugged.

Satish glanced at him, then said, 'We just picked it at random, really. Neither of us had any real plans for New Year's Eve so we thought we might as well do something together, and we fancied going out somewhere different but didn't want to travel too far. We thought about Bristol, but we've both been there loads of times so we just plumped for Oxford instead. It's a beautiful city and, well ...'

He shrugged too, and Steph looked from one of them to the other and back a couple of times, then nodded.

'Right, well, thanks for your time, gentlemen. As I said, just routine, and I'm sure we won't need to bother you again.'

On the way back to the station, they'd discussed the two

men, agreeing that Satish Patel in particular had seemed extremely nervous and twitchy.

'Wouldn't surprise me at all if they had something to do with all this,' Mike muttered darkly as they pulled into the station car park.

But once all the checks had been done – The Bellingham Hotel contacted, the happy discovery that they kept their CCTV footage for up to two months meaning that the images from New Year's Eve and the following day could be studied – the story told by Mary's two work colleagues stood up. They were indeed seen checking in to the hotel just after 3.30pm and leaving again half an hour later, only to return shortly before 1am and not emerging again until nine o'clock the following morning, this time dressed in running gear. Their rooms had been on the fifth floor, and the hotel's security manager had been insistent that they could not have left and re-entered the building during the night without being seen.

'The only other way out is through alarmed fire doors, and there are cameras on those too,' he said. 'And unless they're Batman and Robin in disguise, there was no way they went out through their bedroom windows, is there?'

With the time of Lisa Turner's murder estimated to be between two and three in the morning, it seemed that Edward and Satish were in the clear, much to Mike's disappointment, a feeling shared by DCI Linda Lake, who had, for a few short days, hoped to finally have a decent lead in her case.

Following the arrival of the Diary Killer's latest communication, which implied that somebody knew that Mary had been looking into flights abroad, Steph had as promised also ordered checks on her laptop and tablet. The forensic computer analysts had, as feared, found spyware on both, which they believed had been installed remotely, probably via an email which Mary had innocently opened.

'It means that whoever sent it was able to track what you were doing online,' Steph explained to a horrified Mary. 'So he was able to work out that you're considering going away around the 1st of April. He's a clever one, that's for sure. But don't panic – it's all been removed now and a rock-solid fire-wall's been installed. Just don't open *anything* from anyone you don't know, OK? And the guys are going to contact you and give you some more advice about how to keep safe online going forward. You shouldn't have any more issues, I hope.'

What the analysts hadn't been able to do, though, was give the Operation Shearwater team any information what-soever about *who* installed the spyware, or from where, and so although some peace of mind had been restored for Mary, the investigation was still no further forward. There'd also been an extensive look at what was now known as 'the parent connection', but no evidence had been found that Gregor Ellis, Alice Turner, or John Holland had ever even spoken to one another, never mind met at any point. The theory had not been discarded – it was still the only half-decent one they had – but everyone had begun to lose faith, and in the past couple of days morale had reached rock bottom.

Now, on the monitor in front of Steph and Jess, the face of DCI Bryn Lewis bears a grimace.

'We have just two weeks now until he's threatening to strike here in Cardiff,' he says. 'As we've discussed previously, we're still intending to warn the list of possible victims we've compiled, probably about a week out, to give them time to make some plans. It's a massive gamble, we know that, but if we get it right, and can save a life ...'

His voice tails off, and he rubs his eyes and sighs. Jess turns to look at Steph, and for the first time today Steph sees a spark of energy in her eyes.

Maybe she needed the food and coffee to get her going, she thinks.

'Two weeks. It's not long, is it?' she says, and Jess shakes her head.

'It's not.'

Then she pulls at the collar of her shirt and adds, 'Is it me, or is it hot in here? Can we open a window?'

Steph nods.

'It is hot, actually. It's always too hot in in this bloody place. Drives me mad. Go for it. Open them all, if you like.'

Jess smiles and stands up.

'Anyway, two weeks until Cardiff,' she says over her shoulder as she heads over to the windows.

'Which means about six weeks to us in Cheltenham. God help us all, eh?'

Chapter 20

Monday 15th February

It's Monday morning and I'm at work, although I don't really want to be. Since the arrival of the letter my ability to sleep is worse than ever and I'm even struggling to eat, my stomach constantly churning, my mind racing. After originally telling Lucinda I might come and visit at the end of next month, I rang her again at the weekend to tell her that I probably won't make the trip until later in the year after all, for what's the point in trying to leave the country to escape him now? I was thinking of staying anyway, of course, but the idea of going away was always there as a back-up. Now that it's clear my every move is being watched, there seems no point in even thinking about it. The idea that there was spyware on my computer has really spooked me, and although the police have assured me that my laptop and tablet are now safe to use, the tech guy who contacted me did, in his words, 'urge caution'.

'We've put a really strong firewall on them for you,' he said. 'But a determined hacker can get through the most watertight security defence. It's almost impossible to make a system completely impenetrable, so I'd suggest spending minimal time online for the next few weeks until this threat is over, especially with regards to anything that might indicate any plans you might be making for the dates in question. Same on the phone. Just be mindful, OK? Change all your passwords too, on every site you use. None of your accounts appear to have been hacked or anything like that, which fits with the theory that none of this is to do with money or any sort of financial gain. Wish we knew what it was to do with, eh? But you're as safe online as we can make you right now. Try not to worry.'

Try not to worry.

It's what Jess, who's been checking on me almost every day, keeps saying too. But how on earth can I be expected not to worry, when I can see that, despite their outwardly calm exteriors and reassuring words, even the police are more on edge every day? As far as I can tell, there've been absolutely no new developments in the past week – the note, it appears, was no help at all forensically – and when Jess, in one of our conversations last week, murmured almost under her breath that this killer seems to be 'very focused' on me, my palms began to sweat.

'It all goes back to one of our biggest questions in all of this,' she continued. She was sitting opposite me in a little coffee shop just down the road from The Hub, where she'd asked to meet me for a quick catch up. Her hair was loose that day for a change, soft waves around her face, and she was wearing a pale-pink shirt with a slick of matching lipstick. She's become friendlier lately, more animated, more relaxed around me. I'm starting to really quite like her.

'And that question is, why the killer contacted you in the first place,' she said. She'd been stirring milk into her coffee, and she put the spoon down on her saucer and looked at me. She spoke in a hushed tone, scanning the room first to see if anyone might be listening, but the place was virtually empty, just a couple of elderly women sitting at a window table chatting earnestly, and two bored-looking waitresses behind the counter, engrossed in their mobile phones.

'Why did he warn *you*, and not any of the other victims? Why did he get in contact *again*, to let you know he's watching you? It's almost as if this is some sort of game, and you're the ultimate prize. You're special to him in some way. But *why*? Come on Mary, help me out here.'

She was looking at me intently, her eyes boring into mine, and I suddenly felt uncomfortable again.

'Jess, I have absolutely no idea. I'd have told you ages ago if I had any sort of theory, wouldn't I?'

I smiled at her, and picked up my own coffee mug, but my armpits were becoming damp as well as my palms, my mouth dry. The idea that had been forming in my head about the only way to deal with this was crystallising now, taking on a solid form, and it was beginning to terrify me. *Could I really do it? Could I really go through with what I was planning? And if I did, could it possibly work?* I needed to think some more, to make that final decision, but Jess was still talking, and I realised she was asking me another question.

'... so have you made a final decision about what you want to do yet, Mary? Because we want to keep you as safe as we can, but we are now quite concerned about the fact that he seems to have found ways of keeping close tabs on you, so we're going to have to be clever about it if we're going to take you into some sort of safe custody. If he's savvy enough to find out where you are, a police guard may not be enough. Who's to say he won't, I don't know, try to blow up the entire building to get to you? Oh gosh, sorry, I probably shouldn't have said that ...'

I was gaping at her, aghast.

'You really ... you really think he'd do that?' I stuttered. 'Bomb a building and kill everyone in it, just to kill *me*? Bloody hell, Jess.'

She sank her head into her hands for a moment, then looked back up at me, a contrite expression on her face, her cheeks as pink as her shirt.

'I'm so sorry,' she said again. 'It's just something that was raised as a possibility at yesterday's meeting, and I definitely shouldn't have repeated it to you. I do apologise. It's all speculation, but it's just something we need to think about. We can't risk any more lives. And anyway, we still have, what, six weeks? We might have caught him by then and all this will be behind us, eh?'

I've only told Pete about the new note from the killer. I had to tell somebody, and as he's still the only one other than the police who knows what's going on, I didn't think it would matter. And then I almost regretted telling him, because when I did, something a bit weird happened.

'*Shit*, Mary. Are you OK? This thing is getting out of hand now. Come here,' he'd said, and he held out his arms. I stepped towards him and leaned my head on his shoulder, and he hugged me tightly, his body lean and hard against mine, his hands stroking my back, and I felt myself relax for the first time in days, and then ... well, then, and this is the weird thing ... I felt something else too. I tried to ignore it, but I knew what it was, and it took me by surprise: a little fizz of excitement low in my belly, a sudden, unexpected yearning. I stepped back, smiling at him, telling him I was fine, and that I needed a pee and could he put the kettle on, but once in the bathroom I locked the door and leaned against it, breathing hard.

What on earth was that?

Pete and I have shared hundreds of hugs over the years, but that one felt different, suddenly, and I had no idea why. Why had I suddenly been so aware of the sensation of his body, so close to mine?

I do not fancy Pete, I told myself sternly. *That's the last thing I need. It's just everything that's going on at the moment, it's messing with my head ...*

I've resolved not to think about it. It's almost definitely stress-related, and when all this is over, I'll get myself out there, get on one of the dating apps, find someone to have some fun with. It's been ages since I went on a date, and it's about time I did something about that. And anyway, even if I *was* suppressing feelings for my housemate – which I'm *not* – he has a girlfriend, doesn't he? And it seems to be getting a bit more serious recently too, Megan making subtle noises about the two of them moving in together.

'I know we mostly stay at mine, Mary, so it's really kind of you to let me crash here for a couple of nights,' she said last week. She'd had a leak in her bathroom, the water coming through the ceiling into the kitchen below, and she'd come to stay at ours while the damage was repaired.

'That's OK,' I said. 'Any time.'

We were sitting at the kitchen breakfast bar after dinner, me with a glass of white wine, her with a peppermint tea, naturally. She was wearing a taupe cashmere sweatshirt and matching leggings, so tight that I could see the outline of the muscles in her calves. She'd been for a run with Pete before dinner, and her hair was still damp from the shower, tied loosely in a topknot, little tendrils escaping. Her make-up free skin was creamy and flawless and yet again I felt self-conscious next to her, my fingers straying to the scar on my cheek, feeling its familiar coarseness.

'Well, it's good of you,' she said. 'Although I suppose you do have plenty of room in this lovely big house, don't you? I could be here all the time and you'd probably barely even notice, would she Pete?'

She laughed lightly, and Pete, who was stacking the dishwasher, turned and smiled at her, but he looked a little uncertain.

'Well, your repairs will be done in a couple of days, won't they?' he said. 'Don't worry, Mary, we won't inflict our annoying lovey-dovey couple thing on you for too long.'

'It's fine, honestly, I don't—' I began, but Megan interrupted me.

'Well, as Mary said, she doesn't mind at all,' she said. 'Life's short, my darling. If two people are meant to be together, why waste time being apart? Come here, you gorgeous creature!'

She leapt from her stool and skipped over to him, flinging her arms around his neck and kissing him, her body pressed against his. He kissed her back, but I still thought he looked a little uncomfortable. We haven't discussed it, but I'm pretty sure he's not quite at the stage where he wants to make Megan a permanent fixture in his home, and that makes me happy. I *need* Pete, need him to have a little bit more time for me, just while this is all going on anyway. Afterwards ... well, who knows?

Now, on this Monday morning, I'm browsing the news websites, looking for updates on some of the cases I've been half-heartedly following for potential future articles, and trying to avoid catching Edward's eye. Although Jess, to my immense relief, told me that the police are certain that he and Satish had no connection to the Oxford murder, that the two of them and their movements that night have been thoroughly checked out with no resultant cause for concern, I still feel uncomfortable around them, as well as a little guilty for putting them through what now feels like totally unnecessary police questioning.

Edward confronted me about it, of course. I knew he would, despite DCI Warden's assertion that she would come up with some cover story that wouldn't implicate me. The very next time we were in the office together he was there, hovering over me at my desk, a suspicious look on his bony face.

'Did you tell the police that Satish and I spent New Year's Eve in Oxford?' he said.

No preamble, just come straight out with it, why don't you? I thought.

I looked up at him wide-eyed, feigning surprise.

'What? Of course I didn't!' I said. 'Why on earth would I do that? Why are you asking?'

He stared at me for a few moments, and I thought he looked a little upset suddenly, a sad expression in his dark eyes.

'Well, you've been looking into the case of that lawyer's murder, haven't you? I've seen you. And I told you we'd been there for New Year, and the next thing the police are here in reception. Seems a bit of a coincidence.'

I sighed theatrically.

'Well, that was absolutely nothing to do with me, I can assure you. It's a major murder investigation, Edward. They're probably questioning hundreds of men who were in the city that night. They have loads of ways of tracking people down. Sorry, was there anything else? Because I'm a bit busy ...'

I turned away, tapping on my computer keyboard, and he stood there for another few seconds, then grunted and walked away. When I turned around a minute later I saw, as I knew I would, him and Satish conversing in low voices, eyes flitting in my direction. But since then, neither of them has mentioned it, and Satish even brought me a chocolate éclair back from the bakery when he did a cake run on Friday afternoon, depositing it on my desk with a friendly smile, so I'm trying hard to forget my suspicions, unfounded as they clearly are.

I'm planning to drive to Birmingham tomorrow; I need to get another interview in the bag for the Diary Killer piece and I've managed to fix a chat with a woman called Stella Clayforth, who's one of Jane Holland's cousins. We're meeting at Topaz Casino at midday, and although I've pretty much given up on finding any new connection between me and the other victims at this point, I need to carry on with this anyway. Time is ticking; the promised murder in Cardiff just – I look at the calendar sitting on my desk – two weeks away now. I swallow hard.

And then a month after that …

'Mary! Fancy a drink after work? I'm celebrating. Bloody Valentine's Day behind us at last! I know it's only Monday, but to hell with it. I need to get drunk. Are you up for it?'

Eleanor has suddenly appeared next to my desk, smiling broadly. She's wearing a cobalt-blue roll-neck jumper, which makes a wonderful contrast to the rich red of her hair, piled on top of her head today. I smile back at her, trying to quell my rising anxiety.

'Do you know what? That sounds like a plan, Ellie,' I say. 'I mean, maybe not the getting drunk bit. I have a job in Birmingham tomorrow and I need to be in decent shape for it. But I'm definitely up for a couple of drinks later. Shall we bunk off early and go out around four?'

She grins.

'Perfect. I'll see you then. Laters!'

She winks, and races off, and I take a deep breath.

I need a little bit of normality. A few drinks with Ellie will be lovely, I think. *A couple of hours to forget about all this and have a bit of fun. I don't have to make any decisions yet, after all, do I? About anything. I still have time.*

And yet even as I tell myself that, the little voice in my head, the voice that's becoming louder and more insistent with each passing day, is repeating itself, over and over.

But you already know what you have to do, don't you. it's saying.

You know something he doesn't know. You know something nobody knows. And there's only one way you just might get yourself out of this. Might save yourself from this killer. You're going to have to tell him, aren't you?

Chapter 21

Tuesday 16th February

It did me good to have a few drinks and a catch-up with Ellie after work yesterday; as I drive northbound on the M5 towards Birmingham at a steady seventy miles an hour, I'm feeling a little more like myself than I did this time yesterday morning. I'm still anxious, still permanently exhausted. But I've decided to just take it all a day at a time for now, for what else can I do? So much could change in the next six weeks or so. David in Cardiff might not die; the police may unearth something that leads them to whoever is behind all this at any moment. *I* may not need to do anything at all. So, I've vowed to stay calm and carry on, to use a cliché.

I arrive at Topaz Casino just before midday, pulling into a parking space right opposite the front entrance. Unsurprisingly, the large car park is three-quarters empty at this hour, and after locking my car I stand there for a moment, shivering as a bitter wind tears at my coat and whips my hair across my face while I take in the impressive frontage of the building. It's huge, ten floors tall, all reflective grey glass and concrete, its name emblazoned across the front in blue neon. There's an external lift, also walled in glass, moving slowly upwards, and at the grand pillared entrance I can see two doormen, slick in matching sharp black suits. I've read up on the casino; it's the bigger of the two owned by Jane Holland, and this one is, in fact, reported to be one of the largest in the UK outside London. Open twenty-four hours a day, it has more than two hundred slot machines, a hundred gaming tables and a poker room that can accommodate a hundred and fifty players, with a monthly tournament that attracts gamblers from miles around. It employs more than two hundred people and is almost as famous for its food as it is for its gaming, with whisky, gin and cocktail bars and several restaurants serving an eclectic mix of Indian and western cuisines.

When I give my name at the door I'm ushered past with a polite nod and pointed in the direction of a long reception desk, topped with what looks like glittery silver-grey marble. There are a man and a woman, both also dressed in black – he in a suit similar to those of the doormen, her in a simple shift dress – tapping on keyboards behind it. The woman looks up and smiles as I approach.

'Mary Ellis? Stella is expecting you. She's waiting in the office. Let me take you up.'

She leads me, disappointingly, to an internal lift – *maybe the fancy external one is for high-rolling gamblers only*, I think – and presses the button for the seventh floor. We emerge into a wide, carpeted corridor, its walls adorned with several large pieces of colourful abstract modern art, and I follow her as she walks swiftly to a door at the far end and taps smartly on it.

'Come in!' calls a voice, and my escort opens the door, smiles briefly at me again and then turns and walks away, as a tall blonde woman standing by the floor-to-ceiling windows opposite strides towards me, hand outstretched.

'Mary, nice to meet you. Stella Clayforth,' she says. Her accent is broad Brummie, and although I've never thought of myself as particularly short at five foot nine, she towers above me. Six foot, maybe? She's broad-shouldered and heavy-busted, wearing low-heeled, snake-print court shoes with slim-leg black jeans and a blue silk shirt, sparkling gold hoops in her earlobes. Her eyes are dark grey, and her hair is pulled back into a neat chignon.

She looks very different from her cousin, I think, remembering the photographs of the murdered Jane Holland, who was a petite, slender brunette.

'Lovely to meet you too,' I say. 'And thank you so much for agreeing to talk to me. I'm so sorry for your loss.'

'Thank you. It's been a pretty dreadful time,' she says, and a stricken expression flashes across her face. She leads me to a burgundy-coloured leather sofa, next to which is a low table bearing white coffee cups, a tall cafetière and a plate of delicious-looking miniature pastries. She asks me how I like my coffee and pours it as I take in the room, which is a spacious, bright office, the desk glass-topped with steel legs, a row of sleek metal storage cabinets lined up behind it. There's modern art in here too, splashes of colour against white walls, and the sofa and two matching leather chairs make a comfortable and perfectly positioned seating area in front of the huge windows with their far-reaching views across the city.

Stella sits down on one of the chairs, and when we've both taken a few sips of coffee and exchanged some pleasantries about the weather and how changeable it's been recently, I pull my notebook, pen, and voice recorder out of my bag, check that she's happy for me to record our chat, and repeat the story I told her on the phone, and the same one I told Alastair Turner: that I'm writing a piece on various recent murders which seem to have stumped police.

'Well, Jane's certainly fits the bill,' she says. 'I literally have no clue why anyone would want to kill her. She was just the nicest, kindest—'

Her voice breaks suddenly, and she clears her throat.

'Sorry. I just don't understand it, you know? Especially as no money was taken or anything. She must have been targeted for some other reason – I mean, it wasn't exactly random, was it? Whoever did it came to her house, knocked on her door, and she let them in, for God's sake. The police say that doesn't necessarily mean she knew whoever it was; they say he could easily have been a stranger, someone who just managed to give her some really good reason to let him through the door. Jane was a sweetie, big on charity work, you know? If someone gave her a sob story ...'

She shakes her head, her eyes sad.

'Sorry, listen to me prattling on. What do you need to know for your story, Mary?'

I smile at her.

'No, don't worry, this is all good background. Do you think that's what happened then? Somebody gave her a sob story at the door and persuaded them to let them in?'

She shrugs, her sparkling earrings bobbing.

'Maybe. I mean, she was a very savvy businesswoman – she didn't suffer fools or anything like that. Don't get me wrong – she wasn't a soft touch, but she had such a kind heart. And if we're ruling out someone she knew killing her – because I really, really can't imagine that – then maybe that's what happened. Somebody came to her door saying they needed help or something, and she let them in. But I don't know, Mary. Nobody knows; that's the problem.'

She sighs.

'It's certainly a mystery,' I say. 'So, what do you do, Stella? Do you actually work here? Is this your office?'

Another shake of the head.

'No, this was actually Jane's room. I thought it might be nice for you to see where she worked, get a feel for her maybe? I do work here at the casino though, yes. I've run bars in Birmingham for the past ten years or so, and Jane asked me to join her here a while back, to join the board of directors and head up that side of things. We have three bars, all very different, so it's good fun. Well, *was* good fun. I don't know if we'll ever be able to have fun here again now that Jane's gone.'

She sighs again and picks up her cup. I nod, remembering the few details Jess was able to give me when I asked her about the Jane Holland investigation. She'd mentioned that the casinos were to be kept going after Jane's death, run by a board of directors, but that it wasn't currently believed that financial gain was a motive for the murder. She'd also mentioned that Jane had three cousins whom she was close to, but I hadn't realised that one of them also worked with her.

'Are any of Jane's other relatives employed here too?' I ask.

'Not as such,' Stella replies. 'I mean, not full-time. I have two teenagers – actually, Amy is nineteen and Andrew has just turned twenty now, so not really teenagers anymore. They do a bit of bar work here, and our cousin Gerry's son – he's older – does a bit of security now and then. So yes, she was good about sharing out work when people needed it. But I'm the only one who's ever worked here full-time. We were close, you see, Jane and I. More like … more like sisters, really.'

Her eyes fill with tears, and she stands up abruptly and walks to the window, wiping at her cheeks with the backs of her hands.

'God, sorry,' she says. 'It's still a bit raw, you know?'

'Oh, please don't apologise. I'm the one who should be saying sorry, raking it all up,' I say quickly. 'Are you OK to carry on?'

'Yes, yes of course. Sorry. Right, let's do this. I have a meeting at 1.30 but we still have plenty of time.'

She sits down again, and for the next hour we chat about Jane. About her childhood, described by Stella as a happy, comfortable one, and about her father, the man known as Big Johnny. I already know a little about him of course, from what Jess told me when the police started looking into the parent-connection thing, and from my own subsequent research online. But it's fascinating to hear about him from someone who knew him, and to hear about his relationship with his daughter.

'Yes, there were always rumours about Uncle John when we were growing up,' Stella says. 'But we were always told to ignore them, that it was just jealousy, from people who didn't like how well he was doing. And he was never arrested for anything, you know? And as I said, Jane and I were close. I was round at theirs all the time when we were kids. He was great, good fun, always had time to chat and ask how I was doing at school and all that stuff. And Jane and he were *super* close. She was an only child, and back then it wasn't really expected that a mere *girl*'—she rolls her eyes—'would take over the family firm, especially one like this, but she was set on it from a very young age, and he absolutely encouraged her all the way. He knew she could do it, and he was right. Her mum passing away was part of it, I think; Auntie Lil died of a stroke at fifty and I think that spurred Jane on. I think she was scared the same might happen to her. And look at what she achieved: two of the biggest casinos in the country, a multi-million-pound business. He would have been so proud. He *was* so proud of her, always. She'd already done great things before he passed away, and I know it made her so happy that he was still around to see her success. I hope they're together up there now, raising a glass of bubbly.'

She glances towards the ceiling, and smiles.

We carry on chatting, but after a while I realise it's just like it was in Oxford. Jane Holland was, it seems, a thoroughly nice, caring, successful, hard-working woman. But I can see nothing whatsoever that might connect me and her; nothing at all similar in our backgrounds, our interests, where we've lived, who we knew. Nothing significant anyway, although there is one small, throwaway remark from Stella that makes me wonder, just a little. It comes when I ask about Jane's love life. She was, as far as I know, single when she died, but when I ask Stella if she'd been seeing anyone in the recent past she rolls her eyes.

'Who knows?' she says, with a little laugh. 'Jane was always very secretive about things like that. I don't think so, though.'

I laugh too, and we move on, and for a while, I forget about it. Stella herself escorts me back down to reception, shaking my hand warmly as we say goodbye, and as I leave, I pause for a few seconds in the opulent entrance lobby, studying a vast floor plan of the building that's painted on the wall. The locations of the three bars are all marked, and I wonder which of them Pete and his friends drank in the night they came here back in January.

Was Stella working that night? I wonder. *Was Jane? Did Pete meet her, speak to her?*

I suddenly wonder if I should go back and ask Stella, show her a photo of Pete maybe. But I'm not sure how I could do it without making her suspicious, and anyway, she said she had a meeting now, didn't she? I tell myself to forget it, to stop worrying about things which clearly have no relevance, and head back outside to my car, nodding my thanks to the two men in black suits as I pass. But as I navigate the traffic on the way to the motorway, Stella's comment about Jane drifts back into my mind.

Jane was always very secretive about things like that.

Now, I start to consider the remark properly, and wonder. If Jane had secrets, could that mean something? Could *that* be a connection?

What if this isn't about our parents after all? What if the connection is that we all have a secret? A secret that the killer somehow knows about? A secret he thinks we need punishing for?

I think about that for a while, driving on autopilot, the sun finally breaking through the clouds and warming my face through the windscreen. And then, abruptly, I dismiss the idea again. Because nobody could know my secret. *Nobody*. It's not possible. And killing random people because they all have some sort of secret doesn't make any sense, does it? Not if the secrets are all different, all totally unrelated. Because there's no doubt that our secrets would be different, no doubt at all.

Nobody else could possibly have a secret like mine.

But my secret could save my life. And I'm very nearly there now. I know what I have to do, and how to do it. I also know that this is going to be one of the biggest gambles of my life. It could save me, but it could destroy me too.

I just have to decide if that's a risk worth taking.

Chapter 22

Saturday 20th February

Megan has gone away for the weekend, on some sort of advanced yoga teacher training course down in Devon, something which, if I'm honest, is a bit of a relief. I've felt a bit awkward around her since the conversation about her potentially moving in, and the prospect of spending Saturday evening here at home with just Pete is infinitely more appealing than playing gooseberry again.

We both have a busy day, Pete heading into the office to finish off some urgent work for a client, and me trying to catch up on my washing and ironing and other chores I've been badly neglecting recently. But at seven o'clock, we finally crash in the upstairs lounge.

'Can you be bothered to cook dinner?' I ask Pete, poking his thigh with a bare toe. He's sprawled at one end of the sofa, me at the other.

He turns and squints at me.

'Definitely not. Curry?' he says.

'Sounds like a plan,' I say, and grin at him.

We order an Indian and Pete goes down to the kitchen to get us a drink while we wait for the food, spending several minutes clanking bottles in and out of the wine cupboard before choosing a nice bottle of Rioja. The restaurant is busy and running behind on deliveries, and the curry is late in arriving; it's nearly nine by the time we're spooning it onto our plates, and by then we've finished the first bottle of wine and we're halfway down a second. I'm feeling decidedly tipsy, and even though we're having a lovely, chilled-out evening, my thoughts keep floating off in other directions: Topaz Casino, Stella Clayforth, and poor dead Jane Holland are still uppermost in my mind. Suddenly, I can't help myself. I *have* to ask Pete again about his visit to the Topaz back in January. As we finally put our empty plates aside – the chicken madras with Bombay aloo and tarka dhal was *delicious* – and settle back on opposite ends of the sofa, my left foot resting against his knee, I say it.

'It's such a weird coincidence, isn't it? That you were at the Topaz Casino so recently. Stella told me that Jane was really hands-on, never out of the place really. You could easily have seen her that night, you know. Maybe you *did* speak to her ...'

'And maybe I didn't. Maybe she wasn't there. Maybe she was at the Coventry casino that night, or maybe she just took a night off,' he says, and although his voice is steady, I know him well enough to detect the hint of impatience in his tone. 'And even if I did speak to her, so what? What difference does it make, Mary? Bloody hell. Can we change the subject now?'

'Er, sure. Sorry,' I say, and he looks at me for a few seconds, a curious expression on his face, then swings his legs off the sofa and stands up.

'You need to think about something else for a few hours,' he says. 'Stop dwelling on it all. I'm going to top us up. Here, hand over your glass.'

'OK. Thanks,' I say, and hold out my empty wine glass, and he takes it and leaves the room, leaving me feeling strangely uneasy.

Was that a weird reaction to an innocent observation? I think. *Or am I just thinking that because I'm ever so slightly pissed?*

When he comes back a minute later, he's his usual cheery self, and I try to dispel my sense of disquiet. Pete's right. His visit to the casino has no relevance at all, and I *do* need to stop thinking about it.

And so we drink more wine and talk about other things. Neither of us mentions Megan; instead, we chat about music, and about silly things that happened at work this past week, and about whether we should buy a new barbecue for the back garden ahead of the summer. That, of course, makes me start to wonder yet again if I'll actually even be *here* by the time summer comes around, if I might in fact (despite the continued plotting I've been doing about my possible way out of this), be dead by then. I've told myself repeatedly, *daily*, that of *course* I'm not really going to die on the 1st of April, that it's all going to be fine, but every now and again it still hits me like a punch to the stomach. And now, embarrassingly – and I'm sure mainly thanks to the frankly excessive quantity of wine I've glugged – the prospect of having only weeks to live suddenly seems utterly overwhelming.

'Oh shit. *Shit*, Pete. What's the point in buying a new barbecue? What's the point in buying a new *anything*?' I slur, and I burst into tears. And once I start, I seem to find it impossible to stop. 'This poor guy called David, whoever he is, only has *one* week to live now, and he doesn't even know,' I sob. 'I mean, I'm sure the police in Cardiff are trying their best – all the police forces are. But it's impossible, isn't it? And then ... then it's my turn. And I don't want to die, Pete. I really don't. I'm scared, and I don't know what to do ...'

I bury my face in my hands and bawl. I'm standing up now, and I start pacing up and down the lounge, crying loudly and feeling a growing sense of panic. As I reach the far wall for the second time and stop, tears beginning to seep through my fingers and drip down my arms, I hear Pete say, 'Oh, for goodness' sake. Come here.'

Moments later I feel his hands gently peeling mine away from my face and placing them firmly on his waist. He wraps his arms around me and pulls me close and, eyes closed, I rest my head on his shoulder, my rapid breathing gradually slowing, my heart rate settling, as he strokes my back and whispers in my ear, his lips brushing my skin.

'It's going to be OK. You know that, don't you? It's all going to be OK. Nothing bad's going to happen to you, Mary Ellis. I'm not going to let it, all right? Everything's going to be fine.'

I gulp, and lift my head so our cheeks are touching, and we stand there in silence for another few seconds, his hands still gently running up and down my back. He smells so good, I suddenly realise, a seductive scent of musk mixed with something else – *bergamot, maybe? A hint of vanilla?* I can't help it – I nuzzle my nose into the soft skin of his collarbone, and hear him take a short, surprised breath.

'You smell delicious,' I murmur. 'Sorry. I just needed to sniff it properly. What aftershave is this?'

'I ... I can't remember,' he says softly, and then we both move our heads at the same time, and bump noses, and for one, two, three electrifying seconds our mouths are just centimetres apart, and I can feel his warm breath on my lips. And then, simultaneously, we both release our grip on each other and step backwards, moving apart again, and we both laugh a little awkwardly and agree it's time to go to bed, and we head off to our respective rooms and, well, that's that.

I pull my clothes off and pass out almost immediately, but wake in the early hours, my mouth feeling like someone's poured sand into it and my head pounding. I drag myself out of bed to get water and paracetemol, then crawl back under the duvet and lie awake for a long time, thinking about those few moments with Pete which, despite knowing I have the mother of all hangovers brewing, are crystal clear in my memory.

I don't fancy Pete, I don't, I tell myself repeatedly. *I never have. Why would I start now?*

And yet, for just a few heady, heart-stopping moments, did we almost kiss? I think about that, about our lips meeting, about his tongue slipping into my mouth, for the very first time, and what that might feel like. And, even though I give myself a stern talking to, telling myself that Pete's my best friend, that it was just the booze and the fact that I was so upset that led to us standing in our living room wrapped around each other, I'm not sure I'm even convincing myself. If he had kissed me, would I have responded? Would I have kissed him back? Or would I have laughed, and pushed him away? It's a question I can't answer. Don't *want* to answer.

I have enough problems right now, and getting involved in a messy love triangle with my best mate and his girlfriend is not on the cards, I decide, and I roll over and fall back into a dreamless sleep.

Chapter 23

Monday 22nd February

Cardiff Central Police Station

'A week to go. *One week.*'

DCI Bryn Lewis shakes his head and groans, and Sergeant Hari Hughes, who's sitting opposite him, sighs.

'I know. Not long. It doesn't look like anyone's going to track him down before then either, does it, at this stage? Everything seems to have stalled. So ...'

He raises an eyebrow, and gestures at the piece of paper on the desk in front of him, and Bryn looks at it and nods slowly. It's the David List, as they've been calling it. There are now close to forty names on it; in the past couple of weeks they've added sons of senior police officers, judges, prison and probation officers, and even Davids who are the offspring of some of the city's most well-known debt collectors and money lenders.

There've been extensive discussions and debates about this list, and about the wisdom of potentially panicking so many people, but after numerous Operation Shearwater meetings, a final plan has been decided upon, and Bryn thinks it's as good as it can be, in the circumstances.

Contact with the Davids will begin today. They're to be told that police have become aware of a threat to the life of someone with a similar name to theirs, a threat which has pinpointed Monday the 1st of March as the day when something is likely to happen. They're to be advised to leave Cardiff for twenty-four hours if at all possible; if not, it will be suggested that they take every possible precaution: stay inside, keep all doors and windows locked, and keep the police on speed dial, on a special number set up just for them.

'I'm hoping the suggestion that someone may be after them will persuade at least some of them to leave the city,' Bryn told the team. 'But I'm expecting many to be unhappy about it, and probably quite a few refusing to cooperate. And to be fair, it's quite possibly a pointless exercise. I mean, none of this will stop him if he's really determined, will it? He may well be watching his next victim already, like he seems to be doing with Mary Ellis. He could already be following them. He probably knows exactly where they live, and he doesn't even need to get close to them to kill them, does he? He can set their bloody house on fire with them locked inside it. But we can't take every bloke in Cardiff called David into safe custody, so if we're on the right track, and if we've done our job here in identifying at least some of the most likely victims, well at least these guys will have been warned, and hopefully will be looking out for potential trouble. It's a lot more than poor Lisa and Jane had going for them.'

Each David is, of course, not being given any indication that he is just one of many potential victims, or that the threat to his life is part of a much bigger multi-police-force investigation; neither is anyone being told of any possible links to the recent murders of two women in other parts of the country. Each one is also to be asked, in the strongest of terms, not to speak about this threat to anyone, and it's this aspect that's concerning the team the most.

'I hope to God none of them goes to the press,' Bryn says now, rubbing a hand across his eyes. 'There've already been some critical newspaper reports about the lack of progress in both the Oxford and Birmingham cases, but thankfully nobody's made any connection between them yet, and we want it to stay like that. If we *do* a have a murder in Cardiff – and I'm keeping everything crossed it doesn't happen, but let's see, eh – but if we *do*, and it's a similar thing, a head injury, an early-hours-of-the-morning attack, well, who knows? Some quick-witted journalist might start noticing the similarities with those other two killings and start asking questions. But right now, we're able to carry on doing our jobs and trying to protect these final two victims without a nation in mass panic about a serial killer. The press getting wise to it at this stage could be a bloody disaster.'

There's silence for a few moments. Then Hari says quietly, 'Fingers crossed the Davids keep their mouths shut then.'

'Fingers, arms, legs, the lot,' says Bryn.

He sighs and picks up the list.

'Better hit the phones then, eh?'

Chapter 24

Monday 22nd February

I'm sitting at my desk at The Hub, trying to do some research into a romance scammer case that's caught my eye, but finding it hard to concentrate. The case is an interesting one; the scammer is a fifty-five-year-old Edinburgh man called Tommy MacKenzie, who created dozens of fake profiles on dating apps and struck up relationships with eleven different women, then managed to persuade them to part with a total of more than a hundred thousand pounds by pretending to need urgent medical treatment abroad. I've managed to make contact with three of the women MacKenzie scammed, the others having asked to remain anonymous when he was finally tracked down and taken to court, and one of them has agreed to an in-depth, sit-down interview with me. But it's him I'm really interested in. He's currently serving three years in prison, and no journalist has so far got anywhere near him. I'm hoping to be the first, but my heart isn't in it today, my eyes constantly flitting around the office. A couple of times I notice Edward looking my way and quickly avert my gaze;

once, I meet Satish's eye, and he looks uncomfortable for a moment then smiles. I give him a brief smile back, but I still feel a bit tense around both of them. This jittery feeling was compounded earlier this morning when, desperately needing caffeine, I walked down to the staff kitchen to make a coffee and found Satish there, fishing a teabag out of a mug.

'Oh, Mary,' he said. He glanced at me, a little nervously I thought, and then turned his attention back to his drink, balancing the teabag on a spoon and tipping it into the food caddy by the sink.

'Hi,' I said, inwardly cursing my timing. I walked to the coffee machine and picked up a mug, aware that he was still hovering behind me and hoping he'd just leave.

But instead he cleared his throat and said, 'Sorry ... I was just ... erm ... I was just wondering if you're going to be around on the evening of the 31st of March? It's a Wednesday? It's just that, well, Edward said you might be going away and I was wondering ...'

I whirled around, feeling a little surge of panic.

'Edward said what?'

His eyes widened.

'He said, well, erm, he said he'd seen you looking into flights abroad and that you might be going on holiday? Are you?'

I stared at him, my heart thumping.

Why is he asking me about the night of the 31st of March? That date ... it's the day before the 1st of April, which is the day ...

'I don't know yet,' I said quickly, my mouth suddenly dry, my throat tight. 'It's just something I'm thinking about. I haven't decided when I'm going away yet. And sorry, I need to get back to my desk, I'm expecting a call.'

I picked up my coffee and scuttled past him on wobbly legs, and as soon as I reached my desk I called Jess, telling her about the encounter in an urgent whisper.

'I think you're being paranoid, Mary,' she said. 'And I totally understand why, and I'm glad you're keeping us informed, but honestly, try not to read too much into it. As I've told you, we have absolutely no evidence to suggest either of your colleagues were involved in what happened in Oxford, or in the threat against you. Mr Cooper did see you googling flights, didn't he? Maybe Mr Patel was just asking for some sort of social reason – maybe he's organising an office night out or something? Try not to worry, OK?'

It's becoming annoying, the numbers of times people have said 'try not to worry' to me in the past few weeks, but I knew Jess meant well so I thanked her and tried to get on with my day. But now as I sit here reading about Tommy MacKenzie, I'm struggling to focus, the kitchen incident with Satish still niggling me.

Saturday night and what happened – or didn't happen – with Pete, is still niggling me too, although in a much more pleasant, if rather confusing, way. Yesterday morning, when hunger finally forced me out of bed and downstairs, I found him acting perfectly normally and offering to make me scrambled eggs. The night before wasn't even mentioned, and yet it's still preying on my mind now as I sit at my desk trying to work.

Stop it, just stop it, I think. *You have far, far more important things to worry about than a strange new desire to climb into bed with Pete bloody Chong. And he's dating Megan, remember? Girl code, and all that …*

I vow to forget about it. It's only a week until the Cardiff murder now, if it's actually going to happen. And then the countdown begins. After my meeting with Stella Clayforth in Birmingham, which simply proved yet again that there's no obvious link between me and the other victims other than the parent thing, I've suddenly decided that I need to stop obsessing about it. I'm on my own here, aren't I? I have to forget about *them*, and about the killer's reasons for targeting them, and concentrate on *me*. On getting *myself* out of this, somehow. I can't even rely on the police to do that, not entirely. What if I *do* let them secrete me away somewhere, and the fears Jess let slip actually come to fruition, and he blows up a building or something just to get to me? What if other people die too? I can't let that happen, I *won't*.

There's been enough killing. It's time to stop it.

Chapter 25

Sunday 28th February

Cheltenham Central Police Station

'So, dare I ask, how are you feeling, Bryn? Only a few hours until D-Day now.'

It's Sunday afternoon, and the Operation Shearwater team is trying, although not succeeding very well, to put on a brave face. The mission to get as many potential David victims as possible out of the city for the coming twenty-hour hours turned out to be as tricky as anticipated. Some of the men point-blank refused to go, accusing the police of over-reacting and saying that the threat to an unspecified man with the same extremely common name couldn't possibly be aimed at them. Others were, according to Bryn, 'absolutely bloody terrified' and fled immediately, three demanding police escorts to take them to rural hidey-holes and one booking himself and his entire family straight onto a plane to Los Angeles. But it's done, as far as it can be, and now it's just a waiting game. Looking at the grim expressions on the faces on her screen, DCI Steph Warden can see that everyone is feeling horribly anxious, and totally powerless. There's nothing any of them can do now except wait and see what the coming hours will bring, and the nervous tension emanating from the team is palpable.

'Eight hours and two minutes until midnight, to be precise,' Bryn says. 'And as we know, he could kick this off any minute from then onwards. In fact, I'm expecting a call in the early hours, as that seems to be his preferred time. Maybe, just maybe, we've warned the right bloke. Miracles do happen, now and again. But we have no idea if this theory about how the killer's selecting his victims is correct, do we? So, to answer your question, Steph, I feel sick to my stomach, to be honest. I haven't eaten a thing all day, and that's not like me at all.'

He rubs a hand across his paunch, and sighs heavily. Steph touches her own flat belly and wishes she hadn't eaten the cheese toastie she had for lunch. Her stomach is churning, and the room, as it often does, feels too hot, too stuffy, as if the walls are slowly closing in.

I need some fresh air, she thinks, but Bryn is still talking, his tone melancholy.

'We're screwed, aren't we? We've done what we can, which isn't much, and now we're out of time And my gut tells me we're going to be dealing with victim number three by this time tomorrow, and there's not a damn thing we can do about it.'

There's a long silence. Then DCI Priya Thomson clears her throat. She's wearing a blue and while floral blouse today, her long, dark hair loose around her face.

She looks more like a pleasant primary school teacher

than a detective, Steph thinks. *And I bet she wishes she was, sometimes.*

Priya leans forwards a little towards the camera, her brow crinkling with worry.

'You are going to do what we did in Birmingham though, tonight?' she says. 'Extra patrols, officers keeping an eye out for men walking home alone, all that?'

Bryn is nodding.

'Yes, yes. And keeping their eyes peeled for late-night runners too. But he's good at picking the quiet spots, isn't he? That canal towpath in Oxford, out of sight of any cameras. And if he goes for somebody's home again, well ...'

He shrugs helplessly.

They exchange a few more words, but nobody has anything else constructive to add.

'Right. Well, let's end it there,' says Steph quietly. 'No doubt we'll talk again in a few hours.'

'Good luck, Bryn,' says DCI Linda Lake. 'We'll be thinking of you tonight.'

'We will,' says Priya. 'Keep us posted.'

'I will. Anyone going to bed tonight?' asks Bryn and gets shakes of heads and murmurs of 'not me' and 'not a chance' in reply.

'Speak to you at some point after midnight, then,' he says. 'And if you're a believer, start praying, eh?'

Chapter 26

Monday 1st March

Cardiff

It's just over fourteen hours later when the call comes in. Two police officers, Sergeant Sean Fay and Constable Danny Roberts, are coming to the end of a night shift on patrol in the Llanishen area of Cardiff when a security guard at a local business park makes a panicked 999 call. Immediately deployed, minutes later Sean and Danny arrive to find him, white-faced and sweating, standing over the body of another man in a dimly lit car parking area to the rear of a unit called The Fit Joint.

They can see, even in this pre-dawn darkness, that the man on the ground is quite obviously dead: slumped on the tarmac in an unnatural position next to the open door of a shiny, new-looking black Range Rover, his eyes are wide open, there's a large dent in the centre of his forehead, and his face and clothes are covered in blood. As Sean asks the security guard to step back from the victim, Danny, who's more than a little squeamish, bends to take a quick, closer look then straightens up and backs away hurriedly.

'Christ. I think I can see his brains. Or bone, or something. No coming back from that, poor bugger,' he hisses. 'What the hell's gone on here? I think I'm going to be sick, sarge.'

Sean rolls his eyes.

'Well, if you are, go over there,' he says. 'We don't need you throwing up on the crime scene.'

Danny nods and, hand clutching his mouth now, jogs across to the far side of the small car park, where he leans over a litter bin, retching. Sean, pulling on a pair of latex gloves, crouches down for a few moments to double-check that the motionless victim has no pulse – *no, absolutely, definitely dead,* he thinks – then turns to the guard, who's now leaning against the wall of the building, wiping his forehead with a large, grubby-looking grey handkerchief he's pulled from somewhere about his person.

'Do you know who he is?' Sean asks, gesturing at the crumpled figure on the ground.

The security man nods and swallows.

'It's David Howells,' he says. 'He runs this place. He usually gets in super early, around five. I saw him drive in around ten past this morning, so same as usual. But when I did my usual 6am patrol, I found him like that. Poor bastard didn't even get inside, did he? Nobody else has driven in this morning yet though, so I can't work it out. Must have been somebody on foot who attacked him, maybe, I don't know. Oh God, I think I'm going to faint. I'm so sorry ...'

He starts to slide slowly down the wall and Sean, wondering

what he's done to deserve a vomiting constable *and* a fainting witness, sighs and helps the man lower himself to the ground, instructs him to put his head between his knees and breathe deeply, then pulls out his radio.

David Howells, he thinks. *David. The tip-off wasn't wrong, then. Although it's an extremely common name, obviously. Could just be a coincidence. But still …*

The pre-shift briefing last night had informed them that there'd been an unspecified threat made against a male called David, at an unspecified location somewhere in the Cardiff area, at an unspecified time on the 1st of March – today – which had made them all raise their eyebrows and mutter under their breaths. Now that it has actually happened, and a dead man called David is lying just feet away from him, Sean's wondering what on earth this is all about, and who this man is. For now though, he just needs to get on with his job, so once he's sure that an ambulance and back-up are on their way, he takes a small but powerful flashlight from his pocket and takes a cautious walk around the car park, ignoring Danny who, remarkably, is *still* heaving over the bin.

Sean's been here before; he attended a break-in at a tyre repair shop in one of the other units a few months back, and he knows that the business park is a small one, fewer than thirty companies on site with the security guard stationed in a little prefabricated building just inside the main entrance. It's not gated, no barrier either, so it's very possible that if the guard is correct about seeing no other vehicles entering the park this morning, it could easily have been someone who slipped past on foot who carried out this attack. If that's the case, the CCTV cameras he knows are positioned at the entrance and at regular intervals along the lampposts that line the criss-crossed streets of the small estate may, if they're lucky, have captured footage of the assailant. But ...

He frowns, running the torchlight along the fence at the back of the car park.

That could be another way in, couldn't it? he thinks. This particular unit is at the far end of a cul-de-sac, the building and a fifteen-foot-high brick wall making up two sides of the square plot, and a low wall on the third side dividing it from that of the business next door, with a path running alongside it to give access to the main entrance at the front. But to the rear, there's a fence, about five foot high, and on the other side of it there's a field, or some sort of waste ground; he's not entirely sure what it is, in the dark, but definitely some sort of green space anyway.

It wouldn't be hard for someone to come in that way, he thinks. *Someone with an average level of fitness could easily scale that fence.*

He stands there for a few moments, scanning the ground, looking for anything that seems out of place, but nothing leaps out at him. It's been raining on and off all night, and there are puddles on the uneven surface of the small car park, which probably has enough space for about six cars. It's just started raining again now, and that won't help preserve the crime scene, Sean thinks, knowing that evidence can be destroyed by such inclement weather and wondering if he should quickly find something to prop over the body to protect it. But even as he's considering this, he hears the sirens, and seconds later sees the blue lights swirling in the sky over the building. Barking at Danny to get a grip and come and join him, and telling the security man, who's now sucking frantically on a cigarette, to stay exactly where he is, he heads round the front to greet his colleagues.

Chapter 27

Monday 1st March

I've been awake since 5am, sitting in bed trawling social media and the news websites, a sick feeling in my stomach, a tight knot of anxiety in my chest. It's almost a relief when I see it, a few minutes after seven: just two lines on the South Wales Police Twitter feed, but I know straight away that this is it. This is David.

> @SWPCardiff Officers are currently at the scene of a major incident at Parc Llawndy business park in Llanishen. New Road has been closed and is likely to remain closed for some hours – motorists are asked to avoid the area this morning.

I read it, read it again, then scroll frantically, looking for more information, but there's nothing, so I phone Jess. Over the weekend she gave me brief details of the plans being put into place in Cardiff – about how some cautious warnings had been issued to men identified as potential victims – but

I could tell from her demeanour that she wasn't convinced it would work, and I couldn't help feeling the same. I'm desperate to speak to her now, but she doesn't pick up immediately, so I leave a message, begging her to call me back as soon as she can. It's nearly 8.30 when she does, and by then I'm dressed and pacing up and down the kitchen, aching for Pete. I'm a little upset that he's not here, given the date; given the fact too that he knows how horribly agitated I've been, even more so in the past few days than I was last weekend, on the night when I somewhat lost the plot.

When we almost kissed, I think, then push the thought from my mind.

He *was* here yesterday, and we even went out for lunch, a big Sunday roast at the pub up the road. It's just reopened under new management after a massive refurbishment, and now has plush booth seating and a fancy revamped menu with dishes like truffle mash and mushroom risotto. It used to be a rickety wooden tables, eggs and chips, and sticky laminated menus type of place; I think I miss that, just a little.

But then, not long after we got home and were collapsed on the sofa, bellies full and the first episode of the new David Attenborough nature series playing on the TV, Megan arrived, all glowy and fresh-faced after teaching her Sunday afternoon yoga class in town. I'd known she was coming, of course – Pete had asked me if it was OK earlier in the day, and of course I couldn't say I'd rather it was just us, given the date and how I was feeling – and I made an effort to be nice, and it was fine, I suppose. The original plan, as Pete had to be in work extra-early this morning for a 6am online meeting with some client abroad, was that she'd spend the afternoon here and then go back to hers last night. What *actually* happened though was that the two of them disappeared to Pete's room around six in the evening, whereupon I hastily left the lounge and went downstairs to watch TV in the kitchen instead. Pete's bedroom is next door to the upstairs lounge, and the walls in these modern houses are not terribly thick and, well, you get the picture ...

But when they emerged forty-five minutes later, Pete told me, a little sheepishly I felt, that he was going to spend the night at Megan's instead.

'But ... really?' I said.

I was sitting at the kitchen island, a glass of red wine in my hand, and I put it slowly down on the counter, feeling a surge of disappointment.

'I thought ... well, I mean, it's fine, obviously. But I just hoped you'd be here, you know. As it's the 1st of the month tomorrow and everything ...'

I kept my voice low, aware that Megan was just outside the kitchen door in the hall, putting her coat and shoes on. Pete glanced at the door and then looked back at me, grimacing.

'I know, I'm sorry. But she sort of begged and, well, you know. Things have been a bit tricky recently with all that talk about wanting to move in and everything, so I'm just trying to ... Look, you'll be fine. I'll call you last thing tonight and first thing tomorrow. And you never know, the Cardiff thing might not even happen, eh?'

Except now it has of course. I knew it as soon as I read that tweet, and it's confirmed now by Jess.

'Sorry for the delay in getting back to you,' she says. She sounds flustered.

'I actually slept through my alarm. I never do that. And I've been trying since I got in to get a bit more detail from South Wales, but it's literally just happened about three hours ago, so everything's a bit crazy over there, as you can imagine. But I've spoken to DCI Lewis and yes, it does seem that this is a murder, and yes, the victim's name does appear to be David. And that's all I can tell you right now, Mary, and it goes without saying that this is for your ears only, OK? We'll get more information later and I'll keep you posted as far as I can. And now Steph's just arrived and there's a briefing so ... speak later, right? And Mary, I know I keep saying this, but try not to worry. It's going to be all right, I promise you.'

She says goodbye and hangs up, and I slump onto one of the kitchen island barstools, my legs suddenly a little shaky.

And so much for Pete promising to call me first thing, I think, and for some reason I feel like bursting into tears. I *did* cry last night, in the early hours when I woke, panting, my body bathed in sweat again, my heart beating so fast I could hear the *swush, swush, swush* of it in my ears. I'd been having yet another nightmare, I knew that, but the detail had already gone, leaching out of my panicked brain, leaving just a sense of a dark figure, a roar of anger, a scream of terror. I don't often feel lonely – I like to think I'm quite self-sufficient, most of the time. But last night, it suddenly all became just a little bit too much and I cried, alone in my bedroom, yearning for someone to wrap their arms around me, to kiss away my tears, to tell me that everything, *everything*, is going to be all right.

I probably wouldn't have believed them, of course, because I don't believe it when Jess says it, and how *can* everything be OK after all, especially now, when poor David, whoever he is, has joined the ranks of the dead, just as the diary promised. But it would be nice, would have been nice last night in particular, to have someone to hold me, to whisper reassuring words in my ear.

And now Pete, who's supposed to be my best friend, the only person outside the police who actually knows what's going on, hasn't even bloody bothered to call me …

I'm just starting to feel incensed instead of upset when my mobile rings.

'Mary! I'm so sorry I didn't ring earlier. Are you OK? Any news?'

It's Pete, driving by the sound of it, and I look at the clock on the kitchen wall and wonder why he's not at work. It's nearly nine and he was supposed to be in before six today, wasn't he?

'Where are you? And yes, there's news. It's happened. David, in Cardiff. A few hours ago, at some business park. I don't know anything else yet. Are you driving?'

'Christ. Yes, yes, I'm just on my way into the office now,' he says. There's an edge to his voice, and I know him well enough to know that he's unhappy about something.

'Change of plan this morning. My early meeting was cancelled, which was nice, except now I wish it hadn't been because I ended up having breakfast with Megan instead and we somehow managed to have the mother of all rows. She's still on about us moving in together and … oh shit, it doesn't matter. Will you be OK today? I'm so sorry about the Cardiff thing. And I'm going to have to go now. I'm just pulling into the car park, but we can talk about it properly later, all right? Keep smiling, Ellis.'

'Sure. Smiling all over my face here,' I say, but the line's gone dead. I stare at the phone for a moment then toss it onto the counter.

OK, so a massive row with his girlfriend is an excuse of sorts, I think. But he still could have called earlier ...

I sigh. I might as well head into work myself, because I really need to be around people today. I need to be somewhere busy and buzzy. I need to find out more about David, whoever is he is. Whoever he *was*. And I need to get my head together and stop procrastinating.

I have a month now, just one month, four short weeks. The police only have four weeks too, to try and stop this. To track down whoever's behind it. But if they don't, well, at least we know *who* the next victim is. It's me, isn't it?

The countdown has well and truly begun.

Chapter 28

Tuesday 2nd March

Cheltenham Central Police Station

'David Howells. Forty-six years of age. Single. Owner of The Fit Joint, a company that supplies fitness equipment – treadmills, weights, exercise bikes, that kind of thing – mainly for domestic use. The company's based at Parc Llawndy business park in Llanishen, which is in north Cardiff.'

DCI Bryn Lewis sighs heavily and rubs a meaty hand across his forehead. He looks, Steph thinks, as if he hasn't slept in two days, which is probably quite likely. It's just after eleven o'clock on Tuesday morning, nearly thirty hours since the body of David Howells was found sprawled on the wet ground in the car park to the rear of his business, and the Operation Shearwater team has convened for a briefing. All the faces are sombre, but Bryn looks distraught, his eyes blood-shot, his shirt crumpled.

'The victim is single, so in that way he fits the profile of the two previous victims,' he says. 'But, well, that's it. We got it wrong, guys. We bloody got it wrong. David Howells is the son of Paul, a Tesco check-out assistant, and Angela, an office cleaner. He was an only child, and they're devastated. But no high-profile parent. No crime connection whatsoever, either by profession or when it comes to a criminal record. Not so much as a parking ticket amongst them. So all those people we warned, all the bloody Davids we told to get out of town ...'

He shakes his head.

'But you weren't to know that,' says DCI Priya Thomson gently. 'It was worth a try, wasn't it? We knew the crime connection link was only a hunch, but it *could* have been right, and we *might* have saved the next victim. It was better than doing nothing, surely?'

Bryn shrugs his broad shoulders.

'I suppose so,' he says. 'It's still gutting though.'

He sighs again, then picks up a piece of paper and waves it at the group.

'There is one thing though. Although as I said there's no *crime* link we can find here, Paul Howells did hit the news-papers a couple of years back. He had a lottery win – not millions but a decent whack, around three hundred thousand. He's in his late sixties so he could have retired and had a nice time of it with the money, but he loves his supermarket job so much he decided to carry on with it and the Tesco bosses made a thing of it, and got the local paper in. Not sure if that qualifies him as a well-known or *prominent* parent, but he's certainly well-known in his local community. Well-loved too. And he told us he used some of the cash to help set up his son's business. David had been a personal trainer at a small gym before, not earning much money; his dad invested a chunk of his lottery money to get The Fit Joint up and running.'

There's silence as the assembled officers digest this piece of news. Then DCI Linda Lake says, 'OK, interesting. And you know what, I *still* think the killer's motive could be related to the victim's parents for some reason, even if we got the crime element wrong. I mean, look at what we've got: a judge, a wealthy and of dubious character business owner, a lottery winner ... and next up, a famous author. It still *fits*, doesn't it? None of these are what you'd call ordinary people. They all stand out in some way. Except, well, we still have no idea about *why*. What on earth is this killer gaining from targeting them? It's absolutely not financial, is it? I mean, I'm assuming that no money was stolen from David Howells?'

Bryn shakes his head.

'No. It's just like the others. Just a fast, clean, efficient murder. Nothing whatsoever stolen. It looks like he'd just got out of his car when he was attacked – and the car was a very classy, almost new black Range Rover Evoque, by the way. Still sitting there, keys in the ignition. Cause of death just like the others, a vicious blow to the head, from the front this time. No weapon at the scene. The car park is poorly lit so if our killer was dressed all in black again he was probably lurking there nicely concealed in the shadows waiting for David to arrive. He wouldn't have stood a chance really, poor bugger, fit as he was. He was likely jumped on as soon as he opened his car door.'

'Can we assume still little in the way of forensics, yet again?' asks Steph. Jess, who's sitting next to her as usual, has just opened a packet of chocolate finger biscuits, and she pushes the packet along the table.

'Thanks,' Steph mouths, and takes one. She was too busy yesterday to eat much, and she's suddenly feeling ravenous.

'You assume correctly,' says Bryn. 'Absolutely diddly squat. And nothing on CCTV either. The access roads to the business park and the buildings are all well covered by cameras, but there's no sign of anyone suspicious entering either in a vehicle or on foot in the hours before David arrived for work. Everyone who does appear in the security footage has been identified and has a valid reason for being there, and there's no sign of anyone who was there in the early hours of the morning leaving their own buildings and making their way over to The Fit Joint, nothing like that. David arrived at around the same time every day, according to security. Creature of habit. So if someone was planning this in advance and watching him, it wouldn't be hard to decide on the best time to grab him. Early morning, quiet spot, still dark. Boom.'

'So how did he get into the car park, then?' asks Jess. There's a biscuit crumb on her bottom lip, and she wipes it off, frowning at Bryn's image on the screen.

'Well, our victim's building doesn't have a camera to the rear, just the front,' says Bryn. 'And the car park backs onto an area of wasteland. There was an old chemicals factory there for years, but it was demolished a while back and there are rumours of the land being bought by a developer, possibly for some new fancy apartments, but nothing definite yet. Anyway, our best guess is that the killer came in from there. There's a five-foot fence, very climbable, especially if he's pretty fit, as he seems to be. There's not much in the way of security on that old factory site – there are cameras on the main road at the front, but plenty of access points out of sight of them around the boundary. While it's lying empty all sorts of people have been getting in there: fly-tippers, druggies, you name it. He could have slipped in and out that way in the dark easily as anything. We're checking all the nearby roads for any sightings of an early morning runner in dark clothing but nothing of any use so far. And as we've long known, this killer is smart. Good at evading the cameras. I'm not holding my breath.'

There's silence again, broken only by a sigh from Priya and a muttered 'buggering *hell*' from Linda.

Then Jess says, 'So nothing was stolen – but this guy sounds pretty well off. A nice little business, courtesy of his lottery-winning parents. Who inherits that, now he's dead? Any motive there?'

Bryn shakes his head.

'Don't think so. David Howells was single as I said, no kids. He was a gay man and had had a few long-term relationships but the last one ended a year ago and he'd only had the odd casual date since then, according to his parents, who say they were close and that they knew pretty much everything that was going on in his life. He'd been concentrating on building up the business recently and didn't have much time for romance. We're speaking to his most recent long-term partner, a guy called Darren Edge, to see if there's anything there that might help, but by all accounts the relationship ended amicably and they were still good friends. And sorry, you asked who inherits the business? It'll just go back to his parents, as his closest relatives. At the moment we can find no reason whatsoever why anyone might want him dead.'

'Just like Lisa Turner. And Jane Holland,' says Linda morosely.

'And Mary Ellis,' says Jess quietly. 'She's next now, isn't she?'

'How is she?' asks Priya.

Jess picks up her mug, takes a sip of coffee, and puts the mug down again.

'She's OK,' she says. 'I spoke to her a couple of times yesterday. We're going to get together later this week to make some concrete plans for the 1st of April and the run-up to it. But she's bearing up.'

'It's such a weird one,' says Priya, rubbing her nose. 'This killer must know that by pre-warning Mary that he's coming for her, he's scuppering his own chances of killing her. He's not going to be able to get to her, is he? Unless, as we've discussed before, he does something really drastic. So what was the point? Is it all a double bluff? Is someone else the real victim on the 1st of April, and Mary's being used as a distraction, maybe?'

'Maybe,' says Linda. 'Maybe this thing is nowhere near over yet. Maybe the "two down, two to go" letter was a double bluff too, and we *are* going to receive another diary with more names and more dates. We literally have no idea, do we? And that's what makes all this so frustrating, and so bloody terrifying. I've never felt so helpless in my life.'

As she's speaking, Bryn is leaning to his left, conversing with someone out of sight of his camera. Moments later he's back in vision, leaning forwards with an anguished look on his face.

'Shit. SHIT,' he says. Then, immediately, 'Sorry. Bad news though. One of the Davids we advised to get out of the city has heard about David Howell's murder and put two and two together. It's David Evans, son of Alwyn Evans. Alwyn's been the main crime reporter for BBC Cymru Wales for donkey's years. We asked all of them, *begged* them, to keep this quiet; we even implied that if they didn't they could jeopardise a major police investigation. But David Evans has told his father, apparently, and now Alwyn's making noise with the press office. This could be all over the six o'clock news tonight, guys.'

'*Christ*,' says Linda Lake. 'This is literally the last thing we need. What do we do now?'

There's silence for a few seconds.

Then Steph clears her throat, her expression sombre.

'I think we need to brace ourselves, guys. This could get ugly,' she says.

Chapter 29

Wednesday 3rd March

The last couple of days have been a bit of a blur. I've carried on as normal, on the face of it; I've sat at my desk at The Hub, researching stories, making phone calls, chatting to Ellie and Guy and Stu, and trying, without making it too obvious, to stay away from Edward and Satish. I've eaten dinner with Pete and chatted to him like I always do, even though I'm still a little upset by the fact that he left me alone in the house on Sunday night and went off to Megan's. Then I get cross with myself for feeling like that, because she *is* his girlfriend, and he has every right to go and spend the night with her. It's not as if *my* life was in any danger on Sunday night, after all. It wasn't my turn. But he knew how apprehensive I was, how worried I've been feeling, and a tiny part of me is devastated that he went away for the night anyway, while at the same time the rational part of my brain is telling me not to be so needy, so demanding.

He'll be there for me when it really matters, I tell myself. *In a few weeks' time, when it really is my turn. He'll be there then. Give him a break, for God's sake.*

It's Wednesday, two days since David Howells was murdered. And even though as always I've been scouring the news sites for information, Jess as usual just giving me the bare bones of the case without the detail I crave, after the initial reports on Monday there's been very little in terms of updates. I've stared at his photographs online until I know his face by heart: a good-looking man of forty-six with prematurely grey hair and a matching neatly trimmed beard, a long, straight nose and even, white teeth. The main point of interest in his story is his father's lottery win, which funded the start-up of David's business, but otherwise his life seems unremarkable, and the press, it seems, have been treating this as just another murder, a businessman attacked outside his premises for no apparent reason, another senseless attack in violent Britain. And then, last night, something happened. I'd gone to bed early, exhausted by it all, by the stress and sense of foreboding I know is only going to worsen over the next few weeks. Snuggled under the duvet, with just my bedside lamp casting a warm glow across the room, I'd opened the BBC News website on my tablet for a final scroll through the latest stories, and then I'd frozen.

POLICE 'PRE-WARNED' ABOUT THREAT TO MURDERED CARDIFF BUSINESSMAN

I read the headline again, my heart beginning to thud, and then frantically scanned the article below it. It had been written by crime correspondent Alwyn Evans, a veteran reporter whose work I was familiar with.

South Wales Police were warned in advance about a possible threat to life in the Cardiff area on Sunday night, the BBC has learned. Llanishen business owner David Howells, 46, was found dead in the car park outside his offices in Parc Llawndy in the early hours of Monday morning. It's believed he sustained fatal head injuries in an attack by an as yet unknown assailant.

But it's now emerged that the police were warned of a possible attack well in advance, although it's thought they weren't given precise details about the identity of the intended victim.

A source told the BBC that they believe a number of men with the first name David were contacted by police and advised to 'lie low or, ideally, leave the city' for the twenty-four hours of the 1st of March.

'They didn't say why, specifically, just that they'd received intelligence that an attack may take place and that a number of likely victims were being warned,' the source said.

When contacted, South Wales Police said only that they could not comment, stressing that to do so might compromise an on-going investigation. The search for David Howell's killer continues.

I read the article twice, then slowly put my tablet down. *Shit,* I thought. *So somebody did talk, then.*

When Jess told me that a list of potential victims called David were being warned ahead of Monday, she'd said that the men had all been told in no uncertain terms that the police did not want them to speak to anyone about what was going on, and especially not to the press, officers emphasising that to do so could seriously hamper a major police enquiry. Clearly, someone had blabbed, although whether this would have any impact on the case I wasn't sure. An impact on the perceived ability of South Wales Police to keep its citizens safe, maybe.

But could this make any difference to the case as a whole? Maybe not, I thought.

It was clear that Alwyn Evans still had no idea that the Cardiff murder was actually the third in a serial killer spree. I read the article a third time, still a little unnerved despite my attempts to reassure myself, before switching off the light and falling into a restless sleep.

This morning, the first thing I do after Pete leaves for work is call Jess.

'Yes, DCI Lewis and his team are pretty livid about it. We know which of the Davids talked – sorry, I can't divulge that, Mary. But he's been warned again, as have all the others and the reporter who wrote the story. South Wales have also messaged all the major news outlets requesting that they don't follow up on the BBC piece. They've told the editors that a major investigation is at a critical stage and that further speculation could be extremely damaging. So far, it looks like everyone's playing ball, so fingers crossed it stays that way. We potentially only have one more chance to catch this guy, Mary. We can't have the country in uproar about an on-the-loose serial killer. He could go to ground – we might *never* find him. It sounds scary, I know, but we *need* him to come after you. And on that, can we meet, this week? We need to make plans. Proper plans, as soon as possible.'

I swallow hard, and reach for the mug of coffee in front of me, then realise that my hand is shaking slightly and decide to leave it.

We potentially only have one more chance to catch this killer, Mary. We need him to come after you …

Her words reverberate in my head.

Can I do this? Really?

'Sure,' I say. 'I'm pretty free, Jess. You have a look at your diary and find a time that works for you and let me know, OK?'

'Thanks, Mary. I'll get back to you as soon as possible.'

We end the call, and I sit motionless for a long time. My thoughts are elsewhere at first, racing around my conscious-ness, tumbling over each other as they've had a habit of doing recently, but then, to my surprise, they gradually begin to assemble themselves, lining up neatly in my brain. I've made and unmade this decision a hundred times in the past few days, but now, quite suddenly, I just … *know*. I pick up my mug again, my hand surprisingly steady now, and take a slow sip of tepid coffee, then take a deep breath.

I'm going to do it.

The words are still inside my head, but they're as loud and clear as if I've shouted them at the top of my voice, echoing around the room.

I'm going to do it.

I'm not going to run away. I'm not going to hide in a police safehouse. On the 1st of April, when this killer, whoever he is, finally comes for me, I'm going to be right here waiting. And I think he *will* come. I just have a *feeling*. So I'll be here, ready to confront him. Because it's time he knew the truth, the truth he couldn't possibly know when he added me, Mary Ellis, to his list of victims.

You see, when I tell the story of what happened in my past, the story of the fire, and the people who died in it, and everything that happened after that, I don't actually tell the *full* story. Not to anyone, ever. I never, ever have. Not even to Pete. The story I tell is … well, it's almost the truth. *Almost.* The truth, but just … *twisted* a little.

This killer is after Mary Ellis. Mary Ellis, daughter of the famous Gregor Ellis. He's been very specific about that.

But he can't kill Mary Ellis. It's not possible.

Because Mary Ellis is already dead.

Chapter 30

Wednesday 3rd March

Let me introduce myself. My name is Amanda Archer. It feels strange to say that now, because I've been Mary Ellis for so long that sometimes I forget who I really am. Who I really *was*. I was born in Bristol, only child of a violent heroin-addict mother and a father I never met. One of the other druggies my mum hung around with, I always assume, although she never told me which one, and with a choice like that, I didn't really want to know anyway. My childhood years are ones I've tried, mostly successfully, to forget: a blur of coldness and bruises, of being left alone for hours in a filthy bedsit, of being ostracised at school because of my tatty clothes and greasy hair, of sitting alone in the playground at break times despite the teachers' best efforts to get the other kids to include me in their games. Maybe it was because, back then, schools weren't as hot on child safeguarding as they are nowadays, or maybe it was just because I was so good at pretending that everything was OK, just like I am now; but whatever the reason, my plight wasn't really recognised until

I was nine, when Mrs Lottes, my new form teacher, crouched down beside me one September afternoon when I was, yet again, the last child to be collected after class had finished.

'Are you OK, Amanda? Is everything all right at home?' she asked.

Until then, I'd held the horrors of my home life so tightly inside me that some days it physically hurt, an ache deep in the pit of my stomach that wasn't just down to the gnawing hunger I'd learned to live with thanks to my mother's preference for visiting her dealer rather than the supermarket. But that day, something happened. Quite suddenly and unexpectedly, the dam finally broke, and as Mrs Lottes wrapped her arms around me and tried to calm my hysterical sobs, she told me that from then on, everything was going to change.

'I'm going to make sure of that,' she whispered fiercely in my ear.

I can still remember how soft her jumper was against my wet cheek, the mingled sweet, floral scents of fabric conditioner and perfume, the gentleness of her hands as they stroked my back. And she was right. Everything *did* change. I never went home – if you could call it a home – again. First, emergency foster care: two weeks with a middle-aged couple called Josie and Eric, in whose cosy Redland home I had my own bedroom for the first time in my life and snuggled under a pink Barbie duvet with a white cat called Snowy to keep me company. If I could have stayed with Josie and Eric I might have been all right; I might *even* still be Amanda Archer. But unfortunately, I had to move on to a more permanent placement and, well, let's just say that I didn't find it easy – any of it.

It was quickly realised that rules and routines were alien to me; sharing a home with other children was too, and I was soon labelled as 'difficult', and the so-called 'permanent' placements never actually were. When my mother finally overdosed and died when I was twelve, I retreated further into myself, and my behaviour became even more challenging for those charged with looking after me. And so I bounced along in the care system, from home to home, family to family, and even from school to school – five, in total – never really bonding with anyone, trying to play a game I didn't understand. Remarkably though, academically I slowly began to flourish. Maybe it was my massively improved diet, or the fact that I could actually sleep properly instead of being woken in the early hours on an almost nightly basis by a drugged-up mother and her cronies partying at the end of my bed. Maybe it was that, with my mother's death, I finally felt free of the fear that one day she'd come for me, and take me back to the nightmare that had been my life before. Or maybe it was just that books became a refuge, an alternative world I could lose myself in. Whatever the reason, flourish I did. I loved history and English the most, and by fourteen I was top of the class in both; still an object of curiosity to most of my fellow pupils, still largely friendless, but at least by then with, finally, some self-esteem, and the grudging respect of some of my classmates for my academic achievements.

It was after I enrolled at St George's College in the city centre to do my A Levels that I met Mary Ellis. She'd arrived for the final year as a boarder; the college offered both day and boarding options, and Mary had recently arrived in the

UK with, to the great excitement of many of the students and teachers, her father, a famous author. They were renting a big house in the Cotswolds, and Gregor had, according to Mary, wanted her out of the way during the week so he could concentrate on writing his next novel, although he insisted that she came home every single weekend.

When she first sat down beside me in English class, heads turned and grins spread over faces; we stared at each other for a few moments and then simultaneously grinned too. I was wearing a red polo-neck jumper that day, my long, dark hair falling loose over my shoulders; she was wearing an almost identical red jumper, and her hair, almost exactly the same shade and length as mine, fell in soft waves around her face. She was prettier than me, there was no doubt about that, but otherwise we looked ... well, not like *twins* exactly, but we could definitely have passed for sisters. The hair, the build, the dark-brown eyes; even our noses were similar.

And so, just like that, I finally had a friend. The story I now tell about myself, now that *I'm* Mary Ellis, the story of my upbringing, my past is, of course, *her* story. But our lives had so many parallels that it never really felt as if I was lying, not after a while anyway. I had lost my mother at a young age, and never known my father; Mary had never known her mother, dying as she had when her little girl was just three years old. And although Mary's life since could not have been more different to mine, a whirl of money and privilege, of mansions and private jets, we still found so much common ground. Gregor Ellis, consumed by grief after the death of his wife, had spent the previous fourteen years moving himself and his young daughter from country to country, unable to settle anywhere for more than a few months, throwing himself into his writing before declaring that Germany or Spain or Brazil or wherever they happened to be no longer inspired him, whereupon the bags would be packed and flights would be booked once more. On a far more palatial scale, it was an upbringing reminiscent of my own; Mary, like me, was nomadic, friendless, solitary. And then, in our matching red jumpers, we met in a Bristol classroom, and suddenly we had each other, and within weeks were spending every possible minute together.

The first time she invited me to their rented house, Furnbury Hall, for the weekend I was awestruck. I'd never set foot inside such a grand home before, and the fifteenth-century manor house was, to me, like something out of a film.

People actually live in such places? Real people? I remember thinking, as Mary, smiling widely at the incredulous look on my face and my gasps of amazement, took me on a grand tour of the eight-bedroomed pile, which sat in two acres of manicured grounds with a tennis court and a sweeping lawn with an Italianate fountain centrepiece.

'The original house was built in around 1410,' she told me, as we walked through the Great Hall, with its deep oak-framed leaded windows and flagstone flooring, now used as an elegant lounge. 'But the east wing was added in the late 1500s and the west wing is actually eighteenth century.'

'You have ... *wings?*' I spluttered, and she snorted with laughter. Coming as she did from a relatively modern, though no less magnificent, home in New England, she had been as thrilled by living in such a historical building as I was to visit it.

'Dad quite likes it too,' she confided on that first night, as we sat together after dinner in the wood-panelled room she called the 'snug', Gregor having retired to his study for his usual late-night writing session. The housekeeper and chef – yes, they had staff too, although they didn't live in, leaving each night after the evening meal was cleared away – had gone home, and it was just the two of us, sipping hot chocolate, cosy and relaxed on a big squishy sofa in front of the inglenook fireplace.

'I think we might actually stay here for a while, for a change, Amanda. Great, eh?' she said, and clinked her mug against mine.

I loved that she wanted to stay. I loved her accent too – vaguely American but ... *softer*, I suppose, her years of global travel making it impossible to pin down. I liked to copy it, to try to pronounce my words like she did, and she did the same to me, giggling as she told me that my Bristolian '*r*'s made me sound like a pirate.

And then, less than a year after we'd met, not long after we'd both turned eighteen within days of each other – another strange synchronicity – and just weeks before our final exams, we decided to spend the weekend studying together at Furnbury Hall. By then I had finally left care; I was living independently, in a small, neat little bedsit in Bristol, Mary occasionally crashing there with me after a Friday night out, but still very much expected to spend most of her weekends in Gloucestershire with her father.

That night, he had, unusually, popped his head into the snug before eleven, telling us he was going to bed early. He'd been suffering with a head cold, and said he was tired.

'Can't keep my eyes open,' he'd muttered. 'Don't stay up too long, you two. You have another long day of study ahead tomorrow, remember.'

We'd followed not long afterwards, whispering goodnight on the landing before heading to our respective rooms. It wasn't until I got into bed in the guest room that I realised I was still wearing Mary's bracelet. We'd taken a break from our books mid-afternoon, and had ended up in her bedroom, sifting through her mother's old jewellery box. She'd had it for years, but had only recently started to take an interest in some of the pieces in it: an Art Deco opal ring in white gold, with diamonds set into the shoulders; a pendant in the shape of a fox's head with emeralds for eyes; a sapphire and amethyst tennis bracelet. Mary had slipped her own bracelet off to try on the latter; I'd never seen her without hers, the silver identity bracelet from Tiffany always encircling her right wrist. It had been a gift from Gregor for her sixteenth birthday, and had *Mary* engraved on it in a swirly font. I picked it up to study it more closely as she admired the tennis bracelet now on her arm in its place, and asked her if I could try it on.

'Sure,' she said. 'I think I'll wear this one to dinner for a change anyway.'

And so I'd slipped the silver bracelet onto my own right wrist and then forgotten about it. Noticing it as I slipped under the blankets, I'd shrugged and decided to keep it on for safekeeping. Mary knew where it was, after all – it wasn't as if she'd be worrying about its whereabouts. I'd fallen asleep quickly; when I'd woken, not long after midnight, it was to the crackle of flames, the choking smoke, a nightmare made real.

I can't, even now, so many years later, spend too long thinking about the night of the fire. The fear, the pain. And then, the aftermath. When, by some miracle, I woke up in the bleach-scented, stiff white sheets of a hospital bed, it was to be told by a softly-spoken, auburn-haired police officer that I was the only survivor, the house reduced to smouldering ashes.

'I'm so very sorry,' she said. 'But your father didn't make it, Mary. Your friend too. I'm so, so sorry.'

'But ... I'm not ... That's wrong ...'

I remember swallowing hard, my throat still raw from the acrid smoke, and starting to cough, unable to get any more words out, but desperately wanting to explain to her that she'd got it wrong, that I *wasn't* Mary. Until then, a day after I'd regained consciousness, it hadn't even occurred to me that anyone would think that *I* was Mary Ellis; if any of the doctors or nurses had used that name as they'd been treating me, I must have been too out of it for the error to register. But I'd been wearing her bracelet, after all, the name *Mary* emblazoned across it, hadn't I? And so when the police officer called me by that name, and told me how sorry she was about the loss of my father and my friend, my mind began to race.

'Don't try to speak too much,' she said gently. Her hand was resting on my right forearm, her touch cool against my skin. Below it, where the bracelet had been, my wrist was tightly bandaged, the pain a dull throbbing ache, the burn a deep second-degree one. My head was swathed in bandages too, half of my hair gone, and more serious third-degree burns on the left side of my face; I'd been told too that my left ear had been partially destroyed, that I would need some form of reconstructive surgery.

'And I'm so sorry, but we haven't got it wrong,' she continued. 'You were so lucky, Mary. I know it won't feel like that now, and I'm so, so sorry that you've lost your dad. That fire was so fierce; it's a miracle anyone got out alive. I know this is very distressing, but can you confirm your friend's name? Your housekeeper, Mrs Daly, told us that your college friend Amanda was the third person in the house, but she wasn't sure of her surname, and we need to inform her family ...'

She'd carried on talking, but I'd stopped listening. Through the pain, and the horror, and the grief, there was now one tiny glimmer of light.

They think I'm Mary Ellis. They really do. So what if ...?

Did I tell the truth, put them straight? Just go back to my life, but without Mary now? Go back to my Bristol bedsit, do my exams, try to find a job, struggle on by myself? Or, could this change everything? Change my whole life, from this moment on? Could I do this? Was there a way they could find out, or could I just simply go along with what everyone clearly thought anyway, and just *become* Mary? I looked a bit like her already after all, and with the burns, the bandages ... was it possible? They thought Amanda Archer was dead. That *I* was dead ...

We had the same blood type, I knew that. There'd been a leaflet about becoming a blood donor on the college notice-board, and we'd both decided to do it when we turned eighteen, discovering in the process that we were both O positive. It wasn't such a coincidence really – it's the most common blood type in the world, after all – but it was something which had made us happy.

'We both have positivity literally running through our veins – no negative blood here,' Mary had laughed.

I worried, for a while though, about DNA; we'd learned about it at school, and I was terrified that there'd be some sort of post-mortem that would reveal the truth, that they'd find out that the young woman's body pulled from the fire was not that of Amanda Archer after all. But, I reasoned, where would they get DNA to compare hers to? I had no living family members that I knew of, after all. But what about medical records, dental records? And then even that worry evaporated, when the same police officer returned to see me a few days later.

'The fire investigators are still trying to establish what started the blaze,' she said. 'They think it was probably a stray ember from the fireplace in the snug, but as to why it spread so fast ...' She shrugged. 'These old houses ... so much wood ... It goes up so quickly, and Mary, I know you're keen to hold the funerals as soon as possible. We intend to release the remains tomorrow, so please let your funeral directors know that they can go ahead whenever you feel ready. Again, I'm so very sorry. And you were right about poor Amanda having no family. It's so very good of you to give her a proper send off, and a headstone. You must have been very close.'

'We were,' I whispered.

Closer than you'll ever know, I thought.

Later, when I read the fire investigator's report, I learned that the bodies pulled from the ashes were so badly damaged that no formal identification had been possible – bones, teeth, everything, so damaged by fire and heat that it had been impossible to extract any DNA, or to retrieve anything to compare against old medical or dental records. And everyone knew, after all, who had been in the house that night, didn't they? Gregor and Mary Ellis, and Mary's friend Amanda Archer. If Mary Ellis, with her long, dark hair and her identity bracelet still on her wrist, was lying in a hospital bed, then the two bodies were obviously those of Amanda and Gregor, weren't they?

And so the funerals went ahead, two graves, side by side. I sobbed that day, my heart splintering, the guilt threatening to overwhelm me, the firm, steadying hand of my grandmother in the small of my back. I say *my* grandmother; obviously, it was *Mary's* grandmother, Celeste, swooping in from New York to rescue the burned, battered granddaughter she hadn't seen since she was three years old, since her heartbroken son Gregor had fled the US and refused to return. She'd seen only a very occasional photo over the years, and the similarities between Mary and me, and my ability to imitate her slight American accent, plus my facial burns and bandages, meant that she simply never questioned my identity, not even once. I knew enough about Mary's past, from our long, deep-into-the-night heart-to-heart chats over the months since we'd met, to be able to drop 'memories', little stories about 'my' early years and 'my' father into my conversations with Celeste and others. That, along with simply telling people that the past was too painful to talk about for long, seemed to be enough.

And it was Celeste who saved me, really. From the minute we landed at JFK airport, and she swept me out into an air-conditioned limousine and settled me into a cream leather seat with a cashmere blanket draped across my knees, I began to heal. Not just the physical damage, although she took care of that too, whisking me off to see the very best doctors, paying for me to have the best treatment. It was everything else; the years of feeling as if I didn't belong, of being constantly on the move, of always, *always* feeling lost and insecure. Meeting Mary had started that process, but with Grandmama, as she liked to be called, I was finally home. I adored that woman from the first moment we met; before long, I loved her with every fibre of my being. For the next four years, she gave me everything: my health, my university education, security, love, laughter. Money too, of course. I was her long-lost granddaughter after all. But that, most of the time, seemed unimportant. I *had* money, inheriting Gregor's estate, of course. And then I just had a bit more, when Grandmama finally passed away. But by then what I also had was so much more than just a financially secure future. I'd found myself; I'd finally left my dark childhood years behind me, and learned how to trust, and how to befriend, and how to love. It began with Mary, and her wonderful grandmother had, unwittingly, continued along that path with me. By the time I moved back to the UK, to take up a post-university job in London, I still had some physical scars – even the best reconstructive surgeon in New York couldn't entirely erase the damage the fire had done to my face. But I was content with the work that had been done, the scarring on my face and wrist minimal, my ear partially rebuilt and easy to hide under my hair, which had grown back even thicker than before. And, more importantly, mentally I was healed. Amanda Archer, with her nightmarish past, was long dead. I was Mary Ellis, and I was happy, finally. Apart from the nightmares, of course. The fire will always haunt me, that terrible night of fear and pain and death.

And there's the guilt too, of course. For years, there was the lingering feeling that somehow, somebody would find out the truth; that someone would realise what I'd done, who I really was. But they didn't. Somehow, I got away with it. Everyone from my past thought Amanda Archer was dead, and there was nobody I'd ever been really close to anyway. Even if I did bump into someone I used to know, an old school mate or foster parent or social worker for example, I knew they'd never recognise me as Amanda anyway these days, not so many years on, not with the way I look now.

And Mary had only just arrived in the UK, and didn't really hang out with anyone except me, so the same applied. Now and again over the years I'd get a letter or email from someone she'd vaguely known from her brief stays in Spain or South Africa, someone who said they'd heard about the fire and Gregor's death and hoped that she was OK, but I always ignored the messages, and eventually they stopped coming. I knew that, like me, there was nobody Mary had ever been really close to; I'd been able to fool even her own grandmother, and I was confident too that, if by some huge coincidence at some point in the future I ever ran into anyone she'd actually known, I could easily pull off being her – a scarred, grown-up version of the girl they vaguely remembered.

The guilt never goes away, not entirely. But my life has continued, and it's good. I am, to the whole world, Mary. It's as simple as that.

But the truth is, if this serial killer wants to kill Mary Ellis, he's far, far too late.

She's already long gone.

And it's time to let him know that, isn't it?

Chapter 31

Thursday 4th March

Cheltenham Central Police Station

It's Thursday morning, and I'm having a meeting with Jess. We're in a bright, sunny room today with a pot of good coffee on the table, and I'm feeling strangely calm, now that I've decided. Jess, on the other hand, seems a little tense.

'Are you absolutely sure, Mary? I really need to know that you're certain about this, and the potential risks. You don't feel that anyone's pressured you into it in any way?' she asks, looking at me with a deep frown creasing her smooth brow. She pushes a plate of bourbon creams across the table towards me.

'Here, have one.'

'Thanks,' I say. 'And yes, I'm sure. And no, nobody's put any pressure on me. This is *my* decision.'

'OK, well, great.'

She gives me a half smile, then taps the track pad on the laptop in front of her to wake up the screen.

'Right, well, I'll inform the team that you're definitely

staying at home, then. No safehouse required. Provisional plans for the day are already afoot, and I'll be able to give you all the details by the end of next week, I reckon. I'm just sending an email confirming that you're happy to go ahead, and then ...'

She rapidly types a few sentences, and I take a bite of my biscuit and wash it down with a mouthful of coffee, watching her as she reads through what she's written and then hits the send button.

'Done.'

She looks up at me.

'This could be it, Mary. If we can pull this off ... I mean, unless it's a double bluff, and he's going to strike somewhere else while all our attention is on you. But, assuming that's not the case, and he's really coming to Cheltenham ...' She pauses, shaking her head. 'I mean, he must know that you're going to have police protection. He *must*. You're hardly going to sit there all on your own on the 1st of April. So he obviously thinks he's cleverer than us – that somehow he can get to you anyway. If he does turn up, and we can nab him ...'

'I know. Or it *could* all be a bluff. He might not turn up at all. Or he might wait another day, or another month. But he's been bang on with all the other dates, hasn't he? So fingers crossed, Jess.'

She nods.

'Yes, we know all this preparation might be for nothing. And if he doesn't turn up on the 1st, well, we'll need to come up with a Plan B, and find a way of keeping you safe going forwards until we finally find out who the hell he is. But we'll worry about that later. The best possible scenario right now is that he shows up as promised, and we get our man. And you get the story of the decade, which would be richly deserved.'

I smile at that.

'Thanks. We'll see. It would be a flipping amazing story to write though, if it ends like we want it to.'

I just need to write it very, very carefully, I think.

I've thought a lot about this. I'll have to say in my article that I somehow managed to talk the killer out of harming me, without saying exactly *how*. And if this killer ends up in court and says I told him that I'm not Mary Ellis, that Mary Ellis is already dead? Well, I'll just say I made it up. I lied. I pretended to be someone else in an attempt to save my skin. After all, who are they going to believe? A serial killer, or a respected crime writer?

'Oh, that reminds me, Jess,' I say now. 'I need one more element for the article actually. Can you help me with this? I need to go and chat to a close friend or relative of David Howells. Do you think you could get me a contact?'

She nods.

'I'm sure I can, yes. We're due to have a briefing shortly, as a matter of fact, so I'll see if DCI Lewis can suggest a likely candidate. I'm thinking David's ex-partner, though. I'll get his details for you.'

She makes a note on her pad, then looks at me again.

'At least the bloody newspapers still haven't linked the three cases, despite their nice little splash on our prior knowledge of David's murder,' she says. 'But we're going to have to tell the relatives of all three victims about the connection before your article goes to print, obviously. I know you haven't been exactly straight with them about the real focus of the article you're writing, and they need to know that their loved ones were actually the victims of a serial killer well in advance of any press. And you're still happy to include the police side of this too? To explain why this was all kept from the public, and even from the victims' families?'

It's my turn to nod. It's something she asked me about a while ago, and I'd been happy to agree.

'Of course. I think we can make people understand that it *had* to be kept quiet. The mass panic it would have caused ... I'm really hoping that people will understand that the information the police had to work with was so ridiculously vague that it was just impossible.'

And I really, really do hope that people will understand. I know I need to explain *my* part carefully too, when I'm putting this piece together, to explain why I didn't go public with the diary and the horrors within its pages earlier. There will, undoubtedly, be some who will think the public *should* have been warned, that every Jane and David in the UK should have been given the opportunity to try to shield themselves from harm on the dates in question. But that would have been thousands upon thousands of people, quite possibly all baying for police protection, and that would have been utterly unfeasible. It had to be like this. And if we do manage to catch him now, it will be something, at least. It's a risk I'm happy to take.

Jess is tapping on her keyboard again, and my mind drifts, wondering how the police are going to play this. I still can't imagine how it's going to work. I mean, the other victims were all taken by surprise, outdoors, in the dark, weren't they? But if I'm staying at home, a sitting duck, waiting for him, pre-warned? He must have some other plan for me.

And if I really do get the chance to speak to him, and I tell him the woman he wants to kill is already dead, what if he doesn't care? I think. *What if he attacks me anyway, before anyone gets a chance to intervene? There are so many variables, so many ways this could pan out …*

'You OK?'

I'm so lost in thought that the quiet question from Jess makes me jump.

'Yes! Sorry, Jess. I was miles away.'

She smiles.

'That's all right. Look, let's wrap this up. I'll be in touch as soon as we have everything in place. I'll speak to you later anyway, once I've got you that contact in Cardiff.'

'Brilliant. Thanks, Jess.'

I walked to the police station earlier – it's a mild, dry morning – and as I wander back past the Regency terraces of Lansdown Road, I breathe deeply and try to stay in the moment, admiring the daffodils bobbing their golden heads in the planters on Montpellier roundabout and telling myself there's no point in worrying about what might be to come. The case has taken on a momentum of its own now, and I have to trust the process, trust the police, trust my own instincts. Trust that it will work out how it's meant to work out. And if it all goes wrong, and I do actually die on the 1st of April … well, maybe that will be my punishment. Maybe that's the price I'll have to pay for all the lies I've told, the lie I live every single day.

So be it, I think.

As I turn right along Montpellier Terrace and decide to walk through the park instead of along the road as I head for home, though, I feel a little frisson of fear.

Can I really do this?

But I have to, don't I? If we can catch this killer, it won't make up for what I've done, but at least I'll have helped in some small way to get justice for Lisa, for Jane, for David. Not quite redemption, but something close to it maybe. I take a deep breath, and cross the road into the park.

Chapter 32

Thursday 4th March

Cheltenham Central Police Station

'How was Mary this morning?' asks Steph.

'She was surprisingly OK, I'd say, considering what she's agreed to do. Pretty calm really,' replies Jess.

Steph nods and turns back to the monitor in front of her, clicking on the link which will connect them to the online briefing session and tutting when the screen freezes and she has to refresh the page. Jess watches her, thinking that for once it's actually the normally imperturbable Steph who looks a tad less than calm today. Her dark-brown bob, always so sleek, looks a little ruffled, as if she forgot to brush it this morning, and the fine lines around her eyes are deeper than usual, faint dark circles making her skin look bruised.

Feeling the pressure, Jess thinks. *And I'm not surprised – it's a hell of a position to be in, heading up an investigation like this, with the clock ticking …*

'Good morning, everyone!'

DCI Bryn Lewis's rich baritone booms through the speakers, making her jump, and she stops staring at Steph and turns to look at the big screen, where the by now familiar faces are lined up, ready to hear the latest from Cardiff. As she suspected when she sat down, it doesn't take long.

'Absolutely nothing new to report,' says Bryn, and sighs heavily. 'We've now gone through hundreds of hours of CCTV footage from the night of David Howells's murder, and there's no sign of any suspicious late-night runners or any sodding other thing of any use either. Yet again, whoever's doing this seems to be able to slip in and out of the area of the crime without leaving a trace. Forensically aware, careful to avoid being captured on camera – our worst nightmare. So, DCI Warden, I'm afraid I can offer you nothing to help you as D-Day approaches in your neck of the woods, unfortunately.'

Steph sighs too, and shrugs.

'As I suspected,' she says.

'Did you speak to his ex? What was his name, Darren?' asks DCI Priya Thomson, from the window on the screen marked 'Birmingham'.

'We did,' says Bryn. 'Darren Edge. Nice bloke. He and David dated for about two years and the relationship was pretty serious for a while – they even talked about marriage apparently. But it all went wrong a year or so ago. Darren was a bit younger, late thirties, and David was forty-five at the time, and Darren told us he wanted to start a family, as in, having kids. David wasn't interested in being a dad; he said he was too old and he liked his life as it was, etcetera, etcetera. Anyway, long story short, they decided to go their separate ways, but they were able to remain on good terms and still used to meet up for dinner every few weeks. Darren actually met someone else about six months ago and the new partner also got on well with David. So no animosity there. Darren is pretty cut up about what's happened. He says David was one of the nicest guys you could hope to meet, and he can't imagine anyone wanting to hurt him, which is pretty much the same thing *everyone* we've spoken to has said. No obvious motive at all. And solid alibis all round too.'

'Same old, same old,' says DCI Linda Lake quietly. Then she adds, 'Any more trouble from the newspapers? I haven't seen any follow-up stories?'

Bryn shakes his head.

'No, thank Christ. I'm hoping we'll get a clear run now until the 1st of April with no press interference, fingers crossed. We shall see. How are preparations, DCI ... Steph?'

'Work in progress,' she replies. 'I'd rather wait until everything's finalised before I go into any details. But I'll talk it through with you all before the day. Now, if there's nothing else, can we leave it there for now? I have rather a lot on my plate.'

She smiles, but Jess is close enough to see that it doesn't reach her eyes.

'Sure,' says Bryn. 'Thanks all. Take care, OK? We'll catch up again soon.'

Steph clicks her mouse a couple of times to exit the meeting, then turns to Jess.

'I feel like the walls are closing in on me. I'm going to take a quick stroll round the block. And then we need to get the team together and start thrashing out some plans. Does that sound all right?'

Jess nods.

'I'll come for a walk with you. I could do with some air too. And then we'll get our heads together. Don't worry, Steph, we've got this, OK?'

Steph raises her eyebrows.

'I bloody hope so,' she says.

Chapter 33

Friday 5th March

I haven't been very constructive this week, workwise, and I really need to get back to it properly – it's a distraction, if nothing else – but sitting at my desk at The Hub just hasn't felt like a priority for some reason. As it's Friday though, I decide I might as well take the day off, get my head together over the weekend, and start to focus properly on work again on Monday. Focus on work, and on everything else that's coming up in the next few weeks, of course, even though most of it really is out of my hands.

Jess came through with the contact for me in Cardiff last night; as she'd suggested, it's Darren Edge, a former partner and close friend of David Howells. I email him first thing with my usual cover story, slightly concerned as I do so that he might be surprised that I'm latching onto David's murder so quickly, but to my relief he emails back within an hour.

The police do indeed seem to have zero leads, which is very distressing for all of us. I hold the view that any publicity is good publicity therefore, so I'm happy to chat to you. Could we leave it another few days though? It's still very raw. Would next Friday work?

I'm more than happy to oblige, and we fix a lunch meeting in Cardiff. Once that's done, I potter around the house, getting some chores done, but by four o'clock I'm bored and lonely, and looking forward to Pete coming home. Megan – to my secret joy – is on her travels again tonight, teaching at a yoga retreat somewhere in the Midlands, and Pete suggested this morning that as we've barely seen each other this week, it might be nice to have a movie night. I think, reading between the lines, that he's still feeling a little guilty about heading off to Megan's last Sunday and leaving me here on my own, so I tell him that would be lovely.

'And some bubbly would be nice, if you're passing the offie on your way home,' I said cheekily as he left for work this morning, and he rolled his eyes and grinned.

'Yes, Your Highness. Champagne it is, then. I suppose you deserve it,' he said, and I smiled back.

Now, not expecting him home until at least six, and anxiety starting to bubble up again, I run a deep, fragrant bath, find a soothing piano music playlist and pour the last large glass of sauvignon blanc from a bottle already open in the fridge from earlier in the week. I sink into the bath with a weary sigh, but an hour and several hot water top-ups later the warm bubbles, music and, no doubt, the wine have worked their magic, and I'm feeling calmer than I have been in weeks.

Focus on the moment. Don't look too far ahead. One day, one hour, at a time, I keep telling myself.

By the time I hear Pete open the front door and call up the stairs to ask if I want him to open the Champagne immediately and bring a glass up with him, I'm snug on the sofa in a long-sleeved T-shirt and sweatpants, my feet bare, the lamps on and Adele's latest album playing quietly through the ceiling speakers.

'Well, this is all very nice!' says Pete, as he walks in, two flutes of pale straw-coloured liquid in hand. He passes one to me, and I take a sip. It's cold and delicious, the bubbles dancing on my tongue.

'Mark at Montpellier Wine had a few already chilled, so I bought three bottles,' he says with a wink. 'I know what you're like, Ellis. Right, I'm just going to get changed and then we can order some food. I fancy Thai, what do you think?'

'Fine by me,' I say, and raise my glass. He winks again and leaves the room. Minutes later, he's flinging himself onto the other end of the sofa and reaching for his own glass, and once we've ordered the food – spicy squid salad, a beef massaman curry and a chicken pad thai – we chat easily about his day, and then he fills me in on some gossip he's heard about an old mutual friend of ours from our London days, a guy who's just allegedly left his wife for a barman he met on a night out in Soho. We don't talk about Megan at all, or about the diary, or the murders, or what's due to happen in a few weeks' time, and it's just ... just so *nice*. So normal. Me, and my lovely friend, my housemate, having a drink and chatting and laughing and putting the world to rights on the perfect Friday night in.

By the time the food arrives, in true Pete and Mary fashion – *how many times have we done this?* – we've already drunk the first bottle of Champagne, and by the time we've eaten, on our knees in front of the TV, the second is on its way out too. It feels wildly extravagant – Pete certainly didn't buy the cheapest bottles on the shelf – which isn't normally my style, but for some reason that doesn't seem to matter right now.

Strange, isn't it, how the prospect that one might die in a few weeks' time changes one's perspective on almost everything, I think, as Pete clears away the plates. When he comes back up into the lounge after dumping them in the kitchen, he sits down right next to me, his knee touching mine.

'Another drink?' he asks, and I nod. He refills my glass and then tops up his own. It's after 10.30pm by now; *The Graham Norton Show* has just started, a programme we both love, but tonight I'm finding it difficult to concentrate on the chat. Maybe it's the combination of the bath, the alcohol, and the big meal, making me a little woozy. Or maybe – and if I'm honest, I think this is what's really distracting me – it's the feeling of Pete's muscular thigh against mine, the way his fingers keep brushing against my hand as he picks up his glass to take a sip and then puts it down again on the floor in front of the sofa.

Stop it, you idiot, I tell myself firmly. *It's just the booze, and the stress …*

But now my mind is flitting back to that night a couple

of weeks ago, when I had my meltdown and I thought for a few intoxicating seconds that we were about to kiss, and how confused I felt about it, wondering what I would have done if he'd actually made a move. And suddenly, quite unexpectedly, I know exactly what I'd do. I turn my head to look at him, and I don't feel confused at all. I *want* him to kiss me, I realise. I want to feel his hands on my body, his lips on my skin.

Where has this come from? And why now? And what about Megan? And what the hell am I going to do about it?

As if he can hear what I'm thinking, Pete turns to look at me too. For a moment, it's as if there's an electric charge fizzing between us, the air almost crackling.

'Are you OK, Mary? Really OK, I mean? There's just a few weeks ...'

He says the words softly, his dark eyes fixed on mine, but it's not the conversation I want to have right now and I hold up a hand to shush him.

'Not now, Pete, please. When ... when will Megan be back?'

He hesitates for a moment before he answers.

'Tomorrow lunchtime, I think. But ... things aren't great ... I ... Oh, it doesn't matter.'

He swallows, and am I imagining it, or has he edged a little closer to me on the sofa? I can feel the heat from his body now, hear his quickening breathing, and my stomach does a little backflip, my heart rate speeding up.

This is ridiculous. Is something happening here? I think.

And then I'm not thinking at all, because Pete is leaning towards me, closer and closer until our noses brush. And then suddenly we're kissing, hesitantly at first, but then his hands are in my hair, and mine are gripping his thigh, and I know this is wrong, that it shouldn't be happening, but I simply don't care, because it's ... it's just *so damn good*. I feel Pete's hands moving down my back now, sliding up under my top, warm against my skin, and I know I want this, I *need* this. I groan softly, and in one swift movement he's pulled my T-shirt over my head and his lips are trailing downwards from my collarbone, butterfly-soft kisses that make my insides feel as though they're melting. I reach for his belt buckle, and he doesn't stop me.

The sex is incredible – passionate yet gentle – and afterwards we lie there on the sofa, legs entwined, my head on his chest, both silent except for our laboured breathing.

Finally, I angle my neck so I can see his face and say, 'Well. That was nice.'

'*Nice?*'

His eyes widen, and for some reason I give a little snort of laughter, and then we're both laughing, tittering like naughty school children until eventually he wipes his eyes and grunts.

'Urgh, my leg's gone to sleep. Shift, Ellis!'

I sit up and we both grope for our clothes which are scattered across the floor, and pull them back on. Then we look at each other again, a little sheepishly this time.

'Erm ... do we need to talk about this?' I say. 'I mean, Megan ... I feel dreadful ...'

'I think Megan and I might be done, actually,' he says quickly. He's standing up, refastening his belt buckle, and he sits down heavily on the sofa and reaches for his half-full glass of champagne. He takes a mouthful, swallows then adds, 'I just don't think we're on the same page. She's been going on about us moving in together, as you know, and ...'

He pauses, takes another drink, then continues.

'Well, I like her and everything, and things were going really well for a while, but now I just don't know ... Sorry, Mary, I'm not explaining this very well. But I think this'—he gestures vaguely at me, and then at himself—'well, this just proves it, I suppose. I can't be in love with her if I've just done that with you, can I? And we need to talk about what's just happened, yes. But maybe not right now? I think I need to end it with Megan first, and then ... God, I'm not looking forward to that though.'

He sighs, looking anguished, and I sit down beside him and squeeze his hand. I'm not sure how I'm feeling. *Do I want Pete and me to be a thing now? Or did I just need sex, something to take my mind off everything that's going on?* I'm so confused. I really have no idea, but I look at Pete, my lovely, lovely friend, his head in his hands now, and I feel a wave of sympathy.

'Look, don't stress about it tonight. You and I are fine, OK? We don't need to talk about this now at all. And just sleep on it, the Megan thing. We've been drinking, and you've had a long week, and things will be clearer in the morning. Are you seeing her tomorrow night?'

He nods.

'Supposed to be, yes. It's one of her mate's thirtieth birthday, and she's rented a private room at Hotel du Vin for a bit of a party. Ahh, shit, Mary. You're right. Let's have another drink and I'll forget about it 'til tomorrow. And you're sure we're OK? It's a bit of a weird one, you and me, after all this time, isn't it?'

He raises an eyebrow and gives me a cheeky grin, and I smile back.

'Very,' I agree. 'But, well, it's just one of those things, isn't it? Let's not analyse it too much, not tonight. Go on, top me up.'

He taps his hand to his forehead and stands up.

'Aye aye, cap'n,' he says, and I laugh.

We settle down again, and I decide that, having not wanted to talk about it earlier, this might actually now be a good time to finally tell Pete what I've decided to do on the 1st of April, so I do. His eyes widen as I explain that I'm not going to go anywhere; that I'm going to stay here and let the killer come to me, if he dares. For one crazy moment, I wonder if I should just carry on and tell him *everything*, the whole truth about me and my life; tell him that I'm not Mary Ellis at all, and that's why I'm taking this chance. But the moment passes, and I know I can't. How can I, after all these years? It would be impossible, horrendous. So I just tell him that I'm going to risk it. That the killer will obviously know the police will be waiting for him, and that if he comes after me anyway and is apprehended, what a story it will make. And that the police are currently making plans and will fill me in as soon as they can. At this point, he raises a hand.

'Well, I hope those police plans include me staying here in the house with you, because there's no bloody way I'm going anywhere.'

My stomach rolls.

'Pete, look, that's so lovely of you. But I don't know ... I mean, the police ...'

No! I think. *No! How can I tell the killer I'm not Mary Ellis if Pete's here? I should have known he'd offer to stay. I didn't even think …*

'Mary, I'm staying with you, end of. Don't ask them, *tell* them, OK? You're the one putting your life at risk here so they can catch their killer. Although, as you say, he's going to know they're going to be protecting you, isn't he? I don't really understand how he thinks he can get to you.'

I swallow hard.

OK. It'll be OK. It will look too odd if I say I don't want him here. I'll find a way round this somehow. Don't panic. Don't. Panic.

'Right, well, I'll have to run it past the police, but … thanks Pete,' I say. 'And yes, we're just going to have to wait and see, I suppose. I'm trying not to think about it too much, to be honest. One day at a time, you know?'

There's silence for a moment, Pete nodding slowly. The he leans towards me, and his lips brush my cheek, before he sits back against the cushions again.

'OK,' he says. 'But it's a lot, all this. So, I'm here, right? For whatever you need, over the next few weeks. You only have to ask.'

His gaze is fixed on my face, and he looks so serious suddenly, an intense look in his eyes that I've never seen before. Still trying to calm myself down, I stare back at him, and a shiver goes through me.

Why is he looking at me like that? Is it lust? Fear? Or something else?

Then he smiles.

'Right, Mary Ellis. Time to open that last bottle, I reckon.'

He leaps from the sofa, and heads for the door.

Chapter 34

Friday 12th March

'Oh, hi Mary. Leaving us so soon?'

I've just pushed open the front door of The Hub's reception area, heading for my car and my lunchtime meeting with Darren Edge in Cardiff, and running through the questions I want to ask him in my head, so the unexpected sound of Edward Cooper's voice startles me.

'Oh! Hello, Edward. Yes, just leaving on a job. Got to rush, sorry!'

He steps aside to let me pass, but not quite far enough, so my arm brushes his jacket and I get a whiff of body odour, a hint of sweat and stale clothing.

'Have fun!' he calls after me, and I can't help it: I shudder as I walk quickly away. I haven't seen him for a week or so – I assumed he was on holiday or something – and Satish hasn't been in much for the past week either, which has been somewhat of a relief. On Wednesday, when I stopped by Eleanor's desk for a quick catch-up, he walked past and paused for a few seconds, looking as though he wanted to interrupt our conversation, but I steadfastly ignored him, keeping my eyes fixed on my friend. Out of the corner of my eye I saw him glance from me to her and back again and then scuttle away, his cheeks reddening.

'What's up with him?' hissed Eleanor.

'No idea,' I whispered back. 'I think he's been hanging around with Edward too much. I thought he was OK, but I'm starting to think they're both real oddballs.'

'Aw, don't be mean. I think they're both quite sweet. Just a bit shy, I think.'

Sweet? Really? I thought, but she was still talking, telling me a story about a complaint she'd just had from a client who'd hired one of her artists to do her make up for a party.

What she forgot to tell me was that it was actually a *fancy-dress* party. And the theme was "movie monsters", and she was going as some alien thing from a film called *Attack the Block*. I mean, I've never even heard of it, but apparently the creatures are like a cross between a wolf and a gorilla with thick, black fur and luminous, turquoise fangs. She had some sort of costume but it didn't have a mask, so she was expecting Amy to do her face to match. The poor girl did her best but seriously? A furry face and turquoise teeth? Give me a break ...'

Eleanor snorted, which set me off too, and I was still giggling on my way back to my desk, feeling Satish's eyes on me but ignoring him. I haven't seen him since then, and now that I know Edward's in today I'm glad I'm heading out of the office. I'm clearly a horrible person, but the less I see of the pair of them at the moment the better, even if some people do think they're 'sweet'.

I don't turn the car radio on as I drive the seventy or so miles to the Cardiff café where I've arranged to meet Darren. I feel like I need the silence today; there's so much *stuff* buzzing around in my brain. Pete, for a start. It's been a week now since we had sex, and neither of us has mentioned it since. And, unless anything's happened this morning, as far as I know he still hasn't ended his relationship with Megan either. I'm *definitely* a horrible person, aren't I? How could I have done that – slept with another girl's boyfriend, even if I *have* known him for so much longer than she has? It was a dreadful thing to do, and I'm still not sure why it happened. Pete does seem certain their relationship is over though, although he decided not to ruin her excitement about her friend's birthday party by telling her last Saturday.

'She's been looking forward to this do for weeks, Mary. I just can't do it to her, not tonight,' he said, and went off to Hotel du Vin with her for the evening as planned, and then back to spend the night at hers, although when he finally came home late on Sunday afternoon he told me they'd literally just *slept* together the previous evening.

'She was so drunk she pretty much passed out as soon as we got in,' he told me. 'You know Megan – she doesn't drink that much, so when she does, it doesn't always end well. And she was so hungover today, all she wanted to do was lie on the sofa and have me bring her coffee and water on repeat. She wasn't in any sort of fit state for a serious chat. I'm probably not going to see her for a few days now, we're both so busy at the moment, but I'll do it later in the week, I promise."

'No need to promise *me*,' I replied. 'Nothing to do with me, Pete.'

He looked at me a little strangely when I said that, and I shrugged and headed upstairs for a bath; we didn't talk about it again when I came back down, and indeed haven't since. But it's true. It *is* nothing to do with me. If Pete wants to end things with his girlfriend, that's up to him. I'm not putting any pressure on him, because I'm not even sure how I feel about him, how I feel about *us*, or even if there *is* an us. Yes, I've thought about last Friday, of course I have. I've felt a ripple of desire when I remember how his fingers ran up my inner thigh, so gently, so seductively, and I've tried very hard not to look at those fingers when he's handed me a mug of tea or passed me the black pepper at dinner, worrying that my eyes might give me away. And I know, without a doubt, that I love Pete – I've loved him for years, as a friend, as one of the few people in the world I'm really close too, someone who's always there for me. But has that love slowly, imperceptibly, changed into a different kind of love over the years, and is that why what happened on Friday happened? Or was it just sex?

It was great sex, that's for sure. More than that: it felt natural, easy, as if we'd done it a hundred times before. It felt ... *right*, I suppose. But maybe that's just the difference between having sex on a one-night stand with a stranger and doing it with someone you've known for years, someone you already have feelings for, someone you already love. It doesn't mean we'd be right as a *couple*, I keep telling myself. That might not work at all, even though I already know how well we get on, how easy it is to live with him, how much we make each other laugh – all the good stuff, the things that would be at the top of a relationship wish-list, if I were ever to write one.

And throw in great sex too, and, well ...

I shake my head as I drive off the slip road onto the M4, trying to banish the intrusive thoughts. Whatever happens with Pete will happen; I need to concentrate on more pressing issues, like the small matter of whether this serial killer is going to turn up on my doorstep in a couple of weeks' time, if between us the police and I can stop him murdering me, and what I do about Pete being there. I told Jess he's insisting he stays at home with me on the day, and at first she said she didn't think it was a good idea at all.

'It's another life we'd potentially be putting at risk, Mary,' she said.

But after discussing it with the team, she called me back.

'We already know this killer has been keeping tabs on you, so he'll know exactly who lives in your house. Moving Pete out would serve no real purpose, and it'll probably mean you'll feel calmer, won't it, having your friend there? So, fine. He can stay.'

Pete simply gave me a satisfied-sounding 'Good,' when I told him, leaving me to carry on with my secret worrying about how I can tell the killer what I need to tell him out of Pete's earshot. It's something I'll have to worry about on the day, I suppose; we're still waiting to hear the police plan too, which they now say they're going to keep close to their chests for a bit longer, something which seems to be frustrating Pete.

'It's your bloody life at stake here. They should be keeping you fully informed. I'd be demanding answers, if it was me,' he's said more than once over the past few days, until I finally told him to please just leave it. He grumpily obliged, but I can tell that he's growing increasingly anxious, whereas the whole thing has taken on a somewhat surreal feeling for me now. The clock is ticking, and I'm very aware of that, but I'm still taking it one day, one hour, at a time. And this hour, I need to concentrate on Darren Edge, and the murder of his ex-lover. *I still have an article to write when this is over, after all*, I think as I pull into a parking space just up the road from Peterkins Café just before 1.30pm, our designated meeting time.

Llandaff, to the northwest of Cardiff, is like a city within a city; I've just driven past its twelfth-century cathedral, but the area, on the banks of the River Taff, has a cosy, small-town feel. There's even a pretty village green, but the High Street is bustling, and as I lock the car and walk the hundred metres or so to the café, I spot at least three enticing boutiques and a florist's shop, a beautiful display of elegant hand-tied bouquets in its window. This suburb is where David Howells lived, which is why Darren suggested we meet here, and I feel a pang of sorrow as I push open the door of Peterkins and scan the room. The place is small and busy, most of the tables occupied: a couple of groups of young women, buggies and babies tucked in around them, chatting and laughing over coffee and cake; an elderly couple talking animatedly in one corner, heads close together; and just one man sitting alone at a high bar-style counter at the back. He catches my eye and raises a hand.

'Mary?' he mouths.

I nod and smile, then weave my way between the tables,

dodging a waiter holding aloft a tray with a precariously balanced teapot and a stack of mugs, and slide onto the stool next to his.

'Darren. So good of you to agree to this. How are you?' I say.

'Still in shock, I think,' he replies.

He's already ordered a mixed platter of crackers, meats, and cheeses, and a pot of tea for two, and he pours me a cup and offers me milk and sugar, before helping himself to some food. He's a good-looking man, probably in his late thirties, and sporting, like David did in the photos I've seen of him, a neatly trimmed beard, although Darren's is dark. He's wearing a denim shirt, a leather jacket slung over the spare seat next to him, and he has a heart-shaped signet ring on the little finger of his left hand. His eyes look sad.

'I still can't get my head round it,' he says, once we've both had a few sips of tea. 'It seems so senseless. Why kill him, and not take anything, or break in, or … well, there just seems no reason for it. It's just … sick.'

His accent isn't Welsh – I think it's West Country, maybe Devon, and has a soft burr.

'I know. I'm so sorry. The police seem baffled too, which is why I've taken an interest,' I say.

I pause, not wanting to elaborate too much on why I'm writing the article, but he's nodding.

'And I appreciate that, as do his parents. I did run this past them, after I spoke to you, just to make sure they were OK with me talking to you, but they were fine with it. They're like me – they think that any publicity we can get can only help. *Somebody* out there knows who did this, and why, don't they?'

'They do. So, can you tell me a bit about David? About his background, hobbies, that sort of thing, just to get us started?'

I pull my notebook and pen out of my bag, deciding the café is a little too noisy for the voice recorder, and open the pad at a fresh page. Darren sighs.

'Sure. I mean, he was just an ordinary guy really. Nice working-class family, did OK at school but sport was always his thing. He was on the school football team, and he was good at athletics too; he still has a drawerful of medals he won for the hundred metres, the high jump, all sorts.'

He grimaces.

'Sorry, he *had* a drawerful of medals. I can't believe I have to talk about him in the past tense now, it's just ... ridiculous. Anyway, he did his A levels and then went on to do some sort of personal trainer diploma and worked in various gyms around Cardiff for years. He came out as gay in his mid-twenties, I think, and there was a bit of the usual hassle around that, you know. Twenty years ago things were a bit different to nowadays. I'm not sure his dad took it very well at first, but David said he soon came round; he's a decent bloke, Paul – he was always very good to me. We're still pally now. So, you know, David's life was fairly standard, I suppose. He worked hard, had a few relationships, enjoyed a night out now and again and the odd holiday – Spain, Portugal, nothing too exotic. And then of course his parents won the lottery, so that made everything a bit easier. They helped him set up The Fit Joint, and that was a new lease of life for him. He still worked really hard – he was usually in his office at 5am. But being his own boss, seeing his business grow ... he just loved it.'

Darren's voice cracks, and he stops talking for a few moments, obviously struggling to compose himself. I don't say anything, cutting a piece of Camembert and putting it on a cracker, giving him time, until finally he takes a deep breath and says:

'Sorry. This is hard. We met a little while after he set up The Fit Joint. It was at a dinner party with mutual friends who thought we'd hit it off, and they were right. I don't really believe in love at first sight, but it was definitely lust, and things progressed pretty quickly. But eighteen months or so down the line, I don't know ... something changed. I started to yearn for a family, to have kids, you know? And for David, that just wasn't on the agenda. He liked life as it was, and children were never in his plans. And so we gradually drifted apart, and finally it just ended. We stayed friends though – and I mean *real* friends. I'm with a guy called Eric now, and we're hoping to get married and maybe try to start a family soon ...'

His cheeks flush a little as he says this, and I smile.

'That's great. I'm happy for you,' I say.

'David was too,' he says. 'He really was. He liked Eric a lot, and he was genuinely pleased that things had worked out for me. I was planning to ask him to be godfather, if we'd been lucky enough to have a baby, but now ...'

His voice breaks again, and this time his eyes fill with tears.

'Shit. *Shit.* Why the hell did this happen to him?' he hisses, then hastily looks around the café, as if checking that his language hasn't offended anyone, but nobody seems to be looking at us.

'I really don't know. I wish I did,' I say.

We pause to eat a little of the food, and then start chatting again, but just like in my interviews with Lisa Turner's brother and Jane Holland's cousin, there's nothing in anything I learn about David Howells that rings any bells, no connection that I can see between any of us. A barrister, a casino boss, the owner of a fitness business, and a crime writer. No common ground, no common friends or interests, no shared history. Nothing.

When we say goodbye, and Darren walks off down the High Street, shoulders hunched against a rain-spattered wind that's sprung up while we've been talking, I sit in my car for several minutes, staring into space, my mind whirring, thinking about Darren's anguished question.

Why the hell did this happen to him?

If I do get to confront this killer, will he tell me? I wonder.

Will he finally answer the question that we've all been asking, since the very beginning? Will he tell us *why?* If it's somehow connected to our parents, after all? Or if it's us, specifically, he's after? Lisa Turner, Jane Holland, David Howells.

And Mary Ellis.

Who he can't kill, because she's not here.

I start the engine and pull away slowly, trying to breathe deeply. I feel more confused than ever, I realise. I want to do something *good*, something that might make a real difference. But am I completely insane to even think of confronting this madman? My hand shaking, I press the handsfree button on my steering wheel and call Pete.

Chapter 35

Friday 12th March

It takes a few attempts to get hold of my housemate, and by the time I do manage to speak to him I'm tearful and panicky, sobbing as I tell him, without going into detail, that I'm suddenly terrified about what's to come.

'Mary, calm down. You're just having a mild panic attack or something. I'm going to be with you, OK? I'd never let anything bad happen to you, you know that, don't you? Come on, breathe. Of course you're scared; you wouldn't be human if you weren't. But I promise you, you're going to be all right.'

Gradually, gently, he talks me down, and by the time I'm back on the M4 I'm feeling better, especially as he tells me he'll be home tonight after all. He'd been due to see Megan as promised but, I suspect to his relief, he'd had to pull a last-minute late shift in the office, so she decided to go out with friends instead. At seven, when I'm back in Cheltenham and snuggled up on the sofa, he texts to say he'll be home between 10.30 and 11, adding:

Grabbing some fish 'n' chips on the way back. Want some?

I decline, thanking him but telling him I'm not hungry, and that I'm exhausted and planning an early night.

Can't keep my eyes open. Would love to see you when you get in but might be asleep at this rate!

I text back, and he replies with a sad face emoji. For some reason, that makes my heart flutter a little, and although I really do feel wiped out, as the clock ticks round to 11 I'm still valiantly trying to stay awake by watching TV in bed, choosing one of my favourite old episodes of *Sex and the City*, the one where Carrie and Mr Big meet for lunch and end up falling in a lake. Even though I'm expecting Pete's arrival, I don't hear the front door opening or his footsteps on the stairs, so when there's a sudden tap on my bedroom door I jump, instantly on full alert, my heart thumping,

'Bloody hell, Pete. You could have called up the stairs or something. You scared the life out of me,' I snap, as he pokes his head into the room.

'Oh, bugger. Sorry babes.' He walks in, coat still on, takeaway bag in hand, a contrite expression replacing the grin on his face.

'I should have thought, especially at the moment. Would a chip do as an apology?'

I glare at him, my heart still racing, then sniff. There's a rather enticing aroma coming from the bag in his hand, and my stomach growls.

I haven't eaten since lunch, have I? Maybe I am hungry, after all.

'Possibly,' I say. 'What else is in that bag?'

He smirks.

'Knew you wouldn't be able to resist. Battered plaice, onion rings, mushy peas. And two forks.'

I sigh.

'Damn you, Chong. You know my weak spots, don't you? I can't resist an onion ring.'

And, it seems, for some reason at the moment I can't resist Pete Chong either. He gives a whoop and leaps onto my bed, but after only a few minutes of nibbling on the contents of the bag, he leans across to wipe a dribble of tartar sauce off my chin and then, very slowly, runs his finger across my lips, and my stomach flips. Our eyes meet, and we stare at each other for a few long moments. And then we're kissing, panting, our hands ripping at each other's clothing, and as I'm already in bed and wearing just a T-shirt, it's not long before I'm naked, groaning with pleasure as his fingers roam my body. The sex is, as it was the first time, delicious, and afterwards he stays with me, one long, muscular leg thrown across mine, his breath warm on my neck. I lie there for a few minutes, feeling the gentle rise and fall of his chest against my back, trying to process how I'm feeling.

Even more guilty, about sleeping with another woman's boyfriend *again?* Definitely.

But happy?

Also definitely, I realise, and whether that's a good thing or not, I'm simply too tired and emotional to figure it out now. I fall asleep with my fingers entwined in his and, I'm pretty sure, a small smile on my face.

Chapter 36

Saturday 13th March

I wake with a start when my alarm, the weekday one I forgot to turn off, rings shrilly from my bedside table at 7am. My first thought is about how disgusting my room smells.

Why? Why does it smell like this?

Then I remember, and sit up slowly, first looking at the takeaway bag on the floor, cold, greasy-looking chips spilling out of it onto my cream carpet – *and, seriously? Is that a piece of batter on the end of the bed?* I think – and then turning to see Pete's sleepy face on the pillow next to mine.

'Stinks like a fishmonger's in here,' he mumbles. 'Morning.'

'Oh bloody hell, Pete. We really need to stop doing this,' I reply. 'How did that happen? We can't even use booze as an excuse for last night. We were both stone-cold sober.'

'I know.' He sounds more awake now, rubbing his eyes and then propping himself up against the headboard.

'I mean, I don't know. And ... oh shit, is it seven already? I need to get back into the office – we have a few more hours to do on that rush job this morning, and I said I'd see Megan at lunchtime. I'm absolutely going to talk to her today, OK? I need to get it over with, especially after ... Oh hell, I'm so sorry, I just don't have time to discuss any of this now. Do you mind?'

The guilt is rushing over me again – *poor Megan* – but Pete is on the move, and without waiting for a reply, he pushes the duvet back and climbs out of bed, scrabbling on the floor for his clothes. He clutches them self-consciously to his naked groin as he bends down and drops a clumsy kiss on my forehead.

'Have a good day,' he says; then, turning back to look at me as he reaches the door, adds, 'And you really need to think about cleaning your room one of these days, Ellis. I think I can see an onion ring in your slipper. Look, there. I mean, honestly, you're such a slob ...'

'YOU CHEEKY—!'

I grab a pillow and lob it at him, and he ducks and runs from the room, laughing. I lie down again, grinning myself now, but the smell of the stale food is too much. An hour later the room is clean again, windows flung open to allow some fresh air in, and I'm showered and downstairs making breakfast, and wondering how to spend the day. My mind is once again full of uncomfortable thoughts about my feelings about my housemate and what we've just done, as well as the usual bubbling anxiety over the bloody Diary Killer, and all I know for certain is that I don't want to sit and dwell on any of it.

'Distraction, that's what I need,' I say out loud to the kettle.

I end up wandering round the shops in Montpellier for a few hours, coming home with a pair of slouchy cream linen dungarees, an inky-blue ceramic vase, and a box of candied fruit cannoli from the Italian bakery, none of which I really need, or indeed want. I've just sat down in the kitchen with a cup of tea and some mushroom pâté on toast, when I hear the front door open, and two people chatting animatedly.

Pete and … oh no, really? Megan. It's bloody Megan, I think.

I look frantically around the room, almost tempted to run and hide behind the little sofa. Then I realise that would be ludicrous behaviour, and stay where I am, bracing myself.

'Oh, hi, Mary,' says Pete, as they walk into the kitchen. 'I … erm, I didn't know if you'd be here or not. I thought you might have gone shopping or something. Sorry … we, erm … we won't be here long. I'm just picking up some stuff to take over to Megan's …'

He looks as awkward as he sounds, and I smile stiffly, trying to ignore what I'm sure is a suspicious expression crossing Megan's face as she looks from Pete to me and back again.

For goodness' sake, Pete. Just tell her it's over. What's all the delay? I think. *You're just making it worse.*

But of course I don't say it. Instead I say brightly, 'Oh, that's OK. I *was* out shopping, yes. I've just got in actually. Just having a quick lunch …'

I gesture at my plate, and Megan frowns.

'Why are you two being weird? Have you had an argument or something?'

'No!' I exclaim, at exactly the same moment as Pete says: 'Yes! We have …'

We both fall silent. *Shit! Shut up Pete,* I think, and Megan takes a step backwards, eyes flitting from one of us to the other.

'Oh. So which is it, then?' she says, her voice cold.

'It wasn't really an argument,' I say lamely, looking at Pete. He looks back at me and ...

Oh, come on! Is that really a hint of a smile I can see?

'No, it wasn't,' he says, and turns to Megan. 'More a disagreement. We're fine. Nothing to worry about. Look, I'm just nipping upstairs to get a few things. Help yourself to a tea or whatever. I'll be two minutes, OK?'

He skips, a little too eagerly in my view, from the room, and Megan turns to me, fixing me with a cool gaze.

'What was the disagreement about, Mary?' she asks.

'Erm ...' My mind races. 'Oh, it was just that Pete came home late from the office last night with a takeaway, and he went to bed without clearing it away. The place stank of fish this morning, and we had words. Nothing major.'

'Oh.' She looks somewhat mollified. 'Actually, I did think I could smell something when I came in. Men, eh? Can I just grab a glass of water?'

'Of course, go for it.'

She gives me a small smile, and I smile back, relieved.

Dodged that one, then, I think. *But we can't go on like this, we really can't ...*

Megan opens the cupboard where we keep the glassware, then heads for the sink and turns the tap on, filling her tumbler before turning back to look at me. She's wearing a fitted pink hoodie and skin-tight grey leggings with little white stars all over them, her body looking taut and toned. Her long blonde hair is pulled into a neat top-knot, and she seems to be wearing no make-up other than a slick of mascara, her skin fresh and glowing. I wonder, not for the first time, why Pete is bothering with me when he has this gorgeous creature.

'So, what are you up to at the moment, Mary? Anything exciting happening?'

Megan puts her glass down on the counter, and I shake my head and take a sip of my tea.

'Not a lot,' I say. 'Same old, same old.'

'Oh.' She sounds mildly surprised, and her blue eyes widen.

'I thought Pete said you were going away for a bit? At the end of the month?'

My heart skips a beat.

He told her I was thinking of going away? When? And why would he do that? He promised me he wouldn't say a word ...

I stare at her for a moment, then shake my head.

'Erm ... no, change of plan,' I say. 'I *was* thinking about going on a trip, yes. But I've changed my mind. I might take a holiday a bit later in the year instead.'

'Right.' She's definitely looking at me with a strange expression on her face now, one I can't read, but it's making me feel nervous. A knot of apprehension begins to form in my stomach.

'So you'll be here, then? For the next few weeks? Here, in the house?'

Her voice has a hard edge to it, one I haven't heard before.

'Yes. Not going anywhere!'

I keep my tone light, breezy even, not sure what's going on, and then almost clap with relief as Pete reappears, duffle bag slung over his shoulder.

'Pete! So, you won't be back tonight, then? Because I might see if Ellie wants to come round,' I say.

'Ah, good idea. No, I won't be back tonight. See you sometime tomorrow?' he replies, but he's looking more at the wall behind me than he is at me, the awkwardness in his manner persisting. Then he says, 'Ready, Meg? Let's go. Bye, Mary. Give my regards to Ellie.'

'Sure,' I say, but he's already left the room, his footsteps heading down the hall towards the front door.

'Bye, Megan,' I say quietly, but she doesn't reply. Instead, as she follows Pete out of the room, she turns for a moment and looks at me. I stare back, and my chest tightens.

Why is she looking at me like that?

Megan is beautiful. But now her face tightens, her mouth curling into a sneer, and there's something in her eyes, an expression that makes my whole body tense. She looks ... she looks *evil*.

'Bye, Mary,' she says, and her voice is low; there's a hint of menace in her tone that chills me. She stares at me for a few more seconds, then turns away and follows Pete down the hall. Moments later I hear the front door closing, and they're gone.

Chapter 37

Monday 15th March

'**M**ary? Are you very busy? Could I have a quick word?' I'm so engrossed in what I'm writing that I didn't hear Satish approaching my desk, but suddenly he's there, standing behind me, and I frown as I turn to look at him. He looks as if he's used some sort of new styling product; normally artfully messy, today his thick, dark hair is lying perfectly flat on his head.

'I'm actually right in the middle of something. Can you give me fifteen minutes or so?' I say brusquely. 'I'll come and find you.'

'Sure. Sorry,' he says. He stands there, fiddling with his navy and red striped tie for a few seconds, looking uncomfortable, then turns away and scuttles back to his desk. I watch him go, sigh, and type a few more words, then stop.

Damn. I've lost the flow now, I think.

I'm trying to start putting my article together, and it was going rather nicely until bloody Satish interrupted. I can't write the main piece yet, of course: the section about my encounter with a serial killer who had my name on his hitlist, and how

I managed to evade him and live, hopefully. I can't write that until a) it actually happens, and b) I work out how to write it without revealing the truth to my readers about my big, fat lie of a life. But I'm trying to put the other bits together, those about the lives – and deaths – of Lisa, Jane, and David. I wrote Lisa's part first, and now I'm on to Jane, trying to sift through my notes from my chat with Stella, and trying very hard not to be distracted by thoughts of Pete and, more importantly now, of Megan.

The conversation we had in the kitchen on Saturday and the – well, *scary*, quite frankly – look she gave me as they left has been preying on my mind, anxiety prickling my skin every time her face flashes into my head.

Does she know – or suspect – what Pete and I have been up to behind her back? I keep thinking. *Is that it? Or is it something else? Why did she look at me with such … loathing? Hatred, almost?*

A shiver runs down my back again now, like a cold finger caressing my spine. I texted Pete after they'd left, asking him to call me urgently and to do it from somewhere private. It took nearly two hours for him to get back to me, by which time I was furious as well as anxious.

'I had to wait until Megan was in the shower,' he whispered. 'What's wrong? Has something happened?'

When I angrily challenged him about why he'd told Megan I'd been thinking of going away at the end of the month, he seemed bemused.

'I told her that ages ago, when you first suggested it as a possibility,' he said. 'I said you might be planning a little break. It was just so she wouldn't think it was strange if you suddenly disappeared from the house and we hadn't said anything. She doesn't know anything else, I promise. Nobody does. Come on, Mary. What do you think I am?'

I felt a little embarrassed then for what suddenly felt like a massive over-reaction. Of *course* he would have had to give Megan some sort of explanation if I suddenly vanished for a couple of weeks. And so I apologised, blamed it on stress, and let him get back to her. But the way she looked at me, the way she *spoke* to me, is still bothering me, giving me an uneasy feeling deep in my guts.

And what the *hell* is Pete playing at with her, anyway? Yet again, he spent Saturday night with her and all day yesterday too, not arriving home until so late that I was already asleep, and leaving for work before I got up this morning. I'm assuming, as I haven't heard anything from him, that he still hasn't managed to get out of the relationship, and I can't get my head round it. It's not about me and him, it *really* isn't; more that this just isn't like Pete. I've never known him to do the dirty on a girlfriend; never known him to two-time. He's a straightforward, honest kind of guy, and that's one of the things I love about him. So to behave like this ... it's out of character. It's *odd*.

I shake my head, trying to force myself to concentrate on my work, but it's no good. And now I have to go and see what Satish wanted, although talking to him is the last thing I want to do right now. Reluctantly, I stand up and walk slowly towards his desk, where he's rummaging in his top drawer. As I reach him, he pulls out a brown envelope, then sees me and stuffs it back into the drawer again, his cheeks reddening.

'Mary! Oh. Thanks. Erm ... well, what it was ... erm ...'

I wait impatiently, wondering why he's suddenly looking so flushed.

'Well, do you remember I asked you a while back if you're around on the 31st of March? Have you decided yet if you're going away at the end of the month? You weren't sure back then, but it's only a couple of weeks away now so I was just wondering ...'

'Why on earth do you want to know that?' I explode. I know I've pretty much shouted the words at him; he visibly recoils, and I can see out of the corner of my eye heads at the nearest desks turning towards us. But I can't help myself.

Again, asking me about where I'm going to be at the end of the month? What the ...? I think, and I can feel the anger building, like a tight fist inside my chest.

'It's none of your bloody business whether I'm going away or not,' I say, still far too loudly, my voice quivering. I suddenly feel like crying, or thumping the wall, or pushing Satish off his chair, none of which would be a good idea. He's looking at me wide-eyed now, his mouth slightly open, eyes blinking at me from behind his rectangular glasses.

'I'm sorry. I just ...'

'Oh, just keep away from me. You *and* Edward. Leave me alone, OK?' I say, and I give him what I hope is a withering look and stalk away, ignoring the curious stares I'm getting from the handful of other people who are in. But my heart is pounding, my legs are wobbly, and by the time I make it the few metres back to my desk and sink gratefully into my chair I'm feeling a little light-headed.

What the hell? I think. That's the second time he's tried to find out what I'm doing on the 31st of March. *That must mean something, whatever the police think, surely? What if he and Edward aren't directly involved, but are passing on information to the killer, maybe? What if they're helping him find out where his victims are going to be on the day of the murder? That could be why they were in Oxford on New Year's Eve, couldn't it? And—*

Oh shit …

Something else has just struck me. The envelope Satish was pulling out of his drawer as I approached, and then hastily shoved out of sight again? It was a *brown* envelope.

The letter I got from the Diary Killer was in an envelope just like that, wasn't it? Or am I being ridiculous? A brown envelope isn't exactly unusual in an office, is it?

My hand shaking, I pick up my mobile phone, stand up – Satish has his head down at his desk, not looking in my direction now, thank goodness – and head for the kitchen. Thankful to find it empty, I shut the door and dial Jess's number. She picks up almost immediately.

'Hi Mary. Everything OK?'

'Jess, no, not really. Something strange has just happened, and it's really stressed me out. Have you got a minute?'

'Of course. What's up?'

I tell her, and she listens, making sympathetic noises, but when I've finished she's silent for a few seconds, before saying, 'I hear you, and I understand why you're still concerned. And I will of course pass this on to the team. But honestly, Mary, those two have been ruled out. There's absolutely no evidence—'

'But JESS! It's the second time he's asked me about that

weekend. He's trying to find out where I'm going to be. Surely that's suspicious?'

I can't keep the exasperation out of my voice, and Jess again falls silent for a few moments, then replies, 'I just don't think it is, Mary. I think you're oversensitive and nervous, and nobody could blame you for that. Look, you know it's going to be pretty much impossible for anything bad to happen to you on the 1st of April, don't you? Just hold on to that, and try and keep your nerve. Just take a few deep breaths, make yourself a coffee, and focus on something else. It's going to be OK. Trust me.'

'I … OK, Jess. Sorry. I'm sorry.'

I stand in the kitchen for a full five minutes, leaning motionless against the worktop, trying to calm myself. Jess is right, isn't she? It's going to unfold how it's going to unfold, and I need to keep it together. I only have to do this for two more weeks. And at least Satish is fairly likely to leave me alone from now on, after the way I just reacted. And so I do as Jess suggested. I take some deep breaths, make a strong coffee, and walk reluctantly back to my desk.

But I still feel horribly on edge, and I glance over my shoulder towards where Satish sits, and see that Edward has now arrived and is crouching by his chair, the two of them engrossed in yet another quiet conversation. They're not looking in my direction, but even so a little tremor runs through me.

There's just something …

I shake my head slightly, trying to suppress the feeling of foreboding. I'm going to drive myself mad if I go on like this. I turn resolutely back to my screen, and begin to type.

Chapter 38

Monday 29th March

Cheltenham Central Police Station

'Three days. We have *three* days. Every detail needs to be pinned down now, OK? There's no room for error. Let's go through the plan one more time – Mike, you talk us through it – and let's see if there's anything outstanding. Let's go.'

DCI Steph Warden is pacing up and down, DC Jess Gordon and DI Mike Stanley watching her from their seats at the conference table, sheets of notes and diagrams laid out neatly in front of them. They only sat down a few moments ago, but there's already a tense atmosphere in the room, and as he gathers his thoughts Mike glances surreptitiously at his colleagues. Jess looks anxious, her usually smooth brow furrowed, hair scraped back, hands clenched tightly around her mug of tea. And Steph looks as if she hasn't slept well for days. The boss's cheeks are pale and hollow, as if she's recently lost weight, and there's a stain on the front of one leg of her tailored black trousers.

I'm not surprised, Mike thinks. *This is the big one. The other forces had the date of the promised murder but an impossible task in pinpointing the victim. We know exactly who the victim is, as well as the date. If he's really going to attempt this, and we screw up …*

He doesn't even want to think about it, and he feels a wave of sympathy for Steph, who will bear the brunt of their superiors' anger if this goes wrong. She's good, he knows that. Tough, determined, bright. But is she bright enough to foil the Diary Killer?

Are any of us? he thinks, as he stands up, walking to the whiteboard by the window. Despite huge renewed efforts by the entire Operation Shearwater team over the past two weeks, they're still no closer to identifying the killer than they were back in January, when this all started. Thursday will probably be their last, and maybe only, chance to catch him. It still seems impossible to Mike that the guy will actually show up, but hey. He's clearly insane, and they have to go through the motions, just in case. And if he does appear, and they manage to catch him … *wow. Just wow.*

Mike clears his throat.

'OK, so let's start inside.'

He taps the sketch on the whiteboard, a plan of Mary's house and the surrounding streets.

'This is number 21 The Grove in Montpellier. Home of Mary Ellis. Tomorrow we go in and do final checks on all the door and window locks and fit a panic button in a discreet place in each of the main rooms of the property. These will not give an audible alert in the house itself, but we'll be warned immediately that something has gone wrong so we can get straight in there. We're also fitting bullet-proof window panels throughout. They're installed inside, behind the primary glass. They can withstand bomb blasts as well as bullets, in case he decides to try a sniper style attack or chuck something through a window. Not his style, if the previous murders are anything to go by, but we're trying to cover all bases. We've also fitted powerful motion-sensor lights on both the front and back of the property. We've decided against hidden cameras or listening devices; Mary told us she was uneasy about having them in the house and as we should have clear visuals of anyone who does manage to get in there, we agreed that it's probably not necessary. Unless the guy has an invisibility cloak, there's no way he'll get in without being seen, even in the dark.'

He pauses, then points to the roof of the neatly drawn house.

'To cover every eventuality, we're also sealing off the chimney, and access to the attic, just in case he has any plans to gain access to the house via the roof space. It's a terrace, so potentially if he was able to get into the attic of one of the adjoining houses, he could break his way through. It's unlikely he'd be able to do that quietly or unobserved, but even so. Essentially, all of that will mean the house will be a sealed box, with nobody able to gain access unless one of the occupants lets them in.'

Steph, who's stopped pacing and is now leaning against the wall at the back of the room, nods.

'Great,' she says. 'I mean, I guess the only other thing he could try is flying over the house in some sort of aircraft and dropping a bomb on the roof. But as you say, that would be so far away from his usual style ...'

'Agreed. And we'll be warned of any unusual aircraft activity in the area in advance too; that's already in place,' says Mike.

'And fire isn't likely either,' adds Jess. 'He'd never get close enough to try to set the place alight without being spotted. I feel like we've covered everything.'

'So do I,' agrees Steph.

'Great. So ... inside the house there will be Mary Ellis, obviously,' Mike continues.

He pauses for a few seconds to take a sip of water. His armpits feel clammy, and he's desperately hoping he's not developing sweat patches on his shirt. Then he taps the upstairs living room area on the house plan.

'And with her will be her housemate, Peter Chong. He's been thoroughly vetted as we know, and he's Mary's closest friend. He's adamant about wanting to stay in the home to help protect her and keep her company, and she's keen to have him there. He'll also be another pair of eyes and ears and, should the worst somehow happen, a first line of defence for Mary, as it'll take us a minute or so maybe to get in there if we need to.'

'But he's been warned not to do anything stupid? Not to try any heroics?' asks Steph. 'We don't want *two* victims. I mean, we don't want *any*, obviously, but ...'

'Yes,' says Mike. 'He's been briefed. He knows that if anything does happen, the first thing he does is alert us. The two of them will be in the house, on lockdown, from 6pm on Wednesday evening. They've been advised to confine themselves to this first-floor living room as much as possible, so we know where they are; they can go to the bathroom or downstairs to the kitchen to get food and drink, obviously, but we've requested that they base themselves in that room for the period in question, including sleeping there. We don't want them heading off to individual bedrooms. They need to stay together.'

There are a few seconds of silence as the three of them stare at the whiteboard. Then Mike points at the street in front of number 21.

'Next, outside. We've gained access for the period to the currently vacant top floor flat in number 18, just opposite Mary's. We'll be able to watch the entire street from the windows of that flat, as well as the front of the house. Everything will be put into place gradually over the twenty-four hours prior, and as discreetly as possible. We'll use officers dressed as furniture delivery drivers to move the surveillance equipment in and all personnel moving into positions around the target will be in plain clothes. If he's nearby and watching the house, we don't want to scare him off.'

He runs a finger along the street drawn on the plan.

'We'll also have officers stationed at various points along the street and in adjoining roads. We have a couple of dummy roadwork vans at the junctions so we can keep an eye on any potential suspects entering the street, and'—he points to the rear of number 21, where Mary's patio garden leads via a gate into the large courtyard garden of the apartment block behind it—'we will also be taking over a vacant ground floor apartment in Grove Court itself. It's not quite opposite Mary's back gate but just to the left, *here* ... and has a good line of sight to her property. Again, there's no way anyone will be able to get in through her back gate or over her fence without being seen. He'd have to get through the security gates to access the apartment block courtyard first, plus Mary's back gate will of course be locked too. So access from the rear is probably even harder than from the street at the front.'

He stands back, scanning the board. He doesn't think he's left anything out, so he turns expectantly to Steph, who's still standing at the back of the room, her face expressionless.

'And I think that's it, ma'am. If he does show his face, I can't see how we won't be able to nab him.'

Jess turns to look at Steph too.

'What do you think?' she asks.

Steph remains silent for a few seconds, staring at the board. Then she exhales.

'I think we're ready,' she says.

Chapter 39

Tuesday 30th March

I'm starting to feel sick. It's Tuesday afternoon, and there are now approximately thirty-three hours to get through until the 1st of April officially begins. Suddenly, it's starting to feel real. All day, my house has been crawling with people fitting bullet-proof panels over the windows, nailing the loft hatch shut, wiring in panic buttons and generally making me feel more unsettled by the minute, although I'm fully aware that they're trying to make me feel the complete opposite.

'Peace of mind, eh?' a plump, smiling shaven-headed man in a blue boiler suit said with a wink, as he lumbered down the stairs carrying a toolbox. I have no idea how much these people know about what's really going on here; I suspect the police haven't given them many details, and that they think I'm some sort of paranoid security obsessive, but I'm not asking them any questions and they're simply getting on with their jobs, clearly following orders not to bother me. I'm not sure what the neighbours are thinking about what's going on, but as I don't really know any of them apart from

Dinah next door, I don't really care, and I pre-warned Dinah, simply telling her I was having a little overdue maintenance work done on the house and saying I hoped she wouldn't be disturbed too much.

I did put my foot down when hidden cameras and listening devices were mooted though. I don't mind all the other measures they're putting in place; I welcome them, because with everything that's being done I really can't see how anyone is going to get anywhere near me. But if he does, somehow – *if* – I can't risk the police being able to overhear our conversation. As for Pete, my only plan is still to play it by ear. Scream at him to go and get help, maybe, so the killer and I are briefly left alone? I know there won't be much time anyway, maybe only a minute or so, if someone does get into the house, before the police are swarming in. So hopefully, telling him what I need to tell him will stall him just long enough ...

So, no cameras and no bugs in the house. I told Jess I simply couldn't handle being watched and listened to in my own home, not on top of everything else. I told her the very idea was making me feel panicky, and she spoke to DCI Warden and some of the other senior officers and they agreed not to fit anything except panic buttons. Pete backed me up too – he insisted on being there when I had the conversation with Jess, and he told her that we both felt quite strongly that there was no need for what he called 'spyware' inside the house. He's not here at the moment; he told me earlier, yet *again*, that today is, finally, the day he's going to end things with Megan because yes, surprise surprise, they're still together. I've given up asking him about it now, fed up with his vague explanations as to why he's still been continuing to put it off. We haven't slept together again since the night of the fish and chips; I haven't seen that much of him, actually, over the past couple of weeks. He's been incredibly busy at work, and then had to spend a few days in London at an Accountants Association conference, so I've been trying to keep busy too, arranging a few nights out with the guys from The Hub, getting my head down to finish the Diary Killer article as far as I can, researching some new stories to get my teeth into when this is all over.

If I'm still alive.

The thought still creeps into my head from time to time, but I resolutely push it away, trying to stay in the moment. Pete left for Megan's half an hour ago; he said he'll be home as soon as he's told her it's over, but I'm not holding my breath. In the meantime, I'm skulking in the kitchen, where the men and women tramping around the house have already finished their work. I can hear them upstairs though, somebody hammering in the lounge directly above, and the whine of an electric drill in the main bathroom on the landing. I run the tap and fill a glass with water, then sip it as I stand by the window, staring out into the quiet street. My gaze rests for a few moments on the windows of the top floor flat opposite, where I know the police have set up some sort of surveillance station, but there's no sign of any activity; the curtains are open but the spaces between them are empty and dark.

I thought the bullet-proof panels fitted over my windows might impede my view of the outside world, but I'm relieved to see that they don't; they seem to be made of some sort of acrylic or polycarbonate, and they're crystal clear.

'Virtually indestructible,' said the young woman who fitted them earlier, standing back and scrutinising her work with obvious pride. 'Bullets, storm damage, repeated high-force impacts – none are a match for these.'

She wiped her hands on her overalls, nodded at me, and marched out of the room. She was a tiny woman, probably not even thirty, with blonde hair in two bouncy pigtails, and it gave me a moment of pleasure to see the obvious satisfaction she took in what was really a most unusual job. I get to keep her handiwork in place afterwards, too, apparently; a nice little bonus, I suppose, although I'm not sure how much it will add to the value of the house. I doubt bullet- and bomb-proof glass is on many home-buyers' wish lists, to be honest.

I'm still staring absent-mindedly out of the window, smiling as an elderly lady in a bright-blue coat walks slowly past, a fat poodle in a matching doggie jacket that looks as if it may have been hand-knitted ambling behind her. And then …

I gasp, and slowly back away from the glass.

Is that …? It is! It's bloody Edward Cooper, walking along the pavement. What's he doing here, in my street, in the middle of the afternoon? I think, and back away further, aware that my breathing has quickened.

Outside, three or four metres away, Edward has stopped walking. He's wearing running gear, trainers and black leggings, and a fitted black hoodie, and he reaches into a pocket and pulls out a piece of paper. He glances at it, looks at my house, then shoves the paper back into his pocket. And now he's walking again, getting closer, until at the end of the short path that leads from the pavement to my front door he pauses, eyes narrowing, as if he's double-checking he's in the right place. He takes a step closer, then another. And then I hear the front door open, and see one of the workmen step out onto the path. He's holding a phone to his ear, and takes a few steps away from the house, maybe trying to get away from all the noise, the hammering and the drilling, because he turns and tilts his head towards the first-floor lounge window, frowning as he does so, then carries on talking. On the pavement, Edward has frozen, staring at the man, an uncertain look on his face. As I watch, he looks over his shoulder, then back at the house and the man standing outside it. And then, as if he's suddenly made a decision, he turns and begins to jog quickly down the road, not looking back. Seconds later he's disappeared, out of sight.

What was that?

I realise I've been holding my breath, and exhale, relief flooding through me.

He was definitely coming here, wasn't he? He only changed his mind because that man appeared. What did he want? Was he hoping to find me here alone? And how did he even get my address?

I don't like this. I don't like this *at all*. Wishing desperately that Pete would hurry up and come back, I decide to call Jess.

The poor woman's going to think I'm absolutely bonkers, I think, as I wait for her to pick up. *She'll think I'm obsessed with Edward and Satish.*

But that *was* weird, right? For him to suddenly appear outside my house, clearly about to knock on the door, only to change his mind and scurry away again? That's not normal behaviour. If he wanted to talk to me about something, he could have just called me, couldn't he? Why somehow sneakily acquire my address, and just turn up out of the blue?

'Hi Mary. How's it going there?'

'Jess! Yes, the work's all going fine, as far as I can tell. They're all very pleasant and efficient. But Jess, that's not what I'm calling about ...'

I tell her, and she's silent for a few moments as she always is when I ring her to report something like this, clearly thinking about it.

'Well, nothing actually happened, did it?' she says. 'He just went away. I agree it's a bit strange, but with all the security measures you're going to have in place by the end of today I really don't think you have anything to worry about. Maybe he was out for a run and just happened to find himself in your street? Maybe he thought about popping in to see you and then changed his mind? And in your current completely understandably rather anxious state you put two and two together and made six? Try to relax, Mary. Look, you've got your panic buttons now, so feel free to use them at any point if you feel there's an imminent threat, OK?'

'OK. Yes, I will. Sorry, Jess. And thank you. I'll see you soon.'

I end the call, feeling slightly better. The panic buttons *do* give me more peace of mind, but I still think I'm right about Edward. Whatever Jess may think, he wasn't just out for a run and happened to end up in The Grove. He was *definitely* on his way here. But he's gone now, and I need to get through this day somehow, to occupy my mind with something else. I settle down on the sofa at the far end of the kitchen and scroll through the TV movie channels, settling on a cheesy American film about a young woman raised by her single parent mother in New York, who then discovers her long-lost father is a British aristocrat. By the time it's over, the work in the house has also been completed, the team waving and smiling as they say goodbye and leaving me greatly impressed that the place looks immaculate, every speck of dust neatly swept up, every piece of furniture that had to be moved perfectly back in position. Then I check the time, and frown. It's after six, and Pete *still* isn't home. I don't want to call or text because I know he's obviously busy, but ...

How on earth can it be taking this long? What's he doing?

I sigh, despairing of the whole situation, and then hear my stomach growl and realise to my surprise that I'm actually quite hungry, so I find a barbecue chicken pizza in the freezer and turn the oven on. I eat my dinner in front of the TV upstairs, sipping a glass of merlot, and then drink more wine as I watch three episodes of the latest series of *Married at First Sight* back to back. At ten, I give up on Pete and go to bed, head swimming from the alcohol and the stress of it all, and I fall asleep quickly, only to jolt upright sometime later, knowing I've heard a door slam somewhere downstairs. My heart is thumping, my eyes wide as they scan the dark room, terrified that somebody's there, waiting to pounce. It's nearly midnight, and for a moment, almost rigid with fear, my hand hovers near the panic button that's discreetly hidden on the side of my bedside table. But then I hear footsteps on the stairs, and the familiar click as Pete's bedroom door opens and then gently closes.

Pete. It's just Pete. He's home, finally, I think, and I slump back onto my pillows, my heart rate slowing. I hear him moving around, the toilet in his en suite bathroom flushing, and then there's silence. I pull the duvet tightly around me and fall back into an uneasy sleep, dreaming of shadowy figures floating past my house, and the scream of a siren, loud at first and then fading away into the distance, the shadows melting away as the sound does, until all is calm and quiet once more.

Chapter 40

Wednesday 31st March

I think I now have some small inkling of what it must feel like to be a prisoner on Death Row, counting down the hours to execution. It's just after eleven in the morning, just under thirteen hours until the 1st of April officially begins, and I suddenly feel as if I want to make a bucket list; to spend the next thirteen hours doing all the things I love to do, just in case.

'I should have done it sooner! I should have been doing this for *weeks*. Why didn't I do that? What's wrong with me?' I say to Pete, and he rolls his eyes.

'Don't be ridiculous. You don't need a bucket list. You're *not* going to die tomorrow, OK? But if it makes you feel better, let's do something nice this afternoon. We're going to be cooped up here for long enough over the next day or so. So come on, what's on your silly list?'

'Erm, well, I don't really have one,' I say, feeling a little foolish. 'I was just wishing that I *had* made one, ages ago ...'

Pete looks at me with an exasperated expression.

'Right. Well, you always love going to the Farm Park. So, come on. We'll go there for the afternoon, get some fresh air and have tea and cake in the café. And then lockdown. Sound like a plan?'

I nod.

'It does. It sounds like the *perfect* plan. Thanks, Pete. I'll just run up and get my jacket.'

I take the stairs two at a time, suddenly desperate to get out of the house. I'm still experiencing waves of dread about what's to come, but I'm trying to take today hour by hour, minute by minute, savouring every moment of the time we have left before midnight strikes.

I'm like Cinderella's twisted sister, I think, as I put my phone, some cash, and a lip balm into my favourite tan leather handbag and pull a lightly padded navy jacket from its hanger. It's a dry, sunny spring day but there's a chill in the air, winter still nipping at April's heels.

Cinderella's carriage turns into a pumpkin and her ballgown to rags at midnight. I become a potential murder victim, and risk having to reveal that my entire identity, my whole life, is a lie.

I shiver, and pull my jacket on, turning the collar up and fastening the buttons, trying to focus on having a nice afternoon with Pete. We still haven't really talked about him and Megan, and how yesterday went.

'You got back late last night,' I said casually, as we drank coffee together in the kitchen earlier, me still in my dressing gown, hair in a messy bun, him in his running gear, saying he needed a caffeine injection before his daily ten kilometres.

'How did it go? How did she take it?'

He sighed, forefinger rubbing at a little mark on the countertop.

'Not well,' he said, frowning at the mark. 'It took … it took longer than I thought it would. Lots of *discussion*. But it's over. For good. Time for a new start.'

He looked up and his lovely eyes met mine, and for a few moments we just sat there, staring at each other. Then he said, 'Can we talk about it another time? Let's get the next twenty-four hours out of the way first. I'm going for my run. I'll see you later.'

He glugged down the last of his coffee, leapt from his seat and left, leaving me to wonder how Megan had managed to make discussions about Pete wanting to split up with her last for … *how long was he gone? Eight, nine hours?*

I hope she's OK though, I think now, as I run back downstairs, ready for our afternoon out. It's never nice, going through a break-up, and she did seem to be very fond of Pete. But he's right; we just need to get through tonight, and tomorrow. There'll be plenty of time for worrying about everything else later, and right now he's waiting for me in the hall, car keys dangling from a finger.

'I'll drive,' he says.

We have, almost to my surprise considering how much we both have on our minds, a very pleasant afternoon. The Farm Park is an easy fifteen-mile drive from Cheltenham, and it's quiet on this Wednesday afternoon in term time, so when we've parked and bought our tickets we find just a handful of people wandering the paths between the paddocks. We do a circuit of the rare-breeds trail, smiling at the antics of the Golden Guernsey goats and admiring the ball-shaped hats of feathers atop the heads of the Crested Ducks. We buy cow-shaped handmade chocolates in the gift shop, and sit by the window in the café, drinking Earl Grey tea and eating lemon drizzle cake, and watching Herdwick lambs running around under the watchful eyes of their mothers, their black, teddy-bear-like faces almost smiling. At four, we finally decide we should call it a day, and we drive home in silence, both of us lost in thought.

Minutes after we get back, Jess is at the front door, carrying a large cardboard box which she thrusts towards me.

'We know it's going to be a long night, and a long day tomorrow too, potentially,' she says. 'So we thought this lot might come in handy. Call it a little thank you from the team for what you're about to do, Mary.'

'Gosh. Thank you. What is it?'

I put the box down on the floor of the hall and crouch to open it, Pete peering curiously over my shoulder.

'Wow!' he exclaims. 'Is that Stinking Bishop? I can smell it from here! That's my favourite cheese in the whole world. How did you know?'

I wrinkle my nose. The box is packed with delicious-looking food: a bag of saltine crackers, a little tray of cured meats, a jar of blackberry and apple chutney and another of almond-stuffed olives, a box of stem ginger biscuits, a truckle of Isle of Mull cheddar, and, yes, definitely Stinking Bishop. It's a local cheese, named after the pear variety used to make the perry that the cheese is washed in. Its flavour is actually reported to be surprisingly creamy and delicate, but it has such a pungent odour that I've never been able to get close enough to try it. Pete, on the other hand, is obsessed, gleeful every time he comes across it for sale at a farmers' market or spots it on a restaurant menu.

'*I* flipping told her how much you love it a few weeks ago,' I say, standing up again. 'We were chatting about picnics for some reason, and you asked me what my favourite snacks were, didn't you Jess? I mentioned it then, as one of my *least* favourite things, but I said how much you loved the smelly old stuff. Very sneaky, Jess. Very sneaky indeed. But thank you so much. This is far too much.'

Jess is smiling, two spots of high colour on her cheekbones.

'You deserve it,' she says. 'You've been brilliant through all of this. We know it hasn't been easy. But it's nearly over now. Let's just see what happens over the next twenty-four hours or so. If he dares to show his face, and we can bring the murdering bastard in, well ...'

'We'll think of this as a last supper then,' says Pete, then winces as I punch him in the arm.

'Pete! Don't even joke about it, please,' I say, and his face contorts apologetically.

'Bad joke,' he says. 'Is everything in place, Jess? Everyone at their posts for midnight?'

'If they're not already, they will be soon,' Jess replies, glancing over her shoulder at the house opposite. 'I'll be across the road with Steph and a few of the others. Are you both happy? You know what to do if anything – and I mean *anything* – happens?'

'We do. We've been well briefed,' I say. 'Steph's come round to go over it with me at least three times now, and Pete's heard it all twice. All good.'

We stand there for a few moments, looking at each other, and then Jess suddenly takes a step forwards and before I know what's happening, she's wrapped her arms around me and pulled me in for a hug.

'Good luck, Mary,' she whispers, before quickly releasing me again, her cheeks even more flushed now.

A little startled by the unexpected physical contact, but touched too, I reach out a hand and squeeze her arm.

'Thank you, Jess. For everything. And good luck to you guys too. It might be a long night.'

'We'll see. Take care, right? Both of you. See you on the other side.'

She nods at Pete, then turns and quickly walks away, heading for her car which I can see parked a little further down the street.

We watch her go, then Pete says:

'That was ... well, quite nice, really, wasn't it? Are you all right? I'll unpack this lot. Time to double-lock the door and get this party started, I think.'

He bends down and scoops up the box, and I nod.

'I'm OK. I might go and have a soak, actually. I'll see you in a bit.'

'Good idea. I'll be up in the lounge. See you shortly.'

He's already marching down the hall, heading for the kitchen. I turn back to the front door, making sure that it's locked and bolted, then walk slowly up the stairs to the second floor and head for my en suite bathroom. I turn the taps on and scan the row of bath oils on the shelf next to the window, finally selecting lavender and jasmine. I normally find the fragrance relaxing, but I'm not sure it will work today; the strangest feeling has begun sweeping over me. It started as I watched Jess turn and walk away, and it's intensifying. As I strip off my clothes and climb into the warm water, sinking into it and breathing deeply as it laps around my shoulders, I'm trying desperately to stay calm.

Come on, Mary. Pete is here with you, I tell myself. *And we're surrounded by a huge safety net. Nothing bad can happen, nothing at all.*

And yet the bad feeling is still getting worse. The back of my throat is aching, and I have a chill deep inside my chest despite the warmth of my bath. I'm surrounded by people who want to help me. And yet I feel completely alone, I suddenly realise.

Why? Why do I suddenly feel like this? As if there's actually no one who can really help me at all. As if whatever happens next is *entirely* down to me. There are tears running down my cheeks now, dripping from my chin and mingling with the lavender-scented water, and I let them flow, lying there sobbing until the bath cools and I start to shiver. Then I clamber out, get dressed again, and head back down to the lounge.

Chapter 41

Thursday 1st April

Tick. Tick. Tick.

There's a big digital clock on the mantelpiece in the lounge of number 18 The Grove, and Jess is watching it, mesmerised.

23.57.

23.58.

23.59.

00.00.

'It's midnight,' she whispers, then wonders *why* she's whispering, and repeats the words again in a normal voice.

'It's midnight. Here we go, then.'

They all look at each other, just about able to see each other's faces in the dark room, illuminated only by the streetlights outside. There are five of them in the first-floor flat, normally a part-furnished rental that's currently unoccupied, the landlord more than happy to let the police pay a handsome sum to take it over for a couple of days. The lounge is at the front, directly opposite the first-floor lounge of Mary

Ellis's house across the road, but it couldn't be more different to her bright, spacious room; it has an ancient grey carpet, stained and fraying, and its only furniture is a small dining table with two rickety wooden chairs and a sagging brown leather sofa. They'd brought their own with them: fold-up chairs and tables to put their equipment on; a kettle, toaster, and microwave to use in the small galley kitchen. There's no central heating, just an old four-bar electric heater sitting in the blocked-up fireplace, but the room still feels stuffy, Steph groaning that she couldn't stand it and cracking open the windows an hour ago, just enough to allow a hint of the cool night breeze to float in.

'Here we go indeed,' she says now. She and DI Mike Stanley are sitting at the window, staring at the street below. Behind them, Jess and two other officers – she's only just met them today, but their names are James and Miriam and both seem efficient and experienced – are getting regular updates from the other surveillance sites, those on adjoining streets and in the Grove Court apartment at the rear of Mary's house. So far, there's been no activity out there whatsoever, other than a few late-night dog walkers and the occasional couple ambling past, none of them approaching or even looking at number 21 The Grove. But then, thinks Jess, nobody was *expecting* any activity, not before midnight. But now ... well, now it's the 1st of April, and she can feel the sudden tension in the air, can hear Mike shifting in his chair, can see Steph wiping the back of her hand across her brow.

She's nervous, she thinks. *We're all nervous, aren't we? And I can't even imagine what Mary's feeling like ...*

'Anyone want a coffee?' she says. She has the sudden urge to get up and do something, to get out of this dark room for a few minutes and busy herself in the bright kitchen.

'Thanks, that would be good,' Steph replies over her shoulder, and there are murmurs of 'yes, please, thanks Jess' from the others too, so she gratefully stands up and leaves the room, walking down the short corridor with one cramped bedroom and a tiny bathroom leading off it and opening the door to the kitchen with its cracked worktop and 70s-style tiles.

'They have lobsters on them. Who wants lobster tiles in their kitchen?' she'd hissed to Mike when they'd first toured the flat, and he'd grinned.

'Hey, how do shellfish get to the hospital?' he'd replied, and she'd frowned.

'What?'

'In a clambulance,' he'd said with a snigger, then ducked as she pretended she was about to throttle him. She smiles now as she remembers the terrible joke, checking the water level in the kettle and switching it on.

'Shit! Shit! Look!'

She turns as she hears the low, urgent exclamation from the lounge, and seconds later she's back in there, seeing all four of the others gathered at the window, peering down into the street.

'What? What's going on?'

Mike's leaning forwards, binoculars pressed to his eyes.

'There's somebody outside the door,' he says quietly. 'They just walked quickly down the street from the north end and down the path. They're wearing dark clothes and a hoodie, so

I can't even tell if it's a man or a woman, but I think they've just rung the doorbell ...'

'It's very late for a casual caller,' says James. 'After midnight on a Wednesday night? But do we really think our killer's going to just ring the doorbell?'

'He did in Birmingham, remember? With Jane Holland,' says Mike. 'Although, to be fair, she wasn't expecting him. We *are*, so ... what do you want to do, boss?'

'Hold fire, just for a minute,' Steph replies. She's staring intently through her own binoculars, her jawline tense. 'There's a spyhole in the front door, so they won't open it if they don't recognise— Oh, hang on ...'

Jess, who's just reached for her own binoculars and is trying to focus them, hears Mike gasp. The front door is opening slowly, and then they can see Pete Chong standing there, the lights on in the hallway behind him. The figure on the doorstep is clearly talking, gesticulating, and Pete stands there, listening, and then quickly glances over his shoulder. Then he turns back to the visitor and says something.

'Bloody hell!' says Mike. 'Is he ...?'

She hears a low whistle from James.

'He is,' he says. 'He's letting them in.'

Across the street, the visitor steps into the house, and the door closes.

Chapter 42

Thursday 1st April

'It's OK! It's just Megan! We're coming up,' calls Pete from the hall, and I let out a long, shaky breath.

Megan? What the hell is she doing here? And why on earth did Pete let her in? I think, even as my head swims with relief. We were still awake, of course, sitting in the lounge as instructed, the TV showing some late-night comedy hour that we weren't really watching. We'd put together a cheese board to nibble on after dinner, with the cheddar and Stinking Bishop Jess had brought round, and we'd opened a bottle of shiraz, but neither of us really felt like drinking, taking only a few sips before pushing our glasses away.

'I'm not feeling it tonight, are you?' Pete muttered, and I nodded in agreement, although I noted with some amusement that he still wolfed down a generous portion of his smelly cheese.

When the doorbell rang, just after midnight, my heart practically leapt into my throat, my body involuntarily curling into a ball on the sofa, pressing into the cushions as if I was trying to vanish inside the fabric. Pete hesitated for a moment, locking eyes with me, before he jumped to his feet and headed for the door.

'Pete! No!' I shouted after him, but he was already halfway down the stairs, calling:

'I'm just going to see who it is. I won't open it!'

Now he appears in the doorway looking a little sheepish, Megan a couple of steps behind him.

She looks dreadful, I think. She's wearing black skinny jeans and a plain navy hoodie, and as she walks into the room she pulls the hood down, revealing unbrushed hair and red-rimmed eyes, puffy from crying.

'Sorry, Mary, but ...'

Pete gestures at his now ex-girlfriend, and I nod. I can't be angry, not with her in this state.

'Come in and sit down, Megan,' I say gently. 'Are you OK? Would you like a drink or something?'

She shakes her head, then looks at Pete.

'I just wanted ... I just wanted to speak to Pete. I'm really upset. I went for a long walk, and I just ended up here somehow ...'

She walked? From Prestbury? It's miles, I think.

Her words sound slightly slurred, and I realise that she's been drinking, a faint smell of alcohol now obvious. She sniffs, and a tear runs down her cheek, but she doesn't seem to notice.

'I didn't want us to split up, and I just wanted to see if ...'

Her voice breaks, and she sinks slowly onto the opposite end of the sofa and begins to cry quietly.

Bloody hell, I think.

Pete is still standing, shifting his weight from one foot to the other, looking from me to Megan and back again as if he has no idea what to do next. He looks pale, almost as if he's in shock. I'm about to tell him to say *something*, for goodness' sake, when from somewhere a mobile phone starts to ring shrilly, making us both jump. Megan, still sobbing, face buried in her hands, doesn't even look up, and I scan the room, seeing Pete's phone on the side table, its screen flashing. He grabs it.

'Hello? Oh, I'm so sorry, I should have thought ... yes, it's fine, it's just Megan, my girlfriend ... well, my ex now, we've just split up and ... yes, I know, but she's really upset, and I thought just for a few minutes ... yes, yes, OK. I understand. Thanks. Speak later.'

He ends the call, and gestures at me to follow him out of the room, pulling the door gently closed behind us.

'That was the police,' he whispers. 'Telling me off for letting her in. But I couldn't leave her on the doorstep, could I? She's clearly drunk and ... well, you know. She looks so bloody sad. The cops aren't happy; they said not to open the door to anyone else, even if we know them. Listen, I'll have a chat with her. I'll try to make her feel a bit better and let her sober up a bit, and then I'll call her a cab – is that OK? Could you give us a few minutes?'

I sigh.

'Sure,' I whisper back. 'Just let me grab my phone and I'll go down and make a pot of strong coffee. She looks as if she might need it.'

'You're the best,' Pete says quietly, and he takes my right

hand in his and presses it to his mouth for a second, before releasing it again.

'Oh shush,' I say, but I can still feel the soft pressure of his lips on my skin, and I feel a little flutter of pleasure.

He smiles, and together we walk back into the lounge. As we do so, Megan turns to look at us, and to my surprise she's no longer crying. Slowly, she stands up, her eyes narrowing, and I see a strange expression flash across her face.

'Very cosy, you two,' she says coldly.

'What? Don't be silly, Megan. We're just worried about you,' I say, trying to keep my tone light, but she takes a step towards me, then another, and as I look at her, puzzled, her face suddenly contorts with rage and then she's reaching for me, fingers curling as she stretches out her arms, hands moving towards my neck.

'You bitch!' she spits, and I feel a lurch of fear.

What is she doing?

I feel her long nails graze my skin, and I step backwards.

'Megan!' I screech. 'What's wrong with you?'

I look desperately at Pete, but he's standing there motionless, as if in a trance, eyes fixed on his ex-girlfriend, and a sudden, horrifying suspicion slams into my brain.

It couldn't be. Could it?

Suddenly it's as if everything's happening in slow motion. Megan's still coming towards me, her beautiful face twisted into an ugly snarl, but my mind is racing, thoughts whirling through my head.

Is it possible?

Think, Mary. Think. Could Megan be the Diary Killer? The

way she's acted towards me recently ... where was she on the nights of the other murders? I have no idea what she did on New Year's Eve, but ...

I gasp, the thoughts still churning even as I take another step backwards, my fear spiking now, trying to get away from her. I remember the night of Jane Holland's murder, when Pete took a late-night call from Megan and headed off to be with her. I think about how they were together again on the night of David Howells's murder, and how Pete didn't call me until much later than planned the following morning, telling me his work plans had changed at short notice. A little whimper escapes me.

Could he be in on it too?

I think about how he told me he'd come with me if I was moved to a safehouse. How he insisted on staying here with me tonight. How he was so vocal about having no cameras or listening devices in the house. Was all that so he could *kill* me? Suddenly, I think I'm going to be sick. The fear is paralysing.

No, please, no. Could they really be in it together? Is that why he kept saying he was going to finish with her, and then didn't? Is it really over now at all? Or is this all part of a plan? Her turning up here acting all upset so I'd be OK about him letting her in? Oh shit, SHIT. Am I crazy? Am I imagining all this? But if I'm not, why isn't Pete doing anything? Why isn't he stopping her?

'PETE! Help me!'

He still appears to be frozen to the spot, his face looking even paler than it did a few minutes ago, his eyes wide, but my scream seems to jolt him into action.

'MEGAN!'

He jumps forwards and grabs her around the waist, pulling her backwards, away from me.

'MEGAN! What the hell are you doing?' he shouts.

For a few moments, she struggles violently, hands still clawing the air, trying to get closer to me. Then, quite suddenly, her body goes limp.

'Sorry ... I'm so sorry,' she gasps. 'I've had a few drinks. I just thought that you two ... I didn't mean to ...'

And now she's crying again, tears streaming down her cheeks, her slender shoulders heaving. She turns in Pete's arms, and buries her face in his chest, and he looks at me helplessly.

'What do I do?' he mouths.

I'm shaking from head to toe, and I stare at him. I have no idea what to say, no idea what's going on here.

Can I trust him?

But he just saved me, didn't he? I think, frantically. *He must be still on my side; he must be. And Megan ... she's just drunk, that's all. Neither of them is the killer; they can't be. I'm being ridiculous. I've got this all wrong ...*

I swallow hard.

Calm down. Act normal.

'Deal. With. It,' I mouth back, and I pick up my phone from the arm of the sofa and leave the room. But I'm still shaking as I stagger downstairs, and when I make it to the kitchen I lean on the counter for a long time, trying to stabilise my heart rate, breathing slowly and deeply.

Keep it together, I tell myself. *Of course Pete and Megan aren't involved in any of this. Don't get paranoid, not now. Get a bloody grip, woman.*

302

I inhale again, exhale slowly, and look at the clock on the microwave. It's 12.25am and I feel exhausted, wobbly from the adrenaline that's just surged through my body. I get myself a glass of water and sit down, but the thoughts are still racing through my mind.

Pete was definitely away on the nights of Jane and David's murders. With Megan, or so he said. But what about New Year's Eve? He was in Dublin on New Year's Eve, visiting his mother, wasn't he? He wasn't in Oxford, murdering Lisa Turner. But how do I know he was in Dublin, really? Have I ever seen any photos, any evidence?

I can't remember, and I can feel a tight little knot of fear forming again, low in my belly.

He'd visited Jane's casino a few weeks before she died. And both he and Megan are runners ...

'No! No, stop it!'

I shout the words then stand up, take a few steps towards the door, and stop, breathing heavily.

This is ludicrous. All this stuff is just coincidence. Pete and Megan were dating; it stands to reason they're going to spend lots of nights together. And what possible reason would either of them have for killing all of those people, or for wanting to kill me? Pete just stepped in to stop her attacking me, for goodness' sake ...

'Stop it. Just *stop*. It's not them; it's not,' I say out loud. 'Pete's my *friend*. More than a friend now, maybe. Stop this. Think *properly*.'

Suddenly, I'm a little calmer.

It's just stress, messing with my head, I know it is. The

pressure of all this, it's bound to have an effect. I can't let it do this to me. I won't. *Just make some coffee, come on …*

Then from upstairs, I hear the lounge door open, and moments later, the click of Pete's bedroom door as it opens and then closes again.

Why have they gone into his room?

I feel a fresh ripple of panic. For a few seconds, I stand stock still, listening, but all I can hear is a soft murmur, two voices in conversation, and I take another deep breath, willing the panic away.

It's OK. Everything's OK. They just want somewhere private to chat, I think. *Stop bloody over-reacting. He'll talk to her, we'll get her a cab, and then it'll be just us again. Everything's fine. You're going to have a heart attack if you carry on like this.*

I listen for a few more seconds, then turn and walk back to the coffee machine.

Chapter 43

Thursday 1st April

DI Mike Stanley leans back in his chair with a soft groan, and glances at the clock on the mantelpiece. 1.45am. They've just watched a taxi pull up outside number 21 opposite, and the woman they now know to be Peter Chong's ex-girlfriend clamber into it. Mary called Steph half an hour ago, explaining that the woman, Megan Walker, had been distraught after Chong ended their relationship and had come round in an inebriated state wanting to talk things through.

'She was in a bad way – she lunged at me at one point, and for a moment I thought ... Well, anyway, Pete stopped her, and it's all fine. She's just come downstairs, and I've given her some coffee and she seems calmer now,' she said. She was making the call from the downstairs toilet, she said, leaving Megan to finish her drink in the kitchen.

'Pete's having a lie down, apparently. He looked really drained earlier. I think it's taken the stuffing out of him a bit, her turning up like that. He's in his room, and yes, I know we agreed to stay together in the lounge for the night but I'll

Jackie Kabler

just leave him to rest for a few minutes and then I'll go and wake him up, don't worry. And I've ordered Megan a cab, so don't panic when you see it stopping outside, OK?'

The taxi has left now, and the street is quiet once more, a light rain falling, spattering the windows. There've still been no reports of any unusual activity from anywhere nearby, and even though they're less than two hours into the day, Mike's starting to wonder yet again if all this is a waste of time. He knows it has to be done – of course it does. This killer has been true to his word with all the other dates and all the other victims. But to give Mary three months' notice, and still turn up to try and kill her? He just can't see it happening, and he can already feel boredom setting in.

'Tell us a story, boss,' he says suddenly.

Steph, sitting to his right, turns to look at him, and even in the darkness he can see the surprised expression on her face.

'Pardon? How old are you, five?' she says.

He laughs.

'Not a bedtime story. Tell us about some of the big cases you worked on before you transferred to Gloucestershire. Go on, to pass the time. You had a couple of serial killers, didn't you? Tell us about the one in Manchester. The Ashford Mall killer?'

'Oooh yes, go on,' says James, and Miriam, who's been sitting at the back of the room, pulls her chair a little closer to the others.

'Think you might have to now, Steph,' says Jess, and Mike can hear the smile in her voice.

Steph sighs.

306

'OK, but keep your eyes on the road, and one ear on your comms, all of you, OK? We can't forget what we're here to do, even if it does seem eerily quiet out there at the moment.'

She clears her throat.

'It was the second serial killer case I'd been assigned to. Five victims. I'm sure you all know the basics – it was all over the news back then. Builders were working on a big, new out-of-town shopping centre, the Ashford Mall, and suddenly they're digging up bodies. Three at first. Two of them were later identified as sex workers who'd gone missing a couple of years before; the third was a man, an older guy in his sixties or seventies. We still don't know who he is to this day, which has always bugged me.'

She pauses, leaning forwards in her chair as there's a sudden movement in the street below.

'It's just a fox,' says Mike quietly, and Steph gives a soft laugh as the creature scurries across the road, pausing to snuffle at the patch of grass outside Mary's next-door neighbour's house before scampering away down the road.

'Anyway, there was little in the way of forensic evidence – the building site had been flooded a number of times over the previous two winters, which hadn't helped. But we did find that all the victims had a matching injury, and *this* wasn't ever made public: they all had a broken finger on their left hand. The ring finger.'

'Wow,' whispers James. 'Weird.'

'That rang a bell for me,' Steph continues.

Her voice and the rhythmic *tick, tick, tick* of the clock are the only sounds in the shadowy room, four pairs of eyes fixed on her silhouette in the window.

'I remembered a rape case, a year or so before, in Leeds. The victim wasn't killed, but she was beaten and the ring finger of her left hand was broken. She had other broken bones too – her nose, a couple of ribs – but I got hold of her statement, and she said her attacker had deliberately chosen that finger to break. She described how he gripped her hand between his knees and then carefully lifted her ring finger and snapped it.'

'Oh my God. Poor woman,' says Miriam.

'Pretty horrific, yes,' says Steph. 'But her rapist had been caught, and was already in prison ...'

'Cole Carter,' says James. 'I remember. Evil-looking bastard.'

'That's him,' says Steph. 'So we talked to him. He denied murdering anyone, of course, even when we pointed out the finger thing. But then we spoke to his cellmate, who told us that Carter had told him stories about his big back garden in Manchester, where he'd buried a load of bodies. The guy didn't believe him at first, but when he heard we were questioning him, he thought he should share. And it turned out that some years before, Carter had lived in a bedsit adjoining the waste ground that became the site for the Ashford Mall. That piece of ground was, apparently, what he referred to as his back garden.'

'Bloody hell.' James lets out a low whistle.

'Indeed. So we carried on digging and found two more bodies. Two more missing sex workers. Same broken fingers. And this time one of them was much more recent – he must have killed her just before he was arrested for the rape. We were able to find DNA evidence, and matched it to Carter. When we confronted him, he broke down and told us everything. He couldn't understand how he'd been caught – that was the weirdest thing. He didn't seem to realise that blabbing to a cellmate *and* leaving a calling card like that on every victim *and* leaving DNA at the scene might be a bit of a giveaway. Quite stupid really. You expect serial killers to be a bit brighter, don't you?'

There's silence in the room for few moments, broken only by the sound of a car driving slowly past outside.

'Shame we didn't get one of the stupid ones, isn't it?' says Miriam. 'We get one who's already got three police forces baffled. Four, if you count us.'

'Well, the game's not over yet,' says Mike. 'There's a long day ahead. Did you ever find out *why* he broke their fingers, by the way, boss?'

Steph shakes her head.

'No. He would never say. Now, enough bedtime stories. Mike, can you give Mary and Pete a buzz, check everything's OK over there now their visitor's gone?'

'Will do.'

Mike picks up the handset on the table next to him and dials Mary's number. He listens as the phone rings and rings, and then clicks onto voicemail.

'Hi, this is Mary Ellis. I'm busy right now, so please leave a message ...'

Strange, he thinks. Frowning, he dials Pete's number. This time, the phone rings for longer, but after thirty seconds or so the same thing happens.

'Hello, Peter Chong isn't available right now ...'

'Uh-oh,' he says. He puts the handset down, scraping a hand across his cropped black hair.

'Guys, I'm not getting an answer from either of their phones. They're just ringing out and going to voicemail.'

'What? Try again,' says Steph.

He does, but the same thing happens, and as he puts the phone down he can feel his scalp beginning to prickle. He clears his throat.

'Boss, they're not answering. I don't know how anything could have happened with so many eyes on the place, but I think something's wrong.'

Chapter 44

Thursday 1st April

When Megan's gone, I quickly tidy up the kitchen and then go back upstairs to find Pete. I don't really like to disturb him if he's having a quick nap – it *is* nearly two in the morning after all – but at the same time I don't really want him to sleep in his room. I'm already feeling anxious at being awake on my own, still jittery from what happened with Megan and the stream of irrational thoughts it triggered. I tap on his door, softly at first and then, hearing nothing, more loudly.

Come on, Pete. Wake up.

I wait a few more seconds – still silence – then sigh and push the door open. He's lying on his back on the bed, still fully dressed, eyes closed.

'Pete. Pete, wake up,' I say quietly. He doesn't move, so I repeat the words, a little louder this time, but he's clearly sound asleep, so I walk over and shake his arm gently.

'Pete! Come on, wakey wakey!'

He doesn't move, not even a flutter of an eyelid, and I stare at him, feeling a little tingle of unease. This isn't like Pete;

I've had to wake him up many times over the years, and he's normally bolt upright as soon as I call his name.

What's wrong with him?

'Pete. Pete, please. You're scaring me. Wake up. PETE!'

Nothing. Starting to feel a bit panicky now, I lean over him, taking his hands and squeezing them, saying his name over and over. And then I pause, listening. His breathing doesn't sound right, I realise; it's too slow, with long gaps between breaths.

'Pete! What's wrong?'

I look frantically around the room, but everything looks the same as it always does.

What's happened to him? Did Megan do something? He's not just asleep, is he?

It's almost as if he's been drugged, and now I can see that his face is even paler than it was earlier, his skin clammy.

'What did you do, Megan? You little cow, if you've done something to hurt him ...'

I scream the words, shaking Pete harder, willing him to open his eyes, but his head just lolls to the side, his mouth slack.

'PETE. PETE, PLEASE. WAKE UP!'

I'm starting to hyperventilate. I can hear a faint musical sound now, a familiar tune playing, far in the distance, and for a moment I think I'm hallucinating, and then I realise it's my mobile phone ringing, downstairs in the kitchen. My phone. I need my phone, I need to call an ambulance, but I don't want to leave Pete. What if he stops breathing? What if he starts choking? His phone; I can use *his* phone, can't I? I whirl around, looking for it, but I can't see it anywhere, not on the bedside table or on the duvet or on the windowsill.

Where is it?

Pete's never without his phone; he's like a teenager in that regard. It's *always* with him; it *must* be here. In his pocket maybe? I pat him down, running my hands over his jeans, even – with a grunt – rolling him onto his side so I can check his back pockets, but it's not there.

'Shit! Where is it, Pete? Where's your bloody phone?'

He doesn't reply, of course.

Did he leave it in the lounge, maybe?

I quickly lean over him again, my ear to his mouth, making sure he's still breathing. Then I run the few steps across the landing to the lounge, checking the coffee table, the sofa, the mantelpiece, but there's still no sign of it.

I'm going to have to go downstairs and get mine. I'm going to have to risk leaving him up here just for a minute, I think, so I run back, light-headed with fear now, check again that he's breathing, then race down the stairs, almost falling down the bottom three steps in my haste.

I've just grabbed my phone from the kitchen worktop and I'm about to dial 999 when I hear the doorbell ring, and I spin around in panic, the phone slipping from my grasp and falling to the floor.

NO! Not now, please! I think, and a wave of dizziness hits me, so intense I think I might actually fall over. I lean heavily against the counter for support, hearing the doorbell ring again, more insistently this time.

Go away. Please. Go. Away.

I realise I'm sobbing and my heart is pounding, little sparks dancing before my eyes, and then suddenly I hear a voice, calling my name from outside the front door. It's faint, but it's a voice I recognise, and relief washes over me.

Jess. It's just Jess. I take a deep breath, and another, and the dizziness starts to recede. A few seconds later I'm in the hall, fumbling with the locks, flinging the door open. I grab Jess by the hand and pull her inside.

'Jess! Oh my God, I'm so glad— It's Pete, there's something wrong, I think it was Megan, we need an ambulance, please ...'

'Mary! Mary, slow down. What are you talking about? What was Megan? Where's Pete?'

She takes both of my hands in hers and forces me to stand still, her expression one of absolute confusion. I gulp in some air, feeling light-headed again, realising I'm not making any sense.

'It's Pete. He's ...'

'Mary, we've been trying to call Pete, *and* you,' she says, interrupting me. 'Neither of you have been answering your phones, that's why Steph sent me over to check that everything's OK. Why haven't you picked up? Breathe, OK. Tell me, slowly.'

'OK. OK, sorry.'

I pause for a couple of seconds, trying to collect my thoughts, but the panic is rising again. I've left Pete up there on his own for too long. What if he's got worse while I've been down here? What if something terrible's happened?

'Something's wrong with Pete. He went for a lie-down and now I can't wake him up, and his breathing's all funny, it's like he's been drugged or something, but I don't even know how that's possible, unless Megan did something to him while she was here ... Oh God, Jess ...'

'Drugged?'

She's still looking at me with a bewildered expression.

'And I did hear my phone, but I was upstairs trying to wake Pete up, and I'd left it down here, and I can't find his anywhere, I looked for it to call an ambulance but it's just vanished, I didn't hear it ringing either ... Jess, please, we need an ambulance ...'

My words are tumbling over each other, my voice shrill with fear, and she nods, seemingly finally understanding.

'Why didn't you use your panic button? OK, never mind. Come on, show me where he is. I'm first aid trained so I'll have a look and yes, if we need an ambulance I can radio ...'

'I forgot, I was freaking out ... Thank you! Thank you so much!'

I wrench my hands from hers and bound up the stairs, feeling like an idiot for forgetting the house is rigged with panic buttons and yelling at her to follow, and seconds later we're both in Pete's room. He hasn't moved, but as I rush over to him, my heart hammering in my chest, I see that his breathing doesn't seem to have worsened, which calms me just a little. I turn to Jess.

'See what I mean? He's unconscious. I'm scared, Jess.'

'OK. Let me just make sure he's stable, and then I'll radio and get an ambulance here right away. Don't panic, all right? I'm sure he'll be fine.'

She walks to the other side of the bed and sits down carefully beside Pete, lifting his eyelids and then putting the back of her hand against his pale cheek, frowning as she does so. She's just begun to check his pulse when the radio on her belt crackles.

'Oscar Sierra One, Oscar Sierra One receiving Oscar Sierra Five, over.'

It's Steph's voice, and my stomach rolls.

Has something else happened?

Still holding Pete's wrist, Jess fumbles at a button on the side of her radio.

'Oscar Sierra Five, go ahead, over,' she says.

'Please confirm all safe and well, over.'

Jess looks at me and hesitates.

'Not really, are we?' she mouths. I shake my head, and Jess releases Pete's hand and says, 'Medical assistance required. Over.'

There's a few seconds of silence, and then Steph's voice again, her tone urgent now.

'I'm coming in. Front door open, please. Over and out.'

Jess looks at me.

'Mary, please go down and open the door. Pete's pulse is very weak – we're going to need that ambulance quickly, OK? You let Steph in and I'll radio for help. Go!'

She leans over Pete, her fingers touching the side of his neck now, checking his pulse again I assume, and a fresh wave of fear swirls in my stomach.

Please don't die. Please don't die. I repeat the words over and over as I stumble down the stairs, tears pricking my eyelids. As soon as I open the door, Steph is pushing past me, her face tense.

'Where is she, Mary?'

'She?' I'm confused.

'You mean Jess?'

I gesture vaguely down the hallway, and Steph looks around and then back at me.

'No, Jess is fine,' I say. 'It's Pete. Something's wrong with him, Steph, and I'm so scared. I think Megan must have drugged him, and we can't wake him up. Jess is calling for an ambulance ...'

'Christ!' Steph runs her hands through her hair, takes a step towards the kitchen and then turns back.

'He's still alive though, right?' she says. She sounds panicked, I realise. She's normally so calm, so focussed, and a shiver runs through me.

Is there something she's not telling me?

'Yes. He's upstairs. Steph, what's wrong?' I say.

She bites her lip, her gaze flitting towards the staircase and then back to me.

'Mary, look, I don't even know how to say this, but I think we've screwed up, big time. I think ... I think it's Jess. Did Pete eat that cheese?'

I wrinkle my brow, wiping the tears from my cheeks with the backs of my hands.

What on earth is she talking about?

'Did Pete eat the *cheese*? The cheese Jess brought? Yes, he had some earlier. I don't understand. What's that got to do with anything? And what do you mean, you think it's Jess? You think *what's* Jess?'

Her hands are in her hair again, fingers clawing at her scalp.

'Oh God, Mary. I mean, I think it might be Jess who's behind all this. Jess who's the killer ...'

'Wh-what?'

What did she just say? No, come on …

She takes a step towards me and presses a finger to her lips. 'Shhhh, please.'

She looks over her shoulder, towards the stairs, then back at me.

'Look, I know it sounds impossible, but hear me out.'

Her voice is low and urgent.

'Think about it. It's something that's been niggling at me for the past day or so, but just now when she volunteered to come over here to see if you two were OK, I don't know … it all makes sense, Mary. She's been so quiet in all of the Operation Shearwater meetings, listening, taking it all in. But what if it was her, all along? She's a runner. She doesn't work nights generally, so she could easily have travelled to all the murder scenes overnight and been back at her desk the next morning. She knows every inch of your house, and all the security measures we've installed. She even said early on that if you wanted to go to a safehouse, she'd go with you, do you remember that?'

I nod, and feel a wave of nausea.

But Jess? Really? I wasn't sure about her at first, but recently … Am I seriously that poor a judge of character?

And then I remember the morning after David's murder in Cardiff, and how I couldn't get hold of Jess, and how when she finally rang me back she told me she'd been late to work because she'd slept through her alarm.

Could the real reason she was late have been because she'd been trying to get back from Cardiff in the early morning traffic?

I feel faint again, black spots dancing in front of my eyes, and I reach for the wall with one hand, trying to steady myself. Steph is still talking, and I force myself to focus on what she's saying.

'That spyware on your computer – the techs said it came in via email, didn't they? You and Jess exchanged emails all the time. And she must have sent that letter in the post too. She knew you were thinking of going abroad and she needed to stop you. She needed you *here*, where she could get to you. And she was so insistent on getting that cheese for Pete – she must have put some sort of drug in it, knowing Pete would eat it and you wouldn't. It was a way to make sure he was indisposed so that she could come in here and kill you without him getting in the way. She knew you'd let her in. It all makes sense, Mary. I'm so sorry. So very sorry. But I'm almost certain—'

My legs buckle.

But why? Why? And … oh God, oh God …

'Pete,' I say weakly. 'She's up there now, on her own with Pete.'

'WHAT? She's with him? Why didn't you say? I assumed she was in the kitchen!'

Steph's eyes widen, and the look of horror in them makes my stomach lurch.

'No, she's upstairs too. She had her hands on his neck as I left the room, and I thought she was just checking his pulse but … what if … what if …?'

'Christ. She's going to try and kill him too, isn't she?'

Steph gives me another anguished look, then turns and runs for the stairs.

Chapter 45

Thursday 1st April

Somehow, I'm moving again, my limbs weak, my hands tingling, my heart beating so hard I can feel it thumping against the wall of my chest. But I'm running now, running up the stairs, just a second behind Steph.

Please, let him be OK. Please.

'Where is he?' Steph yells, as she reaches the landing.

'First on the left,' I shriek, and she lunges for the door. Jess is still sitting on the bed, staring down at Pete, and as we bolt into the room she turns around, looking startled. Terrified, I look at the inert shape on the duvet, and I see that his face, so pale before, is now almost grey, ghostly looking, his lips tinged with blue.

He's dead, isn't he? Pete's dead. No, no ...

'WHAT HAVE YOU DONE TO HIM?'

I scream the words at her, and her eyes widen.

'What? Nothing. I've just—'

She stops talking suddenly, and a horrified expression creeps over her face.

'Steph? What are you ...?'

I turn to see Steph stalking across the room towards the bed, her mouth set in a grim line, right hand raised. In it, she's clutching Pete's tennis trophy, the one he keeps in pride of place on a shelf by his bedroom door, a fond memory of a hard-fought battle with his biggest rival at his former tennis club in London. It's big and heavy, a thick engraved glass panel on a marble base, and as she reaches the bed Steph lifts her arm even higher and then ...

'Oh my *God*!'

I gasp as she smashes the trophy against the side of Jess's head. Instantly, Jess's body crumples, and she collapses onto Pete's chest, blood running down the side of her cheek. She twitches, once, twice, and then stops moving, her lips slightly parted as if she's about to speak, her eyes closed. Appalled, I take a step forwards, and I see a flash of white under the mess of blonde hair and blood.

'Steph ... *Steph*? Is that—? Is that bone? You've shattered her skull! My God ... why?'

Steph is panting slightly, eyes fixed on Jess's slumped body, the trophy still dangling from her hand. She bends down slowly and puts it on the floor, and then straightens up again.

'I had to stop her,' she says. 'She's probably already killed Pete. And you'd have been next, Mary.'

I feel sick suddenly, my legs weak again. I look around the room, but there's nowhere to sit except the bed, and that's already horribly occupied. I swallow hard, trying to quell the nausea.

'But with two of us here ... I mean, we could have

overpowered her between us, couldn't we? You didn't have to *kill* her. And now we'll never know, will we? We'll never know *why*. Why she did it all.'

Steph's eyes are locked on mine, but she doesn't say anything, and for a few seconds there's complete silence. And then I hear a siren, a rhythmic two-tone whine, getting louder, getting closer.

An ambulance? Is that an ambulance?

Pete's curtains are open, and suddenly the room is awash with blue light, flashing on, off, on off. It *is* an ambulance, and it's right outside. *But that means …*

'She called an ambulance,' I say frantically. 'She called an ambulance for Pete. So she *can't* have been wanting to hurt him. That doesn't make sense. Maybe it's *not* Jess, Steph. Maybe it's not her at all. Maybe you've got it wrong, and now—'

Steph is still staring at me, her face expressionless. And then, without warning, she throws back her head and starts to laugh, a low, throaty chuckle.

What the hell? What's she laughing at?

'What the …?' I splutter.

'Oh, Mary. Mary, Mary, Mary.'

She's not laughing anymore. Instead, she's looking at me intently, head tilted to one side. I look back at her, feeling so confused I'm starting to wonder if *I've* been fed some sort of drug too. I can't seem to think properly. My head is heavy and fuzzy as my brain tries to make some sort of sense of all this. I desperately want to check on Pete and on Jess too now, and I'm waiting for Steph to explain, to help me understand, but she's still just *looking* at me. Out of the corner of my eye,

I think I see something moving on the bed, and I turn, my heart thudding, but Jess is still lying motionless, Pete too, both limp and silent, so I turn back to Steph, and I'm just about to ask her to please, p*lease* tell me what's going on, when she raises a hand.

'Maybe I've got it wrong, Mary? Oh no. *I* haven't got it wrong. It's everyone else who's done that.'

She smiles, a peculiar, cold little smile, and takes a step towards me, and I feel a quiver of fear.

'What ... what do you mean?' I whisper.

She moves another step closer and leans her face towards mine, so close that I can feel her warm breath on my cheek.

'What I mean, Mary Ellis, is that of course it's not Jess. Jess Gordon, a serial killer? She's far, *far* too stupid for that. And now those two are out of the way, we can finally get to the good bit. Honestly, I thought you were brighter than this, Mary. Haven't you worked it out yet?'

I take a step backwards, trying to move away from her, aware that my chest is tightening, my breath coming in ragged gasps, but she grabs my upper arm, her grip so tight I whimper in pain.

'Worked ... worked *what* out?' I gasp.

She smiles her nasty little smile again.

'That it's me, you moron. It's me. I'm the Diary Killer.'

Chapter 46

Thursday 1st April

'You ... you can't be. You're in charge. You're running the investigation ...'

She's joking. She *must* be joking. But she doesn't look like she's joking. She's stopped smiling now; she's even let go of my arm, but the way she's looking at me ...

'Steph, please ...'

She shakes her head slowly, her lip curled in disgust, her eyes cold, as if I'm something unpleasant to behold.

'I am in charge, yes. I've been in charge of this from the very beginning. Just not in the way you all thought.'

The doorbell is ringing now, the paramedics obviously trying to gain access, and I turn to look at Pete, deathly still on the bed, Jess too, *two* people now who very urgently need medical help – or maybe it's already too late, and even as I'm thinking this, I'm also wondering how the hell *I'm* going to get out of this nightmare, because I believe her now. I believe that Steph, DCI Steph Warden, is the killer. I can see it in her eyes, the menace, the hatred. The madness. I can smell her sweat, and now as I back away, trying to move towards the doorway, she's bending down, picking up the trophy again, and I know it will only take her a couple of seconds to swing it at me and bring me down too, and I have no idea what I'm going to do. None.

And I thought I could talk my way out of this? Faced with a crazed murderer? What the hell was I thinking? How deluded was I? I think, and I'm panicking now, my chest so tight that every breath is painful, my palms slick with sweat.

I need to talk to her, I have to buy some time, because surely the other officers in the house across the road are still watching? Surely, if the paramedics can't get in, the police will come and investigate? I just need a minute or two, and they'll be here, won't they?

'Why? Tell me why, at least,' I stutter. 'If you really are going to kill me, what difference does it make? Why me, why Lisa and Jane and David? What's the point of it all?'

She smiles again, swinging the trophy slowly back and forth, back and forth. I can see the muscles in her forearms bulging, and I know there's no way I can fight her off, absolutely none. She's far stronger than me, far fitter.

Time. Buy some time.

'They'll be here in a minute or two,' she says. 'They'll think it was Jess, you see. I'll tell them I arrived just in time to see her attacking you, so I had to whack her to try to save your life. Unfortunately, I was too late. You're dead, and she's dead too. I'll check that in a minute – I think she's gone, but if not I'll finish her off, along with your friend Pete. We chose that lovely food box we sent you together – did you enjoy your last supper, by the way?'

She smirks, and my head swims.

'Jess told me how much he loves that awful cheese, so I popped some strong sedatives in it for him, but of course it was her who delivered it to you, so they'll think that was her too. And then, while he was unconscious, she strangled him. That's what they'll think ...'

She laughs, then her face grows serious.

'I'm sorry about Pete, really. Collateral damage. But he would insist on staying here with you, playing the hero, so ...'

She shrugs. From the bed, there's a crackle, and then a tinny voice. Jess's radio. Someone trying to get hold of her, wondering what's going on. Steph turns, stares at it for a couple of seconds, then shrugs again and turns back to me. My head is reeling, trying to take it all in, trying to understand what she's saying, and now, with horror, I realise that she's going to get away with it. Because she is, isn't she? She must have realised, when we didn't answer our phones, that her plan had worked, that Pete must have eaten that drugged cheese, so she sent Jess over to kick off the final act. In a couple of minutes' time, the other police officers will be in here and they'll find three dead bodies and Steph, the woman who's been doing such a sterling job leading the serial killer investigation. And when she tells them that Pete was already dead and Jess was in the process of killing me when she arrived, well of *course* they'll believe her, won't they?

Oh God, oh God, oh God ...

'Why? You still haven't told me? *Why?*' I scream, and the doorbell is ringing again. *When will someone come? When? Please, please ...*

'Just eleven per cent of serial killers are women, did you know that? That's the most recent estimate, anyway,' she says.

She looks animated suddenly, as if she's a university lecturer imparting some fascinating facts. She's still swinging the trophy, and my gaze is darting from it to her face, up, down, up down.

'I found that fascinating as a child – murder in general, but serial killers in particular. It's why I joined the police. And then I worked two serial killer cases, and you know what I realised? I realised that they were stupid. Two stupid men, who killed and then got caught. And it made me wonder if I could do better. I wondered if it would be possible to kill people literally right under the noses of the police and get away with it. To even tell them who the victims were going to be in advance. I mean, obviously I made it a little tricky for them with the earlier three. But you – well, they had the name, the day, the place, and they've still screwed it up, haven't they? Thanks for not wanting cameras or listening devices in the house by the way. I could have disabled them, but it would have made things trickier. That was a great help.'

She laughs again, her eyes bright now, excitement flashing in them. I inch backwards, a tiny movement she doesn't seem to notice.

'I mean, of course Jess gets the glory for the first four. Well, five now. But this is just the start, you know? Maybe I'll send another diary after today. Maybe I'll do something different next time. Because this is far from over. It's only just beginning. It's a game, and *I* know how to play it.'

There's a voice coming from the radio on *her* belt now, but she doesn't seem to hear it. I take another tiny step away from her, but she's still talking, her eyes feverishly bright, the trophy swinging in ever bigger arcs, and I wonder at what point she'll swing it at my head, and my stomach contracts. The doorbell has stopped ringing, and I wonder if that means the paramedics are now seeking advice from the police, and the police are wondering why nobody in this house is responding, and if someone will be here soon to find out why. And then I think about the front door being closed, and how they'll have to break it down, and how that will take more time, and I don't have time, I don't. Time is running out so quickly now ...

'Ah, you asked why, didn't you?' she says. 'I'm so sorry, I failed to answer your question. Well, this is why.'

Abruptly, she stops moving her arm, the trophy hanging at her side now, and in the sudden stillness I think for a second that once again, I see a tiny movement from the inert bodies on the bed. I want to look, but I keep my eyes locked to hers, waiting, wanting her to keep talking, because if she's talking she's not killing me. And then I think how ridiculous this all is, how impossible it can be that this is real, and yet ... it is, isn't it?

'Tell me,' I whisper.

She's crazy, isn't she? I think. *She's insane.*

'Ah, it's a bit of cliché really,' she says. 'I had a shitty childhood. I mean, *really* shitty. Abuse, neglect, all of it. My father ... anyway, he died when I was twelve. And my mother, well, she was just plain nasty. Vile. A pathetic excuse for a mother. I have no idea why she went ahead with a pregnancy, because they didn't love me, or want me, I know that. I don't remember a single kind word, a single cuddle. I was unpaid household labour, mostly. They even used to go on holiday without me – can you imagine? I was nine the first time. Home alone for a week, barely any food in the cupboards, getting myself to school, terrified on my own at night ... and when they *were* there, well, it was almost worse.'

She pauses for a moment, staring at the ceiling, her jaw tense. I swallow, my throat parched and sore.

'I'm so sorry,' I whisper.

She looks at me again, her face expressionless.

'My so-called *mother* is in a care home now. She's never apologised, never, for what they did to me. And yet, I never fully walked away. How stupid am I? I even go and see her now and again, play the dutiful daughter, but honestly? She can rot in hell for all I care, the sooner the better. So, you know, I had to pretty much bring myself up. I had to work two jobs to get through university. No help from anyone, ever. Everything I've achieved has been down to me. *Me*, and me alone. And yet, growing up I saw people all the time who just didn't have to make that effort. People who had it easy. Family money, support, the best of everything. People who did well in life because they had everything handed to them on a nice, big, shiny plate. That's not achievement. That's *lazy*. And I started to hate those people, you know? I mean, really *hate* them. Hate them so much I wanted to kill them. That's just a thing people say, sometimes. *Ooh, I could kill him.* But because I'm mad, unhinged, whatever you want to call it – and yes, I know that too, I'm sick, even though I hide it well ...'

She laughs. I'm standing in front of her, motionless, horrified, terrified, but she's still talking, and that's good, isn't it?

Keep talking, Steph. Please, keep talking.

'Well, I just took it a step further, and decided I wanted to become Britain's most notorious, un-caught serial killer – because that's what I'm going to be, you know. And *those* people would be my victims. It wasn't hard to find them. I could have picked anyone, really. They're everywhere. I decided they'd all have to be single though. No kids. I didn't want any children to suffer. I'm not an animal. So I browsed local newspapers. I thought I'd choose people who'd actually got *publicity* out of their family connections, you know? *Bragging* about it. And there they all were. Lisa Turner, a barrister in a posh Oxford chambers, spouting off to *The Times* about there not being enough female judges. *Boohoo*. Jane Holland, with her massive casino business, but not through her own hard work – all left to her by *daddy* – all over the papers with her goodie-goodie charity work. David Howells, with his oh-so-generous lottery winner parents. And you fitted the bill perfectly too, of course. With your rich, famous papa, who left you a fortune so you can piss about pretending to be a writer. Your byline on all those articles. Never interviewed a serial killer, though, have you? I knew you'd like that. I knew you'd start trying to work out who was behind it, so that was an extra little challenge for me. But you were clueless, weren't you? You'd be nothing without your father's help. You *are* nothing. You're a nobody. And in a minute, you'll be a *dead* nobody, Mary Ellis.'

Her voice has been growing louder and louder, and now she's practically shouting, spitting the words at me, and I'm still backing away, almost at the open bedroom now, edging my way towards the landing. She's following me though, and

I know now that I have to say it, that I have one last shot at this, and that the Operation Shearwater team did get that one detail right, after all; this *is* all about our parents. It is, and now I have to tell her, tell her that Gregor Ellis is *not* my father. Tell her that, in fact, my background was very much like hers: tough, lonely, abusive. Tell her that I get it.

Because I do. I know what a childhood like that feels like. And how it never really goes away ...

I take a breath.

'I'm not, Steph.'

She frowns.

'What?'

'You want to kill Mary Ellis. You want to kill Gregor Ellis's daughter, the one who had the fancy upbringing and ... and all of it. But you've got this one wrong, Steph. I'm *not* Mary Ellis. Mary Ellis is already dead.'

Chapter 47

Thursday 1st April

She stares at me, her body frozen to the spot, and for the first time since she walked into the room her expression is one of uncertainty.

'What ... what are you talking about?' she says.

'Mary was a friend of mine,' I say. I take another step backwards, and I'm in the doorway now. She doesn't move, her brow crinkled. Her radio is crackling again, and downstairs I can hear hammering on the front door, someone shouting, but she seems oblivious to all of it, her face a picture of confusion.

'I grew up very much like you did, by the sound of it, Steph,' I say. My heart's still pounding so hard I feel light-headed, but for the first time I feel a tiny sliver of hope.

She's listening. If I can just keep her listening to me for a little bit longer ...

'I never knew my dad, and my mother was a drug addict. My upbringing ... it was awful, Steph. I was taken into care when I was nine, and I moved from foster home to foster home, and, well, it was hard. Maybe not as hard as yours, but

332

still ... horrible. And then I met Mary, and her dad, Gregor, and I got a taste of a different life. A life with money. A life of privilege. I didn't plan for it to happen, but I went to stay with her for the weekend and the house caught fire. And, well, when I woke up in hospital, everyone assumed I was Mary. We looked quite alike, you see, and I was wearing her identity bracelet, and my face was burned and all bandaged up and ... they just thought I was her. And so I thought about it and realised I just might get away with it ...'

'You're not Mary Ellis.'

She says the words slowly, her eyes narrowing.

'No,' I whisper.

'So who are you, then?' she asks.

I swallow. It's been so many years since I've said it out loud.

'My name is Amanda Archer,' I say quietly. 'Gregor died in the fire, and Mary did too. But everyone thought it was me who'd died. My name is on the gravestone next to Gregor's. I'm a nobody, Steph. I stole my life. I stole my inheritance. It's all a big fat lie.'

For a moment there's silence, both of us just looking at each other, and I think what a weird pair we are: the police detective who's actually a serial killer, and the daughter of a famous author, who's actually a massive fake. And then she shrugs.

'OK. Well, that's a freaky little coincidence, isn't it? I could have used *that* little nugget of information rather nicely, if I'd known. You're a bit smarter than I thought, aren't you, keeping that juicy secret. But it doesn't make any difference, not really. Fine, so life might not have started well for you. But you still benefitted, didn't you? This house, your money in the bank, all of it. You still have it all, with no effort.'

'No!' I yell the word, and her eyes widen.

'No effort? Do you know what it's like, pretending to be someone else every day of your life? Living a lie, wondering if someday somebody will find out and it will all come tumbling down? *No effort?*'

Her eyes widen, and she smirks.

'Ah, poor little rich girl. Give me a break.'

She's looking at me with contempt now, her tone scathing, and for a moment I want to tell her that yes, I agree with her.

She's right. It started badly, but I have had it easy for the past fourteen years. I know that. I have no reason to complain. None. Maybe it's payback time. Maybe I do deserve to die, for what I've done. But I don't *want* to die, not here, not like this ...

'I don't like doing this indoors,' she says, unexpectedly. 'It's too enclosed, too warm. It's hot in here, isn't it? I get claustrophobic indoors, especially when it's stuffy. That's why I like to kill outside. Much more fun. Much more *pleasant*.'

I swallow hard and see that there's a sheen of sweat on her forehead now, and that her eyes look glassy, as if she's not quite well.

'But hey, needs must. Bye bye, Mary. Or Amanda. Or whatever,' she says, and she takes a step towards me, and then another, the trophy raised above her head. In an instant, her face changes again, eyes flashing with fury, the madness back, and suddenly I know with a deep, sickening certainty that it's all over. I tried, I failed, and time has run out.

I shut my eyes, pressing my knuckles into my sockets,

waiting for the blow, for the pain, for the inevitable darkness. And then I hear a grunt, and a rustle, and a groan, and a heavy thud, and I slowly move my fists away from my face, and my mouth falls open in shock.

Because Pete is standing there. Pete, still white-faced, blood stains across his shirt, swaying slightly on his feet. One hand is clutching the door frame, and in the other he's holding a glass dome, an ornament of some sort. I blink, trying to focus. It's a snow globe, the snow globe he keeps in a drawer in his room and brings out every Christmas. The snow globe he bought in a little store just off Central Park in New York – our favourite city. It's streaked with something red, and my gaze continues downwards to where Steph is now lying on the landing carpet, groaning softly, blood running down her forehead.

'Pete. *Pete.*'

My voice cracks.

'I love you,' he whispers, and he drops the snow globe and stretches out his arms. I step into his embrace, just as I hear shouts followed by an enormous bang from downstairs, and the sound of wood splintering.

Chapter 48

Friday 2nd April

'One coffee, dash of milk.'

I put the mug down in front of DI Mike Stanley, and he nods a thank you. I perch on the stool opposite his at the breakfast bar and take a sip of my own coffee. It's black and strong and much-needed; I feel exhausted, mentally and physically, my body aching, my head fuzzy from way too few hours' sleep over the past two days.

It all still feels a little surreal, like a nightmare I haven't quite been able to wake up from. The minutes after Pete – Pete, my hero, my love, maybe even my future now, if I'm very, very lucky – crept up behind Steph and attacked her, undoubtedly saving my life, are a blur. The front door crashing open, the sound of yells and pounding footsteps on the stairs, Steph moaning on the landing carpet, Pete's legs giving way, me sobbing and trying to support his weight before sliding to the floor with him. And Jess, poor Jess, still immobile on the bed behind us.

She died; Jess died. They said it would have been almost

instantaneous, that she was unlikely to have suffered, such was the intensity of the blow. Blows very similar, it's now emerged, to those which killed Lisa and Jane and David. I'm still trying to come to terms with that; from being someone I wasn't sure I even liked a few months ago, Jess had become a big part of my life, a reassuring presence, and I feel a deep, aching sadness that her life ended like it did, a sense of intense loss which has surprised me.

Pete's OK, or he will be. He's in hospital, recovering from the huge dose of barbiturates that Steph laced his cheese with. It was lucky, his doctor said, that he hadn't washed it down with too much of the wine we opened but then didn't feel like drinking – the combination of alcohol and drugs may well have been fatal, but as it is it's thought he'll make a full recovery.

I came back home this morning. Pete's bedroom is now a murder scene, of course, and I spent last night in a hotel, while police processed it. It didn't take long – it was pretty clear what had happened, after all. They're sending specialist cleaners in later today, and I can't bring myself to even glance into the room, not yet. But this morning they said I can move back home, if I want to, and so I'm here, for now at least.

There are so many unanswered questions right now: Steph, her head injury inflicted by Pete not a serious one as it turned out, only a glancing blow which stunned her for a minute or so but is unlikely to have caused any serious damage, has only just started being questioned. But she is, according to DI Stanley, so far being surprisingly open about what she's done.

'She's admitted everything. She said she really thought she'd get away with it,' he told me on the phone when he rang first thing this morning to ask if he could come round for a chat. 'But now that she's been arrested, she says she might as well tell us exactly how she did it. I think she's rather enjoying it, from all accounts. She fooled everyone, for such a long time. It seems to be bringing her some kind of sick pleasure. She enjoyed watching us all running round in circles and going down rabbit holes that led us in completely the wrong direction. That so-called crime connection between the victims' parents, for example. She knew we'd got that wrong, but she loved how much time we wasted on it.'

Now, he's telling me about the drugs she poisoned Pete with.

'They were her mother's; she's in a care home down in Cirencester, and she's an insomniac apparently, so they give her pretty heavy-duty sleeping pills. Wow, Steph really hates her mother, doesn't she, by the way? Can't say I blame her really, but anyway, she always timed her visits for when they were doling out the evening drugs, and persuaded the staff to let her help her mother take them. I mean, it wasn't hard – she's a senior cop, isn't she? They knew that, so they trusted her. Of course, she just stuck the pills in her bag, until she had a nice little collection, then crushed them and mashed them into your friend's cheese. It's such a strong one she figured the smell and taste would mask the drugs, and it obviously worked.'

I shake my head, my heart twisting as I think about how close I came to losing Pete.

'She's sick. Evil,' I whisper.

'Evil, and clever,' he says. 'It's like it was her own little personal challenge: warning four different police forces in advance, and you, well, that was to be her moment of glory. Killing a woman at the centre of a police ring of steel, and still believing she'd get away with it. If it hadn't been for Mr Chong, she probably would have. We'd all have believed that Jess was the killer, and that Steph was the hero who tried to save your life.'

He pauses, rubbing a hand across his eyes.

'Poor Jess,' he mutters.

'I'm going to miss her,' I say quietly.

'Me too,' he replies.

And then he tells me everything else they've learned so far. How Steph had taken a chance when she sent me the diary, hoping I'd read it and report it to the police as soon as I received it, and getting nervous when it took so long. She'd transferred to Gloucestershire two months earlier, knowing that when the serial killer case came in, her track record would ensure she'd be assigned to it.

'She says that if you'd never read the diary, she'd have found another way to do it all. But she was pretty ecstatic when you did,' he says. 'And she seemed very pleased with herself for picking April Fool's Day for your murder. She laughed herself silly over that one. She's been laughing a lot, actually. It's creepy. She said she really enjoyed that interview with your two male colleagues too, the ones who went to Oxford for New Year? The interview she took me along to. She loved how much time that line of enquiry wasted. Well, they all did, didn't they?'

He tells me how she used the PNC – the Police National

Computer – to help plan the murders and access information.

'It's illegal, of course, to use it the way she did. Every use of the PNC is logged and there are daily audits, but there's also PNC data on other databases which aren't subject to the same audits. Misuse is a serious disciplinary matter, and if it *had* been picked up, we might have been onto her sooner, but we've been understaffed in a lot of areas recently, and so she got lucky that no red flags were raised.'

He sighs and shakes his head.

'She was able to access vehicle and driver files, all sorts of stuff. It was easy for her to find home addresses, and check the location of CCTV cameras and that kind of thing too, of course. And then she just made sure her shifts worked around the murders. It was why she chose victims who all lived in locations within ninety minutes' drive or so from here. Easy to get back and appear as normal in the office the next day.'

'She said to me that she preferred to kill outside. That was a bit weird,' I say. My throat sounds raspy and dry, and I take another sip of my drink.

He nods.

'Yes, in retrospect she was always going on about needing fresh air and complaining about how overheated the station is. But to be fair, we all moan about it. It *is* always too hot. But it made her stir crazy. She says now that she was locked in a cupboard a lot as a child, for the slightest misdemeanour. It made her claustrophobic and panicky, and ever since she hasn't been able to think straight in stuffy rooms. So, yes, she killed them all outdoors, so she'd be less likely to make a mistake. She talked her way into Jane's house with her police badge, and told her she needed to show her something out in the garden. She just sneaked up on the other two in the dark. She parked her car in a CCTV blind spot, hid a heavy hammer under her jacket and ran to the murder locations, and then ran back to her car again afterwards. Simple, really. And she's so forensically aware that she obviously made sure she didn't leave any usable evidence behind, although she admitted she did get a bit twitchy each time, waiting for the lab report. She didn't bring a weapon here to kill you because she'd already earmarked a few things she could use here in the house when she came round to brief you ahead of Thursday.'

As he carries on telling me what Steph's revealed, I realise that she, of course, did all the things she told me Jess had done. Sending the spyware to my computer in an email, knowing it would be found and removed but loving how frightened it made me feel. Sending me that letter in the post, to stop me thinking about fleeing abroad.

'She said that if it had all worked, if she'd been able to pin it on Jess like she'd planned, the fact that Jess was so quiet, so withdrawn a lot of the time, would have helped. A lot of people think Jess is – *was* – a bit odd, you know? But she and I were friends. She was actually just really, really shy. She's struggled with confidence her whole life, and she found meeting new people extremely difficult. It's one of the reasons she became a family liaison officer. She knew she'd have to get close to lots of different people and she thought it might help her. And she was getting there, too. She was terrified of you when she first met you, but she was genuinely fond of you by the end.'

I feel tears stinging my eyes when he says that, remembering the way Jess hugged me so unexpectedly on the doorstep on Wednesday evening when she came round to drop off the food box.

'Poor Jess,' I say. 'All she wanted to do was help. It's so sad, so bloody unfair ...'

'It is,' Mike says, and there's a look of real sadness in his eyes, a bleakness, and I wonder if he might have been a little bit in love with Jess, and my heart twists.

'Anyway, I'll leave you in peace for a while,' he says abruptly. 'We'll need to get a formal statement from you, maybe on Monday? Take the weekend to try and get your head together. I can't even imagine how stressful the past few months have been for you. And give our best to Mr Chong, won't you? We'll need to chat to him too, when he's feeling up to it, but we've already reassured him he won't be facing any charges in relation to the assault on DCI Warden.'

'Good,' I said. 'Thanks, Mike. You take care.'

When he's gone, I walk slowly upstairs to the lounge and curl into a corner of the sofa, pulling the grey blanket we keep on the side over my legs. I'm going to go and visit Pete again this afternoon, and while part of me is longing to see him, anxiety is nibbling at the edges of my mind, anxiety that's been building since he staggered out of his bedroom and saved my life.

He hasn't said a word about it, not yet. But is it possible that he heard some of what I told Steph? About me not being Mary Ellis? About my real identity, and what I did?

He appeared on the landing just *after* I'd told her, I know that. But what were her last words to me?

'Bye bye, Mary. Or Amanda. Or whatever ...'

He *must* have heard that, surely? It was just seconds before he attacked Steph. And yet, when I visited him last night, all he did was tell me again that he's realised he loves me, and not just as a friend. He told me that if there's any chance I might feel the same, that he wants to try and make a go of it, as a couple. And I wrapped my arms around him, and told him that there's nothing I want more, because, to my own immense surprise, that's how I feel now. I still don't know where it's come from, why our feelings have changed so much, why it didn't happen years ago. But I'm too happy to question it, and they do say – whoever *they* are – that the best relationships are the ones that start with friendship, don't they?

And so I snuggle under the blanket and try to force the thoughts from my head. Pete had been drugged, after all. His recollections of the whole night are incredibly hazy, he says; he just remembers waking up to feel a heavy weight across his body, pushing poor Jess off him, and then becoming aware of some sort of altercation on the landing. He says he vaguely remembered that I was in some sort of danger, although he couldn't remember exactly what, but he decided he needed a weapon and grabbed the snow globe from his drawer, before stumbling to the door to see Steph about to bring his tennis trophy down on my skull.

If he did hear what we were talking about, he'd surely have mentioned it by now, I reason. Which means it's just Steph who knows, and clearly she hasn't told anyone about it yet, because Mike would definitely have said, wouldn't he? So there's nothing I can do except wait for her to tell and then deny it. She's clearly crazy, after all, so I just stick to my plan and say I made it up. I would have said anything to save my life when I knew she was about to kill me, wouldn't I? I'd have lied through my teeth to her …

And I'm good at that, of course. Lying. I've been doing it for years, to everyone. Even now.

Because I lied to Steph too.

Not about everything, of course. But, once again, I altered the story a bit. I had to. That story about Mary, and the fire, and what I did afterwards, well, that's actually not a *hundred* per cent true.

There's more.

Chapter 49

Monday 5th April

Pete's home from the hospital. He was discharged last night; it's only a ten-minute walk from here, but I drove round to pick him up, and he kept his hand on my knee for the entire duration of the short trip back to The Grove. He still looks pale, and he's a little wobbly on his feet, but he's got the old Pete twinkle back in his eye, and that makes me so happy. It's a bit peculiar, this change in our relationship; we both slept in my bed last night, neither of us wanting to go into his room ever again, and certain now that we need to leave this house as soon as possible. We're already making plans, talking about me selling up, him selling his rented-out Cheltenham apartment too, and us getting a place together. It seems fast – it *is* fast – but we've known each other for nearly nine years now, after all. We know this is *right*.

We talked a lot, last night, wrapped around each other in the dimly lit bedroom. We talked about Megan, who called both of us over the weekend, apologising profusely for her 'appalling behaviour' and telling me that despite appearances, she was horribly insecure when it came to men, and had been constantly worried that Pete and I were carrying on behind her back.

'I've had some really bad experiences, in the past,' she told me tearfully. 'And I was far too full-on with Pete, I know that. I was far too intense. I just thought, "finally, I've got a good one", you know? And now I've driven him away, and it's something I'll have to live with. I'm just glad he's OK. I'm glad you both are.'

She said she'd wanted to spend a romantic few days alone with Pete in our house last week, and had been making all sorts of plans to surprise him with, which was why she'd been so angry to find out that I wasn't going away after all. And she solved the mystery of Pete's missing phone for us too, admitting that she'd taken it with her when she'd gone off in her taxi.

'I knew his PIN,' she said. 'And I wanted to check for messages from you, in case you really were carrying on behind my back. I'm so sorry. I'll stick it through the letter box, and then I won't bother either of you again. Look after him, OK?'

I promised her I would, and then felt horribly guilty again, because of course we *had* been 'carrying on behind her back', although not for long. It was probably best if she didn't know that though, for now at least. The little detail of us now being a couple is still one we've managed to keep under wraps, even though the story hit the news last night, with lurid headlines about the Diary Killer, the cop-turned-serial killer who'd managed to kill four people, and about me and Pete, the two who escaped. I've had to disconnect the house phone and turn my mobile off, so unceasing are the calls from journalists, and from friends and colleagues too, both current and former. The press have taken over the street too, camped outside, waiting for us to appear; good old Dinah next door has been trying to shoo them away, but with little success. We've decided we *will* go out and speak to them soon; give them a little something in the hope that they'll go away. But not just yet. Right now, we want it to be just us, hunkered down, curtains closed. Just *us*.

I've told Pete that I briefly suspected him and Megan of being the killers. But of course, all the things I was so concerned about *were* just coincidences after all, in the end. Them being together on the nights of the murders, Pete happening to visit Jane Holland's casino once – all perfectly innocent after all, and Pete's mild annoyance when I repeatedly acted strangely about his casino trip absolutely justifiable.

'I just couldn't understand why you kept harping on about it,' he said.

'But why did you take so long to finish with Megan?' I asked him, and he told me that every time he tried, she'd get hysterical, telling him how damaged she was after her father left her mother when she was very young, how the experience had scarred her, how she'd been treated so badly by so many men that she wasn't sure if she could take it again.

'I genuinely thought she might hurt herself, you know?' he said. 'I didn't want to tell you, partly because she begged me not to tell *anyone* how fragile and messed-up she was, and partly because I thought you might not believe me anyway; I thought you'd think I was just making excuses. I knew I needed to end it, but I was scared, and I didn't want her harming herself because of me, so I kept putting it off. I'm sorry; I'm an idiot.'

'No, you're not. You're a very lovely man, Pete Chong,' I said. 'Megan was right. You *are* one of the good ones.'

Early this morning, before too many members of the press pack had arrived to spend another day knocking on my door, I sneaked out through the back gate and spent an hour in the police station, giving my formal statement about what happened here. On my way back, I thought about the tragic deaths of Lisa and David and Jane, all such good people, all murdered for such a stupid, pointless reason. I thought about how much time both the police and I wasted in looking for connections between us that simply weren't there. And now I've just walked into The Hub, and I'm bracing myself for more questions, because of course everyone here has seen the news stories by now too, and so far I've ignored all the messages they've sent me, which isn't really fair. Plus, I need to get back to work, anyway; I need to finish writing my article. I've already had a dozen emails from editors wanting my story, and I need to pick one to give it to, as soon as the police give me the go ahead.

'Mary! Oh, Mary. I'm so happy to see you!'

It's Eleanor, racing across the room towards me, long locks flying behind her, holding out her arms as she hits the brakes. I bend down to hug her, and she squeezes me hard.

'I can't believe what's happened to you,' she says, when she finally lets me go. 'And that you kept it to yourself all this time. I mean, we knew something was going on, you hinted at that, but we had no idea it was anything as huge as this. I understand why you had to keep it under wraps, but it must have been *so* hard. Have you got time for a coffee?'

We take our drinks to one of the little break-out areas at the far end of the room, and I settle down on the big, lurid pink sofa, Eleanor tucking her wheelchair in next to me.

'So, spill,' she says.

I tell her the whole story, carefully editing my account of my conversation with Steph, of course, and she listens wide-eyed, her mouth dropping open in horror when I tell her about the final moments on the landing.

'Oh. My. God,' she gasps.

'But, you know what,' I say, when I've finished. 'For a while I actually thought Edward and Satish might have something to do with it.'

I tell her why, and she claps a hand to her mouth.

'Oh Mary! I know exactly what that's all about, but I promise I only found out last week. The only thing those two have been plotting is how to get you to go on a date with Satish. He's crazy about you, you numpty.'

'He's ... he's *what*?'

She starts to giggle, and explains that last week a flustered Satish took her aside and asked her if she could give him some advice.

'He's had a crush on you from day one, but he says he's rubbish with women, and he thought you were way out of his league. So he enlisted Edward to help, although I'm not sure why, given that he's probably just as inept. Anyway, that's why Edward kept hanging around you, trying to find out more about you and impress you with stories about Satish: their interesting weekends away, the fact that they're fit runners, all that stuff. He was trying to make you see Satish as a bit of a catch. It all went a bit pear-shaped when they were questioned by the police – Satish is from a really strict family, he's never been in any sort of trouble in his life, and it really freaked him out. But even when Edward told him he suspected that you had reported them, the poor guy was still in love with you. He bought two tickets for Dua Lipa in Bristol and he wanted to invite you along, but the gig was last Wednesday night and you'd told Edward you might be going away so Satish wasn't sure if you'd be around. He said he tried a couple of times to ask you but you were acting a bit weird with him, so in desperation on the day before the gig last week, when you weren't at work, he asked Edward to go round to your house to ask you if you'd like to go. I gave him your address, I'm so sorry. You'd taken a few days off so I didn't want to disturb you by calling to ask if it was OK, and I didn't think there was any harm in it. Edward's all right, deep down, honestly. But he screwed it up apparently – he lost his nerve and didn't even knock on your door.'

I laugh, understanding finally dawning.

It all makes sense now, I think. *It doesn't stop me thinking that Edward's a bit creepy, but I suppose he was only trying to help his friend …*

'Well, that clears that up,' I say. 'But sorry, Satish. I already *have* a boyfriend.'

I wink at Eleanor, and she almost drops her coffee mug. 'You have a WHAT? When did this happen?'

We spend the next hour chatting, before I head back to my desk feeling light, happy, and for the first time in a very long time, optimistic about the future. It's nice to know that everything's out in the open now, that I can come to work without being suspicious and on edge. No more confusion, no more lies.

Except for one, of course.

The real story about me and Mary Ellis can't ever be told, not even to Pete. And even if he did, in his drugged state, overhear what Steph and I were talking about outside his bedroom door on that awful night, and one day he remembers it, he'll still only know half the truth.

Pete's one of my very best friends in the world. But the reason I can never, ever tell anyone, even him, the full truth about what happened fourteen years ago is because I need to protect another friend.

One of the other very best friends I ever had: Mary Ellis.

You may ask why I need to protect someone who's dead, who died in a fire more than a decade ago. And I probably wouldn't, if she really had.

But you see, the real truth is this: Mary Ellis isn't actually dead at all.

Chapter 50

Monday 5th April

When I first met Mary, we had an immediate connection. But it wasn't just that we looked, and sometimes dressed, a little alike. Mary was, despite her wealth and her outwardly luxurious, exciting life with her famous father, desperately unhappy. Gregor Ellis, although he clearly loved his daughter in his own way, was also the most controlling person I've ever met, before then or since. He wanted Mary to live her life exactly as he did; he had few friends, and rarely spoke to any of his relatives, even his mother, telling his daughter that relying on family members was a weakness, that one had to make one's own way in life and that the only way to measure success was by the amount of money one could make.

When Mary's mother had been alive, he'd been different – or so *his* mother, Celeste, told me, when I went to New York to live with her and asked her to tell me stories about 'my' childhood. Back then, he'd been ambitious, and a little anti-social, but nothing like he was in his later years. Losing his wife changed him, made him fold in on himself, and he took

Mary into his cold, enclosed little world with him. She'd never met most of her relations, and few had even seen photos of her since she was a toddler, which made it all much easier for me, of course, later on.

Life was far from easy for Mary, despite the fancy homes and private jets. And when the time came for her to start thinking of going to university, and planning her career, Gregor simply refused to let her have much say. She could go to university, he said, but she must live at home with him for the duration; she could study what she liked, but when she graduated there would be no question of her going out into the world on her own. She would stay with him, and work from home, possibly even become a writer like he was. I believe now that this was probably his deluded way of trying to keep her safe; he couldn't stop her mother from dying and leaving him, but he could at least try to stop Mary from coming to any harm and leaving him too. But back then, we both saw only the injustice, and the unfairness of his actions. Mary knew that, once she turned eighteen, he'd have no legal right to stop her doing anything, that he couldn't, and wouldn't, keep her locked up in a basement; but she also knew her father, and she knew that if she tried to go against his wishes, he could make life very difficult for her.

'He's done it before, with staff who've crossed him. He's made up stories about them stealing from him and reported them to the police, stuff like that. You can do a lot when you have as much money as he has,' she whispered to me one night when I was staying with her, and he'd retired to his study to write.

'He's already told me that if I try to leave, he'll ruin it for me too. He'll make me unemployable. I hate him, Amanda. I *hate* him. I hate being his daughter. I want to go far, far away where nobody knows who I am, or who my father is. I'll die if I don't.'

And that's what gave us the idea.

I'll die if I don't.

We planned it so carefully. For Mary, her father simply not being around anymore, and her being free to do what she wanted, wasn't nearly enough. She wanted to be *entirely* free of him, free of all of it. She didn't *want* to be Mary Ellis, daughter of the great, exalted Gregor. But she was convinced that if she simply vanished, her wider family, even though she barely knew them, would never stop searching for her, and that she'd spend her entire life looking over her shoulder.

'It's only him that stops them being involved in my life,' she told me. 'Once he's dead, they'll want me back in the family. I can't just disappear, it won't work. Mary Ellis *has* to still be around, somehow.'

And so, we made our plan. To make it work, we needed a third girl, and Laney was the obvious choice. She was a young homeless kid, the same age as us. She often slept in a doorway near our college, and we'd give her sandwiches and chocolate sometimes, feeling sorry for her. We talked for hours, Mary and I, about whether we could really do it, whether we could sacrifice Laney for our own ends. But we were eighteen, with all the bravado and selfishness of youth, and both of us were damaged and unhappy and wanted a better life. We thought, back then, that this was the only way we could get it.

If I could go back in time, would I change what we did? Yes, yes, *yes*. It haunts me, wakes me in the small hours, feeds my never-ending nightmares. It made me think, more than once, as the Diary Killer saga unfolded, that finally I was about to get my punishment; that I deserved to die, and die horribly, like Laney did. Sometimes, I can't believe we really did it. But it's too late now. Too late for regrets. Too late to change anything. Too late for Laney, anyway.

She had no family, or none who gave a damn about her anyway, and when we invited her to stay the night at Mary's that weekend she couldn't believe her luck. Dealing with Gregor was easy; we doctored his dinner with some of his own sleeping pills, in the hope that he'd go to bed earlier than usual and sleep soundly as we carried out our plan. We got lucky there too, because he had a cold that day, and wasn't feeling great anyway, so when he started to feel sleepy after dinner he stumbled off to bed immediately, muttering about viruses and how they drain your energy, leaving us to look at each other gleefully.

We'd hidden Laney in one of the outbuildings, telling her Gregor didn't like visitors but that we'd smuggle her in when the coast was clear, and she was delighted to be brought inside to sit in front of a warm fire and be fed roast chicken and red wine. We waited until, sleepy from the booze and the heat, she asked if she could go to bed too. And then we started the fire, and we said goodbye, Mary and I hugging tightly before she grabbed the small bag of belongings she'd packed, handed me her identity bracelet, and slipped out of the house. She'd left her old passport and birth certificate in an envelope in

Gregor's car outside, telling me to say he'd been about to open a savings account for me or something of that sort, and had put the documents in his glove compartment ready to take to the bank in case they needed proof of my identity.

It made things easier for me, having those, and I didn't ask any details about *her* escape; how she'd organised it, who helped her, where she was going. We both decided it was better for me *not* to know, for what I didn't know I couldn't reveal. And if our plan worked, everyone would think *I* was Mary anyway, so her whereabouts wouldn't be in question. All I knew was that it involved a fake passport, and it had taken money – lots of money – to pull off, money she'd somehow managed to steal from her father's bank account. Again, I didn't ask. I simply waved her off, tears running down my cheeks, and then I went to bed too, and waited for the fire to take hold.

It didn't take long. We'd spent hours at the library, researching fire accelerants, hoping that the blaze would be so fierce it would be impossible to find the cause, but deciding that if questions were asked I could simply say I'd heard a break-in downstairs shortly before the fire started, and that the intruder must have set the place alight.

I say it didn't take long, but of course I needed to delay calling the fire brigade for as long as possible; we knew nobody else would do it, the housekeeper and chef long gone home, the house's location so remote that no passing car or pedestrian would see the flames until it was too late. I needed to wait long enough to hear the screams from Gregor and Laney's rooms, and – terrifyingly – I needed to get burned myself. That was part of the plan, and my memories of those seemingly never-ending minutes still infest my nightmares too; Mary's bracelet, the one with her name engraved on it, searing my skin; my chest burning as flames licked my curtains and smoke stung my eyes; the wails of terror from the two people I'd locked in their rooms, quietly turning the keys I'd slipped from their doors earlier in the day. I finally dialled 999 then, on the extension phone on my bedside table, but by then my room was well alight, and I can still feel the fear that gripped me, hear the sound of glass splintering, remember the feeling of the sickening realisation that my own hair was on fire.

And so they died, Gregor and Laney. It was, we thought, the only way. We'd discussed swapping places without involving anyone else at all, of course; could Mary just run away, head abroad, change her name and start again that way, without us hurting anyone other than Gregor? Could I just simply slip in and take her place once the housekeeping staff had left for the night? But we thought that would raise too many questions: why Mary's best friend Amanda, who often stayed overnight, was never seen again after the fire, why she didn't attend Gregor's funeral. What if the police started looking for Amanda, suspecting *her* of starting the fire maybe, and then discovered the truth? It was neater, tidier, easier, to make everyone think that Amanda had died and Mary had survived. We *needed* that second body. It was Laney who was going to be the potential problem, but we'd researched death by fire too, in those hours in the library, and of course back then DNA analysis techniques were much less advanced than they are now. We knew that if human remains were very badly burned, it was very difficult to extract useable DNA, and that even identification by dental or medical records was likely to be impossible. And poor Laney had nobody to miss her anyway; no family, few friends other than a handful of other street people. She was just another homeless girl who drifted away, never to be seen again, no questions asked.

We got lucky in more ways than one, I know that. The old house had no fire alarm, just a few smoke detectors, melted into mush by the blaze; I told police I hadn't heard them screaming their warning until it was too late, and they believed me. We got away with the locked bedroom doors too, although that worried me for a while. But they were never mentioned, and so I assumed the ferocity of the fire had concealed that for us as well. As for the funeral, even though I was still heavily bandaged I couldn't risk getting too close to anyone who might have known either me or Mary; instead, I clung to Celeste, telling her I was too distraught to speak to *anybody* and, like a fierce mother tiger, she batted away well-meaning attendees, not allowing anyone near me, not even Furnbury Hall's chef and housekeeper, and whisked me away as soon as the coffins were lowered into the ground.

And so it all worked out beautifully. Mary got away, to start her new life. Everyone thought I was Mary, and so I became Mary Ellis, and moved to America to live with 'my' grandmother. And it was assumed that Laney was me, the real me, Amanda Archer. But it's Laney who lies in the grave next to Gregor's; Laney who I weep for on the rare occasions that I visit the graveyard in Thornton. I don't go there for Gregor, because why would I? He's nothing to me, after all. It's Laney's death I regret, more than I can say.

My burns, my scars, are my lasting reminders of that night, and of what we did to her. I deserve these scars, this disfigurement. I don't feel guilt about Gregor, not really. He'd lived a life. But Laney; I think about her every time my fingers brush against the lumpy, pitted skin of my cheek, or catch a glimpse of my deformed left ear in the mirror. It's her face that floats through the dreams that never leave me. Who knows what her life could have been, had she been given the chance? It torments me, but it's far, far too late to make any sort of real amends now. And to even attempt to do so would not only destroy my life, but Mary's too.

Because we're still in touch, you see, Mary and me. We're still friends, the closest friends imaginable. She got back in touch once she was free, once she was settled. She's not Mary anymore of course; she's achieved what she wanted: a life of her own, a career she loves, with no links whatsoever to Gregor Ellis. Those links are all mine now; I took them on, in return for a life of security and comfort that I could never have imagined as a child. The money I inherited was rightfully hers of course, and although she argued against it at first, saying she wanted to make her own way in the world, I insisted that she have half of everything. I couldn't have lived with myself if I'd kept it all. It was her birth right, after all, and I carried on arguing with her about it until, finally, she gave in. And so, every sum I've ever received: birthday cheques from her grandmother and other relatives, the ongoing book royalties, all of it, I split, transferring fifty per cent of everything to her bank account. At the end of it all, we've both got what we wanted.

And now I need to speak to her, because although I messaged her as soon as I could on Thursday morning to reassure her I'm still alive, I haven't had a chance to tell her properly about how all this turned out. I've kept her updated every step of the way of course; in fact, it was her idea for me, as a last resort, to confess to the killer that I'm not really Mary Ellis at all. And now I have so much to tell her. Especially that, for now at least, our secret is still safe. I pick up my phone, and dial her number.

Epilogue

One year later

'Over there ... look! An elephant! An actual elephant!'
Pete nudges me, eyes bright with excitement, pointing frantically, and I laugh.

'I see it, I see it! They're not exactly hard to miss, are they, you twit?'

'I know, but ... wow!'

I laugh again. His enthusiasm is contagious, and I lean over to kiss him on the cheek. In the front passenger seat, Lucinda rolls her eyes and smiles.

'You two lovebirds,' she says. 'Makes me sick.'

'Aw shut up. You're just jealous,' I say, and she laughs and sticks out her tongue at me.

She already loves Pete though, despite her sarky comments. She told me as much on our first night here, when we went to sit on her veranda and have a cold beer together while Pete went to take a shower.

'I always thought you might end up together, you know, from the way you've always talked about him,' she said. 'Even though you always denied you had those sorts of feelings. I just had a hunch.'

'Well, I never did. But I'm so glad you were right,' I said and we clinked bottles.

We're married now, Pete and I. He proposed at Christmas, less than nine months after we officially got together, and neither of us saw any reason to have a long engagement. We got married last week, the first week of April, just after the anniversary of that horrible night when Jess died in Pete's bedroom, and he came close to death himself.

'It'll give us some happy beginning-of-April memories, maybe,' he said, when we finally decided on the date. 'Instead of the nightmarish ones. Now, where do you want to go on honeymoon? Where's nice in April?'

It had to be Botswana, of course. I'd wanted to come out here for so long, and I haven't been disappointed. Lucinda has moved now, no longer on her project in the Okavango Delta but living on the Moremi Game Reserve in the northern part of this beautiful country. She's part of a team investigating the mysterious deaths of hundreds of elephants in the past year, first in Okavango and now here. It's thought to be down to some sort of water-borne bacteria, a toxin made by microscopic algae, but nobody seems quite sure yet, and although her job can be distressing at times, Lucinda is in her element here, even helping to fund some of the ongoing research. She doesn't spend much on herself; she prefers to use her money to help others. It's something I'm going to start doing too, now, I've decided. My career has soared since I wrote the Diary Killer piece; I've even been offered a book deal. Following in 'my father's' footsteps. Oh, the irony. But I already have more money than I need, and I'm thinking of setting up a charity to help young homeless women, in memory of Laney. Lucinda thinks it's a wonderful idea, and something she can support too, if only from a distance. She has no plans to return to the UK, and I don't blame her.

I look at her now as we bump along in the open-sided jeep, her dark hair, so similar in colour to my own, ruffled by the warm breeze.

Mary Ellis, I think. *You'd never have had this life if we hadn't done what we did, would you? Neither would I. It would all have been so, so different.*

Mary Ellis is free now. She's Lucinda Graham, and she's happy. We don't look much alike at all these days. Her skin is deeply tanned from her years in the sun, her haircut short and practical. We both know what a terrible thing we did; both know that one day, all this could still fall apart. Even if Pete's drug-erased memories don't return, Steph, who's now serving a life sentence, might eventually tell someone that Mary Ellis, the one who got away, isn't Mary Ellis at all. I don't really understand why she hasn't done that already, and it bothers me. Maybe what I told her about our similar, grim childhoods *did* make a difference after all, who knows? But if it happens, it happens. We know we deserve to be punished, and we'll deal with it. At least we'll have had *this*. For now, life is good. And none of us knows what the future holds, do we? Your entire life can change in a single moment.

I grab hold of my husband's hand – *my husband!* – and squeeze it, and he tears his eyes away from the elephant just long enough to nuzzle his nose against my ear and say quietly, 'I love you, Mary Ellis.'

Lucinda must have heard, because she turns round in her seat again and gives me a small, knowing smile. I wait until Pete turns away, pulling his phone from the pocket of his gilet to take yet another photo. Then I mouth:

'And I love *you*, Mary Ellis.'

Lucinda smiles again, then winks.

'Right back at ya,' she whispers.

Acknowledgements

This is my fourth psychological thriller, and as always there are so many people who played a part in it. I must begin by thanking Anna Powell-Smith, founder and director of the Centre for Public Data, for being so incredibly helpful when contacted by an author with a list of bizarre questions about how one could calculate the approximate number of Janes or Davids living in a particular UK city. Thank you so much, Anna, for taking the time to point me in the right direction (and even do some of the maths for me!). Your patience and kindness are very much appreciated. More useful data came from the BBC News and Office for National Statistics websites, and I once again had invaluable advice from former senior police detective Stuart Gibbon. For this book I created fictional versions of all of the police forces involved; all irregularities or mistakes in police procedure are mine or written with artistic licence! Along with crime historian Stephen Wade, Stuart has also written a series of comprehensive guides which cover all aspects of crime and policing, and which I find incredibly useful: essential reading for crime writers or any true crime fans!

Others I must give a special mention to are:

My 'day job' manager Sean Fay – you are now a cool cop in one of my books. See Chapter 26. You're welcome.

My friend, June Kelly, CEO of Makeup Junkies International, inspiration for the character of Eleanor in this book, and one of the most vibrant, energetic, positive people I know. Thank you for all the fabulous eyeliner, and for making me laugh so much I usually ruin it. Bring on the glitter cannons!

My wonderful agent, Clare Hulton. You already know how grateful I am for everything you've done for me, but I'll carry on telling you regularly! My amazing editor Kathryn Cheshire, who plays such a massive part in the success of my books, and the entire, fabulous, hard-working team at HarperCollins One More Chapter, who continue to punch way above their weight. (We got our UK Amazon Kindle number one finally this year, hurray!) My copy editor Lydia Mason (I love your "Dunh! Dunh! Dunh!" comments when I write an unexpected twist!). Lucy Bennett, who designed the gorgeous cover for this book. The HarperCollins teams in the USA, Canada and Australia (it was so exciting to see one of my novels also hit the number one spot in Canada, thank you so much!). And the brilliant team at ILA, who handle my foreign rights, including Nicki Kennedy, Jenny Robson, Katherine West, Elizabeth Guess, Alix Shaw and Jack Viney. My books are now published in seven languages around the world, something which still blows my mind.

Of course, huge thanks as always to my husband JJ and my fantastic family and friends – your support is immense and unwavering, and I love you all. To the bloggers and book reviewers who devote so much time to supporting authors – you are all incredible, thank you so much for everything you do. To the running community, and the friends I've made through my crazy long-distance challenges: being out there with you is one of my very favourite things in the world (and so many tricky plot issues have been resolved on the trails too – I'm not sure I could write if I couldn't run). To everyone who buys, reads and listens to my books – I am so very grateful. None of this would be possible without you. And to the lovely members of my monthly Instagram book club (two years and counting now!) and everyone who takes the time to send me social media messages about my books. You make me very happy.

Thank you all so much.

Enjoyed *The Murder List*? Make sure you've read all of Jackie Kabler's books!

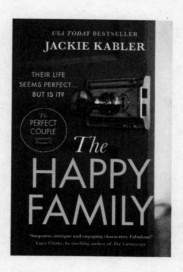

A mother who disappeared …

When Beth was 10 years old, her beautiful, wild mother Alice disappeared. Beth's life since hasn't always been easy, but now she's settled, with a successful career, a loving family and a beautiful home.

An unexpected visitor …

Then one day there's a knock at the door. Alice has returned. Desperate to rebuild their relationship, Beth invites her mother to move in.

A life that comes crashing down …

At first, everything is wonderful. But then Beth's friends start to drift away, strange things happen at home, and rumours about Beth begin to circle. Someone is out to destroy Beth's newfound happiness. But who? And how far will they go?

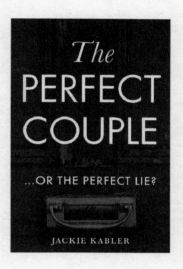

A devoted wife …

A year ago, Gemma met the love of her life, Danny. Since then, their relationship has been perfect. But one evening, Danny doesn't return home.

A missing husband …

Gemma turns to the police. She is horrified by what she discovers – a serial killer is on the loose in Bristol. When she sees photos of the victims she is even more stunned … they all look just like Danny.

Who would you believe?

But the police are suspicious. Why has no one apart from Gemma heard from Danny in weeks? Why is there barely a trace of him in their flat? Is she telling them the truth, or is this marriage hiding some very dark secrets?

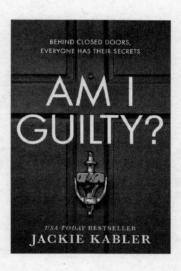

BEHIND CLOSED DOORS, EVERYONE HAS THEIR SECRETS

AM I GUILTY?

USA TODAY BESTSELLER
JACKIE KABLER

I never thought it would happen to me …

One moment I had it all – a gorgeous husband, a beautiful home, a fulfilling career and two adorable children. The next, everything came crashing down around me.

They said it was my fault. They said I'm the worst mother in the world. And even though I can't remember what happened that day, they wouldn't lie to me. These are my friends, my family, people I trust.

But then why do I have this creeping sensation that something is wrong? Why do I feel like people are keeping secrets? Am I really as guilty as they say? And if I'm not, what will happen when the truth comes out …?